BLOODLINE

The Book of the Black Tower
Volume 3

Nick Bastin

Chiselbury

Published by Chiselbury Publishing,
a division of Woodstock Leasor Limited,
81 Dovercourt Road, London SE22 8UW

www.chiselbury.com

ISBN: 978-1-908291-68-4

Acknowledgements

I would like to thank my friends and family for their support in the writing of this book. Their encouragement and enthusiasm has helped keep the ink flowing on to the page. I would also like to thank Ewen Henderson for writing an absolute cracker of a tune for The Reel of the Red Banner – you can find a recording on my website (www.nick-bastin.com) – and for correcting my consistently poor Gaelic. I encourage you to check out his fantastic music.

Finally, I want to salute the former residents of St Kilda, for their tenacious grip on that wonderous archipelago over millennia, and the Gàidhealtachd, for its endurance in the face of centuries of oppression at worst and ambivalence at best. May there be brighter days ahead.

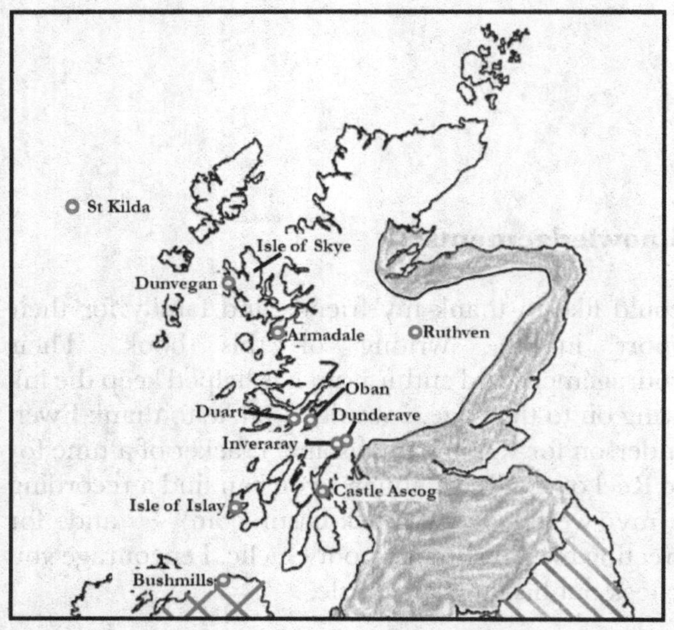

The Free Republic of the Gaels

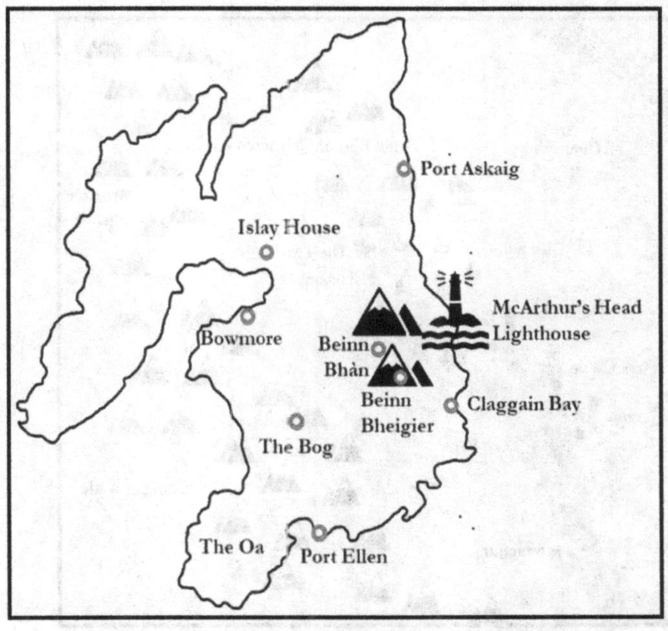

Isle of Islay

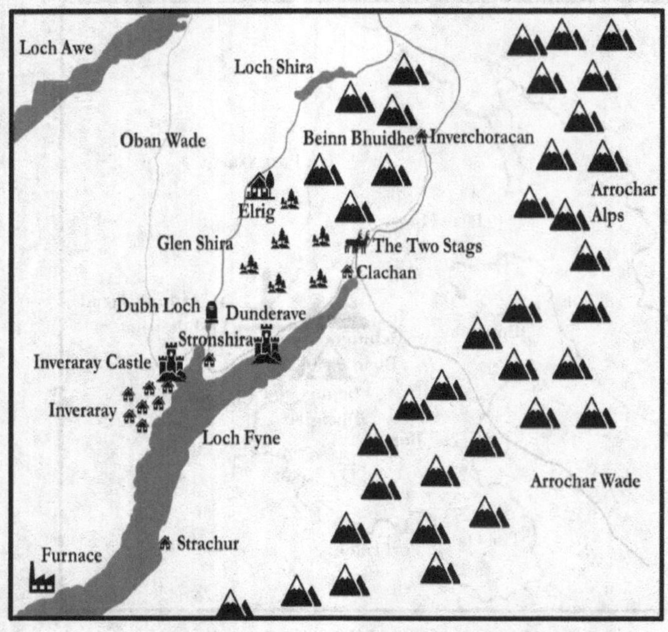

Dunderave and its surroundings

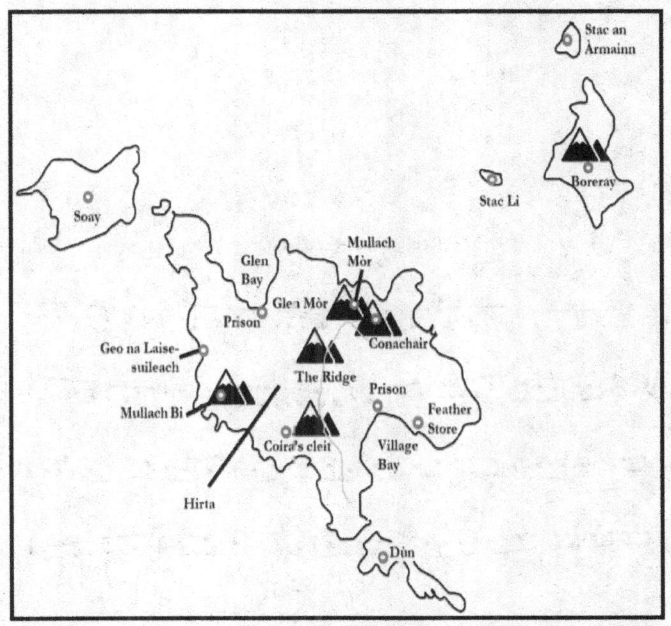

St Kilda Archipelago

The Reel of the Red Banner

Ewen Henderson

Full notation available at:
https://www.nick-bastin.com/music

Following his unexpected victory at the Battle of Culloden in 1746, Prince Charles Edward Stuart became King of the Gaels and split the highlands and islands of Scotland from the rest of Britain. Upon his death, Am Poblachd Shaor nan Gàidheal, The Free Republic of the Gaels, was declared. Since then, the Gaelic Republic has maintained its culture and language, ploughing its own idiosyncratic furrow to the present day, a constant irritant to its larger and more powerful neighbour......

Prologue

29 January 1788, Oban, The Kingdom of the Gaels. It was a shitty town, little more than a village. In Italy, his Master had estates that were larger. The houses were mostly poor hovels, roofed with turf and straw from the fields. He couldn't imagine his Master ever entering one. He had done so once, out of necessity, to seek shelter from the appalling weather. But he wouldn't do so again in a hurry. The verminous bites of lice and fleas had kept him awake the entire night and the smell of shit, both bovine and human, was almost unbearable. He'd heard that some pressed their excrement into the floor, not only to save venturing outside in winter, but also to heat their hovel as it rotted. Come the spring they would dig it out and spread it on their fields to feed their crops. Heathens! Why his Master would leave Rome and his beloved Palazzo della Cancelleria for this pigsty was a mystery that eluded his grasp. He cursed and spat a gobbet of phlegm into the mud, this pervasive damp was filling his Italian lungs. He needed sunshine and civilisation.

"Monsignor Angelo?"

He turned to look at the enquirer, a raggedy man dressed in the bizarre parti-coloured, woollen blanket that the locals tied around them as a form of clothing. In contrast to his muddy and travel worn clothing, the man's many weapons shone with quality and care.

"Si, Si, yes, yes. I am Monsignor Angelo Cesarini."

"I am your humble servant Alexander Gordon. I am

Groom of the Stole to his Majesty King Charles. I am to bring you to the Palace immediately. We do not have much time. He is weak."

He nodded and followed as Alexander Gordon made his way through the muddy streets of the so-called capital.

"Where are your roads? Why do you not have pavements? With so much rain and mud, surely they are necessary?" Angelo asked. In all his travels in Europe he'd never encountered such an impoverished scene.

Alexander flushed, clearly embarrassed. "Ah yes, I must apologise for the state of our streets. You must understand that for the Gael the metalled road is an innovation of the enemy. Before the Liberation, there was a time that the Kingdom tried to conquer us with roads, the work of the twice-cursed General Wade. But now we are free they are not tolerated. Gaels trust to the hill and the sea as their only highway, as they have done for millennia. The hills and rivers are our bulwark against tyranny. They kept out the Romans and will yet keep out the Kings and Queens of Edinburgh and London."

They walked up the slippery, muddy slope towards the tall round edifice that squatted above the town. Its heavy black granite columns and arcades echoed the mighty Colosseum in Rome. The contrast with the surroundings could not be greater; King Charles had chosen a good template to project his power and authority. On entering the mighty doors, Angelo felt for the first time that perhaps this was a patrimony worthy of his Master. The walls were hung with the finest tapestries and the extravagant gilt furniture and artwork spoke of an opulence and culture that he had not imagined possible from the impoverished surroundings outside.

Alexander led him up a sweeping staircase to the King's private apartments. Portraits of the Kings and Queens of Scotland and England were scattered casually up the towering walls, speaking to lineage, authority and the divine right to rule. Far above him, painted on the huge ceiling, coral pink clouds and baby blue skies swirled above a bloody battlefield. In the centre stood an elegant figure, sword in hand, clutching the bloody head of his vanquished foe whose corpulent body lay prone at his feet.

"Tiepolo?" Angelo asked. He knew the answer already; no one could mistake those frothy oranges and pinks.

"Yes, some say his greatest work. The King lured him here to paint it and then wouldn't let him leave until he was satisfied. It shows the moment of King Charlie's victory over the oppressor Cumberland at the Battle of Culloden. From that moment we were free."

A small group of heavily armed men intercepted them at the top of the stairs. Again, they were dressed in the outlandish attire of the Gaels, but this time there was no denying the fineness of the cloth, an exuberant tableau of colour. He'd heard so many stories of these exotic wildmen of the north. He half expected them to have two heads or the bulbous brows of the great apes. In fact they were polite and comely, with shapely muscular limbs; that would please his Master if nothing else.

The men waved Alexander Gordon through, but searched Angelo swiftly and expertly for any hidden weapons. Finally satisfied, they let them pass into what Angelo presumed were the King's apartments. Alexander led him through one suite of rooms after another, each more richly decorated than the last; heavy oak carving and the finest Chinoiserie papers lined the walls and sumptuous works of art caught his eye. He remembered many of them from the family's long exile in Rome, the Palazzo Muti must have been emptied. His Master, Cardinal Henry, would doubtless feel quite at home. Their footsteps echoed on the parquet floor as they strode through chamber after chamber, until finally they arrived at the King's bedroom. Alexander knocked once and then entered.

The bed the King lay on was enormous, its canopy soared a full twenty feet above them. Its heavy cornice held sweeping curtains of the deepest green velvet surmounted at each corner by sprays of ostrich plumes. Behind, gold and silver thread outlined the arms of the King in a lustrous affirmation of his royalty. Angelo smirked; vanity had always coursed through Prince Charles – perhaps the insecurity of the exile – and now that he was a King he was free to express his insecurities to his heart's content.

Despite the room's grandeur it smelt of death's approach: pyretic sweat, stale piss and shit's foul fetor hung like a cloud around the magnificent bed. In its centre lay a wizened old man. Puffy and pale, he was clearly very ill. Angelo was shocked; could this be the same athletic youth he remembered from all those years before?

"Your Majesty, it is Monsignor Angelo Cesarini. He has come from your brother Cardinal Henry in Rome to make the arrangements for the transition."

The King held out his hand. Angelo kissed it. The King tried to sit up a little, to be able to see properly.

"Dear Angelo, what a surprise. How many years has it been? Far too many I fear. And now I have so little time left. I thank God for your safe arrival. How is my brother? I trust he is well and that he is keeping God's work."

"Your Majesty, he sends his love and the especial blessing of His Holiness the Pope for your passage from this temporal kingdom to the eternal paradise of God. He is praying for your soul. Your brother Henry has sent me to smooth his way. The Pope has furnished him with troops and a fleet to come and take possession of his inheritance. With your departure from this world, your gift of this Kingdom for the glory of God and the Holy Catholic Church has caused much joy and celebration in the Holy See."

"Oh, has it now."

"Yes, the Pope himself sees it as a turning point in the Church's fortunes. For centuries we have been pushed back by the tide of Protestantism, by the poison of Calvin and heresy of Luther. Now the See will strike back and regain a lost kingdom, the first of many. We have already had letters of recognition and alliance drawn up with King Louis of France and Joseph, the Holy Roman Emperor. We are confident that we can keep the Kingdom from intervening; they are still so preoccupied with the Americas after all. This will bring your brother much glory in this world and you much in the next."

"Will it indeed?"

Angelo studied the pasty face of the King, there seemed a hesitancy in his voice that Angelo did not like.

"Do you like to read?" The King asked, changing the subject.

Angelo was taken aback by the bizarre question. He was here to consolidate the submission of a nation to the Church, not to discuss literature.

"Sometimes. I can recommend the bible; it is food for the soul."

"Ach! Stop it with your false hypocrisy. I am a King not an idiot! For my brother to send such a philistine, shows how little he knows me yet. If he had the courage he would have come himself. But he never had the gingambobs for it. Staying in Rome wrapped in Cardinal-red luxury while I trod these hills and fought and killed to build a nation and free my people from oppression."

The King swept up some books that were lying on the table next to the bed and threw them weakly at Angelo.

"Montesquieu, Arouet, Rousseau — these are what you should be reading you fool. There is a storm coming which will sweep away the corruption of the past, to free all peoples. When I landed at Loch Nan Uamh with seven good friends more than forty years ago I could not have foreseen my destiny. Yes, I came with dreams of conquest, to seize for my father what he'd ever failed to seize for himself. But what I learned during those months and the years that followed is that these fine people, who took me up when I was but a Prince in rags, who set me to lead them to death or destiny when I could give them nothing but hopes and dreams, they deserve their liberty. Liberty from Kings or Princes, Popes and Bishops, the liberty to choose for themselves, the liberty of culture and practice, of language and law making. Do you think I fought and killed Cumberland with these bare hands to lay this people on a Papal platter like some communion supplicant? They are sick of the gall-duine coming and telling the Gael how to live. And so am I."

Angelo's ears burned; the blood rushed to his cheeks giving away the fury that rose from the pit of his stomach. Could it be true? Was it possible that this dying failure of a King, marooned in his shit strewn hovel of a city, surrounded by impassable mountains and populated by the violent and ignorant, would deny his brother and the Pope!

"You are unwell your Majesty, you know not what you say. This arrangement has been foreseen for many years; you cannot change it now."

"How dare you tell me what I can do!" King Charles seemed to grow in stature, a shadow of his past vigour returned, if only for an moment. "My mind is made, and all your blethering will not persuade me from the rightness of my choice."

Angelo stared at the husk of a man. He could strangle him now. He was sure the Cardinal would absolve him of regicide, given what was at stake.

As if reading his mind, the King shouted at the top of his voice "Curaidh Mòr!" A side door opened in the panelling and out stepped a grim-faced Gael dressed in fine red, green and azure tartan, a steel pistol drawn in one hand and his dirk in the other. "Ah, Gillebrìde, my thanks for your swift attendance. I think it is time for Monsignor Cesarini to leave. He has my message. The time for Kings is over here. On my death will come a new nation, a nation for the Gaels and by the Gaels, a Gaelic Republic to deliver for our people what has so long been denied them."

Angelo raged. "You are a fool! An old and stupid fool! The rain and damp has rotted your brain! You think that this cesspool of misery can survive, with the Kingdom at your gates and the power of France and Rome against you!"

"We shall see. But as our friends in the Americas have shown us, there are some things stronger than kingdoms and princes, and the pursuit of liberty will surely overcome them all. Gillebrìde, please take the Monsignor to the port and see him aboard his vessel. If he gives you any trouble you have my permission to put a bullet between his eyes."

1 – Armadale

Present day, Armadale, Isle of Skye. Alasdair MacGregor had been following the target for at least an hour. The walk would have taken half that time if it hadn't been for the target's intoxicated state. The wind rustled the trees' freshly minted leaves and the damp ground underfoot absorbed any sound as he followed. He had taped his gear carefully so that no clinks would give him away and the highland night was dark, no moon or even starlight to show a shadow.

This was his favourite part of any job; he knew the objective; the target was blissfully unaware. The voyeuristic thrill of watching the quarry carry on their life unaware of the plans in motion around them. Like scoping a distant deer on the hill, that feeling of power, to be the arbiter of death with the smallest squeeze of the finger. All the while, the distant victim stands oblivious to the choices being made around and about them. He had known Griogaraich colleagues become addicted to the stalk, the power of watching from afar, or close up, tucked within an arm's reach without the target's knowledge. It wasn't healthy to take it too far; but on a night like tonight, wrapped in shadow and with the adrenalin pumping, he was in his element.

The curve of the rocky bay swept in an elegant near semicircle, dotted with mooring buoys and assorted boats. The target meandered his way along the shoreline stopping every now and then to pick up a stone and fling it at the water with a twist of his wrist. They never bounced more than twice, at least not that Alasdair could see. Hums and whistles came out of the darkness, interspersed with occasional bursts of full canntaireachd as the target worked through some complex pìobaireachd notation. Alasdair was no expert of the big music of the bagpipes, but he thought he recognised some of the tunes hidden deep in the variations. In any case, he was delighted that the target was so busy distracting himself; this job was difficult and dangerous enough as it was. He was a long way from any backup and with the present state of unrest in the country strangers in the night would be met with force first, questions later.

He'd sat in darkness outside the Ferry Inn waiting for the target to drink his fill and turn for home. This being the Isle of Skye it rained intermittently, everything from stair rods to that thick cloaking sog that permeates clothes and lungs. He wasn't bothered though; little could compare to a wet winter walk on Rannoch Moor, the Griogaraich's wild home. After several hours watching the doors and windows of the Inn, begrudging his target the warmth and conviviality of the bar inside, he had been heartily relieved when at last the door opened and the well upholstered figure of Pat MacArthur filled the frame. Even in these difficult times, the fulsome hospitality of the Ferry Inn could be measured in MacArthur's meandering stagger homewards.

But all journeys must eventually come to an end, and MacArthur finally started to make his way from the shore towards a long, low, white-harled building with an imposing crenelated tower rising at its centre. The medieval theme was further echoed in the ashlar-framed pointed windows sunk into the façade and the double lancet window in the upper floor of the tower.

From his reconnaissance, Alasdair knew that the entrance to Armadale, the home of Sorley MacDonald, Chief of Clan Donald, Warden of the Isles, lay up the hill to the right. He was very keen to avoid rousing any interest from Armadale's security, an unscheduled visit to the Castle was definitely not part of his brief. He ducked behind a tree to check his watch, it was just after midnight, the tide meant that he had to be back at the rendezvous by 1.30am. He didn't have much time to waste.

MacArthur swayed over the lawn in front of the building and headed for the black front door. Fumbling his keys, MacArthur dropped them twice in quick succession. Wheezing, he leant on the door with one hand while he scrabbled to pick them up with the other. Finally successful, MacArthur stabbed the key in the lock and opened the door, falling through it with a curse as it swung open. The door was then kicked shut with a definitive thunk, returning the night to the wind and rain.

Alasdair waited for ten minutes, following Pat MacArthur's progress inside as the lights came on and went out in the different parts of the building. Only when the building was dark except for two shafts of light from the lancet windows in the tower did Alasdair make his move.

Given the hour and the weather he was pretty confident that no one was likely to be passing. His only concern was security surveillance. Breathing out, he stood up straight, put his shoulders back and walked confidently and as bold as brass across the lawn to MacArthur's front door. Resisting the urge to look around him, he pulled the lockpicks out of his sporran, selected the most likely size and slid it into the lock. It was a dumb lock in any case, no challenge to an expert, and within a few seconds, a little pressure and a twist of his wrist, the lock opened with a snick. The door swung inwards revealing a pitch-black corridor beyond. He closed the door softly behind him.

Fumbling in his left sleeve pocket he fished out a pair of glasses, putting them on and depressing a button on the right-hand hinge. The ultra-high frequency whine as they powered up seemed deafening in the confined space, but the hallway went from black to brilliant shades of green as the night vision kicked in through the lenses. He could now see the stairs as clear as day. He climbed them, keeping to the edge of the tread nearest the wall to minimise any squeaks, grateful for the thick Axminster carpet that was an assassin's best friend.

He paused on the half-landing, the room beyond was dark and still. He turned and looked up the next flight. There at the top of the stairs a crack of light was showing on his night vision as bright as a sunbeam at the top of the door. That must be the room with the lancet windows where Pat MacArthur, his target, was. He needed to do this as silently as possible if he was going to be able to escape.

He checked the charge on his pistol. The Atelier had only delivered it to him that week and this was its first outing on a job; it had better work. The tiny LED at the top of the handle showed green, it was good to go.

He approached the door, easing it open a crack. He could hear MacArthur rustling paper on the other side of the room. Putting his face flat to the wood of the door he could just see the plastic shell of the light switch inside the jamb. Taking a deep breath, he exploded into action, pushing through the door while flicking the switch and turning out the lights. The room went black, but his night vision showed MacArthur as clear as day standing by a bookshelf on the far side of the room, his mouth gaping in surprise.

Alasdair pulled the trigger; the barrel spat a single blue bolt of energy that hit Fat Pat MacArthur square in the chest. Unseen by the human eye, the bolt delivered a payload of 5 microcoulombs of energy straight into Pat's already over-burdened heart. Given the size of the charge it is likely that Pat would have dropped dead of a coronary even if he hadn't been elderly and overweight. As it was, and given his condition, his heart exploded under the impact. Certainly, no sound came from his lips as he fell to the floor, smashing his head on the edge of the bookshelf for good measure.

Alasdair cursed MacArthur's ungainly fall, waiting to see if it had been heard by any outside.

Silence reigned.

Now all he had to do was finish the job and get on his way. It was one of the most bizarre and frankly unpalatable requests he'd ever had, but the client had been very specific, and they wanted photos, and they'd paid a lot for the privilege. He sighed, better just to get on with it. He pulled, MacArthur's body around to the sofa, kneeling it on the cushions with the head facing over the back. Then he hunted round the flat to find all the elements that he needed. It didn't take long and ten minutes later he was back outside, sweating from a combination of effort and stress. Once he was safely across the open lawn and back into the shadows by the shore he broke into a jog. He needed to get to The Rose in June in time to catch the tide; he needed to be far away before anyone found the result of his evening's work.

2 – The Morning News

President John Lamont poured himself another cup of coffee, but it was no good. He burst out laughing again, creasing up, doubled over, tears rolling down his face. He took a sip from his cup, the coffee briefly grabbing his attention as it scalded his tongue, but even that couldn't stop another gush of laughter erupting from deep down. He picked up his tablet again to check that he hadn't imagined the news. It was at times like these that he missed Allan Stewart; he was a man that would have appreciated the joke. There it was on the home screen of The Oban Raven, the Gaelic Republic's leading newspaper, in inch-high bold black type: Armadale Arse Assassin's Ambush. Below, in glorious technicolour was a photo of the pasty posterior of a dead, late-middle aged man with his kilt over his head and the bass drone from a fine set of ebony and ivory bound highland bagpipes shoved up where the sun never shone. The cherry on the cake, was that attached to the bass drone, hanging limply in the air, was the official pipe banner of the Warden of the Isles himself, Lord Sorley MacDonald.

It was just too hilarious, and it took Lamont a good twenty minutes before his giggles reliably subsided. Whoever had done it certainly knew how to rile MacDonald; his Cliù must have fair ruptured with the insult. He thought about calling Sorley, just to rub it in a bit, but decided that might be taking it too far. Anyway, he had plenty of others wanting to snigger about it with him; his phone barely stopped all morning with pings and chirrups as messages flooded in. Being

President of the Gaelic Republic could be tough, but this was one of the days to savour. He really hoped that MacDonald didn't call to ask him to take action, he wasn't sure he would be able to keep a straight face.

As if triggered by these thoughts, the phone rang. He swore and looked at the screen trying to compose himself; it was David Brown.

"Ah David, how are you? Trust that you are well and that the sun is shining in Oban?" He was feeling very convivial, his spirits lifted by the morning's entertainment.

"I'm well thank you, although it is raining cats and dogs here. Did you see The Raven?"

"Yes, I did! Hilarious isn't it! I mean terrible, really awful, the poor man….."

"Yes, a terrible murder. And carried out just yards from the entrance to Armadale itself. An unusually bold assassination don't you think?"

Lamont was amused by Brown's reluctance to see the funny side; he was so strait laced.

"What makes you think it was an assassination? I just thought it was the selfless act of a music lover. Or maybe it was a kinky sex game that got out of hand? You know those Sgitheanachs; anything goes up there on the Isle of Skye!" And another wave of uncontrollable laughter burst out of him.

David Brown was evidently unimpressed, the tone coming down the phone was uncharacteristically icy.

"John, may I remind you that the Hereditary Piper to Lord MacDonald has been slain and his body abused in a foul manner. You may find it amusing but I can assure you that Lord MacDonald and his ten thousand fighting men do not. I have had him on the phone for much of the last two hours demanding that the Seanadh censures MacLeod of Dunvegan. He is convinced that it was MacLeod's hand behind this; apparently there has been some bad blood between this man and MacLeod's own piper. Professional jealousy or some such. Anyway, to say that he is on the war path is an understatement. He has summoned back all his overseas units and is concentrating his forces for a full out assault on MacLeod's positions. The island is descending into all-out war. You need to do something!"

Those last words were like a cold slap to Lamont's face – he needed to do something! He smarted from the accusation; how dare anyone talk to him like that, let alone Brown! His good mood evaporated and was replaced by a rising, seething anger.

"How dare you tell me, the President, what I should do. May I remind you of your place. I am fully aware of my duties and don't need you to remind me of them! Now fuck off!"

He swiped the call closed and sat fuming for a good ten minutes. He knew it was pointless being intemperate with David Brown, who responded better to empathy sprinkled with a few judicious threats. He needed him to remain onside though. In the meantime, he thought back to MacLeod and MacDonald; this little conflagration was an absolute godsend. With the two Wardens of the Isles squabbling bloodily among themselves, it left him free to wait until they'd exhausted each other before stepping in to clean up the remains. If the citizens of Skye suffered a little collateral damage along the way, well that was just the price that had to be paid. But he did wonder who the assassin had been, he could really use a man like that, what a sense of humour!

3 – Burning

The column of vehicles pulled out of Port Ellen in a ribbon of trucks and Kats rounding the beach that ran up to the malting sheds of the distillery. No puffs of smoke showed from the pagoda roof; the kilns were shut. Bruce MacVey directed the driver of the lead vehicle to turn left just before the corrugated grey hulk. The road followed the shore and he looked out of the window onto a flat calm sea. They passed a charming sandy bay; Islay was more beautiful than he had expected. He could see why it had been such a focus of Clan rivalry over so many centuries. While there was a lot of useless bog in the middle and a rugged flank to the east, much of the rest was good farmland, something that was a rarity in the Republic.

Of course, no one was going to get rich selling cattle or growing wheat. No, the main economic export was the wet gold produced by the herd of distilleries that dotted the fields and coves of the island. Ever since the founding of the Republic, whisky had been an important part of its identity, used to grease the wheels of realpolitik as it made friends and forged trading agreements around the world. After half a century of unfashionable obsolescence on the back shelf of the world's bars, it had now been reborn as the aspirational connoisseurs' drink of choice for the up and coming of the globe, be they Chinese, Indian or American. And the unique whisky of Islay commanded a price that made its peaty alchemy, that transformed barley, water and yeast into hard cash, highly desirable.

For all the bullshit about MacLean's much vaunted

Cliù as being the reason she wanted to seize Islay, MacVey knew that the whisky revenue stream was equally important. How else were they going to pay and motivate their followers? If the rapidly escalating Clan war worsened, they may need to call in redshank units to support them and that would cost. Their initial priority on landing had been to secure the distilleries and safeguard the stocks. The Kilarrow and Mulindry distilleries were the only ones that escaped them, their Campbell owners having successfully torched the warehouses creating an alcoholic firestorm that was the definition of scorched earth. No matter, there was plenty of other supply to fill the gap and there had been a relentless flow of barrels off the island to bottlers and shippers in the Kingdom and further afield.

But today was not about whisky.

He led the column as it wound its way inland from the seashore. The landscape was more open here, few trees could withstand the relentless Atlantic winters. A drystone wall ran along the roadside safeguarded with barbed wire. Sheep looked up from their grazing, unimpressed by the passing phalanx of noisy, dirty machinery. They rounded a standing stone, enduring evidence of mankind's long presence on the island. He looked at the list on his phone, their destination was just past the next collection of houses.

He turned to his drone operator. "What can you see?"

"Not much, there is a little bit of movement but nothing that we should be worried about. No hostiles that I can see. The biothermal imaging shows seven individuals."

"Good. OK, I want you to stay in here and keep an

eye on the wider perimeter when we arrive; I don't want anyone to catch us unawares."

They turned a corner and pulled into a tidy farmyard filled with a maze of stock pens, a tractor and a few stacked bales of silage. The vehicles spread through the yard disgorging black clad men carrying a variety of weapons. His driver pulled up in front of the door to a whitewashed stone building, a few fish boxes and lobster pots neatly stacked to one side. MacVey got out and stretched; it had already been a long day. Above him the drone hovered briefly, before starting to circle in an ever-larger pattern.

The door opened and a middle-aged woman came out – why did they always send the women first, he wondered, as if that was going to make a difference.

"Can I help you?" She asked, the waver that caught in her throat betrayed her fear, despite her apparent confidence.

"Are you Eleanor MacIvor?"

"Yes, I am."

"Is this Dubhach Farm?"

"Yes, it is. Why do you ask? What are you doing here? Why are you bringing armed men to our home? We've done nothing wrong."

"Well Eleanor, you MacIvors are a well-known Campbell sept. You have chosen to ally yourselves with MacCailean Mòr and have done very well out of that for a long time. But I am afraid to have to tell you that today is the day you start paying."

"What do you mean? I don't understand. We're just farmers; we've been farming here for centuries. Who are you to come and tell me otherwise!"

"Davy," MacVey turned to one of his men, "take

Mrs MacIvor and put her in the truck. Men, I want you to search every building. We know there are another six of them. They might be armed so be on your guard."

"What are you doing?" Eleanor MacIvor shouted, her anger and fear now unmistakable. But she knew what was coming. "We are MacIvors, we aren't even Campbells. We just live here, peacefully. You can't throw us out. We've nowhere else to go!"

MacVey stared at her stony faced and unmoved.

"I suggest you shut your Campbell bitch mouth and get in the back of the truck before I change my mind and decide to hand you over to my men. They'll soon fuck those Campbell genes right out of you, and if you're really lucky, maybe leave a MacLean brat behind in your belly. Then you'll be welcome to stay right enough."

She flew at him, slapping at his head with her hands. He just laughed, easily catching her wrists and throwing her to one side for his men to bind. He went back to the Kat and pulled out a jerry can. Then, entering the house he walked around it, room to room, admiring the neat domesticity while leaving a trail of petrol. Pictures of children and drawings from school projects were pinned on the walls, a well-worn three-piece suite, flatscreen telly and games console; it was all so predictable, he'd already seen it dozens of times. He heard a scuffle upstairs, the sound of breaking glass and the thump of something or someone falling.

"Everything OK up there?" He shouted.

"Aye, I just caught one of the runts trying to hide under the bed. I got the fucker though."

"Great, stick 'em in the van, we deal with them later."

He walked into the kitchen. A pine table filled most of the room, littered with ingredients. Someone had been baking. He sloshed more petrol on the table and for good measure went and turned on the gas hobs. Then carefully leaving a trail out of the back door he stood in the yard. He called to make sure everyone was clear of the building before taking out the cigarette case he always carried in his breast pocket. Using his thumbnail, he split the silver and took out one of the few remaining cigarettes. He needed to get some more. He patted down his pockets to find which had the box of matches. Success! He struck one, then a second, cupping his hands to allow it to catch properly before the wind blew it out. He drew the smoke into his lungs, enjoying the bite and the mild rush. He then carefully put the match to the petrol, standing well back as it rushed towards the house in an orange streak, hungrily mounting the steps and passing through the open door. The gas explosion shattered all the windows and smoke started to pour through them; a choking, black acrid smoke that caught at the back of one's throat, the smell of burning homes and broken dreams.

4 – Impotence

Brighid had never seen MacCailean Mòr look so distracted. He had been pouring over maps of Islay with a stream of duine uasal for much of the morning, making notes and discussing options. It was clear that none of them seemed that appealing. It was almost as if each time he got an answer he didn't like, he called for another opinion. His frustration was growing.

Archie Ban Campbell of Skipness was the latest in a long line of duine uasal to discuss their views of the situation. Balding and grey-faced due to perpetual five o'clock shadow, Archie Ban was no oil painting, but for Brighid he was one of MacCailean Mòr's most reliable and least excitable advisers. He told the facts as he found them and was not prone to the self-aggrandisement or posturing that some of the others were in the presence of their Chief.

"The reports coming in from Islay are disturbing, with the population being brutalised by Bruce MacVey, Catriona MacLean's commander on the ground. MacVey is making himself exceedingly unpopular and has been deliberately bating the community. His first act was to set up his headquarters in Islay House at Bridgend. That was where he welcomed Catriona MacLean when she visited to assess her prize. The Shawfields have wisely fled to Tarbert, leaving only their son Iain Og behind to help with the resistance."

"There are units of MacLeans going house to house checking on peoples' identities; anyone with the surname Campbell is being evicted or having their house torched. We've already seen dozens of homes in

Bowmore, Port Charlotte and Port Ellen go up in flames. Apparently, MacVey has a list of names considered to be Campbell septs or supporters and that list is his judge, jury and executioner. He is also bringing in MacLeans burned out of Tiree or Rum to be resettled. Everyone else is keeping their head down, hoping that he won't come for them."

"The resistance has had some success; at Sunderland they managed to catch a column of MacLeans in a trap, shooting up the first and last vehicle of the convoy before picking off the rest. Not that it made much difference in the end, Sunderland was burned to the ground and anyone the MacLeans could lay their hands on got shot or strung up."

"How many troops does she have on the ground?"

"Hard to say exactly, but she has certainly reinforced since her initial landing. I expect she now has somewhere around 2,000 armed men on the island, and obviously she still has considerable forces on Mull to defend herself from attack there. She seems to have relinquished control of her other island territories – Rum, Coll, Tiree - for the time being. MacDonald's forces have attacked them, just burning and looting mostly."

Archibald Ban rubbed his thickening stubble, Brighid thought it was growing darker by the minute: "My biggest worries are the defences that MacVey has already established on the island." He pointed at the map, jabbing his finger at three corners of the island. "He has set up missile batteries here at McArthur's Head guarding the approach to the Sound of Islay from the South; here, at Rhuvaal guarding it from the north and finally here at Portnahaven on the western tip, which basically commands all of the west coast. Any approaching ships are vulnerable to being sunk before they get anywhere near the island."

"Goddamit! When is Ardkinglas getting back and how many men is he bringing?"

"They are currently transiting to N'Djamena; it took them some time to strike camp. There are about 650 men, and we hope they will be back by next week."

"What about Strachur and Otter?"

"I am afraid that their contract cannot be shortened, so they will need to stay in post for the time being. We have a break clause at the end of the year, we can try then."

"That's no good! I need them now! This is hopeless." MacCailean Mòr's shoulders slumped.

"Sir, I am afraid to say that I agree. We can currently field about 5,000 men, well-armed and supplied. But given the substantial force that would need to remain on the mainland I don't think we have enough, unless the resistance on the island can materially disrupt the defence. In any case, the challenge remains getting them there."

"What about Ardbreknish? I need the Kilmartin Company to be operational. Has he been discharged from the Infirmary?"

"Yes, he was discharged a week ago. He is obviously still weak, but he is undergoing rigorous physiotherapy and I would expect him to be back on full operational duty in a fortnight."

"Good, that is something I suppose." MacCailean Mòr sighed. Then turning to Brighid, he asked: "What do you think we should do?"

Brighid was taken aback; as MacCailean Mòr's

partner, she'd sat in a lot of these discussions, but no one had ever asked her for an opinion before. All the military men with their complex stratagems, they seemed so clear and confident. What experience did she have that could add to their years spent in the battlegrounds of the world? She paused, the last thing she wanted to do was say something stupid.

"Who is this MacVey? What do you know about him?"

Archie Ban turned to face her. "He is a well-known military figure, with a long background in counterinsurgency in places as diverse as Libya, Iraq and Afghanistan. Perhaps as important as his military experience was his relationship with Catriona MacLean; she was fostered with his family as a child, the MacLean's must be one of the last clans to still maintain such an old-fashioned practice. That she would send such a trusted Lieutenant, one that was so close to her emotionally as well as strategically, only further underscores her commitment to holding the island. He is proving himself a capable if cruel leader, unfortunately."

"As you say yourself, you don't have enough men or transports for a frontal assault. And if you did try, you run the risk that she might sink your ships as they cross from the mainland. You'd be sitting ducks in all that open water. No, I think that you need to find a way to cut the head off the snake. Either take her out or this Bruce MacVey. She'll be hard to reach, but with a small team and the support of the resistance on the ground, have you got a chance of getting hold of MacVey? If you can take him out of the game, maybe that will cause her to think again. Or at least it would disrupt the defence sufficiently for you to be able to consider an assault, particularly if you take out the missile battery at McArthur's Head. Then you would have a better chance of being able to land troops anywhere you liked along the southern coast."

Archie Ban was now totally focused on Brighid: "But how do we reach MacVey? He always travels in a large convoy; it would be suicide to try."

MacCailean Mòr was now flushed with excitement, his eyes bright: "No, we need to separate him from his entourage, and I think I have the perfect solution."

5 – The High Adjudicator

Lamont didn't like the tone of the email, there was an underlying threat that he did not appreciate. He felt as though he was being summoned like a naughty schoolboy to go before the headmaster. Who the fuck did Balfour think he was anyway? He might be First Minister of Scotland, but Lamont was the Head of State of one of the oldest republics in the world. A nation that did not take kindly to orders and threats, especially from the Kingdom.

The last time relations had been this bad was when Mrs Thatcher, the Kingdom's belligerent Prime Minister in the 1980's, flushed with her military success in the Falklands, had 'liberated' Inverness and the Black Isle from the Republic. Losing their second biggest city and the best farmland in the whole country had been a huge blow to their esteem. Years had been lost in arbitration, both at the EU and the UN. Fortunately, Thatcher's own party had stabbed her in the back and deposed her before she could snatch any more territory, and her successors had been keener to build bridges. They generally had enough problems on their plate without stirring the Gaelic pot.

Now Lamont was being summoned to Edinburgh for a summit to discuss the security situation and some issue with the Bombay Canton Bank. Publicly it was being dressed up as a visit by the new Head of State to the Republic's nearest and closest neighbour, a cosy fireside chat. But he had been on enough of those phone calls from Balfour to know that underneath there were some burning resentments. He could tell it was serious; not only would Balfour be there, but Westminster itself was deigning to send a Minister to represent the Kingdom's interests.

He needed a distraction for the Kingdom's media, something that smacked of strong government but didn't risk quenching the inferno that was building nicely on the west coast. Now that he was the President, he was forced to be aloof from the day-to-day executive so using the Comhairle was out of the question. He had to use another route. Fortunately, Clan, Canun and Cliù were a guaranteed and intoxicating brew and he meant to use them all to the full.

He telephoned security to make sure that a detachment of Gallowglass, the Black Watch's most elite unit, were ready to accompany him. He couldn't be too careful in these difficult times. The Presidential motorcade swept across town finally stopping outside a Georgian doll's house of a building high up on the hill above the city. It was almost square with a five-bay façade. The top floor was filled with tall arch-topped windows underneath a heavy entablature, while the ground floor was heavily rusticated in the style of a Florentine Palazzo. Its architecture intentionally spoke of doughty duty and stern rigour.

Although he was familiar with the outside from a thousand newscasts, he had never been inside before; to be fair, it was a building most citizens spent their entire lives trying to avoid. A single steep flight of steps led up to the entrance door over which in heavy gold letters read the words Cùirt-Chanun – the Court of Canun.

Leaving his Gallowglass outside, he swept up the steps. Blinking as he left the gloomy entrance, the marble lined hall beyond was bright, powerfully lit by a glittering crystal chandelier that he thought better suited to a ballroom than the highest court in the land. The receptionist approached him.

"President Lamont, I believe you've come to see the High Adjudicator?"

"Yes, she is expecting me."

The receptionist led the way up the stairs to a wide landing under a glass cupola. Ahead were a fine pair of mahogany doors twice as tall as he was; the patina of centuries had given them a warm but imposing glow. On one it said in neat gold leaf Àrd-Bhritheamhand, Cùirt-Chanun, on the other in English High Adjudicator, Court of Canun. The receptionist opened one of the doors a crack and slipped through into the room beyond, returning moments later and throwing both doors dramatically open, she ushered him inside.

Acres of Aubusson carpet stretched away from him to a heavy partner's desk the size of a small car. On the other side, sat a small, neat, middle-aged woman with elegantly coiffed hair and a Chanel suit. She smiled as he approached, standing to shake his hand; it was quite a stretch over the mass of the leather-topped desk.

"Camilla Brehon, delighted to meet you Mr President." She said, inviting him to sit. "How can I and the Court of Canun be of assistance?"

"Thank you, Camilla. And I appreciate you seeing me at such short notice; these are challenging times for us all. The reason for my visit is a terrible and egregious breech of the Canun, the like of which this country cannot tolerate if we are to prevent a slide into total chaos. As you know, I am a strong believer in law and order, and most particularly in justice. The Canun plays a critical role in managing and mitigating the tensions that bubble up in our society and it does it in a way that is swift, fair and generally welcomed by all. However, it has come to my attention that there has just been a terrible breech of the Canun resulting in the death of Allan Stewart, an innocent servant of the Republic."

"You may remember, that after the cruel murder of their last Chief and the burning of Dunderave, by the Campbells, the Clan MacNachtan were placed under the protection of the Comhairle. I was given the grave responsibility for their care and sent my best man, Allan Stewart, to protect them from any further depredations. At great personal risk Allan based himself at the Castle, working hard to deliver the security that all deserve in our society."

"Following a disagreement with a local hothead, there was an escalation which led to a full-blooded combat under Canun. After a fair fight Allan, who had clearly won the contest and was about to deliver the winning blow, was murdered by a third party who intervened in an utterly depraved, merciless, unlawful and dishonourable manner."

Camilla Brehon looked suitably aghast: "That's awful. I'm so sorry. We must take the firmest action. Particularly at this time, when the security situation is so fragile, we must set an example that such law breaking will not be tolerated. Do you know who was responsible?"

"Yes, his name is Gillespie MacNachtan and I demand that he be brought to justice and feel the full force of the law."

6 – Gaming

Shonique's house was small but warm and Gillespie was coming to appreciate that luxurious quality the longer he stayed in the Republic. His old home had been draughty and mostly unheated except during the depths of winter. Some of the more far flung and less used toilets in the house had pails of salt left next to them to be added to every flush to stop them freezing. He had come to love the way Shonique would walk around the house in a silk slip, its hem skimming the top of her toned thighs, an erotic flourish that would have been unthinkable if they'd been at his home in Antrim.

The warmth of the bed and embrace of her arms were hard to leave, but he had to go to work. After living a frenetic otherworldly existence for much of the last few months, the stolid mundanity of having to get up at a set time and walk along the loch to clock in at the gaming operation was a welcome change. He was relishing the predictability, not to mention the office banter, which was chiefly led by Fiona. Kirstie was a slightly more aloof presence in the workplace, well suited to giving directions and making decisions she sat apart, as if conscious of the need to maintain a certain distance, both in her position as a business leader and as Chief-in-waiting.

Gillespie had been put to work on the restoration of the Castle, managing the budget and sourcing quotes from artisans and builders across the Republic and beyond. He enjoyed the thrill of the chase, rootling out suppliers of unusual services and negotiating with them to deliver what he hoped was going to be a building truly fit for the 21st century, and not just the 15th. The best part of it was that whenever he asked a question about budget, there always seemed to be more forthcoming. Money was not something that was talked about openly, but it was clear that the Clan had prodigious resources hidden away and the repairs to Dunderave were taken in its stride.

Aside from running the gaming busines, Kirstie spent a lot of her time on the Clan's hardship fund, dispensing stipends and subsidies to a wide range of individuals and businesses. Following the burning of the Two Stags and the murder of three Clan members by the Lamonts, Kirstie not only settled benefits on the widows and widowers affected, but had also issued a grant to Dolina, the owner of the Two Stags, to rebuild. Gillespie had come to realise that it was this access to resources, combined with the requisite security, which was what held the Clan together. Yes, the Chief sat on top, the arbiter and dispenser of these resources and benefits, but if there was nothing to share then pretty soon they would find themselves Chief of nothing; the Clan would just drift away to find other sources of opportunity. People didn't switch lightly but moving on and taking the name of another Clan was always an option and having had such a close brush with total deliquescence, Kirstie was now deploying all of the Clan's resources to bolster its members.

Checking his watch, Gillespie knew he didn't have time for breakfast and instead grabbed a banana from the fruit bowl and dashed for the door. The walk from Clachan to Dunderave was never less than enervating; if the sun shone then it was glorious, if the rain poured it was bracing. He didn't mind either of those extremes, the only days he begrudged the trudge was when it was grey and dull. Zinc-flat highland skies had a way of sucking the joy out of even the dramatic landscape of the Arrochar Alps. Fortunately, there was always the loch to look at; it was ever changing; the wave patterns sliced and diced by the wind's keen edge, or the passage of boats and shifting buoys of lobster pots. It was the best commute he'd ever had.

Arriving at the gaming centre, he punched in the passcode and went inside. The smell of fresh paint and the gleaming white walls were a contrast with the charred ruin they'd found only a few weeks previously. After the destruction wrought by Allan Stewart and the Lamonts, Kirstie had decided to keep all of the operations in the cloud, so there was no further need for their own servers. With their satellite dish back up and running they could access capacity anywhere in the world in the blink of an eye. Most of the Clan worked remotely, there being no need to physically go into the office, but the available desks were always filled by a diverse crowd who came in for social reasons.

Welcomed by a scattered chorus of "Madainn Mhath!" from around the room, Gillespie opened up his laptop. Having cleared his inbox of overnight emails, he settled in to breaking down a spreadsheet of costs for roof timbers and fire-retardant systems.

He gradually became aware of another sound that was competing with the hum of the air conditioning and winning, the sweeping rhythmic chop of a helicopter. Yes, there it was. It was coming closer.

His co-workers stood up and ran to the window.

"Look there, military by the look of it. What are the markings? Can you see?"

Very calmly but firmly Kirstie ordered everyone to leave the unit and head for the protection of the Castle proper. Gillespie grabbed his gear and followed the crowd out of the door. Whatever this was about, it was the last thing the Clan needed right now. All they wanted was peace and quiet.

Fiona pointed, her finger tracking the fast-approaching group of black, bug-eyed machines. There were three of them, all painted in the same dull flat black. Painted on the underside of each was the screaming head of Medusa, her hair a nest of snakes, her neck dripping blood. They circled Dunderave looking for a spot to put down.

"It's the Skua Squadron for fuck's sake, what the hell are they doing here? Quick get inside the Outer Ward now!" Fiona pushed Gillespie ahead of her across the open ground to the steel blast door. He gawked at the helicopters' menacing insectoid threat. The noise was deafening and the downdraft from their rotors lashed at his hair and clothes. Kirstie came last, slowly and deliberately closing and bolting the door after her.

Two of the helicopters landed, their rotors slowing, while one hovered stationary in the air above: squat, unmoving, threatening, the noise and buffeting of the downdraft a constant reminder of its deadly presence. A helmeted figure emerged out of one of the helicopters, ducking under the sweep of the still-turning blades, he approached the Castle gate. His walk had the easy confidence of a man that carried a very big stick, who knew its potency and was not afraid to use it. He was about to push on the entry phone when Kirstie opened the door and let him inside; it was pointless to equivocate.

He was wearing a pilot's black jumpsuit, a pistol strapped to the webbing on his chest, but otherwise had no obvious weaponry. As he came through the gate, he took off his helmet, revealing a square head and even squarer jaw, the black fuzz of his crew cut undisturbed by the maelstrom from the hovering gunship above. On his chest were marked his name, rank and the Medusa's Head.

"My name is Captain Andy Singh. I need to talk to Kirstie MacNachtan urgently."

Kirstie was taken somewhat aback by his directness.

"I'm Kirstie MacNachtan. What are you doing here?"

"I'm here with an arrest warrant from the Court of Canun for one of your clansmen."

"What?!" Kirstie shouted, cupping her ear as if she was struggling to hear over the roar of the engines.

"You heard. One of your clansmen, a certain Gillespie MacNachtan, has been charged with breaking the legal safeguards under Canun, leading to the extra-judicial murder of one Allan Stewart. He must accompany me to Oban to stand trial."

Gillespie felt his blood sink into his shoes. They wanted him? For killing Allan Stewart, that psychotic, evil bastard? It hadn't crossed his mind that this could happen, that it was even a possibility. Here in the Republic of all places? He looked around; the MacNachtans all stood slack jawed, as stunned as he was. All except Kirstie, who looked him straight in the eye and raising a finger pointed straight at him, said:

"That is Gillespie MacNachtan."

7 – Judas

"How could you just let him be taken like that? After all we've been through together!" He smacked his palm on the table for extra emphasis, the sharp sound causing everyone to flinch.

"C'mon Charlie, what choice did she have?" Nin said, in his most conciliatory tone.

"Nin, don't get me started. You of all people can back me up on this. She didn't even try to defend him. She just handed him over like Judas fucking Iscariot."

It was Kirstie's turn to defend herself: "Look Charlie, I know you are very upset; we all are. It was not something I ever imagined having to do. But you know as well as I do that there were three Skua gunships literally over our heads. What the fuck else do you expect me to do? Just one of those could have taken out all of the Clan at the castle and turned the rest into a smoking ruin. We don't have any defences against that, as well you know. Would it really be better for us all to die in a pointless blaze of glory?"

"I have to think about the Clan, not just Gillespie. I have got thousands of peoples' lives and livelihoods to consider and protect. Even if we had somehow got Gillespie out of there, are we really going to be able to defend ourselves against the Watch?"

"So, we are just going to leave him to the tender mercies of John Lamont, are we? The same John Lamont of the Sorrows from whose dungeon we had to liberate you!"

"I don't need you to remind me of John Lamont," Kirstie's voice was cold as ice, "I have the scars to remind me every fucking minute of every fucking day!"

Charlie realised he had overstepped the mark and, holding his hands up, apologised: "Look I'm sorry, I know you went through hell in that godawful place, which is why I am so worried about what is going to happen to Gillespie. He's not tough like you, he's just some flatlander that has got mixed up with us. This was our problem not his. He saved LeroyMar's life when we were all standing around watching him be slaughtered, our hands bound by the stupidity of Cliù. Do you think that psychotic cunt Allan Stewart gave a shit about Cliù? Do you think he had a fucking microgram of Cliù in his whole body? No!"

Both Nin and Kirstie were looking at the floor, they both knew the answer but neither wanted to acknowledge it.

"What happens now? Where did they take him?"

"He is currently being held at the Court of Canun in Oban. The trial is scheduled for next week."

"Jesus, they aren't hanging around are they? Does the Clan have access to any specialist lawyers? If not, I can probably ask my mother, she is bound to know someone."

"There's MacNeas," Nin offered, looking a little sheepish.

"Niocal MacNeas? The Weasel? You've got to be kidding me. Surely the Clan can get someone else?"

"I don't know what you mean," Nin replied, "he has always been very reliable for the Clan. Got old Duncan Tapaidh out of countless scrapes."

Charlie snorted, "Well if you really think that the Weasel is going to get Gillespie off this then you are even dumber than I thought."

"You think I'm dumb do you?"

They both stood staring at each other, anger flushing their cheeks red. The room held its breath.

It was Charlie that broke the tension, putting his hand on Nin's shoulder. "Of course, I don't think you are dumb. After everything he has been through, I think that Gillespie deserves the best chance we can give him. I was just wondering whether the Weasel was the man to do it. What's his win rate?"

"Put it this way, MacDonald of Barrisdale has him on a retainer, and Pete MacAlistair used him to get off when he murdered that James Campbell with a boathook. If we need someone to go up against the State, I can't think of a better candidate. He won't be bribed or cowed. You can go through the entire roll of the Writers to the White Rose and not find a more qualified or battle-hardened lawyer."

Charlie looked at Kirstie, "What do you think? Have you ever met this man?"

"No, I haven't. But if he is a Writer to the White Rose, then he has to be up there with the best, the WWR are the elite."

"OK, well I'll go to Oban right now to try and meet him and organise Gillespie's defence. We don't have much time."

Several hours later Charlie found himself in a leafy garden square in Oban. It wasn't a part of the capital that he was familiar with; for a start it reeked of money. Most of Oban was set on a steep hillside, leading from the harbour below to the Riaghaltas above. White Rose Square was one of the few places where a sufficient footprint had been terraced to allow a garden square to be carved out of the hill. It wasn't as big as the squares of New Town Edinburgh or stucco-fronted Belgravia, but the fine ashlar stone buildings and heavy bronze railings sent a strong message of quiet power. In the middle was the emerald green of the WWR bowling green, set about with demi-lune beds of roses that had wakened from their winter slumber but were yet to flower. Certain to be white, Charlie thought, lawyers not being renowned for flights of creative fancy.

He drove slowly round the square until he came to an imposing building with shallow Doric pilasters lining its imposing piano nobile. A gleaming black door of the deepest jet was surmounted by a finely carved fanlight of delicate swags holding the single Latin numeral for ten. X marks the spot he thought as he parked in front. He fumbled with his phone to pay the parking charge; the capital's wardens being notorious for their insatiable voracity and assiduity.

He approached the lustrous door. On the right-hand side of the jamb were a series of small silver plaques, each carrying a name; MacAuley, MacCunliffe, Cameron, MacRory, MacDonald, Nicholson - down and down it went – Fletcher, MacLanahan, Mackechnie, Fraser, Smith and finally MacNeas. He had to rub it free of tarnish to make sure, the dull blackened metal a contrast to the burnished rectangles above. He went inside.

"Hello." Charlie tried to keep his voice normal, swallowing his nervousness. "I'm here to see Mr Niocal MacNeas. Where should I go?" The busily masticating receptionist could barely be bothered to lift her eyes from her phone to ask him to first sign in and then take the stairs to the fifth floor.

"The fifth floor?" Charlie asked, just to be sure.

Could the building even have five floors?

She flicked her eyeline to him for a nano-second, simultaneously incorporating a glacial eyeroll and a nod of her head, before returning to her screen.

Tossing an obsequious "Thank you so much for your help" over his shoulder, Charlie turned to climb the stairs; cost, heritage and James Gillespie Graham architecture seemingly not allowing for a lift to be installed. By the time he got to the garret on the fifth floor, he was sweating from the climb and the accumulated heat that had risen from the floors below. In contrast to the twelve-foot ceilings of the first floor, here he practically had to bend double. Feeling altogether less confident than when he'd parked only moments earlier, he knocked on the grimy door that bore the name Niocal MacNeas, WWR.

"Come in, come in." Came a cheerful voice from inside.

Charlie turned the handle; the ribbed brass was slippery with decades of palm grease; he snatched his hand back peering at it in the dim light before wiping it on his kilt and going in. If erudition was measured in dust and dilapidation, then Niocal MacNeas WWR was a very learned man indeed. The attic room was hung with shadow, piles of books teetered, feathered with scraps of paper tucked hither and yon. A well-worn passage had been carved through this moraine of knowledge over the lozenges of a fine Bukaharan Tekke, the blood red madder the only slash of colour in the otherwise monochrome room. A small desk was tucked into the solitary dormer window, a shaded light cast its illuminating pool on dog-eared files and old newspapers several layers deep. On top of this lay a feint ruled pad of yellow A4 paper and a rotary pencil. Niocal MacNeas had his back to the door, his tweed-framed bulk absorbing most of the light, fugitive beams silhouetting his unkempt hair in a frizzy halo.

"Come in, come in, dear boy. Come and tell me what your problem is, and we shall see how I can be helping you."

8 – Taken

It was the first time Gillespie had been in a helicopter. He didn't know if it was the surprising lurch of the machine into the air or his general sense of terror that made his stomach sink through the floor. There wasn't much space in the back, and for all of the short journey he stared down the barrel of a pistol that his captor casually trained on him.

His thought process was spasmodic, floundering between white hot indignation to self-pity by way of utter dejection. How could Kirstie have just handed him over? After everything they'd been through! Hadn't he helped to rescue her from a fate worse than death in the Lamontation's dungeons? Hadn't he killed the Clan's greatest oppressor, liberating Dunderave and allowing their way of life to return to a semblance of normality? She hadn't even tried to shield him. She had just given him up at the first time of asking. The memory of her pointed finger cut him as deep as any blade.

What was he going to do now? What would happen to him? How could he defend himself? Would the Clan come to his aid? Why hadn't he just stayed in Antrim and rebuilt his house? Why did he think that he needed revenge? What was he thinking!

He didn't notice the length of the flight; his brain was whirring too fast. But it wasn't long before they landed, the roar of the rotors slowly subsiding, allowing his brain to think coherently for the first time since he had been taken. The door of the helicopter slid open, and he was manhandled out of the aircraft on to the flat roof of a large building. As he was led to the stairwell, he could see the distinctive shape of the Riaghaltas in the distance and the sea beyond; he was in Oban!

His hands were bound, and the black-clad figures pulled and pushed him on a discombobulating journey of concrete stairwells, corridors and endless sets of self-closing doors. Occasionally, they would hold these for him and occasionally they would allow them to swing closed in his face. Was it deliberate? It was hard to tell. One caught him a sharp blow to his temple knocking him backwards. The sullen throb it left behind matched his mood.

Finally, they entered a white painted room filled with several rows of brightly coloured hard plastic seats and a glass box that ran along one wall. There was a scattering of other occupants, all sat looking dejected and with tied hands. A couple even had their hands bound to their feet through a belt at their waist – they were clearly the most dangerous. The oppressive smell of stale man-sweat hung heavily on the air with no air conditioning or fans to stir it.

Gillespie was marched up to the glass box. Inside was a pretty young clerk, her thick black hair bound up in bun. He smiled; she scowled.

"I need to register you and to confirm some details please." Her Gaelic was fast and had an accent that he struggled to understand; he wondered if she was from the Outer Isles. He bent down to the speaker to try and hear what she was saying.

"Can you please confirm your full name, patronymic, any identifying given names, Clan, date of birth and address." She pushed a sheet of paper and a grubby biro across the counter.

He thought briefly about giving his address as Dunderave or Elrig, but instead put his home address in Antrim. He swithered over what to put for Clan; at that moment he felt abandoned by the MacNachtans but, on the other hand, what would happen if he put nothing? That would mark him as an outsider – would that be good or bad? In the end, his blood was stronger, and he scrawled MacNachtan in the Clan box.

"I want to talk to a lawyer." It seemed like a logical request to make.

"A lawyer?"

"Yes, a lawyer. Surely, I am allowed someone to represent me?"

"Of course. You get a phone call. You may call anyone you choose. The phone is over there." She nodded at an old-fashioned rotary dial telephone that hung on the wall, its once neatly coiled flex was stretched and limp.

"Do you have a list of lawyers for me to choose from."

She looked at him as if he was an idiot.

"No. What do you think this is, a public library?"

He picked up the handset and tried dialling Eammon back at the farm, maybe he could get the Embassy on the case, after all he was a Kingdom citizen. He wasn't too surprised when the number came back as unobtainable. He went back to the counter.

"I need to make an international call – is that possible?"

"No. What do you think this is, a hotel?"

"If I don't have a lawyer's number memorised what am I supposed to do?"

"Dunno. Not my problem."

"I am a Kingdom citizen; I demand to be given access to my Ambassador."

She sniggered, as did most of the room, but did nothing.

One of the heavy steel doors opened and a pair of prison guards came towards him, casually twirling their batons in a threatening manner. His chaperones from the Black Watch pushed him towards them, before disappearing back the way they had come. The guards prodded him with their batons as if he was a bull in a showring, driving him towards the heavy steel door. He could feel the eyes of the room on him as he went, the occasional titter of laughter following after him. He was almost relieved when the door swung closed behind him cutting him off from their disdain.

9 – Luachrach Prison

Charlie had never been inside the Luachrach Prison, although he had driven past it many times. It sat on an island in the freshwater loch of the same name. To get to it, he had to negotiate the outskirts of Oban, park his vehicle in the shoreside car park and walk over a causeway with checkpoints at both ends, the distance between them a hundred metres of totally exposed concrete jetty. The wind picked up and was driving the water onto the walkway, occasionally spattering him as he passed. He tried to keep his shoes out of the worst of it; they had leather soles and he didn't want them wet; his feet would freeze.

The thick grey cloud threatened snow. He shuddered; somehow it seemed awfully appropriate to Gillespie's predicament. He could taste the chilling damp on the air. Cursing the wind and grateful for his heavyweight kilt which resisted its best attempts at indecency, he finally made it to the entrance. The façade was intimidating. The relentless humidity leached shit-stained streaks of rust from the reinforcing bars just below the surface of its grimy grey concrete skin as if it was haemorrhaging the misery within. On one side stood a twenty-foot-high doorway, large enough to accommodate the transport vehicles, on the other was a chipped and rusted turnstile. Above, capping the stolid concrete below, was a shallow, bright green copper mansard roof.

He pressed the buzzer next to the turnstile.

"I'm here to visit Gillespie MacNachtan."

No answer came, but the LED on the turnstile went

green, and he was able to push the heavy steel bars round; it was a tight fit, even for him. In the lobby waiting for him, a broad smile on his face, was Niocal MacNeas. Charlie let out a sigh of relief; he was glad he wasn't doing this totally on his own. Minutes later they were seated in a small square room, a table in the middle and four chairs bolted to the floor, two on either side. The room managed the difficult combination of being searingly bright but depressingly gloomy. They waited, listening to the distant banging of doors, the screech of sliding gates, snatched shouts and the hum of fluorescent lights.

The door finally opened, and Gillespie shuffled through, hands bound and with a dejected look on his face. Without even thinking, Charlie got up and gave him a hug across the table before being told off by the guard: "No touching! Keep your distance!"

Charlie nodded dumbly and sat down. Gillespie hadn't even been convicted of anything yet and he was already being stripped of his humanity.

"How are you? You bearing up OK? How are they treating you? Nin sends his love; in fact, all the Clan do." Charlie scattered some letters and cards on the table. Gillespie picked up one with a brightly coloured smiley face surrounded by a message that read "Gillepsie you are my hero —An Smàladair! ♥♥♥ Love Mara". His eyes visibly moistened, tears welling at their corners.

"I'm…. I'm…I…dunno, I guess I'm OK." He put Mara's card down and absentmindedly sifted through the others, spreading them out on the table but not really reading them.

Charlie decided to change tack. "This is Niocal MacNeas, he is going to defend you in the Court. He is a Writer to the White Rose, that's the highest category of lawyer we have in the Republic. He has a lot of experience dealing with the Court. Also, I wanted to reassure you that the Clan Hardship Fund is going to pay, so you don't need to worry about the cost. Maybe you should introduce yourself Niocal."

Gillespie stared at the table. MacNeas cleared his throat.

"Maha, yes, my dear boy. Allow me to introduce myself. I have been practicing Canun law now for thirty-five years. There is little I haven't seen in that time. I was a junior on the Rose of Kilravock vs Shaw case way back at the start of my career, and since then have helped Keppoch vs MacSween and Findlay vs Henderson among many others. For a detailed case history, take a look at my website." He pushed a thick vellum card across the table. On it, in almost illegibly florid Italic script, read Niocal MacNeas WWR, Cliù Agus Saorsa - Honour and Freedom – underneath.

Gillespie picked it up and turned it over in his hand, as if looking for something more. He carefully placed it back down on the table in front of him, lifting his eyes to look at MacNeas for the first time.

"OK, Mr MacNeas, Writer to the White Rose, what exactly are you going to do to get me out of here?"

Charlie was relieved that Gillespie was at last engaging. He reached out and gave Gillespie's hand a squeeze, "Don't you worry, Mr MacNeas will have you out of here in no time."

"The case is set for next Monday; they are not hanging around. I must say it is quite irregular. I have made representations to the High Adjudicator, but I am afraid she has dismissed them all."

"But I want it as soon as possible. I've got to get out of here before I go insane or get my throat cut. You won't believe the people that they have in here." Gillespie lifted his hollowed eyes, his haunting stare pierced Charlie through and through.

"Maha, yes, well, that is what we are all trying to do isn't it. Now can we go through your side of what happened please? I have taken witness statements from a number of other sources, including Charles Farquharson," MacNeas nodded at Charlie, "and Ninian MacNachtan, Kirstie MacNachtan and LeroyMar MacNachtan among others. But I need your statement to bind it all together."

They spent the next few hours reliving the events of the night. The attack at the Two Stags, Gillespie's role in freeing the Clan from the burning building, the pursuit back to Dunderave, Allan Stewart's invocation of Canun, LeroyMar's acceptance and Kirstie's clear statement at the beginning.

"You definitely heard her say "Full-blooded"?" MacNeas asked for what felt like the tenth time.

"Yes, yes, Full-blooded: everyone heard." Gillespie's frustration was mounting going over and over the same facts again and again.

"And why did you then choose to intervene?"

"This man was a psychotic killer! He'd just murdered several people by burning the Two Stags down. He slew the Clan's previous Chief and Seanchaidh in cold blood, he'd kidnapped eight of the Clan's children, he tried to kill me and burned my house down…. need I go on?!"

"Yes, but as you, yourself, has said, you only have very peripheral connections to the Clan. It will be challenging to argue that you were defending the Clan's Cliù if you are not an active member. I suppose there is the case of MacDonald vs MacDonald, or maybe Gunn vs Gordon, but even so it is weak."

"Wait," shouted Charlie feeling a eureka thought bursting fully formed into his brain. "That's it, surely!"

Gillespie and MacNeas turned to look at him expectantly.

"If Gillespie isn't a proper member of the Clan how can he be subject to the Court of Canun? He's not even a citizen of the Republic for God's sake. How can he be subject to these laws if he doesn't even know what they are, if he doesn't have any Cliù to defend! Surely, as a citizen of the Kingdom he does not fall under the jurisdiction of this Court?"

MacNeas started to nod his head slowly, "You may just be on to something there, my lad." He reached into his briefcase and pulled out a tablet, swiping through page after page of indices to find what he was looking for. "OK, maha, yes, here it is! I knew it was in here somewhere: Smith vs Grant 1832. This is a precedent where a John Smith of Altrincham was discharged after breaking up a contest under Canun, accidentally killing one of the protagonists, a certain Seumaidh Grant. The Court ruled that as a citizen of the Kingdom he had no Cliù and was not subject to Canun and he was therefore discharged. Yes, by Jove, I think that is it!"

Gillespie was visibly transformed by the news; a flush returned to his cheeks and his eyes were bright with excitement: "You really think that will work?"

"Well, the Law is very clear; the precedent is there.

Even if it is not much used, I really don't see what the Judge can do. They will have to discharge you. It really is a promising development."

Gillespie grabbed Charlie by the shoulders and planted a sloppy kiss on his cheek. "Thank you, Charlie!"

Charlie felt his cheeks flushing red with embarrassment, but he also felt a frisson from Gillespie's touch. He swallowed hard; he hadn't been expecting that. "Great, great, well I'm just delighted to be some use from time to time."

Turning to MacNeas he continued "Do you think you have everything you need?"

"Yes, maha, I think I do. I just need to reacquaint myself with all the details of the case, to make sure there is nothing they can do to slip through the precedent. But it seems pretty cut and dried to me."

Gillespie turned back to look at Charlie. "Thank you so much for everything. I can't tell you how tough it has been in here. Fortunately, they have me segregated as I am only on remand. The vicious bastards in here would chill your blood, I can tell you."

"Never you worry," Charlie squeezed Gillespie's shoulder to reassure him. "We'll have you out of here on Monday, just stay out of trouble till then. We'll get you back to Elrig before you know it. Shonique is dying to see you."

"Yes, I have been thinking about her too, please give her my love. As for coming back to Elrig, coming back to the Clan, I have thought a lot about it, and I have come to realise that this is not my place. I need to go home, to Antrim, to rebuild, to farm; that is who I am. The Republic is another world, and I'm tired of being a fish out of water."

Charlie nodded, now was not the moment for these discussions. There would be plenty of time for those decisions.

"Until Monday, then. Monday and freedom."

10 – Plotting

It had been years since John Lamont was last in Edinburgh and in those days it was just as a junior member of the Comhairle. He'd spent his days in Holyrood committee rooms and his nights at the Wally Dug or Sandy Bell's. This time was different. The Presidential Range Rover whisked him to the Arrochar border crossing where he was met by a fleet of police motorcycle outriders and black Jaguars that escorted him across Scotland to the capital. On arrival, he went straight to Bute House, the First Minister's official residence to have the first of many meetings.

First Minister Balfour put on quite a show, with an official welcome by the Scots Guards and their marching band. Lamont swore that if he had to listen to another rendition of the Garb of Old Gaul he wouldn't be responsible for his actions. Once the ceremony was over, they went inside for tea and the hard work started.

Guy Walker, the Scottish Minister of the UK Government, had flown up from London especially. Walker was short, portly with a round red face and aggressive disposition; Lamont took an almost immediate dislike to him. The first ten minutes of the meeting was filled with the usual platitudes. Lamont didn't mind playing along, as he knew that what was going to come after would be more difficult. Balfour finally seemed to think that he had been slathered in enough soft soap for the opening gambit to be played.

"President Lamont, you know how delighted we are that you have been appointed. Especially after the tragic death of President Fraser - she was so admired – we really value the appointment of a robust leader. As you know, there have been any number of difficult times between the Kingdom and the Republic, but the last few months have been as tough as any in the past 100 years. The Kingdom has suffered; our border force has been shot up, three sailors killed, our businesses looted, and now we face the prospect of significant financial losses because one of your banks has gone bust."

"Strictly speaking, that one's not on us." Lamont interjected. "The Bombay Canton Bank was regulated by the Kingdom, always has been. You can't pin that on the Republic."

"Try telling that to the Chinese," Walker sneered. "I am not sure that they care about the finer points of regulatory alignment between the Kingdom and the Republic. Do you know how much money their citizens have lost?"

"No, should I?"

Walker leant forward, his face shiny, a miasma of body odour seeping across the table. "I guess that you also don't know how much of the Kingdom's Civil Service pension scheme was invested in that Bank either, do you?"

"Nope, can't say that I do. You see, that is not my job; that is the job of the regulator and a role that lies firmly in the purview of those clowns." Lamont flicked a dismissive finger at Balfour and his array of flunkeys, who visibly winced. "And frankly, if you have brought me here to have a moan about things that are not my responsibility, then this is going to be a frustrating few days."

Seeing that approach was getting nowhere, Balfour tried another tack. "Our satellites have been looking at what is going on up and down the west coast of your so-called Republic. From what they can see it is a warzone. Trade seems to have ceased and people are being burned out of their homes. And yet, the Government seems to be nowhere. In Islay there seems to be a concerted programme of cleansing of much of the existing population – very distasteful and simply not something we can tolerate."

Standing up, Balfour started to warm to his theme, pacing up and down on his side of the table using his right hand to karate chop his points of emphasis.

"There is no law enforcement, no attempt to suppress these outrageous acts against human decency. We cannot simply sit by and allow innocent people to suffer in this way. Ultimately, if you can't, or won't, take action then we will."

"The Prime Minister has briefed the UN Security Council and they are pretty relaxed. In fact, even the Chinese and the Russians were supportive, unsurprising really considering how much they have suffered at the hands of your citizens." Balfour sneered. "They see it largely as an internal matter apparently. And as long as we don't raise difficult questions about the Uighurs or Chechnya, then they are quite happy for us to crack on."

Lamont froze. His face must have given him away, as Balfour continued with growing confidence.

"Yes, that's right, you jumped up little shit. We have a green light to do pretty much whatever we want with you. Even the Americans won't put their hand in the fire for you this time. No one there seems to remember the Revolutionary War, more's the pity for you. The French did whitter briefly about the Sans Culottes and their glorious contribution to La Revolution, but no one paid them much mind and ultimately they ended up voting with the rest of the Council. Yes, it was a unanimous decision."

"I am not sure what you want me to do." Lamont replied spreading his hands. "Our security force may be lethal, but it is small. The Black Watch can't possibly fight on as many fronts as are opening up at the moment. I was rather hoping that Lord MacDonald would have suppressed Catriona MacLean by now, restoring balance to the Republic. But it seems that he has gone off on a hare-brained revenge mission of his own against MacLeod of Dunvegan. You Kingdom officials don't know how lucky you are. You don't have to try and contain the psychotic, heavily armed warbands that we have on our side of the border. It is harder than it may look."

"What we don't understand," Walker interjected, "is why it has blown up in the first place. I studied Republic politics at University and have wasted too many hours of my life reading the Oban Raven. I know that this is unprecedented. As the President, we are looking to you to restore order."

Lamont felt that the moment was now ripe for him to make his pitch. "I can assure you there is nothing I want more than to return peace to the Republic. The Gaels have suffered too long under the tyranny of a backward culture beholden to outdated concepts of Clan, Canun and Cliù. Despite being one of the oldest democracies in the world, we still have semi-feudal Chieftains running around as if they own the place. The Clans are little more than organised gangs. Yes, they dress it up in terms of familial bonds and shared culture and opportunity, but really there is little to distinguish them from the Mafia or the Triads. Similarly, with Canun and Cliù, they have no role in a modern society."

Lamont continued: "I have spent a long time thinking about how to bring the nation into the 21st Century and I believe that with the neighbourly support of the Kingdom we can do it. For too long the people of the Republic been weighed down by cultural fetishes. I am determined to do away with all that, to reclaim the Republic's rightful place at the forefront of progressive nations."

"Firstly, I want to disestablish the Clan Chiefs, then I want to ban all the tropes and childish props of their backward past – highland dress will be banned, weapons too, tartan will be expunged, and bagpipes consigned to the bonfire of history. It is impossible to underestimate how important these are to the psyche of the Gael. Like Ataturk I need to smash these conventions if I am to build a modern nation."

"Finally, but perhaps most critically, I want to make English the official language. It is ludicrous that we still rely on such a minority language, it is a barrier to trade and globalisation. Gaelic is not the language of Mars missions and genomic technology; it has no role to play in big data and AI. It is a cultural cul de sac in which the Gaels have been marooned for far too long."

"If I - I mean we - are to effect real change then we need to root these anachronisms out. I am afraid to say it will require a strong hand, and there will be resistance. But together, we have the right side of history behind us. I know we can succeed. And if we do, then this will create a new golden age for relations between our two nations."

Balfour looked taken aback by Lamont's speech, it clearly hadn't been what he was expecting. But he knew Lamont well enough that his sudden reasonableness seemed a little too convenient.

"Well, I must say that I thoroughly welcome this change in approach by the Republic. That the President of the Republic should ask the Kingdom for assistance in modernising is very welcome. And dare I say, more than a little surprising. Do you have any democratic mandate for what you are proposing? Surely, what you are suggesting is highly treasonous in the Republic? How do we know that it is something your people actually want and will accept?"

"As you know, our poor benighted people suffer under the domination of their chiefs, they are not free to speak their minds fully. However, I can assure you that the Seanadh, that great check and balance to our ludicrous Comhairle, and which is voted for by the people, is fully supportive. If you wish, I can arrange for you to speak to David Brown the Chief Clerk of the Constitution, and he can corroborate everything I have said."

Walker turned to Balfour his fat face now carrying a smug grin: "I think that President Lamont speaks a lot of sense. I know there will be great appetite to support this initiative in Westminster. I think it is high time the Republic had a makeover. I am sure you are right that there will be a little resistance, but we all know that you can't make an omelette without breaking a few eggs. But if we have the Seanadh on side I don't imagine anyone will care about a bit of collateral damage."

"Yes," said Balfour. "The Gaelic Republic is dead; it

is time to burn the corpse."

11 – Three Fingers In The Bog

Jeanie Campbell had been known as Three Fingers for so long now she'd almost forgotten her real name. As a child she had been gifted with dexterity, from the petit point that her grandmother had insisted on teaching her, to the clarsach she'd learned at school, her nimbleness had made her stand out. But that wasn't why she was called Three Fingers. No, that had been the result of a teenage dispute that had got out of hand. She rubbed the stump of the finger on her left hand, the nub of bone and gristle was hard and alien. It'd acquired its own character, aloof from the rest of her body. It was changed, different, other. She didn't miss the finger particularly, although it meant forming chords on a guitar was that much harder; but Django Reinhardt had had three fingers melted together in a fire and he was still the greatest guitarist who'd ever lived, so she had no excuse. She just hadn't been fast enough that day, an error that she'd promised never to repeat.

Sweat was pouring off her as she worked through her cuts and guards, the tip of her sword dissecting the air like a conductor's baton: poised, controlled, powerful. She missed her usual sparring partners, but ever since the MacLeans had arrived the sword yard had been shut, so she'd had to work out at home. She needed to keep her fitness levels up if she was to have any chance at the National All-Comers in November, assuming that it was held at all. It was a critical part of the selection process for next year's World Championships, so she assumed it would have to be. Fencing was one of the few sports where the Republic dominated and the national Cliù demanded that they compete.

Slope swords, hanging guard, cut one, inside guard, cut three, St George's, cut two, slip leg, volte, sweep, outside guard, cut seven, traverse, traverse, passing step, cut four, thrust. Her steel sliced and diced the air as she moved. She finally stopped, as much to tie back the annoying strand of hair that flicked back and forth across her field of vision as to catch her breath. She'd thought of shaving all her hair off, the last thing she needed was to be distracted in a bout, but her fierce red hair was part of her brand and her fans around the country would not thank her for cutting it. She restarted, her bare feet swishing over the tatami mat, she always fought barefoot, the only other sounds the cleave of the sword in the air and her breathing. She finished with her famous Mako Leap, jumping high in volte, sweeping the air with steel, before landing in a crouch with an upward thrust.

Panting, she picked up her towel and mopped the sweat that was streaming from her. She could hear vehicles in the distance; who would be visiting at this time? She prayed it wasn't MacLeans. The noise was getting closer, so she quickly locked away her training apparatus and sheathed her sword. She went outside pulling the door closed behind her. She could now see the line of vehicles coming down the track over the bog. Three of them, not so many. She wandered over the yard, dodging the puddles and trying to keep off the gravel; she was still in bare feet.

The vehicles stopped and a young man who could not have been more than twenty two, got out and came to the gate. "Halo, are you Jean Campbell? Is this the

Bog House?"

"Aye, it is. And what is your name?"

He seemed a little taken aback by her directness, bashfully offering "James, I mean Jamie MacLean."

"And what can I do for you James, I mean Jamie, MacLean? Why have you come to my house. Not sure there's anything of interest for you here." She held her arms out as if inviting him to consider the merits of the muddy yard, dotted with flowerpots and the odd tractor tyre.

He seemed caught off guard, stammering, "Its, ah, it's very nice."

"Are you here to burn my house James, I mean Jamie? Are you here to root me out like you have so many others?"

"Er, no, I mean yes. Kind of." He flushed red.

She rolled her eyes, "What exactly do you mean James, I mean Jamie? I've watched you bastards roll across Islay, evicting my friends and fellow Clan and killing those that won't leave. You think I haven't seen the huddled masses at Port Ellen being bundled onto the ferry. And now you have made it here, to me."

Some of his colleagues opened their doors and a couple got out, bolstering Jamie's resolve. They looked much tougher than he did, with all the cold, bluntness of a sledgehammer; there would be no negotiating with them. Jamie on the other hand was green as grass, obviously some tacksman's son sent to do his Daddy's bidding.

"So, how many houses have you burnt today Jamie? Are you going to burn me out next?"

"Look, I don't want to burn any houses. I want to give you fair warning to remove yourself and the belongings you wish to keep before nightfall. Your house has been designated as accommodation for refugees from Rum."

"And what about me, Jamie? What am I supposed to do?"

"You are free to go, take as much as you can, and get the ferry back to the mainland. This is a MacLean island now and you Campbells are unwelcome. You must leave or face the consequences."

"Jamie, there is nothing here, just bulrushes and bog-cotton. What do you think your refugees are going to do with it?"

"That's not for me to say; you have to leave. By nightfall."

He then turned and gestured to his men to get back in their vehicles; they drove away back across the bog.

Three Fingers went inside and filled the kettle, tea was needed. Once the whistle became unbearable she took it off the hob and filled a cup, dunking a Clansman teabag in it along with a slug of milk and two teaspoons of sugar; this was not a moment for Oolong or Darjeeling. It tasted better than the bogwater it resembled, but not by much. It did have a restorative effect though, calming her racing mind. She wandered through the house, it was a small croft, not much more than two up and two down. She had built a kitchen on the southern side of the house though, and that is where she spent most of her time. It caught the sun for much of the day and she could sit and look beyond the soggy green moss of her garden to the deer fence and the sedge brown of the bog.

The bog was part of her. She'd lived here all her life. Like her mother and father before her and her father's parents before them; she was a Bog Campbell and leaving didn't feel right. Who would look after her sheep, few though they were? Who would cut the peats for the distilleries to flavour their whisky? Her family had been doing that for more than a hundred years. What about her design studio and all the projects she had lined up? She couldn't leave all that behind. Finally, there was her dojo; made in a disused outbuilding this was where she had spent so many hours of her life practising. She knew every brick, every beam. Her cups and trophies lined the walls – what would happen to them? The dreams and memories of a family over a century and more were about to be cast to the wind, to resettle and regrow somewhere new, or fall on stony ground and die.

She fingered the blades hanging in her armoury, each of them held memories of competitive bouts contested, won or lost, the memories were there. She picked out her best broadsword, the one with the yataghan profile, running her finger along the shock steel blade, the damascus pattern led her eye along the fuller, no imperfections and the sharpest edge. She put it and her favourite dirk to one side. The rest she bundled up in an old blanket before wrapping them in a bit of tarpaulin. Then she climbed into the roof space, cursing the pain as the joists bit into her knees she crawled as far as she could before tucking them under the eaves. The bastards would have to be very thorough to find them. Satisfied, she pulled the door closed behind her, there was no point locking it.

She stood in her living room and looked to see what she should take. A few photo frames of her Mum and Dad, some candles, a large photo of the Big Strand on a sunny day, a saggy sofa that had borne the weight of too many arses over the years, the seams unpinned, the puckered buttons shed; they were welcome to it. She thought about smashing the TV or the games console out of spite, but even now, deep within her, there was a confidence that she would return. Instead, she scooped up the photos of her Mum and Dad and stuffed them in the bottom of her rucksack with the clothes she would need, her laptop and phone charger. Not much to show for a life.

She didn't want to risk still being there when the MacLeans returned, she couldn't guarantee that she wouldn't do something foolish. She ate what she wanted from the fridge, stuffing as many tins and a bag of rice in her pack for good measure. Finally, she filled her flask with the twenty-year-old Mulindry, the best bottle of whisky that was left in the house – she wasn't going to leave that. She raised the empty bottle to her lips, savouring the last drop.

She stuck the key in the front door, no point making it more difficult that it needed to be. Let them come, let them sleep in my bed and drink my whisky. She wasn't going to leave; she wasn't going to run away back to the mainland. No, she was staying. She'd join with Iain Og and the resistance who were skulking on Beinn Bhàn. Shouldering her pack, she set off through the bog towards the hills to the east. She would be back and if the motherfuckers trashed her house she swore that she would cut them up into little pieces.

12 – Friends and Enemies

Gillespie hadn't slept well; his fellow inmates had kept him awake all through the night. There was always something happening to someone it seemed: grunts, moans, laughs, screams. It was a madhouse of emotions. Sometimes, he sat on his bed and tried to single out an individual noise; who was it, what was their story, why were they still awake at 4am? When he'd first arrived he'd been too terrified to leave his cell. Although his door was open for much of the day allowing him to socialise with the other remand prisoners, he was nervous. When he finally dared to venture out, he eyed the other residents apprehensively, unsure of how to act. He didn't want to come across as a pushover, but he knew acting tough brought its own risks; inviting a challenge was not a mistake he wanted to make.

During the afternoon unlock, he leant against the landing rail and tried to take it all in. It was a Victorian-style jail over four floors with a central atrium strung with mesh to catch thrown objects. Each floor was divided up into sections by steel barred gates. His section had twenty cells and during unlock they milled around their cell doors, a few of the longer stay prisoners speaking together, the newbies, like Gillespie, very much keeping to themselves. He leant against the rail and peered down onto the lower floors. On the floor below was a particularly raggedy looking man with matted hair and a hostile demeanour. He was endlessly shouting threats and pointing at some unseen protagonist on the landing beneath Gillespie. He'd ripped the sleeves off his standard issue white shirt so that the gibbous mass of his muscled arms were on display, the mailed fist holding a cross of the MacDonalds clearly tattooed on his left arm. He looked up; his narrow glittering eyes pinning Gillespie to the rail. The MacDonald's index finger swept upwards to point straight at him, his thumb hammering down as if letting off a shot. He then laughed and disappeared from view.

Gillespie turned his gaze to look down his landing, trying not to catch anyone's eye. There was a tall, pale man, as thin and taut as a whip, two cells down. Gillespie was transfixed by the man's hair, it was the reddest hue he'd ever seen; it seemed to burn, his loose carmine curls flickered like flames in the LED light. The red continued into the stubbly beard that swathed his jaw, only interrupted by a thick white scar on his left cheek. They stared at each other for a moment before the man tuned to speak to his bald, middle-aged neighbour. They then both looked at Gillespie – the bald man pointed – and suddenly the tall man sprang towards him, seemingly covering the fifteen feet in single leap and knocking Gillespie to the floor. Gillespie grunted with the force of the impact as he hit the ground; the weight of the man on top of him. Before he could even put up a defence, the man was on his feet and trying to help pick him up off the floor.

"What the fuck are you playing at?" Gillespie shouted, trying to catch his breath.

"Just saving you from an unpleasant gift from your friend down there." The man gestured over the railing at the wild MacDonald on the floor below, who was leaping up and down laughing.

"What do you mean?"

"Look." The man pointed at where Gillespie had been standing. There was a puddle of yellow liquid on the floor. The man bent down and sniffed the rail. "Mostly piss I would say, with a bit of his Sìol-gin for good measure. Not something you want to be wearing, I would say."

Gillespie had to stop for a moment to fully understand. "What you mean he…"

"Yes, he has a habit of doing that. His little joke let's say. Apart from being revolting, you also don't know what else might be in it. Hepatitis C would only be the start of it."

Gillespie self-consciously wiped his hands on his kilt, even though he hadn't touched any of the foul liquid.

"Thanks. I had no idea."

"You a virgin, then?" The man asked.

"What do you mean…" Gillespie stammered.

"Is this your first time inside?"

"Yes."

"Ah, OK. Well, you need to watch yourself in here."

Gillespie nodded, feeling out of his depth. To fill the silence he stuck out his hand; "I'm Gillespie, Gillespie MacNachtan. Thanks for saving me from that."

"Aye no bother. I'm Davy MacSween. What are you doing in this hole anyway?"

Gillespie had heard a little about the MacSweens and their Redshank units and what he'd heard was hardly reassuring, mercenaries not being known for their moral rectitude. For centuries they had provided highly effective security to those that could afford it and while in theory they were not allowed to operate in the Republic, they instead plied their bloody trade from Moscow to Mogadishu, Guadalajara to Guangzhou.

"MacSween you say" Gillespie said without really thinking.

"Aye, do you have a problem with that?" Davy's green eyes instantly annealed to a glittering edge. "And who the fuck are you to judge me anyway?"

"I'm not judging you. I don't even know you or what you've done." Gillespie struggled to find ameliorating words to pour on the troubled waters that seemed to have sprung between them so suddenly.

"Good. 'Cos there are plenty that do." The tension in the air evaporated as fast as it had arrived. "Anyway, what the hell is someone like you doing in a place like this?"

Gillespie explained the bare bones of his case, not wanting to go into too much detail. But as he spoke the expression on Davy's face changed to one of amazement.

"You killed Allan Stewart? Not THE Allan Stewart from Ballachulish?"

"I don't know where he was from, all I know is that he was an evil bastard that murdered my friends, kidnapped their children, stole their land and burned my house down. He was about to kill my girlfriend's brother; I couldn't stand by."

"I wonder…" Davy was lost in thought. "…If it was that Allan Stewart then you must a hell of a fighter. He was a vicious cunt and no mistake. My God, but there's been many the man, and woman too I'll bet, that has wanted to do that over the years. And as many that have tried and failed. Tell me again how it happened."

Gillespie went through the bloody tale again, about how he'd intervened in the duel, saved LeroyMar's life and battered Allan Stewart from this world with a fire extinguisher.

Finally, when the tale was told in full, Davy stuck out his hand again.

"That'll carry you a long way in here," he said. "Allan Stewart was a man of few friends and many enemies."

Trying to change the subject, Gillespie asked, "What are you here for, if you don't mind me asking?"

Davy suddenly became intense again, coming so close that Gillespie could feel the flecks of spittle on his face. "Never you mind what I've done. Or even what they think I've done."

Gillespie didn't flinch and held Davy's penetrating gaze as calmly as he could; he knew enough to hold his ground. The moment passed and Davy laughed his easy chuckle. "Let's just say that I may have a lot to answer for. It's just a question of whether the charges they have against me this time are the right ones!"

Davy waved down at the wild-eyed MacDonald to attract his attention before calmly and determinedly flicking him the finger, laughing as the man raged back, hurling empty threats across the void.

Davy's bald companion walked over; he didn't offer a name. They stood and watched the wing, Davy pointing out particular characters to Gillespie. They either had an interesting back story or were dangerous and worth avoiding.

"How come you know everyone here?" Gillespie asked, "I thought you were just on remand."

"I am, but I've been through here enough over the years to recognise some of the faces. Some of them don't change."

"Are there many prisons in the Republic?" Gillespie

asked.

"A few, most of the Republic's laws are dealt with under Canun, but this is the biggest, if you don't count St Kilda, and that is somewhere you definitely don't want to end up."

"Have you been there?"

"Nope, thank fuck. You only get sent there for the most serious stuff; not many come back."

Gillespie wondered what lay behind Davy's story. He suspected it was messy.

"When's your trial?" The bald man asked.

"Monday." Gillespie replied.

"You got a decent Brief?"

"I certainly hope so. Apparently, he is a Writer to the White Rose, MacNeas or something."

Davy laughed. "Oh get you! Posh wanker. Writer to the White Rose, my arse. Those are the bastards for it right enough."

The bald man joined in the laughter, drawn by Davy's lead. They stood and talked for a while about the merits of different lawyers and who had the best Brief. It was clear to Gillespie that Davy did not place much faith in Wig and Gown, but the bald man seemed impressed with MacNeas. Gillespie was just glad for the human interaction and being able to forget his fear for a few minutes. His fate was in the hands of MacNeas, he only hoped that he would be up to the task.

13 – Homecoming

After so long lying prone in a hospital bed, Niall Campbell of Ardbreknish was more relieved than he could say to finally be able to walk away. Ever since his near murder by Allan Stewart at that fateful meeting in Dunderave, he had been clawing his way back to health. It had taken a long time for the smoke damage to be cleared from his lungs, that invisible danger ironically taking much longer to heal than the dirk wound in his chest. By a miracle Stewart's thrust had missed his heart by millimetres. Still, a miss is as good as a mile, as his Dad would've said. He was worried about his hand though, and he constantly rubbed the jagged scar that was now etched across its back, kneading and working it. The physio had said that he would regain most of its functionality, but he still seemed to have lost the power in his middle two fingers. What would that mean for his blade work? He'd been defined by his skills with a sword for so long he couldn't imagine a life without them. He resolved to get to the dojo as soon as possible.

The green air of Argyll hung fresh. Everywhere, life was making the most of the good weather, plants were flowering, trees rustled their new viridian leaves and the birdsong on the air was full of lechery. As the taxi drove him over the hill to Loch Awe those joys of spring did not go unnoticed. But they hurt. Ever since he had seen MacCailean Mòr kiss Brighid all those months ago a nail had been hammered in his heart and that metal splinter had grown into heavy, dull weight that pressed on his chest, immutable and unmoving.

He'd turned it over in his head so many times; surely

Brighid was meant for him. Ever since their school days he'd desired her. The more she had spurned him, the more it had driven him on. It had seemed like a game of cat and mouse, but one where the cat would catch the mouse in the end. But she'd got away. He thought of her grey agate eyes, the way they shone out when she was happy and dulled flat when she was cross. She was guileless, a quality that he found undid him. He wanted to hold her in his arms, to run his fingers through that long blond hair, the colour of meadowsweet.

He now regretted the bravura of the playground, all those hours and days, months even, when he could have been by her side. He felt sure he could have made her love him. Instead, the braggadocio of the teenage male had got in the way and by the time he'd come to his senses school was over and she was away. He would still run in to her from time to time, but it was not as easy to meet as it had been at Inveraray High School; she was a MacNachtan after all. These meetings were mostly limited to a few snatched words here and there, the pleasantries and platitudes of adult life. What about the times they'd spent together? When he'd swept her up to the watchtower at Dun Na Cuaiche for a surprise picnic of strawberries and champagne. They'd laid on his plaid and passed the hours in a gentle reverie of sweet nothings. She'd held his hand and given him a kiss. Did that not show his love was requited?

He watched her though, watched her from afar as she kept her suitors at bay. He felt certain it was because she was saving herself for him. But whenever he had built up sufficient courage to ask her directly, like a fairy light in the bog she would vanish only to appear again just out of reach.

Now his Chief, MacCailean Mòr, whom he had served so loyally for so long, had snatched his true love away. What did she see in him anyway? Did she just love the status, the Castle, the thrill of being close to power? Surely, she wasn't so shallow? But MacCailean Mòr had thieved her from him. Plucking her without a care or thought for his feelings, the selfish entitlement of a Chief. A Chief who could have chosen any but had chosen Brighid.

Lying on his back in the Infirmary, day after day, he spent hours exploring the cracks and stains in the plaster of the ceiling, imagining pathways to achieve his desire. The pain of losing her was balanced by the burning resentment he felt to MacCailean Mòr. He'd served him loyally for so long, how could he betray him in this way? He thought of all the jobs he had been on, all the dangers he had faced. But he was done with that now. He could not support a man that would betray him like this.

The taxi stopped outside his house; the silver-grey larch cladding matched his dour mood. He paid off the driver and went inside. The house was quiet with a musty deadness, the double glazing and insulation robbing it of any fresh air over the past months while he had been recuperating. It reminded him too much of the Infirmary.

He sat down on the sofa and looked around. The shelves were filled with more fencing trophies than books; a few of the silver ones were now tarnishing to black but the cheap ones still shone true. Pictures hung on the wall showing him in exotic locations with the Kilmartin Company, fading memories of tours of duty with trusted comrades, some dead, some as good as dead. A blood dark rug brought from Afghanistan, woven with helicopter gunships and AK47s, filled the floor with a forbidding presence, the tools of death almost certainly knotted by the fingers of a child. In the Infirmary he'd questioned whether he could really leave all this behind. But he knew the answer now; his mind was made up, there could be no turning back.

14 - Cùirt-Chanun

Charlie pulled the Kat into the parking place behind the Court of Canun. He looked across at Nin; he was pale. Charlie probably felt as nervous as Nin looked, but he didn't want to show it. Appearing before the Court was not something any citizen of the Republic would submit to lightly. As the highest Court in the land it was taken very seriously. More than just its authority was its position in moderating the Canun, the unique honour code that had kept the balance between the martial heritage of the Gaels and society's need for order and structure. It had been the genius of King Charles the Liberator to find that balance and it had been taken up and developed during the long years of the Republic. Of course, like so many of the Republic's institutions, it appeared antediluvian and anachronistic. How could a modern society still hold with such a code literally written in the blood of its citizens? But it worked.

They met with Shonique and Kirstie in the lobby of the Court. MacNeas was there too, dressed in his robes as a Writer to the White Rose, his faded black gown puckered with white ribboned roses. He swept ahead of them, leading them up an imposing flight of marble steps to the Number 1 Court Room. There they milled around the doors waiting to be called, Charlie feeling the apprehension rise in his throat. Ever since his visit to Gillespie he'd felt confident that the case was a non-starter, that it would be dismissed swiftly as the Court had no authority over Gillespie given his Kingdom citizenship. But now he was feeling trepidatious. Everything about the Court was designed to dominate;

its grandeur, the arcane clothing, the scale of the rooms, even the doors; he felt tiny and insignificant. He was very glad that he was not having to stand in the dock, although it pained him that Gillespie did. Anyway, it would soon be over.

On the stroke of 11.00 a.m., the double doors swung open, and they were ushered inside. It was a large and tall octagonal room, punctuated with lofty scagliola columns and filled with rows of dark oak benches. At the front was a raised dais panelled with more heavily carved oak surmounted by a thick entablature. Behind this imposing screen, sat a single, empty, red leather-backed chair. Before it on the floor of the Court was a wide table which divided the room and beyond that was the meagre dock.

They took their places behind MacNeas as he proceeded to the left side of the central table. On the right side sat Mr Wringe, the Prosecutor, an elderly man with snow white hair and a gaunt, pinched face. He nodded knowingly at MacNeas who returned the courtly nod. The Courtroom slowly filled with people, some of them official, some just spectators, who like the Tricoteuses enjoyed watching justice being dispensed. At 11.15, Gillespie was led out of a side door and marched to the dock. He was dressed all in white, his hands ziplocked behind his back. The guard carefully removed the cuffs before sitting him down. Charlie waved and smiled, trying to send positive thoughts. Gillespie looked haggard, his time on remand had clearly weighed heavily on him. MacNeas approached the dock and leant towards Gillespie clearly imparting some morale boosting words, Gillespie smiled. Charlie was cheered by that.

Nin nudged him and nodded towards an officious looking woman in a cloud of black grosgrain who entered through a door at the back and approached the podium in front of the High Adjudicator's bench.

"All rise." She said in a strong Lewis accent. Nin cracked a smile, even Charlie had to stop himself laughing, it sounded incongruous to have such a country accent in this centre of urban power. Kirstie dug him in the ribs with her elbow; he regained his composure.

They dutifully stood and waited for the High Adjudicator to enter. The tall doorway just behind the High Adjudicator's bench opened and admitted a surprisingly small but poised woman. She too was dressed entirely in black with two parallel bands of Government tartan on each sleeve of her gown. Her face was framed by her full-bottomed wig, its tight white curls sweeping down to her chest. Her throat was bound in simple red linen band, the two ends hanging like bloody gashes on the black of her robes. She had a clipped smile that hid all emotion. She nodded to the Clerk of the Court, to the Prosecutor and MacNeas in turn before taking her place on the high-backed chair on the dais. She peered down at Gillespie who seemed to wilt under her scrutiny.

Gathering her papers the High Adjudicator began.

"We are gathered here today to consider an egregious breech of Canun Law in which the defendant Gillespie MacNachtan intervened in a Contest under Canun between Allan Stewart, an acting agent of the Republic, and a certain LeroyMar MacNachtan. The prosecution alleges that the Contest had been clearly declared a Full-Blooded Contest under Canun by

Kirstie MacNachtan, the acting Chief of the Clan MacNachtan, but that at the consummation of the Contest, the defendant illegally intervened, leading to the extra-judicial death of Allan Stewart. This Court is now in session. Proceed."

As she sat down, the Prosecutor stood up and, sucking in the folds of his sallow cheeks, started his excoriating attack. His description of Allan Stewart painted a picture of a paragon of virtue, a selfless agent of the State dutifully fulfilling his commitments by shepherding the leaderless MacNachtans and protecting them from their predatory neighbours. On at least two occasions the High Adjudicator looked sharply at Nin with a quelling glance as he gasped and fulminated over these fanciful descriptions of Allan Stewart, who they knew was in fact a murderer of the most cruel disposition.

MacNeas sat there calmly making notes as the description of the events of that awful night were laid out. The Prosecutor conveniently omitted Allan Stewart's burning of the Two Stags and murder of several MacNachtan clansmen, instead choosing to focus on the duel itself, its clear convocation under Canun, and the illegal and murderous intervention by Gillespie which resulted in the death of Allan Stewart at the moment of his victory over LeroyMar.

Charlie didn't notice the time passing and felt that the hearing had only just begun when the Clerk stood up to declare an adjournment for lunch. His palms were sweaty and furrowed by his nails after hours of clenched fists; the tension of the Court coursed through his whole body.

The MacNachtan party hovered outside the

Courtroom door waiting for MacNeas to come out. He finally emerged with the Prosecutor, both chuckling over a shared joke. When he spied the huddled group he assumed a more sober demeanour and walked over to join them.

"How's it going?" Asked Nin in his usual direct manner.

"As expected." MacNeas replied with a smile. "They are walking right into the trap. We just need to give them enough rope." He then excused himself as he disappeared to get some lunch.

The MacNachtans milled around uncertain of what to do, it was Kirstie who finally gripped the situation and ushered them out of the Court to a café across the road. Fifty minutes later they were settling themselves back on the hard, wooden benches of the Court for the afternoon session. There was no question that MacNeas's confidence boosted their mood and the rigmarole of the Courtroom was now more familiar. That made it easier to listen as the Prosecutor put the finishing touches to his case, which to their ears seemed utterly damning, before MacNeas finally had his chance to take to the floor.

Rising to his feet, MacNeas seemed to swell in stature as he surveyed the Courtroom, his shoulders thrown back, his hands gripping the edge of his robe.

"Your Honour, I have listened to the case made by my learned friend here and while it has been fascinating to hear this fantastical tale, and whatever the truths that might lie within it, it is founded on an incontrovertible oversight which I put to you must undermine and declare null and void the case in its entirety."

The High Adjudicator looked down from her perch

pinning MacNeas with a flash of fire in her eyes. "Go on." She said, tight lipped.

"Your Honour, I am sure that I do not need to remind you of Smith vs Grant 1832. An historic case I think we can all agree, and often therefore overlooked in the modern era. In that case, the precedent was set - was it not - that citizens of the Kingdom are not subject to Canun law in this situation. Therefore I must move to ask the Court to dismiss this case as it has no jurisdiction over Mr Gillespie MacNachtan and no authority to settle this matter as he is a citizen of the Kingdom."

The atmosphere of the Courtroom changed instantly. The Prosecutor looked taken aback, puffing out his cheeks in astonishment. If the High Adjudicator was surprised, she did well to hide it. She followed MacNeas's speech closely. "Have you quite finished now Mr MacNeas?"

"Yes, your Honour, I rest my case."

"Then I call an adjournment. We shall reconvene the Court tomorrow at 11.00 a.m. for the verdict to be pronounced. Please take the prisoner down. Dismissed."

The Courtroom all stood while she gathered her notes and then swept out of the Court.

After a fitful night's sleep, Charlie again found himself with the MacNachtans loitering outside the courtroom. This morning there seemed to be a different atmosphere in the building, something expectant. Officials were scurrying around primping and tidying the curtains and coffee tables as if to ensure the Court House looked its best. At 11.00 a.m. the tall double doors to the courtroom once again opened and Charlie led the others to the spot they had occupied the previous day on the defendant's side of the room. Again at 11.15, Gillespie was led to the dock. Charlie was relieved to see that he appeared more cheerful today, clearly buoyed by the previous day's hearing.

At 11.25 the Clerk of the Court came out and in her thick Lewis accent requested those in the courtroom to rise. But this time, instead of the door on the dais opening for the High Adjudicator, the double doors at the entrance were flung open and a detail of heavily armed soldiers entered. Charlie could see immediately that they were elite Gallowglass. Then, to their astonishment, President John Lamont entered the chamber dressed in his Plaid of Office as if he had come straight from the Riaghaltas. Scurrying flunkeys cleared a way for him to sit on the front bench directly behind the dock and facing the High Adjudicator's seat.

Kirstie gasped, her face crowded with competing emotions; that her torturer could be sat so close, in plain sight, clearly shocked her to her core. Charlie thought she might be sick. Shonique wrapped her in her arms, Kirstie's head buried on her chest. Charlie had never seen Lamont up close before, his dark hair was frosted white at his temples and parted severely. His cheeks were blotchy, but not with the vigour of the hillside, but of long, dark, scabrous nights, their bilious colour draining into the frigid pallor of his taut bloodless lips. Charlie didn't imagine they'd ever kissed a boy, or a girl for that matter. He shuddered. He looked at Nin who was glowering at Lamont, his chin jutted forward in defiance, his eyes blazing. A hint of a smile flicked across Lamont's face like the popper of a bullwhip; he nodded at Kirstie and then turned his eyes to the front.

Moments later, the door at the back of the dais opened and the High Adjudicator once again took her place on the imposing bench.

"My Lord President, Ladies and Gentlemen, the Court is now in session. I would like to welcome the Lord President to the Courtroom today to observe the serving of justice. I think we can all agree that his presence is a reminder of the importance of Canun to the Republic and its institutions."

"Without further delay, I want to turn to the verdict on this case. Mr Wringe for the prosecution made a compelling presentation, painting an outrageous and violent intervention in a clearly declared Canun Contest. The death of Mr Stewart in this manner was clearly a breach of Canun and punishable by the utmost severity under the law."

Charlie held his breath; he didn't like the sound of where this was going.

"However," the High Adjudicator continued. "Mr MacNeas has raised a valuable and incontrovertible point that this Court cannot ignore. Having carefully studied the detail of Smith vs Grant 1832, I can confirm that the precedent does indeed stand and that as a citizen of the United Kingdom the remit of this Court in this situation does not extend to Mr MacNachtan. I must therefore move to dismiss this case and declare Mr MacNachtan cleared of these charges."

The MacNachtans could not contain their joy, their voices raised in an undignified whoop as they exchanged high fives. Gillespie raised his arms above his head in relief, MacNeas rushing over to shake him by the hand. Kirstie stared daggers at Lamont, leaving him in no doubt of her feelings; her joy of getting one over him palpable. Lamont sat there curiously unmoved, his face not betraying any emotion.

"BUT!" The High Adjudicator continued, silencing the Court instantly with the severity of her tone. All eyes returned to look at the dais and its occupant who had a triumphal sneer on her face.

"In my dual capacity as High Sheriff of the Oban Criminal Court, I hereby find Gillespie MacNachtan of Dunderave, Bushmills, County Antrim guilty of the most heinous act of murder. The cold blooded and cruel nature of this act calls for a severe sentence, one that protects the public from risk. Consequently, I hereby sentence you to a minimum twenty-five-year term of detention at the St Kilda Centre for Retribution and Correction."

She brought her gavel down with a crisp finality. The sound was thunder in Charlie's ears.

"Take him below." She then stood up, nodded at Lamont, and left through her side door.

Lamont now turned to the MacNachtans, slapping his hand on the bench in his mirth. His laughter echoed around the high ceiling of the room, following after him as he gathered his retinue and left the courtroom.

Charlie was shell-shocked, Shonique was in tears, Kirstie was raging, and Nin had to be held back from leaping over the benches and going after Lamont. Gillespie looked destroyed, transformed into a shrunken child as he was cuffed and led away. Tears flowed freely down his face. His last tortured look as he disappeared through the door froze Charlie's blood.

15 – Leaving the bog

The walk across the bog had been predictably wet and tiring. Three Fingers had tramped the soggy mire all her life, but the foot sucking monotony of it still weighed on her mood. She thought back to the house, the home, she'd just left to the depredations of the MacLeans, would she ever be able to go back? She tried to focus on stepping from one top heavy tussock to the next, avoiding the pools between, which could be an inch or a foot deep - the brown liquid gave no clues. When the wind blew, the bog cotton waved, as if wishing her god speed, but her progress was slow. The hills in the distance moved towards her at a snail's pace. This wasn't her usual direction. Normally, she would be walking out of the bog towards the sea, to the Big Strand, where she would swim or hang out with her friends. There were few if any reasons to go deeper into the bog, unless it was to look for a lost sheep or to try and bag a snipe for the pot.

The wind was getting up, blustery gusts fresh from the Atlantic bringing fat, soaking raindrops to pepper her. She tried to measure her distance by clumps of gorse, promising herself a rub of the coconut-scented flowers every time she passed the next marker. Little by little she inched towards her objective of Beinn Bhàn. It wasn't much of a hill, but she knew that behind it was the fold of Glen Leòra and that was where she should find Iain Og and the resistance, such as they were.

Suddenly, her phone started vibrating, its staccato urgency telling her immediately that a drone was nearby. She ducked into the nearest gorse thicket, trying to protect her face and hands as she pushed through its vicious spikes. She curled up into a ball, making sure that she didn't show as a human outline on any heat seeking camera it might be using. At least there were no midges this early in the year. She lay as still as she could until finally her phone stopped vibrating. She dragged herself out of the bush swearing blue at the scratches and cuts it had gifted her. She swiped open the Israeli drone-tracking app on her phone, it was standard issue to all Campbell militia units. It gathered information from an armada of satellites, but she'd never imagined she would be using it in her own back yard. She marked the drone's flight; it clearly hadn't been tracking her but was just circling the island in a reconnaissance sweep. Nonetheless, she was glad to have avoided its closer interest. The last thing she wanted to do was to reveal the location of Iain Og to the enemy.

Finally, she was out of the energy sapping morass and onto the gently rising slopes of Beinn Bhàn. She decided to go round the northern shoulder, not wanting to summit the hill and make herself too obvious to casual observers. As she left the bog behind and emerged onto dryer ground, she made much more rapid progress and was soon climbing down through heather and rough grass into the head of Glen Leòra. Almost as soon as she started her descent the scrub oak and birch became thicker in the tight sided glen. She could feel eyes on her as she walked down, her watchers hidden, but she knew they were there. She started whistling the well-known Campbell tune Baile Inneraora to make clear that she was no MacLean, and sure enough after a few minutes the soft sound of following feet confirmed that the message had been received and a faint, rather tuneless, whistle of Clan Campbell's Gathering came in reply.

The sides of the glen were steep here and she staggered through the thick, damp bracken under the trees as she tried to descend. She reached the banks of the River Claggain, at this stage it was little more than a burn, and as she followed it downstream, the whistling footsteps remained close behind but invisible. Finally, she pushed out of the undergrowth into the floor of the glen where, under a huge tarpaulin spread between the trees and the rock of the hill, sat a ragged bunch of men and women surrounded by an assortment of weaponry, tents and a few Kats.

The tarpaulin had been spread over the mouth of a cave, and it was out of the blackness of the cave mouth that Iain Og Campbell appeared, the peat spade of his beard announcing his arrival well before the rest of his face emerged out of the darkness.

"Three Fingers! So glad you've come! Welcome to our little gathering. I think you are familiar with most of us here." He swept one of his long arms around the assembled group. She knew most of the faces: Fraser, Angus, Kat, Mohammed and Needles and she went to hug them in greeting, but there were a few others who were unfamiliar. They introduced themselves, the stiffness of the formality in great contrast to their surroundings. It was a small band. They looked handy enough, but she thought there would have been more. They were in no way a sufficient force to expel the invaders on their own.

"Now come in here and tell me everything you've heard." Iain Og led her through the narrow cave entrance and down a short tunnel, lifting a heavy curtain to admit them into a wider chamber behind. It barely accommodated Iain's looming figure, but there was enough space inside for a makeshift table illuminated by a few solar powered LED lights. Around the table stood a few more faces she knew, Anndra from the Oa and Gill, the Deputy Head of Bowmore High School, they nodded their greetings. On the table was a map of the island.

Three Fingers took her place at the table and listened to the discussion that was in full flow. Anndra was pushing for a hit and run attack as the MacLeans tried to evict residents in the Oa. The terrain was familiar to them and they would have the advantage. Gill on the other hand wanted to hit MacVey with an improvised explosive device, hidden in a drainage pipe under the road. They knew he was raiding the distilleries to ship out their stock and there was a perfect spot on the Kildalton Road. With three major distilleries within a few miles it was an obvious honeypot for him to raid.

"But let's just say you are successful and you kill MacVey, do you really think that there won't be others to take his place?" Iain Og interjected. "They will just send someone even worse. Look at the reprisals after the Sunderland attack. Whole families strung up, their fields and houses burned. It was indiscriminate; innocent people were killed. Surely, we don't want to risk that again?"

"So, what would you suggest?" Gill asked. "as you can see, there aren't many of us. We can't just go straight at them. And what about MacCailean Mòr? What is he doing? When is he going to be ready to come and help us?"

"We don't know. The reality is he doesn't have any ships large enough to carry the force he needs. He is looking at alternatives, but it will take time."

"Time that we don't have." Anndra replied. "The longer those bastards are here the harder it will be to get rid of them."

Three Fingers listened to the debate ebb and flow. It was clear the group had no shortage of resolve and courage, but the lack of a focused strategy was painful. After twenty minutes of futile discussion, she finally felt ready to contribute. "I think we need to put them on the back foot, make them think before they leave Bowmore. Yes we want to get their leaders, but we also want to demoralise their rank and file. Forget about big spectaculars for the time being, their moment will come. Now we should just be chipping away at their resolve. Sniping, vandalism, picking off a unit at a time; low level hit and run. Let's keep them guessing. Also, no killing, well no more that is unavoidable. We don't want to create martyrs, but wounding and incapacitating the enemy will soak up much more of their resources and demoralise them more."

Looking around the table she could see that she had everyone's full attention.

"Look," she pointed at the map. "Every time they leave Bowmore, to the Oa, to the Rhinns or Kildalton, they should be looking over their shoulder. Let's hit them regularly but with no pattern, keep them guessing. Most importantly, every mobile phone mast should be destroyed as soon as they put it up. We want to feed their fear, their uncertainty; keep them guessing."

Her fresh ideas seemed to energise the group and soon they were busy mapping the known mobile masts and the most likely targets. Iain Og marked the main MacLean bases on the map; their headquarters was at Bowmore, but they had satellite posts at Port Ellen, Port Charlotte and Port Askaig – each strategically located to keep the more far-flung parts of the island under easy operational reach.

Three Fingers allowed the discussion to reach a fever pitch, before she silenced the chatter with the stab of her finger on the map. "That should be our first target. They won't be expecting it and it will send a strong message."

Shadows crowded the map as the assembled group lent in to see the target she had selected, the murmur of assent rapidly filling the air. The target was chosen, now they just had to hit it and hit it hard.

16 – Ardbreknish

Brighid snuggled closer under the deadweight of MacCailean Mòr's slumbering arms, spooning her body into his, enjoying the warmth and the press of his body on hers. He seemed to be enjoying it too. She drew one of his arms around her, clutching it, his only response to cup her left breast in his warm palm. She closed her eyes and slipped back into a doze.

Sometime later she reluctantly opened her eyes to check the time, it was already late. They should get up. She tried to wriggle out from under his arm, but it became strangely heavy and impossible to move. He held her tight. She slipped a hand behind her, tracing a line up his thigh.

"Well, it would be a pity to waste this, wouldn't it?"

MacCailean Mòr laughed and rolled over on his back. Brighid straddled him, easing herself down. This was her favourite way to start the day.

Much later, over breakfast, MacCailean Mòr asked about her plans.

"Well, I've been invited by Ardbreknish for a coffee. I thought I would go over and check how his recuperation is going. He was in the Infirmary for so long, it must be quite strange for him to be at home alone."

"That's very kind of you, I'm sure he'll be pleased to see you. Also I'm keen to know when he'll be fit enough to lead the Kilmartin Company. We need all the men we can get."

"Only men is it you need?" Brighid asked, her face turning suddenly stern before creasing into a smile.

"No, of course we need women too. Anyone that can help free us from those goddam MacLeans."

"How about you? Will you be here for the day?"

"I have to go to see Skipness, he is mustering as many boats as he can in Kilbrannan Sound. He's been sourcing them from all over; the Clyde, Kintyre, as well as across in the Kingdom. We almost have enough, at least for an initial landing. It won't be pretty, but I think it could work. Assuming it's unopposed, that is."

"OK, well, I guess I'll see you later then. I think after visiting Ardbreknish I'll check in on LeroyMar. He is making good progress, but that wound Allan Stewart gave him was deep."

MacCailean Mòr grunted; "No one can say that the Inveraray Infirmary isn't the best at treating edged weapon wounds — after all, they've had a lot of practice!"

"Aye, that they have, sadly, that they have."

Having brushed her teeth and tied back her hair, Brighid went outside. She shuffled some gravel chippings over the shiny black splodges of oil that had dripped from her battered trail bike, before swinging her leg over and firing the engine. With MacCailean Mòr's regular tellings off over her reckless scattering of stone chippings onto the lawn ringing in her ears, she puttered down the drive, only opening up the throttle once past the Castle gates.

The wind on her face and the fresh spring air were enervating. She raced down the Oban Wade, opening up the throttle, enjoying its curves, leaning into its sweeping bends as the road rose out of Inveraray towards Loch Awe. On either side were thickets of birch and aspen, scrub oak and rowan and the sun shone through their leaves, dappling the tarmac. The sky was blue, the powder blue of a highland spring, a welcome change after too many days of rain; she felt good.

Despite the terrible situation with Gillespie, life was better than it had been for some time. The Clan was back in control of Dunderave, cash was rolling in from the gaming business, and that meant that everyone had some money. Of course she wanted the MacLeans to be kicked out of Islay, but mostly that was because she wanted MacCailean Mòr to lighten up, he was so tight wound at the moment. As a MacNachtan it wasn't really her problem, but the sooner Catriona MacLean was booted back to her lair in Mull the better as far as she was concerned.

As she passed Ladyfield she gunned the throttle, making the most of the long straight that opened up ahead of her. The Aray River ran alongside, its bed littered with stones, the water's chittering passage filling the air with its refreshing coolth. Just before Cladich she turned off, following the southern shore of Loch Awe as it tracked westwards. The road was narrower here, and she slowed her pace not wanting to wrap herself around one of the many trees that crowded in on it. The air hung thick with viridity, the trees shielding the tight-tucked twists and turns from the breeze. And then she was out into the sun again, the landscape opening up with the loch on her right and high mountains in the distance. She slowed, approaching Ardbreknish's gate at little more than a trundle, giving its sensor enough time to register her arrival and swing open.

She motored up to the front door and parked next to Ardbreknish's Kat. Unsurprisingly, the house and garden had an unkempt air, the absence of its owner for so long had allowed nature to creep in at the edges. She'd always thought the larch cladding somewhat gloomy. She preferred the old-fashioned white harling that most Republic homes used to have before the fashion for Scandinavian prefabricated homes. On the other hand, you couldn't fault their efficient heating and insulation, highly desirable qualities which trumped most other considerations. She shook out her hair, leaving her helmet on the seat, and rang the doorbell.

The Arbreknish that opened the door was quite a shock. Gone was his youthful bloom, robbed by too many hospital hours; gone was the lustre of his long blond hair, replaced by a lank greasy sheen; gone was the fencer's poise, his spring-loaded step reduced to a sombre shuffle.

"Hello." He wheezed. "How kind of you to come."

The house was musty, all the windows sealed against the still chilly spring air. It had a curiously sepulchral feel, despite the dazzling picture window that opened over Loch Awe. The surfaces were dull with dust and littered with dirty glasses and cups, some of which were growing new ecospheres on the mould flecked remains of their undrunk and now unknowable liquid contents. He clearly wasn't doing well.

"Can I offer you a cup of tea? Or something stronger?" Ardbreknish asked.

"That's kind, it is a little early for me to take a dram. Maybe just a glass of water."

"No problem, I have my own spring here, the water is the best in the county."

The touch of pride in his voice cheered her, and while he went to the kitchen to organise the drinks, she went to the window and looked out. The view was stunning, encompassing the length of the loch from Beinn Cruachan at the head, to the Inverinan Forest across the water and down to Carn Duchara at the far western end.

"So, how have you been?" She tried to sound bright and cheerful to offset the ponderous gloom of the house.

"Better, thank you. At least I can walk now and more or less look after myself. It's been hard."

"Have the Clan been looking after you? Has the social care unit been down to see you?"

"Aye, well to start with. But I haven't seen anyone in weeks now. Seems like they are just leaving me to rot."

The tone of his voice caught Brighid like a thorn, bitter resentment lurking barely below the surface. "No, surely not! Don't be such an old curmudgeon! Barely a day goes by when MacCailean Mòr doesn't talk about you! You know how much he cares about you."

"Well, he hasn't cared enough to come and visit me."

"These are difficult times. He has been very distracted by the situation in Islay, as you can imagine there is a lot going on."

"Yes, Islay, that's all he ever asks me about. When will I be ready to fight for him, to lead the Kilmartin Company. I'm sick of it. Fucking Chiefs think that we exist to run around doing their dirty work. They don't really give a shit about us, about me."

Brighid turned from the window to look at Ardbreknish properly. His sallow face was flat, deadpan, the arrogant spark that had animated it all her life was gone, extinguished.

"You don't mean that." She said the words, but they carried no conviction; he clearly did.

"All my life I've served that man. Fighting mostly,

killing sometimes, always doing my duty for Chief, Clan and Cliù. Well, I'm done with that. I'm sick of it. I want to live. My life, for me."

Brighid was uncertain how to respond. She sipped her water, watching as his face became pinched in sneers and curled in disdain.

"That man, what has he ever done for me? I've run around half the world for him. Earning the Cùinn that keeps him in that fucking castle. What have I got in return? A chest full of steel and a trip to the very mouth of death. And now, and now I find that he has taken the most precious thing in the world from me."

"Don't be ridiculous, what would he possibly steal from you?"

He said nothing, fixing her with his pale blue eyes, watching for her reaction.

"Me? What do you mean? What are you saying? You think he stole me from you?"

"I love you. I always have. Ever since we first met at school, I knew you were meant for me. All these years you've waited for me, fending off others. I've watched you; I know. I was young and stupid; I didn't know how to show you my true feelings. But lying there in the Infirmary day after day, godforsaken night after night, I realised I had to show you how much I cared."

Brighid felt the room start to spin, her head was swimming.

"Don't be absurd. You don't love me; you don't even know me!"

"I want you to come with me, away from this place, away from MacCailean Mòr and all this madness. Let's make a new life, a new life together, far away."

"Niall! Stop it. Stop it right now. I don't want to hear

anymore. I think I should go."

Brighid tried to stand up, but her legs refused to move. She tried to use her arms to push herself up. She fell on the floor. She gasped; the room span faster. He was watching her closely, still sipping his tea, calmly taking it all in.

"What, what have you done, what have you done to me?" The words slurring from her lips were soft and pillowy, stretching away into the distance like pulled dough.

"Help me." She whispered, desperately trying to keep her eyelids open. But it was no good, and they shuttered remorselessly, cutting off the light and casting her into darkness.

17 – Transfer

At least the shaking had stopped. Gillespie had wearied of fighting the uncontrollable spasms that had wracked his body from the moment the judgement had been handed down. Camilla Brehon's sentence had been hammered into his heart one word at a time: guilty, St Kilda, the Centre for Punishment and Retribution, twenty five years. Tears still flowed freely down his face as he thought of his lost freedom, of his foolishness in returning to the Republic, of his misplaced arrogance of wanting revenge. He was a farmer not a fighter. The guard looked away, embarrassed.

He thought back to his childhood days in Antrim, halcyon days of sunshine; exploring hedgerows; lough swimming; sitting on his grandfather's knee while wrestling the tractor wheel; feeding lambs and turning eggs in the incubator; the crack of shotguns in the winter; the smell of autumn bonfires and wet walks with wetter dogs; the stillness of the house in the afternoon; the drift of motes caught by slanted beams of sunshine in the atrium; the sound of a distant piano, tip-toed games of tag; cake and crumpets for tea on Saturdays; the joy of a new fishing rod; the click of the reel; the bitter fizz of that first adolescent beer; snatched kisses and fumbles.

Gone, gone forever.

The jolt of the prison van's axle snapped him back into reality. The driver seemed to take pleasure in speeding over any traffic calming bumps, just to shake up the prisoners in the back. Gillespie would have been thrown from his seat if he wasn't handcuffed to it. The steel of the manacles bit deep into his wrists as they fought the impetus of his body. More tears now came, and unable to wipe them away they flowed freely down his face.

The guard banged on the driver's partition. "If you do that one more time you stupid cunt, I'll fucking open you up when I get out of here!"

The driver laughed, but at least he slowed down.

"And as for you," the guard turned his attention back to Gillespie. "I strongly suggest you stop the fucking weeping before you get to St Kilda. You won't find much sympathy there. They're a right bunch of tough cunts. If they think you're soft, you'll end up as someone's fucksack. And with the paedo rapist scum they have there, I don't think you'd want that. But if they think you're hard, well then they'll compete to be the first to take you down. Cliù rules. Even in St Kilda. In fact, especially in St Kilda." He laughed.

Gillespie struggled to contain his emotions, taking deep breaths to calm himself. The guard might be an arsehole, but he was right; he had to get himself under control. He stared at the guard's battered boots and used the pain from his wrists to focus his mind. The tears dried up.

"We're almost there." The guard said. "And judging by the forecast your crossing shouldn't be too rough."

"Crossing? You mean we go by boat?"

The guard laughed. "Of course you go by boat. There's no landing strip at St Kilda. Even boats struggle to get there for eight months of the year. It's no holiday camp you dumb bastard. It's the end of the fucking world!"

The driver stood on the brakes, throwing the guard against the partition again and eliciting another cloud of threats and expletives. Gillespie's momentum caused the manacles to bite so deep into his wrists that he thought they might snap; he screamed with pain.

"We're here." The guard needlessly added. "And I don't want any fucking trouble from you, or I'll smash your kneecaps. Understood?"

Gillespie nodded, meekly.

"Right, well I guess I'd better unlock you then."

The guard released him from the cuffs and the blood rushed back into his hands, his wrists now ringed with thick bloodblack bruises. He rubbed them gently, trying to ease the pain. The back of the van opened, and a group of heavily armed Black Watch covered him with their automatic weapons while he climbed down the steps.

"Hold your hands in front of you." One of them barked.

Gillespie complied, only to have his hands rebound with a cable tie. Fortunately, it wasn't too tight. He was then marched across a concrete dock to a jetty where a grey navy patrol ship was moored. Encouraged down the jetty by the snub nose of the barrel in his back, he was soon bundled onboard and down the steps of the companionway into the bowels of the ship. After being roughly manhandled down corridors and steep steps he found himself facing a steel door. The guard swiped his card through the reader. The door opened silently, and the guard pushed Gillespie inside, before closing the door with a reverberating bang.

It was a small room not more than ten feet square. There were two berths, one on either side of an integrated toilet and wash basin. Apart from the thin mattresses, the room was entirely made of steel. It smelled of sweat and fear. Sitting hunched like a cornered rat with his knees drawn up to his chin was Davy MacSween, who Gillespie had last seen in the Luachrach Prison. He gloomily acknowledged Gillespie with a jerk of his head but said nothing.

At that moment, the cell filled with the thrum of the boat's engines, the steel surfaces vibrating from the horsepower. Davy jerked back, cocking his head on one side to better hear the engine's tone. He muttered under his breath, pushing himself back into the corner. His fierce face morose, his luculent bottle green eyes looked wet, as if he was about to cry.

Gillespie asked, "How long did you get?"

"Ten years." Davy replied, his lower lip sagging under the weight of the words. "Might as well be a hundred."

"Why do you say that?"

Davy looked at Gillespie anew, as if he was an idiot. "We are talking about St Kilda man! Its brutal. One year there is like ten in any other jail. If the wardens don't get you, then the other prisoners will, and if they don't get you then the wind and the birds will drive you insane."

Gillespie flinched. He'd always assumed that St Kilda was tough, but if even this hardened mercenary feared it then what chance would he have. His guts clenched, his pulse throbbing in his forehead; he took a deep breath, trying to push away the devil that gripped the inside of his throat. Camilla Brehon's face flashed before his eyes, the smirk of triumph as she brought down her gavel, Lamont's laughter rang in his ears. But slowly he forced that devil down, each deep breath dissipating its grip on his insides, until finally it was gone. He opened his eyes; Davy was staring at him.

"Are you OK?"

"Yeah, I guess so. Just coming to terms with my sentence."

"What did they give you?"

"Twenty five years."

"Fuck me. Someone's got it in for you right enough."

Gillespie calmly explained what had happened and how Camilla Brehon had twisted the law to absolve him under Canun but convict him, nonetheless.

The boat lurched forward; the thrum of the engine increased to a roar. Gillespie clenched his teeth to try and stop the vibrations.

Davy raised his eyes to the ceiling and swore. "That's it then, no chance for us now, we are well and truly fucked."

"What were you expecting - a last minute reprieve? Some of your MacSween friends to come and rescue you?" Gillespie didn't mean to taunt him, but the words came out harsher than he'd intended.

But instead of lashing out, Davy seemed to crumble into his corner, his cheeks reflecting the light in two trickles of tears. Gillespie lay down on his berth, trying to give him as much privacy as was possible in the tiny cell.

Soon the boat was thumping up and down as it carved its way up the Sound of Mull. Gillespie was no sailor, and he began to worry about how he would keep his last meal down. He'd last eaten at breakfast that morning; how long was it before food passed beyond recall? He focused on the noise and the vibrations to distract himself, cursing as any big wave threw him against the cell wall.

Time crawled.

Every now and then the rhythm of the boat and thump of the waves changed. Gillespie imagined their progress as they moved from the Sound of Mull into the Hebridean Sea, and much later, having sheltered in the lee of the Western Isles, passing through the Sound of Harris and out into the mighty Atlantic. He could feel that changing geography as the thump of the hull and the pitch of the boat evolved.

He closed his eyes, trying to concentrate on controlling the roiling in his guts. Without warning, a spasm gripped him, a vicious clench that constricted his chest tighter than a python's grip; he couldn't breathe, he couldn't even gasp. A rasping gurgle was followed by dry retch after dry retch. Finally, his diaphragm relinquished its hold, air rushed into his lungs. But like a drowning swimmer, no sooner had he broken the surface to grab a gulp of air than he was back under the waves as his body wracked itself in another bout of savage spasms. He'd never experienced seasickness like it.

Eventually, his body decided there was nothing left to try and wring from him and he lay on his back breathing deeply to quell any possible return. The thin mattress barely diminished the rub of the hard steel on his bones, and he felt the impact of each wave as the hull pounded his joints and spine. He tried to shield his eyes from the unremitting glare of the light overhead; sleep wouldn't come.

On the other bunk Davy was suffering too. His moans and curses were interspersed with wild unearthly groans. Judging by the state of him, Davy had clearly eaten his lunch, and his face and clothes were now splashed with vomit and indeterminate chunks of semi-digested food. The sour smell was oppressive in the small airless room. Gillespie grabbed some of the toilet paper and, having dampened it under the tap, tried to clean the worst of it off Davy's face and out of his hair. Davy was in no state to resist, even if he had wanted to, and the pitiful look from his eyes spoke gratitude for Gillespie's kindness.

This torture went on for hours. There were moments when Gillespie would willingly have stepped off a hangman's scaffold to save himself the continuing agony. But like all the best things in life, even the worst things come to an end eventually. A sudden change in the engine note and a commensurate reduction in the vibrations that had started to pick apart his very being, alerted Gillespie to the chilling reality – they had arrived.

18 – Legacy

Lamont woke with a sore head, but even that could not interrupt his good mood. The throbbing slowly subsided after a few swiftly downed glasses of water; its chlorinated reek made him long for the spring water of the Republic. For the first time in a long while he felt that he was riding the tiger, rather than simply having it by the tail.

His dinner the previous night with Balfour and Walker had been choreographed to impress. A private room above the Portcullis Gate of Edinburgh Castle with magnificent views across the city. Balfour could have picked no better location to convey the relative wealth and power of Scotland and the Kingdom to the meagre resources of the Republic. The diplomatic fripperies of his visit had been relentless and unstinting, motorcades with outriders, military march pasts, inspections of rare Gaelic artefacts at the Museum of Scotland – as if he cared – and the relentless drone of bagpipes that seemed to follow him wherever he went; didn't they know they had enough bagpipes in the Republic for God's sake? He presumed they did it to make him feel at home, but while he cursed the relentless ear-splitting caterwaul, even he had to grudgingly admit that their efforts only showcased the superior quality of Ewen MacEunraig, his official piper in the Republic.

Beneath the pleasantries and gewgaws there was a darker undercurrent that ran blood red through all the discussions of how to submit the Republic to the Kingdom. All sides knew that handled poorly, much blood could be spilt, in the Republic but also in the Kingdom. Instead of a full-frontal occupation which was likely to end in sustained and bloody resistance, something the Republic was well suited to and well prepared for, it made more sense to do it by stealth. Like boiling a frog, Lamont needed the citizens of the Republic to remain placid until it was too late.

With the Kingdom having left the European Union, there was an opportunity to reset their trading relationship in a way that just had not previously been possible. As a first and positive step, he outlined with Walker and Balfour the principles of a Free Trade Agreement that they could move to sign quickly. This would allow much greater access into the Republic for Kingdom goods and services than had ever been permitted before. Unquestionably it favoured the Kingdom as the bigger, dominant partner, as most of the Republic's exports were services, security in particular, but also IT and renewable energy, for which the Republic was a centre of excellence. This first step was vital to open up the Republic; by facilitating trade and travel between the two, spreading ideas and relationships, it would start to break down the ancient cultural barriers that stood between the nations. Lamont knew that many of the Chiefs would hate any agreement, particularly those that made their money arbitraging global tariffs, such as MacKinnon and MacLeod.

But this was only the first step, as once it had been accepted and digested by both populations the plan was to move to a far deeper and more intractable union. Positioned as a Commonwealth, the Union would build on the Free Trade Agreement allowing free movement of people, alignment of laws, currency and fiscal policy. And like a fly caught in the spider's web, once in the Kingdom's grip, the Republic would not be able to wriggle free. Of course, this would be anathema to the Chiefs, and much of the Republic's population, the ignorant and backward who clung to the past. But that destination would remain hidden until they were sufficiently far along that there was no turning back. In the meantime, he would educate them.

Of course there was a price for such access to Kingdom markets. Walker was insistent that there would need to be a disarming of the population. The cultured sensitivities of the Kingdom's citizens were threatened by the average Gael's walking armoury. The need for such weaponry would disappear though once the Canun had been abolished, with no Cliù to defend there would be no bloodfeuds, no stupid duels or need for revenge. Arguments could be resolved in a Court of Law rather than by the slash of a blade.

Lamont readily agreed, he knew this was a critical step, but he wanted to go further. He would outlaw tartan too; to weaken the visual tropes that bound the clans together. That shared identity needed to be eroded, diluted, homogenised, the people of the Republic had to be blended into a more malleable blob; freed from petty clannish identities they would become amorphous and more easily controlled. The education medium would be switched to English to chip away at the mental grip that the Gaelic held on the people. Its backward concepts would be expunged from future generations. This was entirely defensible in the name of progress – who could argue against teaching in the most widely spoken language in the world! Over time Gaelic would slowly dim, and that momentum of decline would accelerate with each cohort of children: initially imperceptible, ultimately unstoppable.

After these points had been thrashed out over dinner, First Minister Balfour had waited until the digestifs to ask the most pointed question: What did he want? The unspoken inference was that he, John Lamont, could be bought. That it was merely a question of Cùinn or patronage. Lamont didn't answer immediately, instead he sipped his Montenegro as the words had rolled around his head. The evening had broken up soon after, but the words didn't go away, they rumbled ponderously around the febrile alcoholic swirl of his mind as he'd lain in bed, and they were still there the next morning. The answer was complex, he didn't want anything that Balfour could give him. After all, Lamont had taken everything he'd ever wanted, he didn't need Balfour's munificence. He wasn't motivated by money or sex, or any such pedestrian motivations. Power was too obvious; yes, it was necessary to achieve his objective, but it was not the destination. No, what he wanted was the most alluring, elusive and dangerous of political ambitions; he wanted a legacy.

19 – Imprisoned

Brighid eyed the door with frustration. It was unlocked, she knew. She had seen Niall come and go without having to use any key or swipe. The illusion of easy egress only made her incarceration all the more painful. She pulled up her sleeve to look at the thick plastic band around her wrist. She spent surreptitious hours trying to work away at it with anything she could find or fabricate – the plastic cutlery she was given with each meal, or the sharp pointed edge of the table. It was no good, none of it made the slightest mark.

When she had first come to, she knew immediately that she was in a strange bed in a strange house. She was no longer on Loch Awe-side. The view from the window looked over a long expanse of green lawn to a wide shallow bay. It wasn't a view she knew and there were no obvious clues. She was still in the Republic of that much she was certain, and it must be the west coast, as the sun set into the sea. Other than that, the only clue was a settlement on the far side of the bay – too far for her to see properly – its white walls yielding no obvious clue at this distance.

She watched the tide roll in and out, uncovering and smothering the sandy foreshore twice a day. The briny smell of the sea filled the room. The surface of the sea loch was ever changing, she could watch it for hours, which was lucky as there was nothing else for her to do. To pass the time she tried counting all the different birds that dived and swam on its rucked and graven surface: black headed Arctic Terns, horned Grebes, Oyster Catchers with their bright red beaks, long legged

Curlews, sombre Scaup and her favourite, the Bar-Tailed Godwit, whose elegant poise and red breasted plumage made it an aristocrat of the foreshore. As a diversion it was effective to start with, but as the hours passed she got heartily sick of the darting freedom they enjoyed.

She'd tried several times to pass through the door, to ignore the pain from the band, the jaggedy, tined shredding of every nerve ending in her body, from her toes to the tips of her ears. The first time she'd felt it she was taken by surprise, and it left her gasping on the floor, unable to move. She tried the door again, the nerve-jangling started as soon as she got within two feet of it, the intensity growing until she felt as if her every fibre was being pulled apart. Her mind froze in a paroxysm of agony, unable to think beyond the most basic survival instinct of getting away from the door, the source of her pain. She threw herself backwards and the pain immediately stopped. It was no good. She went back to the window and continued her vigil, counting the birds and watching the tide. From her vantage point she could see a road that ran beside the bay, vehicles regularly raced along it, going about their business as free as the birds. After a while she realised that they were mostly military vehicles rather than your usual Kats. Her apprehension grew, where had Niall taken her to?

The aftereffects of whatever he'd drugged her with were slowly passing, her groggy mind was clearing. She had to think. From the fixtures of the room, the fancy plaster cornice to the old-fashioned astragals of the window, she was sure she was in a big, old building. It had clearly not been built as a prison, more likely a house. That made her hopeful that if only she could find a way to get beyond the door or out of the window, then she would be able to make good her escape. She scoured the view outside for any clues.

She heard footsteps approaching, more than one person; she turned to face the door, determined to show no fear.

Ardbreknish's wan face was the first to enter, followed by a late middle-aged man with receding hair and a jumbled face that had clearly stopped a fair few blows in its time; his cheekbones, eye sockets and nose all askew, the skin ruddy and pitted. He had the yellow-brown eyes of a fox and in contrast to the lumpen open cast of his face they were razor sharp. He stared at her; a cold appraisal that forced an involuntary shiver down her spine. Her eye darted from his face to his forearm. Catching her glance, the man even turned his arm outward to aid her identification, the red and green squares dissected by white and yellow tramlines of MacLean tartan told her everything she needed to know.

Ardbreknish closed the door behind them and approached her. Brighid tried not to show any fear but could feel the window frame digging into her back as it denied her any further retreat. He smiled; she could have punched him.

"Brighid, so good to see you up and about. How are you feeling? I hope that the Rohypnol hasn't left you feeling too much the worse for wear? I must apologise for giving you such a large dose, but I didn't want you waking up before we got here."

"And where exactly is here?" She asked, trying to keep any trace of bitterness out of her voice. Her relationship with Ardbreknish could now be critical to her survival.

The two men exchanged a glance, before Niall opened his hands as if at a cocktail party and said, "How silly of me, first let me introduce you to Bruce MacVey, who is our host here on the island."

"Island? What do you mean island? Where have you brought me?" Brighid asked as her floundering brain competed to process this new information: island; MacLeans, kidnap, MacVey — that name suddenly seemed very familiar. Her mind cartwheeling back to all those meetings with MacCailean Mòr and his advisors.

"Ah yes, of course, there is no reason you would know. We are on Islay, at Islay House to be precise. Bruce commands all MacLean forces on the island, and he has generously agreed to accommodate us in his headquarters."

"I hope you are comfortable." MacVey asked, the rasp of his voice grating on her ears.

"I would be more comfortable without this infernal device." Brighid held up her arm, the thick plastic bracelet was framed by raised red welts.

MacVey smiled. "I'm afraid that we can't take that off and judging by the marks on your arm, you have already figured out how it works. But as long as you stay in here, it won't cause you any discomfort."

To change the subject, Ardbreknish joined her by the window. "Great view isn't it. You see over there," he pointed at the town across the bay, "That's Bowmore, a charming town. One day maybe we can go and explore it together."

"How long are you planning to keep me here? Don't you think MacCailean Mòr is going to get a little upset that you've kidnapped me. You'll be lucky he doesn't have you pulled apart between two Kats."

"Ah yes, MacCailean Mòr," Ardbreknish's face became hard as flint. "Well, that name doesn't have much currency in these parts nowadays. If I were you I would forget all about that pompous arsehole. He was just using you anyway. Using you for a few weeks, a few months and then you'll be tossed over his shoulder while he moves on. You're just the latest in a long line."

"Don't be a bigger prick than usual, Niall. I'm not sure I can bear it."

MacVey laughed. "Doesn't seem like she is so hot on you after all. Not that that matters." He grabbed Brighid's chin and turned her face towards his, his vulpine eyes flashed. Without thinking Brighid slapped him hard across the face. Her hand stung. He smiled back at her, rubbing the livid red imprint of her fury on his cheek, before punching her in the stomach. She staggered, trying to breathe, but air wouldn't come. MacVey laughed and pushed her backwards onto the bed. He tossed a phone at her; it was hers.

"Open it." He barked at her.

She shook her head, still struggling for breath.

MacVey grabbed her by the hair and held the phone up to her face long enough for it to recognise her and unlock the home screen.

"Right, Ardbreknish. Now's your moment. Don't you mind me, I'll just take some photos. I'm sure MacCailean Mòr will be very interested to see what his girlfriend is getting up to."

Ardbreknish approached the bed, unbuckling his kilt. Brighid screamed.

20 – St Kilda

The wind tore into Gillespie as he left the shelter of the bulkhead door. Its ferocity was unlike anything he'd ever experienced, every corner of his body was being nipped and buffeted, seemingly from all directions at the same time. It was nearly night and the boat was moored in a deep bay surrounded by a horseshoe of steep, high hills; their tops lost to thick mist. In the bottom of the horseshoe was a settlement surrounded by a massive wall that snaked around the foot of the hills. The prison block sat in the middle of the bowl, a brooding black hulk with few lights showing in its blunt façade.

One of the crew pushed him towards the back of the boat where a small dinghy bobbed on the swell.

"We have to get in that?" He asked, wondering why they didn't just moor along the quay.

"Aye, no boats allowed to moor here now. We don't want any rats coming ashore to trouble the birds – at least no rats with tails, you scum are welcome enough."

Davy turned an even paler shade of green. Gillespie couldn't imagine that he had anything left to throw up; he was wrong, and he stepped back just in time as another strangulated gasp spattered the deck. The guard unsympathetically pushed Davy down the steps towards the waiting dinghy, clearly keen to get him off his boat. Soon Gillespie was sat opposite him on the squidgy rubber tube of the dinghy as they made their way from the vessel to the shore.

They made the jetty a few minutes later, soaked to the skin by sea water driven by the lashing wind.

Gillespie felt almost pathetically grateful once he was back on dry land, freed from the pitch and roll of the waves. He helped support Davy as they staggered down the quay under the watchful eye of a couple of prison officers towards a low white harled building with Induction Centre stencilled on the side. A heavy steel door opened at their approach and they entered a searingly bright room crisscrossed with taped yellow lines on the floor to channel prisoners in the right direction.

He was ushered to a booth where a severe looking woman sat behind a Perspex screen. Her hair was gathered up tightly, her face taught; lips pursed. Gillespie was not surprised that she was as ill-tempered as she looked, brusquely asking his name and details without raising her eyes from the paperwork. Once he had been processed, she pointed to a machine that sat on the counter. It had a slot, the size of a letter box in its front with the words "Insert hand here" in blocky red type. She waved her hand at him, motioning him to follow these simple instructions. Gillespie suddenly felt nervous, what was going to happen to his hand in that slot? His brain fizzed as he looked at the ominous black hole, while the woman got increasingly frustrated at his slowness. He looked around the room, no one else seemed to be in pain or wielding bloody stumps, so he gritted his teeth and thrust his hand into the darkness. His wrist was immediately clamped, and he felt a short sharp pressure on the back of his hand, before the clamp was released and he could withdraw his hand once again. Now on the back of his hand was a raised rectangular lump about the size of a postage stamp with a thin red line of blood scribing one side.

"What's that?" He asked holding his hand up to the woman.

"That's your ID chip. Everything in here is controlled by it − opening doors, getting your food, access to privileges: everything. You just hold your hand up to a scanner and it will check if you have authorisation. Now move along. You need to be searched next." She shooed him away to a full height turnstile. Next to it was a sensor with a hand printed on it and he dutifully held up the back of his hand, hearing an audible click and the turnstile released. It was a very tight squeeze and he had to shuffle his feet to get it to turn and deposit him in the next room.

Gillespie had read about the deeply personal nature of body searches in US Supermax prisons and was expecting something similarly humiliating. So he was surprised to see a largely empty room with a tall olive-green box at its centre. On the side, in a florid italic font, it simply said Atelier Thomas Caddell. The guard directed him to first hold his hand to the sensor before standing in front of the box with his arms above his head. No sooner had he done that then he was ushered out of the room for his medical check-up.

A nurse put a tourniquet on his arm and drew off several large phials of blood, popping them into a machine which immediately spat out an analysis of any issues and ailments. A timeworn doctor came over and scrutinised the findings. Gillespie couldn't help notice the grimy nails that gripped the clipboard. "Good, so no hepatitis, A, B or C, no HIV, no tuberculosis, COVID-19, or even gonorrhoea − my, my, you are plain vanilla." He then looked at another sheet. "And no objects secreted where they shouldn't be. That is a relief, I must say, as pulling items out of inmates' arseholes is one of my least favourite jobs. Frankly, it is not what I swore the Hippocratic oath for, and I tend not to be very forgiving of those who force me to rummage around for their drugs or razor blades – you understand me?" He peered at Gillespie over his glasses as if expecting a response. Gillespie nodded.

"Right, well, you are done here. Just go through there and pick up your clothes. After that, the Riaghladair will see you in the auditorium. Welcome to St Kilda."

The doctor waved him through the doorway to a room with a counter running down one side. There, an inmate dressed in an orange kilt and sweatshirt looked him up and down before sliding a pile of prison issue clothes across to him, all in the same lurid orange. He pointed Gillespie to a screen that stood in one corner, where he soon stripped off his clothes and returned dressed head to toe in prison orange, with his other clothes under his arm ready to be deposited in a Perspex box for storage until his release. Gillespie momentarily wondered what the sick stained clothes would be like after 25 years hermetically sealed in plastic. As the box disappeared with the last vestiges of his previous life, he had to stop himself from welling up with emotion.

The auditorium was the size of a small university lecture theatre except instead of looking downwards into a bearpit of academic debate, all the seats looked upwards to a pulpit high above. Each inmate was sunken in what amounted to an open topped box, so although they could see the pulpit they couldn't see each other. Gillespie imagined this was to stop violence breaking out among members of the audience, but it had the unwelcome effect of being even more isolating and dispiriting. On reflection he felt that was probably intentional.

He'd almost fallen asleep waiting for the Riaghladair to show up. The closeness of the wooden walls and the phantasmagoric sway of the sea made him queasy and he closed his eyes to try and cope. But there was no sleeping through the Riaghladair's entrance. The lights were turned up impossibly bright as a figure appeared in the pulpit. He picked up an old-fashioned claw hammer from the lectern which he pounded on the pulpit's wooden rail to command the room's attention. It was deafening through the amplification. Gillespie strained to see the figure properly through the halo of light that surrounded him. He was short, with receding hair and shiny currant eyes that never seemed to blink. He exuded passive aggression.

"Welcome to the St Kilda Centre for Retribution and Correction. I hope I haven't met any of you before, because if I have that means I will have failed in my job, and that would displease me." He scanned the room as if looking for a familiar face. "No? No. I didn't think so. No one ever leaves here without never wanting to return. I make sure of it."

"My name is Mr Ferguson, but you can call me Riaghladair. I run this institution and while you are here you belong to me. You are here because you need to be punished. Spare the rod and spoil the child, as the saying goes. And, believe me, you will be chastised fully for your crimes."

He paused for effect, scanning the room for any tall poppy that might try to resist the scythe. He continued: "And after punishment comes correction. You need to learn, to be taught how to be a civilised member of our society. As one of the oldest Republics in the world, we have a duty to uphold the law, to set an example for others. King Charles the Liberator did not free us, for us to squabble and fight like infants. No, you will learn and when you have learned enough you can return to society to try and repay your debt. Do I make myself understood?"

There was a murmur of assent around the room. But Ferguson was dissatisfied and picking up the hammer he smashed it down repeatedly on the pulpit rail, before again shouting: "Do I make myself understood!"

This time the cheer of assent was clear and unequivocal. Ferguson scanned the room, holding out the hammer and picking out each prisoner individually with it, fixing them briefly with his unblinking gaze, before moving on, soaking up the response.

"And don't you forget it." He said, before turning and leaving the podium.

21 – Agony

MacCailean Mòr hadn't slept, and the night had been cruelly long. As the pallid glimmer at the foot of the curtains had turned into a bright line of daylight, he could put it off no longer and got up. He stared at the phone on the other side of the bed. The inanimate object lay where he'd thrown it the previous night, where Brighid should have been. Its black screen was dormant, but last night it had sucked in his soul through its blunt edged slot and torn it in pieces. He clutched his forehead, squeezing his temples to expunge the memory. Brighid, poor Brighid; he tried to recall the memory of her to the room, her amatory curves, the palm-filling rondure of her breasts, the tuck of her chin and the tight pout on her lips while she slept. It almost worked. But the leering figure of Niall Campbell of Ardbreknish was now soaked indelibly through those memories, a watermark of hate and bitterness.

He pulled on his clothes in a daze. His mind was spinning with a mixture of anger, sorrow, forlorn helplessness, and a need to do something, anything, to rescue her. He thought of convening his duine uasal, calling a Council of War immediately. But he hesitated. He knew that their response would be to push for a full-frontal assault on Islay; Clan Cliù demanded it. That their Chief's partner would be kidnapped and raped by one of their own was too great an insult for any other response. He suspected this is what Catriona MacLean and her lackey MacVey wanted, to push him into acting too soon before he was truly ready. An amphibian assault on an island like Islay, one that was defended by well-armed and able troops, was bound to fail if it didn't have overwhelming force behind it. That or total stealth.

He also knew that Brighid's life hung in the balance. What were the chances of her surviving any assault? Thin, too thin for him to contemplate. Would his duine uasal understand him putting the risk to her life before that of the Clan's Cliù? He knew the pressure from Ardkinglas, Strachur and even Skipness would be hard to resist in a Council of War, and he needed them on his side if he was ever to regain Islay. But he couldn't afford to wait.

He looked in the mirror, swags of blue-black worry lined his eyes; even the bags under his eyes seemed to have bags. He could swear that the flecked grey at his temples had advanced overnight. The slap of cold water on his face snapped him into focus. In that instant he knew who he had to talk to, and he hurriedly dried his face and pulled on the rest of his clothes. Then he was taking the stairs two at a time before jumping in his Kat and tearing down the drive.

Minutes later he was parking among the gently rusting detritus of Elrig's front garden. The curtains were all still tightly drawn but by the time he'd mounted the steps to the blue front door it was already swinging open. Nin welcomed him in, the bloom of his face swathed in stubble, his spiky hair even more unkempt than usual.

"Whatever brings you to my door so early cannot be good news." Nin said, putting a cup of coffee down in front of him at the kitchen table. MacCailean Mòr picked up the cup, the hot pottery defrosted his hands, the scalding acidity prickled his tongue. He gulped down the bolus of black caffeine magic, simultaneously calming his nerves and racing his pulse.

"Its Brighid….."

"What's Brighid?"

"She's been kidnapped, by Ardbreknish. Taken to Islay."

"What? That's madness! Why would be he do that?" Nin's jaw hung open, his blue eyes like saucers.

"It gets worse, much worse." MacCailean Mòr gathered himself, just as Charlie came round the door in his dressing gown. "He has raped her…. They sent me a video last night." Even saying the words made him feel sick.

Charlie and Nin were aghast, speechless. Charlie stood behind Nin, putting his hands on his shoulders. Nin's face had gone white, his eyes red, filling with tears; he stammered but no words would form.

It was Charlie that spoke. "Oh my god! Why would he do that? I know you always said he desired her, but enough to kidnap and rape her?"

"Where is she? We need to get her, to save her." Nin's face was now flushed red with anger. "Let's get her back right now!"

"It's not that easy. Islay is crawling with an army of MacLeans you can't just walk in there and take her back."

"But what are you doing about it? You can't just abandon her. For fucks' sake, you are the fucking Duke of Argyll, the Chief of the Clan Campbell and god knows what else."

"Of course I'm not going to abandon her!" MacCailean Mòr's eyes flashed with anger. "That is why I am here."

"What?" Nin looked up, incredulous.

"I need your help." MacCailean Mòr continued, "My men will be too hot headed, too focused on vengeance, on Cliù. They won't care about Brighid. To them she will just be another victim in a long line. Look at all the Campbells that have been burned out of Islay already, cleansed from their homes by those fucking MacLeans. Look at all the refugees crowded in Tarbert, camping out in the sports hall and Council offices. They are my Clan. They look to me to help them take back their homes; to fight for them first and foremost. And I will. But to do that I need to move freely, I can't have Brighid at risk. They will just see her as collateral damage, dispensable. After all, to them she is just a MacNachtan! Why should they care about what happens to her? I want, I need, to save her − she is my priority. But that is not how my men will see it."

"She wouldn't even be there if it wasn't for you!" Nin's bitter words hung in the air. MacCailean Mòr flinched, his face reddening. The tension in the air was palpable, it sat pregnant as a thundercloud waiting for an ill-judged word to discharge its full fury into the room.

Charlie pulled out a chair and sat down next to Nin facing MacCailean Mòr.

"I think we need cool heads if we are going to help Brighid." He squeezed the back of Nin's clenched fist on the table - like paper wrapping rock − his caring touch earthed Nin's impotent rage. "Come on, let's talk this out." Turning to MacCailean Mòr, he continued. "You obviously came here for a reason, with an idea, a plan to help rescue her. Tell us what you need and how you think we can help."

22 – The Bracelet

Brighid felt so angry with herself. How could she have been so stupid, to go to Ardbreknish, to drink that glass of water. She'd tried to care for him, and this was how he'd repaid her. How could she have allowed him to touch her, to do what he had done. Why couldn't she even call it by its name? Rape, yes it was rape, but she struggled to even form the word in her mind.

After the anger came the numbness, an emptiness that gnawed at her heart. A small silence that grew and grew, crowding out the competing voices in her head with its chilly void. Aloof, she fed the silence, allowing it to grow into a shield, something she could shelter behind, inside. She no longer looked out of the window, no longer counted the birds and their freedom, no longer imagined the places their wings could take them. Instead she stared at the wall, finding and joining the marks, mindlessly conjuring shapes and patterns.

How would MacCailean Mòr look at her now? Raped – that word again – by one of his closest confidants. Betrayed, abused, used. Ardbreknish had taken what she would never give him. MacCailean Mòr, what would he think? Surely, she should have fought harder, done more to protect herself, made Ardbreknish pay a heavier price. A few blows, a few scratches, it didn't seem enough. Had she really done all she could? She tried to picture MacCailean Mòr, but his face came through all fuzzy, as if resisting her recall; she needed the certainty of his understanding, but it refused to come.

As the hours passed, the silent void grew, slowly and

inexorably swelling to fill even these fevered corners of her mind. Its weight smothered the dissenting voices, hermetically gripping her heart in its constricting embrace. She finally stopped struggling and relinquished herself to its stygian shadows.

Time lost its form. Although daylight came and went through the window she never drew the curtains. Sleep came or not regardless of the light. Meals were left and taken away again uneaten; she couldn't stomach them.

Ardbreknish had only come once since the rape. He appeared in the doorway but hadn't dared to cross the threshold. She'd shrunk to the far corner, wrapping her legs with her arms. The silence was her friend and shield, it would protect her. He left.

After the door had closed, she flew at it, hammering on its dumb panels with her fists, shouting his name. But the searing burn of the long-forgotten bracelet stopped her in her tracks, her vision exploding with pyrotechnic starbursts of white, yellow and red pain. The surprise and its ferocity forced the air from her lungs. She collapsed backwards onto the bed. Her hard-scrabbled gasps for air came too fast and too shallow. Slowly, she regained control and the pain diminished, finally disappearing to leave her alone again with her thoughts, that babble of inner voices competing for dominance, the ebb and flow of their arguing driving her to distraction.

But a new, small, distant voice in her mind urged her to do it again; to feel the burn, to fill her mind with its nerve-shredding power. She needed that pain; she could use it; it was hers. And so she approached the door, first bathing in the blistering, white-hot, cauterising agony and then wrapping herself in the sepulchral embrace of the silence within. As the hours and days passed, her existence became defined by red, yellow fire and the balm of her blue, black inner shadow. She began to enjoy the withering scorch of the bracelet, to test her endurance; how long she could bear it? She held her breath and fought back against its riving claws, its ice axe blows, the punching needles, the serrated tearing that raced up her arm and through every fibre of her being. That little voice that resisted the silence, goaded her on, pushing her, baiting her; this was the punishment for her failures, for her guilt. She deserved it. Only the blinding flash of excruciating torment could quieten it. On and on she went, thrusting her hand into the invisible field, recoiling from the impact, regrouping in the silence, trying again.

Until, very suddenly, there was nothing.

Her hand touched the door, no jolt raced up her arm. She waited, apprehensive. She tried again. Still nothing. She retreated to the window, rubbing her arm, twisting the bracelet to give it a better contact against the flesh of her forearm. She approached the door again. Nothing. She sat back on the bed and contemplated the door. It hadn't changed. She looked at the bracelet; it hadn't changed either, but it was no longer working. Had she blown its fuse? Or run down its battery? She didn't know, but it didn't matter, its grip on her was gone.

23 – Village Bay

The howl of the wind was beginning to drive Gillespie insane. It was alive, a constant malevolent force, buffeting and tugging, nipping and biting. It snatched your words and filled your ears with its incessant roar. Even on the shore it was strong enough to blow you bodily across the strand if you stood too proud. All the prisoners adopted the stoop backed shuffle of the islanders, rounding their shoulders and hunching low to offer the least resistance. Up on the tops it was worse. He thought he might be physically blown away by the wind the first time he went up Mullach Mòr, to the radar station on the peak of the ridge that divided the island. It screeched around the summit as if the Cailleach herself was trying to dash him onto the rocks below. Even inside the triple glazed radar station you could feel the demented pounding of the wind's fists on its walls. As days became weeks, the psychological effect of the wind didn't lessen, if anything it grew. A constant and incessant reminder of where he was.

The main prison compound was housed in a squat concrete building in the middle of the bowl of hills in Village Bay. Here most of the prisoners slept and worked in the prison's data processing centre, a mindless, repetitive job which earned the facility money to pay for its upkeep. Prisoners could earn a little extra Cùinn if they hit their efficiency targets and were free to spend that in the rudimentary shop on chocolate or vape juice. No cigarettes were allowed as the

Riaghladair thought them unhealthy and dangerous, but vaping was permitted, and the prisoners enthusiastically adopted the habit, with clouds of vapour known as St Kilda Mist pouring out of any prisoner gathering.

In some ways, life in the prison was easier that he'd expected. Like in most prisons on the mainland, the prisoners shared a cell with one other. During the day they were allowed to move relatively freely around the prison compound – after all, where could they go. The perimeter was the high, dry-stone wall which surrounded Village Bay. Originally, the wall had been built to keep the sheep out of the islanders' crops, but now it was used for keeping prisoners in. Even so, it wasn't as if there were armed guards every 50 metres, as there was no way of getting off the island there was no need to waste resources guarding the perimeter. Anyone found out of bounds knew that their punishment would be harsh.

There were several gates in the wall, the one in the west was for those climbing up the very steep slope of Mullach Mòr to the radar station or to cross the ridge to Glen Bay on the other side of the island. This is where the really dangerous or vulnerable prisoners, the psychopaths and paedophiles, were kept in isolation, in a separate, even grimmer facility. While it was only two miles away as the gannet flies, it might as well have been the other side of the world. It faced straight out into the maw of the Atlantic and Gillespie struggled to imagine how awful it must be for much of the year. He'd looked down from the summit of Mullach Mòr, making out the concrete building on the shore far below, as isolated and alone as it was possible to be.

There was another gate in the perimeter wall to the North which allowed you to climb over the flank of Conachair, Mullach Mòr's close neighbour and at just over 1,400 feet the highest point on the island. On Sundays, the prisoners were allowed out of the North Gate to walk to the top and look out to the island of Boreray and the sea stacs; Stac an Àrmainn and Stac Lì, both towering pinnacles of rock that rose like the teeth of leviathan straight out of the ocean. It wasn't just for the altruistic benefits of exercise that the Riaghladair allowed this privilege, but also to remind prisoners that however bad they thought their existence it could always get worse. The hardest nuts to crack were sent to consider their failings on Stac an Àrmainn for a couple of months. With barely any shelter and the need to catch their own food, few returned. Whether they threw themselves willingly from its cliffs to gain release from their purgatory or fell in the incessant hunt for seabirds to eat on the Stac's vertical cliffs it was hard to say.

He shared his cell with Robbie MacRae, a one-time successful music promoter who had filled the clubs of Oban and Stornoway with pounding house music to a loved-up congregation of top-off, arm waving ravers. His misfortune was to be too successful and the Chiefs in the Comhairle did not like his dulling of the martial instincts of their clansmen and women. Consequently, he had been incarcerated for fifteen years for tax evasion and was now nearing the end of his term. Gillespie found him convivial company, although when stoned on the illegally produced cannabis-derived vape juice that circulated in the prison he could bore on for hours about endless rare remixes and so-called "banging" tunes.

That said, Gillespie thanked his lucky stars that he
hadn't been put in with one of the hard men, the ones
that would scoop your eye out with a spoon and eat it
in front of you if they thought you were looking at them
in the wrong way. Many of the prisoners had served in
their Clan's independent company, providing all sorts
of security services around the world. They were inured
to violence, especially as it was often the only way to
have their voice heard in the world. The Riaghladair
understood this and ensured that once their daily data
processing tithe had been completed more life
enhancing classes were available. Gillespie was detailed
to the literacy class, helping fellow prisoners to read and
write – particularly English, of which many had failed
to develop more than a rudimentary knowledge. He
enjoyed having this more positive role and swiftly made
some useful acquaintances who in return helped steer
him through the minefield of prison life.

He would occasionally meet up with Davy
MacSween, and if it wasn't raining too hard they would
sit on the shore and look at the sea. Around the prison
Davy assumed the cock-sure swagger of a member of
one of the most powerful groupings in the facility. The
MacSweens were famous for their heavily armed and
professional mercenary units, the Redshanks, and
unsurprisingly quite a few ended up on St Kilda. This
gave Davy a powerful Ceann, or roof, to shelter under;
if anyone messed with him they would have to answer
to the whole group, not a prospect many fancied. The
MacSweens generally kept to themselves, but Davy
would seek Gillespie out, as if the fragile shared bond of
their boat journey was a bridge back to a more normal
world.

Davy also kept Gillespie updated on all the political machinations that plagued the prison. With so much disruption along the west coast, tensions inevitably spilled over and it was as well to know what was going on before trouble came and found you. Gillespie arranged to meet Davy in the canteen. It had been a few days since they'd last met, and Gillespie found himself unexpectedly pleased to see Davy's violently red hair bobbing across the room towards him. Sitting down at the table, Davy grabbed his wrist in welcome using the MacSween grip.

"How you doin'?"

"Not so bad, yourself?"

"Well, I would feel a whole lot better if those MacLeod and MacDonald cunts could stop battering each other. We MacSweens have friends on both sides and their continual "you're either with us or against us" bullshit is getting on my tits. Anyways, how are the wee Clan Nechtan getting on?"

"I think I'm the only MacNachtan in here. We are but a small Clan that minds its own business, not like you mighty warriors."

Gillespie could joke with Davy, but he knew better than to be so loose tongued around others. They sat and spraffed for a good half an hour, before the bell sounded for the afternoon shift. Gillespie rubbed his eyes in anticipation of another four hours staring at a spreadsheet. Just as he and Davy were getting up, an altercation erupted at the far side of the canteen. The room surged towards the brawl, shouting partisan support for the various participants in the melee. Gillespie struggled to make out what was going on, but Davy whispered in his ear.

"That's the Loch Hourn MacDonalds taking on the Raasay MacLeods, should be interesting. Ooof.....!" Davy exclaimed, as a beefy protagonist punched his shaven headed opponent head over heels. One of the Raasay MacLeods then rammed the edge of a meal tray into the big man's throat, sending him choking to the ground before repeatedly smashing it into his face. The crowd bayed its approval. Before the other MacDonalds could salvage the situation, the guards were on them, hosing them with pepper spray and reducing the maul to a mindless, writhing mound. The doors to the canteen were then sealed while the Riaghladair was sent for.

When he arrived he did not look happy. Dressed in a dark grey kilt and jacket he looked the very epitome of officiousness, but his little currant eyes became as hard as basalt beads. Standing over the subdued and sullen group of men, all of whom were red faced and weeping copiously from the pepper spray, he folded his arms behind his back like a headmaster addressing naughty schoolboys.

"What do you think you are doing bringing your petty squabbles into my prison!" He shouted. "I cannot, and will not, tolerate such behaviour." One of the prisoners tried to speak in their defence and was silenced with a glare that could have cut stone.

"Which of you started this?" Silence swept the room.

"Okay, well let me rephrase that. If you don't tell me who started it, then you will all have the same - two weeks in the Cleit."

This time a ripple went around the crowd, but an answer came not. Cliù meant that no one was going to co-operate, and he knew that as well as any.

"Fine, have it your way." Turning to the guards he said: "Take this scum to the ridge Cleits. Two weeks, no less."

There was a palpable intake of breath around the room.

For Gillespie the punishment Cleits didn't bear thinking of. These were small drystone cells, roofed with turf, most of them not much bigger than a crawl in fridge; not enough space to stand and barely enough to turn around. Originally, the islanders used them to store food – the coursing wind through the gaps between the stones dried the gannets and puffins they'd relied on for nourishment and the turf on top finished the job; the living roof sucking out all remaining moisture. The Riaghladair had a whole range of them he could use, sited in different locations to put a particular spin on the torture, the one constant being the desiccating cold and the perpetual wind roar which drove the incarcerated out of their minds. The ridge Cleits were particularly exposed up on the high slopes of Mullach Mòr, catching the bite of the wind full bore. Gillespie felt the fear in the prisoners' eyes as they were led away.

The rest of the occupants of the dining hall shuffled out under the penetrating gaze of the Riaghladair, his unblinking eyes seeking out any vestige of defiance. Once outside, and well away from the canteen, Davy felt confident enough to slap Gillespie on the back.

"Serves those cunts right! Two weeks in the Cleits should cool their boots, eh?"

Just then, Gillespie saw a strange woman shrouded in black walking across the strand. The wind picked and puffed at her outlandish attire, billowing her loose-fitting clothes into an ever-shifting cloud. She walked tall and straight, no St Kilda stoop for her proud shoulders. Her head held high, she stared straight ahead, as if not seeing all the leering prisoners. Her hair was tightly tied back and was as white as the cresting waves in the bay behind. Her high cheek bones and strong jaw accentuated her hollowed cheeks and sunken eye sockets. She would once have been beautiful, but her face now had the gaunt pinch of someone double her age. Gillespie was mesmerised by this apparition and stared after as her long stride quickly covered the shore and she disappeared among the long row of islanders' houses.

"I didn't know they had women prisoners here." Gillespie said, almost to himself.

"No, they don't. At least, not officially." Davy replied.

"She's clearly no islander."

Davy laughed. "No, she's no islander. And if you look up the prison's records you'll find no trace of her either. One day she was brought here against her will and has been held here ever since. I saw her on the shore begging the last boat to take her with them, every week it's the same. The islanders just ignore her. They know it is not worth their while to help her, not unless they want their very skin flayed from them. Apparently, she lives in a Cleit - imagine that, choosing to live in one of those hell holes! No wonder she's gone out of her mind."

"But who is she?"

"That, my friend, is Lady Lamont, the wife of our dear President."

24 – The Idea

Shonique quietly closed the door to the ward behind her and set off down the long corridor to the lifts. LeroyMar was making good progress and was in high spirits. The wound to his gut had been serious, how could it be otherwise, but miraculously Allan Stewart's thrust had missed his most vital organs and while he'd lost a couple of feet of his small intestine, the doctor assured her that he would make a full recovery. She felt more relaxed about his condition after he came out of the induced coma they'd put him in while he healed. She hated seeing him lying corpse-like surrounded by peeping machines; he'd always been so vital, so to see him hovering in the nether world between life and death pained her deeply, however confident the doctors were.

Once outside, she flagged a Tagsaidh to take her back to Clachan, absentmindedly staring out at the stippled surface of Loch Fyne. As the Tagsaidh passed Dunderave she could see her fellow Clan hard at work repairing the castle. The roof had already been fixed and from the outside the castle was looking much better after the unwelcome depredations of the previous months. As they pulled into Clachan, she told the driver to drop her at the Two Stags, she needed a drink more than she needed to go home. Of course, the shell of the Two Stags was still charnel black and roofless after the fire, but Dolina had borrowed a marquee from Davy Hendry so she could continue to slake the thirst of Clan members. Intended for weddings, it was double lined and wholly convivial, as long as the drinkers learned to avoid the support poles as they wove their way to and from the bar. When it rained, a small stream ran the length of the tent, soaking the hessian flooring and any incautious drinkers' feet. None of that mattered though, what did was the welcoming smile on Dolina's face as Shonique entered.

"What can I get you? Your usual?"

"Clàireat, make it Left Bank and a large glass please."

Shonique looked around to see who else was in. Tam and Davy, the Clan's topers-in-chief were sat on their stools by the bar, swapping chat with anyone who looked lonesome; in another corner sat Don MacNachtan with a group of fellow musicians surrounded by a blizzard of notation. There were a few unfamiliar faces too, but her focus was attracted by Fiona and Kirstie who were sitting in a booth and waving her over. She hesitated, while she was always happy to spend time with Fiona, Kirstie was a different matter. Ever since she'd handed Gillespie over to the Black Watch with barely a pause, Shonique felt a flush of anger whenever she'd seen her. Over the weeks that had diminished, not least because of the time they'd spent together in the Court of Canun, but nonetheless she still felt on edge around her. However, their welcome could not be ignored, and she threaded her way through the tables towards them.

"How's your brother?" Kirstie asked, her brow furrowed in concern.

"He's ok, getting better. They've stitched his guts back together and he seems to be healing up well. So, all good." Turning to Fiona, Shonique asked: "How's wee Mara getting on after her ordeal?"

"Ach yes. She is quite her old self, almost as if it never

happened. It's amazing how quickly kids can move on with their lives and forget such horrible experiences. I'm sure we could all learn a thing or two in that respect."

Shonique decided that now was as good a time as any to have it out with Kirstie. She needed to bury the hatchet if she was to stay in Clachan, she couldn't afford to fall out with the Chief.

"Look, Kirstie…."

"I know what you are going to say. And I'm sorry. Really. It was a horrible thing to have to do. You think that I don't feel shame for doing it? But what was the alternative? They would have taken or killed him anyway and probably a lot of others too."

"But you didn't even try to shield him, you just handed him right over…"

"No individual is bigger than the Clan. And in the last few months we've had a very tough time; we've almost been snuffed out." Kirstie snapped her fingers like a pistol shot. "But being Chief is about leading, taking those difficult decisions. Yes, and it's also about judging Tulloch Gorm or Ghillie Callum at the dancing competition and handing out prizes at the farm show, but the substance is delivering and protecting our collective good. I wish I could have done something, anything, else, but it wasn't to be."

Shonique sipped her wine. She knew that Kirstie was right, but it still rankled. She couldn't imagine LeroyMar giving up so easily. A sullen black cloud descended on the group, the silence growing into an insurmountable obstacle. Just when Shonique thought she was going to have to leave it was Fiona that dispelled the mood as quickly as it had formed.

"Well, I don't know about all that Chiefly nonsense.

All I know is that my man got his head blown off running a fool's errand, and that fool was our last beloved Chief but one, Duncan Tapaidh. They're puffed-up wankers mostly, full of their own self-importance, present company excepted of course." She nodded at Kirstie. "However, we can't do much about that, what we can do is think about how we can help Gillespie."

"What do you mean?" Shonique asked, scoffing. "Don't tell me you're going to bake a nail file into a cake to help him break out!"

"Break out! I like your thinking! Yes, how can we help to break him out, that's what I want to talk about."

"Don't be ridiculous. No one has broken out of St Kilda in more than a hundred years. It can't be done." Kirstie said definitively.

"What happened to all that leadership guff you just spouted? I don't care about what others have failed to do, I only care about what we can, together, do." Fiona was fired up now. "No one imagined that we were going to be able to rescue you from the Lamontation's dungeons after all. No one imagined that we were going to be able to save our kids and wrest Dunderave back from the grip of that murderous bastard, eh! So, all I'm asking is that we have a think about how we might be able to spring Gillespie. It must be possible; everything is always possible with a bit of thought and hard work." She took a deep draw on her vape, before exhaling two jets of mist through her nostrils like an angry dragon.

"OK, I like your confidence." Shonique leant in. "But what do we even know about St Kilda?"

Kirstie's eyes were now lit up with enthusiasm and she drew a rough map in the spilled beer on the table with her finger outlining Hirta, the main island, like two croissants laid back-to-back. "It's a long way out, way beyond the Outer Isles, forty miles or so into the Atlantic Ocean proper. The only way in or out is by the naval patrol ship that takes prisoners and supplies there once a week, weather allowing. There are weeks and weeks of the year when it is too rough for them to get anywhere close. Even helicopters can only get there on the calmest days."

"The main prison is here in Village Bay," she pointed at the crook of the right-hand croissant. "With the really dangerous prisoners kept here in Glen Bay." She indicated at the left-hand croissant. "All around the outside are near vertical sea cliffs, well over a thousand foot high. The only place you can moor a boat is in Village Bay. There is nowhere else. That is why it is so secure."

Fiona stared at the map. "And I can't imagine they are going to let us just sail in and ask for him back are they…."

"No."

Shonique took a sip of her wine. "I think we need to approach this as if we were on a job, as if the Black Tower Company was commissioned to do it. And if that was the case, we would do a whole lot more recon before we started to plan anything. We would want to know exactly what was going on on the ground and ideally have someone on the inside."

"And how do you propose to do that?" Kirstie asked.

"We need to do some digging, try and find a prison guard or a local that can help us out. Without that we won't be able to communicate with Gillespie for a start. C'mon, you guys are the computer whizzes, surely you can sweat the team to try and scrape some useful data."

Kirstie nodded thoughtfully and turned to Fiona. "This might be the time to pull a favour off those creeps on Tor – you know the ones we caught trying to crack our code – they owe us big. Those dark web wankers certainly have their fingers in all sorts of pies, I'm sure they'll be able to rustle up something, at least to get us started."

The sense of hope transformed their mood; together anything was possible.

Fiona raised her glass in toast; "Cheers Ladies, let's get this done!"

25 – Dark Web

The next morning Shonique rose early and jogged over to Dunderave where the gaming operation had been reconstituted. Ever since Allan Stewart's destruction of their original offices, the Clan's programmers had worked remotely, relying on the cloud to deliver services to their global customer base. Since their recapture of the Castle, Kirstie took over its ground floor, arguing that as the Clan's main source of revenue it was important for it to be more defensible. And as she was interim-Chief no one felt much like disagreeing.

It was cramped with crowded desks and constant battles over the right temperature for the newly installed air conditioning, but it had a buzz, that atmosphere when motivated intelligent people mobilise behind an idea. You could almost feel the brain power at work as the Clan picked itself up off the floor, dusted itself down and started to punch its weight again in the global on-line gaming space. Kirstie was at her hard driving best, pushing the development team to evolve new iterations to keep their customers hungry for more. New formats were rolled out and more games were in testing, the operation was humming.

Shonique was no programmer, but she did have a knack for putting her finger on key issues and opportunities; she was instinct not data-led, and that occasionally brought her into a conflict with Kirstie who was all about hard empirical facts. Shonique had empathy though and she'd learned that it was a critical and rare quality.

She scanned her retina to open the gate into the outer ward, waving greetings to various Clan members as she crossed into the passageway that led to the Courtyard of the Fountain and the main entrance to the Castle proper. Soon she was pulling up her chair behind Fiona's desk to watch her at work.

Fiona sipped her Orinoco-brown tea and fired up her computer. She opened the Tor browser and tapped in **www.queenofclubs668.onion**. "Brace yourself, it could get a bit messy in here."

The browser opened an innocuous looking page dominated by the jealous eye of the Queen of Clubs from a pack of playing cards. There was a chat box and a string of threads below where users were discussing card counting stratagems, cheat codes for online games and stolen card details.

"Now, let's see if our favourite Korean kkangpae is on here…." Fiona addressed a message to a handle tagged Don Seokga whose profile picture showed a spread of cards under a perfectly manicured hand with a whopping orange Padparadscha Sapphire on its third finger.

"Who's that!" Shonique asked. "He looks interesting."

"Well, that's one way of describing him I suppose. He's one dangerous motherfucker that's for sure. He hacked us a few years ago and almost shut us down. It was only thanks to Kirstie's skills that we managed to trace him and turn the tables. We've gathered quite a lot of dirt on him in the meantime, something he knows and which I now intend to leverage."

In the chat box a single word appeared:

Annyeong

"He's online, that's Korean for hello." Fiona typed back:

Annyeong hasimnikka

"That's me being super polite."

Characters now started to rapidly flash up on the screen:

It's been a long time, I thought you had gone away. Why do I get the feeling you might want something?

And why might you think that? You know I just love to talk with you, and it's not just to benefit from your great insights and charming personality, I know you are the only person who can help with a difficult problem I have

Fiona looked at Shonique, "This guy loves a bit of soft soap."

You're too kind. What do you want?

Well, since you ask. I am looking for juicy information on anyone that lives on this island

Fiona flicked over the location of St Kilda.

Anything you can find gambling, pornography, drugs, I need a lever

Let me take a look. What can you trade?

Bitcoin?

Ha, ha 😊 *– don't be stupid, I can see this is a prison island. That's official business, if you want me to hack that, its gonna cost more than mere money*

OK. What do you have in mind?

A lengthy discussion ensued where their Korean gangster protagonist made all sorts of outrageous demands, including access to all their users' bank card details. In the end, Fiona agreed to allow him to cashout $10m of dodgy bitcoin through one of their gaming sites, conveniently laundering it for him in the process. He logged off with the promise of returning the next day with what he had found.

"Do you trust him?" Shonique asked.

"No!" Fiona scoffed, "but he is a very talented hacker, and he has a web of contacts on the other side of the world that we don't have. That might be critical if we are to find what we need."

"What is it that you hope he might be able to find?"

"To be honest, I'm not sure. But St Kilda is remote as fuck and that gives us two possible opportunities. The first is that all their data traffic is routed through one fibreoptic pipe, passing through one server to connect it to the world wide web. This means we can tell exactly which data to pick through. The other point is that if you were stuck on a rain-lashed lump in the middle of the Atlantic Ocean you're gonna want some entertainment to take you outside your miserable existence. I'm hoping that some of our St Kildan friends might have some exotic tastes that we can exploit."

"What if they are all god-fearing religious types?"

"In my experience, they are the worst of all, so let's just hope they spend a lot of time on their knees."

The next day, Shonique found herself sat back in the chair behind Fiona, watching as she logged back into Tor, the dark web browser that gave access to the seedier and more nefarious side of life online. Once again, the jaundiced eye of the Queen of Clubs scrutinised them as they logged into her digital kingdom.

Annyeong, my little Gaelic friend, you are back. You must want this information very badly…. makes me wonder if I am charging you enough

Annyeong to you too, and don't start patronising me or I might just send your mother those pictures of what you get up to in your

*twisted Gangnam club. Yeah? I wonder what she would say, or
do, to you?*

*Surely you wouldn't do that to your old friend? Anyway, I'm
only messing, I have found some interesting information....don't
you want it?*

Shonique could almost feel the tug of the cursor as it
winked on the screen – what had this odious creep
found and how could they use it? Fiona kept her cool,
taking another slug of her coffee before returning to
type.

*Of course, I'm sure it will be fascinating, you are the best
hacker I know. If there is something to be found, I'm sure you'll
have found it*

*Ha ha ha! Flattery, flattery, my sweet little silver tongue. When
this is over, why don't you come to Seoul, we could have fun....*

Can you just give me the fucking information, pretty please

*OK, OK, so I found some interesting things...who knew that
on such a small island there could be so much filth ☺, my faith
in humanity has been restored. But I know you are not interested
in tits and bums – shame, shame - you want something more how
can I say, degrading? OK, so I will leave to one side the Minister's
tastes since, while a little dirty and very kinky, I doubt they will
get your Gaelic blood racing. No, I have something better for you.
There is a guard and he likes to gamble. Small time, you know,
online gaming, a little horse racing, some game called shinty - wtaf
is that anyway? - he is reckless, sometimes makes big bets, some he
wins, some he loses....*

So far, so boring

*Of course, so impatient you are, it took a lot of hard work to
get this, hacking his stupid gaming account and everything.
Anyway, he especially likes to play poker, Omaha High, on a
gaming site run by some acquaintances of mine in Macau*

And??

And, judging by his bank statements with a little help we can push him over the edge. If you want, I can talk to my Chinese acquaintances. I'm sure they can do me a favour, you know, shuffle the pack a little. They don't like doing it, but they certainly can. Then if he bites, we can run up a big debt for you to do with as you wish

Fiona looked at Shonique her face flushed with excitement.

OK, that is interesting

But if I do this for you, I want those Gangnam pictures. And I want you to fuck off out of my life – understand? Do we have a deal?

Sure, but I need his balls in a vice, I don't want him able to walk away

Ha ha ha! Don't worry, by the time my Chinese friends have finished with him he will be putty in your hands

26 – The Oath

From the afterdeck of The Revenge the Riaghaltas looked forbidding. It squatted on top of the hill above Oban dominating the city. Its granite arcades bound the politics and ambitions of its lawmakers to it like a malevolent web that none could escape. Sorley MacDonald had spent much of his life there, ever since he'd first visited the Comhairle, the Council of Chiefs that made up one half of the Republic's legislature. He had initially been impressed, not just with the building and its echoes of Imperial Rome, but with the cut and thrust of debate in the chamber, a place where swords may have made way for words, but the encounters lost none of their vigour or viciousness. Nowadays, he came here reluctantly, with President Lamont, the so-called Treòraiche, filling the streets with Black Watch, the Capital was becoming a police state, even while the rest of the nation burned. But he'd had to come today, even if it pained him to admit it.

Ever since Lamont visited him aboard The Revenge to encourage him to take on MacLean and her land grab of Islay, he'd become increasingly suspicious of his motives. While Sorley was the first to admit that he'd wanted to win Islay back, he now began to regret his impetuosity. His northern war with MacLeod was going badly and after some early territorial gains their frontline had settled into stasis. Losses on both sides were heavy. His lands on Skye were under pressure from the MacLeods beyond anything that had been seen in hundreds of years and whilst he was still holding his own, it was costing him – both in Cùinn and men. It couldn't go on indefinitely.

Meanwhile, Catriona MacLean was digging into Islay, cleansing it of its Campbell residents and repopulating with her own. He hadn't really made any impact on her, apart from burning out some of her people on Tiree, Rum and Coll. He now knew that he could not take it from her, he just wasn't strong enough to fight on two fronts. But he was damned if he was going to allow her to have it. He needed allies. That was why he'd answered the President's summons to come to the Comhairle; he'd made up his mind to try and approach MacCailean Mòr and offer his help against MacLean. Although it stuck in his craw that he would be helping his ancient enemy if he could force MacLean to disgorge her prize that would at least return the Republic to its previous finely balanced status quo.

When he shaved that morning, he'd been shocked to find the first scattering of grey sprouting in his thick black hair. He initially looked for tweezers to pluck out this unwelcome evidence of age and stress but rapidly decided that it was a fruitless task. Instead, he made an especial effort with his appearance; he wanted to manifest his full authority as the Warden of the Isles. He wore a kilt and crosscut jacket in the green and white tartan that belonged to him alone and he pinned a fly plaid to his shoulder with the Clach Geal, the ancient rock crystal of the MacDonalds that was supposed to bring victory in any task. His sporran was made from the head of a golden eagle, symbolic of his power and heritage, and his stockings were tied with his finest Cladich garters. Finally, he buckled on his best Ferrara blade and dirk to complete the whole.

He ordered Keppoch to get his tail of duine uasal ready, there was no way he was going to set foot ashore without a serious bodyguard. He didn't think that Lamont would try anything, but as for the other Chiefs, it was hard to say. With thirty heavily armed duine uasal behind him and the old killer, Keppoch, at his side, he disembarked The Revenge and started the steep walk up the hill to the Riaghaltas. Even the usually blasé residents of Oban, who were quite used to seeing the Chiefs strutting around the town, stopped to look. Once they'd climbed the hill to the imposing entrance arch, he and Keppoch left his men to wait while they went inside. Keppoch had arranged to meet his other Chieftains so that they could enter the Chamber together as a show of strength: Barrisdale, Clanranald, Glengarry and MacAlister all primped and puffed in their finest. As they entered, their unity caused a ripple around those present, its message immediately understood.

As they took their places, he looked around the room. MacLeod wasn't there, probably wisely, but he was represented by his own posse of supporters with the MacLeods of The Lewes and Raasay present, as well as MacAskill and MacCrimmon. Down the other end, sat Gunn, and Graham but no sign of Gordon or MacKenzie who were clearly staying out of trouble. The Campbells, came in next all swathed in their sombre dark blue and green tartan, but no MacCailean Mòr to lead them, and last but not least came the MacLeans of Torloisk, Ardgour, Dochgarroch and Dunconnel trotting along behind, but no Catriona MacLean.

Everyone was in their finest clothes, the formality of

a Presidential summons requiring that Clan Cliù was upheld, and the room positively hummed with the colour from all the different tartans. The benches were packed with almost every Chief and Chieftain, it was undeniably impressive sight. Not since Gerald Ford visited the Comhairle on his tour of the Republic back in the 1970s had the Chamber been so splendid.

At the appointed hour, Speaker Urquhart rose to his feet under the spreading wings of his eagle backed throne and called the room to order.

"My Lords, Ladies, please." A hush quickly descended on the room, all except for the MacIans who were bickering with their Stewart neighbours, but finally even they were silenced. "Can you all please be upstanding for the President of the Republic." And with a sweep of his arm the mighty double doors at the end of the chamber were thrown open and in strode John Lamont. He was dressed in his Plaid of Office, with the Liberator's penannular brooch holding it in place at his left shoulder, and four eagle feathers were borne in his bonnet, an honour reserved exclusively for the President. In front of him, the Gall-òglach, processed with an ancient Claidheamh dà Làimh, the great two-handed Sword of State. Behind him came the senior Captains of the Black Watch, their faces grim.

The President took up his place in King Charlie's Seat, a rather modest chair beside and below the overblown Speaker's Throne, embodying the unmistakable message that the Republic transcended above any mere individual. The room sat down and waited to hear what the President had to say.

"My Lords, Ladies, Chiefs and Chieftains, thank you for your welcome here today and for the privilege of addressing you. I come not with easy words, I am afraid, but with tough choices. As you know, our great Republic is currently riven with violence at great cost to our people. Their State is struggling to uphold the law, their homes are under threat, their lives and livelihoods hanging in the balance, all at no fault of their own. As Chiefs, under Canun and Cliù, you are bound to offer protection and shelter to your Clan and yet so many of us are failing in this task."

"Do not think that this has gone unnoticed – either here in Oban, or in Edinburgh and London. Our friends and enemies are all deeply interested in our troubles and where they might lead. If we cannot grip this situation then we risk having solutions imposed on us from outside. Something that the Republic could surely never countenance."

He paused for effect, nodding graciously at the sound of supportive cheers, before continuing.

"Our great nation was forged by your ancestors in steel and blood. A heavy cost was paid to create this great institution and the laws that protect our people, our culture and our way of life. We cannot allow this national bloodletting to continue. But if it is to stop and for Cliù to be upheld, then action must be taken."

Sorley wondered where Lamont's speech was going, it was already highly unusual for a President to address the Comhairle in this manner.

"A few among our number are the source of much of the turmoil our nation is feeling. If they could but find resolution to their squabbles, then surely peace would return. Is it fair, I ask you, for all to suffer for the vainglories of these few?"

The room murmured its assent. Sorley noted some

of the Chiefs of the smaller clans, like Tam Mathieson and Jimmy Singh Davidson were more ardent in their support, waving their order papers vigorously and encouraging those around them. Sorley began to feel nervous; he didn't like where this was going.

"MacCailean Mòr has lost lands his ancestors have held for centuries, his people burned out and dispossessed, scattered by the cruelty of Catriona MacLean's illegal occupation of Islay."

"More than that, great insult has been done to my Lord Sorley MacDonald, whose hereditary piper was found murdered, the body desecrated, and the Chief's very own pipe banner abused and debased! Is there any wonder that the west coast is ablaze!"

Sorley felt his pulse throb, adrenalin spiking in his system, the room fading at the edges as he concentrated on Lamont's words.

"And so, my Lords and Ladies, as President I feel beholden to act. To break this destructive deadlock. To restore peace and bring an end to these petulant and selfish actions prosecuted by a few at little cost to themselves but great cost to the nation and our people. However, words are not enough. I understand that Cliù also demands resolution. To that end, I summon the High Adjudicator of the Court of Canun, Camilla Brehon, to attend the Chamber and pronounce a settlement under Canun so that Cliù may be honoured but peace may also be restored."

The room erupted in a tumult of shouting, waving arms and pointed sgian dubhs. Sorley felt cold rage grip his throat; how could Lamont do this? All along he had been encouraged by Lamont. He'd had his approval, his backing. The idea that Camilla Brehon was going to be the arbiter; it was ludicrous. She was more used to settling petty feuds to keep clansmen in check, what authority did she have over him or the other chiefs! He looked across at the attendant Campbells, MacLeans and MacLeods, all of whom were also still and silent among the raging mob of the chamber, all trying to process Lamont's move, to be ready to counter with their own.

Speaker Urquhart shouted and flailed his arms trying to call the room to order, finally directing the Gall-òglach to pound the pommel of the Sword of State on the wooden podium, its thunderous blows commanding the room to silence.

"Calling the High Adjudicator." The double doors once again opened, and this time the solitary figure of Camilla Brehon picked her way up the aisle to the Speaker's podium, her slow but steady progress stalked by the eyes of the room.

President Lamont turned to her. "High Adjudicator, the nation is bleeding, and the Comhairle asks for your judgement. How can Cliù be assuaged under Canun and the violence that wracks the country be ended."

Camilla Brehon drew herself up and cast around the room, Sorley held her gaze.

"My Lord President, it seems that some of the members of this Chamber have been too swift to use force of arms to achieve mastery over others. Blood has been spilt and the institutions of this great nation have been undermined, ignored and damaged."

The room held its breath. She continued.

"I therefore direct, under the jurisdiction of the Court of Canun, that all members of this House must renew the oath of fealty that they swore on their accession to the Republic and its institutions, including submission to the titular role and authority of the Presidency, our Head of State, currently invested in John Lamont, the Treòraiche. All must complete this act by Liberation Day or be charged with sedition and punished to the full extent of the law!"

27 – A Secret Target

The orders came in late the previous night. Iain Og had pulled her to one side after dinner to tell her and Fraser. He wanted to keep the circle tight. There must be a reason for it, but he certainly wasn't telling her yet and she knew better than to ask. Following their briefing, she and Fraser talked about who they would take with them. To move effectively over the difficult terrain, the team had to be small, but they also needed to be tough. She chose Angus and Fraser chose Kat. She felt confident that this gave them the right blend of skills; she had the blade work down, Fraser was the tactician but was also a crack shot, unsurprising given his decades as head stalker on the hill; Angus was as blunt as a shovel but was the only one of their group who had knowledge of explosives. He had cannily emptied the Learach Quarry of all of its dynamite shortly after the arrival of the MacLeans and made quite a name for himself with his improvised devices. Finally, there was Kat, Islay's own parkour queen. She could tic tac or vault her way over any obstacle, and if they were going to be able to break into their target they would need her at her mercurial best.

None of the wider group knew what was going on, the fewer that knew the greater the chance of success. Nonetheless, she felt a bit guilty when she sat with Needles over breakfast and made polite small talk; it almost felt like lying, but it had to be done.

She'd spent the rest of the morning sharpening her sword until she felt that its yakiba edge could split the atom. It always drew a lot of interest from her companions, the yataghan profile being unusual amongst Gaelic fighters. The forward curved blade with its cinched belly gave it great balance and tremendous chopping power in the cut. She was also sure that the profile confused her opponents who were more used to fighting against straight weapons. She idly traced the stamp of Andrea Ferrara with her finger, following the Hamon pattern of mountains and trees along the temper line, before turning the sword in her hand to catch the laser etched motto "Not drawn without reason, not sheathed without honour" that ran along its humped back. The sword had been a gift from the Ferrara Atelier and was created especially for her when she won her first international competition. She knew how much love and knowledge Ferrara's smiths had poured into it and she relished seeing lesser blades shiver and bend under the impact of her shock steel.

Having finished tending to her sword, she turned her attention to the more mundane task of stripping and cleaning her assault rifle and the SIG P226 pistol that she filched from the group's small armoury. She loaded several large clips with a variety of different bullets, putting dots of nail varnish on each so she could tell which was which; one dot on the jacketed hollow-points, two on the ballistic tips and three on the solid copper slugs, which she figured she might need for maximum penetration power if their opponents were wearing body armour. Finally, she grabbed a few energy bars and a can of spray-on field dressing.

Outside the cave entrance, she joined Kat and Fraser who were rubbing dark camo stick on their faces and hands. A small group gathered around them, some enquired where they were going, but most knew better than to ask. Iain Og came over to see them off. He grasped each of their hands in turn.

"Remember, you must take down the satellite antenna first, that will buy you the time you need. Understood?"

Three Fingers nodded; it had only been the fifth time he'd told her.

"And I'll bring the rest of the group to back you up, but we won't be able to get within a mile of the target without being seen. So, you are really on your own. Of course, you'll have the element of surprise, so don't waste it!"

Fraser waved him away, irritated with his fussing, and started moving them out of the camp following the burn north east, before climbing the steep flank of Beinn Bheigier, the highest point on Islay. A feeble sun tried to pierce the grey clouds above them but without much success. Across the Sound, the Paps of Jura were wrapped in a dank soggy mist that spoke of heavy rain.

They stuck to the rough heather and tried to avoid the bald patches of quartzite rock that littered Beinn Bheigier's higher slopes; they didn't want to be seen by any prying MacLean eyes. Keeping well clear of the summit, they jagged their way around the hill's shoulder before dropping down towards the Phroaig river buried in the crease between the peaks. There was good cover, and they now made quick progress towards Islay's north coast. As night began to fall, they found a steep sided burn that over many millennium had cut a deep channel into Beinn na Caillich Beag, the last hill before their destination. Here they sheltered from the mizzling rain and waited for the true dark of night to fall.

Three Fingers ate some of her energy bars and drank

from the burn, its chilly water was vivifying after the long walk. It was too early in the year for midges, thank goodness. The little bastards would love the shelter of the burn, with its damp bracken and scrubby birch trees. She gave thanks for the cool nights which still kept them at bay. A thread of salt was carried on the breeze; they were close to the coast now. The next part was going to be tough. The approach on a target was always the most challenging part, given the need to remain hidden until the last possible moment.

The gloaming finally eased into night and as the last fingers of daylight relinquished their grip on the western horizon it was time to move. She pulled on her night vision goggles, immediately immersing herself in their green-hued underworld. Progress was naturally slower now, but as they were nearly at the target they had to be more careful. She could see the whole Sound of Islay in front of her. The shore of Jura was so close she felt she could almost jump across if it wasn't for the raging current that surged to and fro twice a day through the Strait, the power of the Hebridean Sea squeezed through its mangle of steep cliffs and saw-toothed rocks.

As if on cue, she saw their target for the first time as the beam of the McArthur's Head lighthouse swept the shore and out to sea. She could only see the very top of the lantern, the shaft was hidden by the steepness of the hill. Although very remote, this was a strategic location given its command of the approach from the mainland and entry to the Sound of Islay. To warn sailors of the dangers, the lighthouse had been built into the sea cliffs, pitched on the very edge of a yawning drop. Its graceful concave pillar surrounded by a drunken ribbon of high wall that encircled a grassy compound. This wall was one of the obstacles they had to overcome.

McArthur's Head was also where the MacLeans had sited one of their missile stations to defend the island. It had a commanding view of the whole Sruth na Maoile, encompassing the east coast of Jura, Gigha, Kintyre and all the way to Antrim in Northern Ireland. No one could approach Islay from this direction without being sunk. That was why they had brought Angus and his little bag of explosives.

The weather was deteriorating, with the wind rising and rain pouring down. She expected that the MacLeans would have thermal imaging alarms, so their final approach had to be quick and decisive. Using the magnifier on her goggles she hunted the top of the lighthouse cupola until she found what she was looking for. She grabbed Fraser's arm and whispered in his ear while pointing to the slender mast surmounted by a pineapple-sized plastic casing. Between the wind and the rain it was hard to communicate, but Fraser nodded, slipping the rifle from his back and uncapping the telescopic sight. The shot would be tricky. Lying on the ground, Fraser couched behind the stock and eyed the sight. He made a few adjustments to the magnification before chambering a round and sliding off the safety. Three Fingers continued to watch the plastic pineapple, willing it into pieces. Fraser's first shot missed; his allowance for the wind clearly insufficient. Cursing, he shouldered the stock again, holding his breath as he lined up the cross hairs with the distant target. This time there was no mistake and Three Fingers saw the satellite antenna disintegrate. She wondered how long it would take the MacLeans to realise their communications were down, and that it was an enemy bullet that had done it rather than the forces of nature. Now was a race against time for them to press home their advantage of surprise.

They moved swiftly over the last stretch of open ground to the lighthouse wall. She had no idea exactly how many MacLeans were inside, but they had to get over that wall before they were discovered. Fraser and Kat were in the lead, while she and Angus covered them. There was no sign of any guards; given the curtains of rain and squalling wind they were probably sheltering inside. The entrance gate was firmly closed though, but that was no impediment to Kat. With a running jump she sprang into a wall pass, using her momentum to take several steps up its face before gripping the top of the parapet and vaulting clear. A few moments later the gate opened, Kat waved them through into the upper compound.

The missile station was right in front of them; four needle sharp missiles mounted on either side of a ball-shaped tracking system. Stacked next to it under tarpaulins were mounded boxes of ammunition; the MacLeans were clearly well prepared, for an assault by sea at least. Along the far wall was the accommodation block and as they crossed the compound the first MacLean burst out of the door. Kat dropped him with two neat shots to the chest. Then all hell broke loose. Floodlights came on, bathing the compound in brilliant white light. Three Fingers tore off her goggles, her vision briefly ablaze with dazzling starbursts. Sheltering behind the missile station with Angus, she covered the door of the accommodation block, steadily threading shots through the doors and windows to keep the defenders holed up. Meanwhile, Fraser and Kat disappeared behind the low wall that led down to the lower compound and the lighthouse itself.

The sound of gunfire echoed through the night, with bursts of automatic weapon fire coming from at least two of the windows. She wasn't sure how much longer she could hold them back.

"C'mon Angus, how much longer do you need?!"

She glanced down at Angus who'd unslung his backpack and placed it beneath the undercarriage. He was busy fiddling with something in the top of it.

"Almost there, just a few more seconds….."

In the moment that she was distracted, the remains of the door were kicked open and a group of MacLeans poured out. She dropped one and winged another, but the next pull on the trigger produced nothing but a dull click. Casting aside her assault rifle, she tore the pistol from her chest webbing, picking off another MacLean who was trying to outflank them. But even with the shelter of the missile station she could hold them off no longer.

"Let's go, now!"

No answer came from Angus. She looked down. He was lying on his back, his forehead a bloody mess. His eyes open but unseeing. In his open hand lay a black plastic detonator the size of a cigarette lighter, a red light flashed insistently.

"Fuuuucking hell! Fraser, Kat where the fuck are you, you motherfuckers? I need back up, now!"

A MacLean got to the missile undercarriage and began to snatch shots at her through the structure. Unfortunately for him, one of his legs was sticking out and she just managed to clip his kneecap. In that moment of respite, she scooped up the detonator and rolled backwards behind the shelter of the inner wall, wildly firing in an effort to keep the MacLeans back. Just as her pistol clicked empty, a welcome burst of automatic weapon fire came from behind the wall, momentarily scattering her pursuers.

"Fraser! Thank fuck! Where the hell have you been!"

"Trying to cover your arse! Where's Angus?"

She opened her palm to show him the detonator.

"They got him. I hope this is live."

"Do it." He said, simultaneously grabbing her and pulling her below the cover of the wall.

Without hesitating, she pressed the button and threw herself to the ground. For a second there was nothing; her mind filled with paralysing fear: what if it wasn't armed? Then came the crump of the explosion, followed by a second bigger blast and a rolling fireball that billowed over the wall. Occasional further explosions followed, as the ammunition pile started to go up. They were sheltered from the blast by the wall, but a huge spike of flame tore into the sky and earth and rocks started to fall with the rain. She pressed her face against the foot of the wall, trying to shelter from the deadly deluge. Her ears rang with a dull high-pitched whine. After a few moments she pulled her head up. Fraser had vanished.

She staggered to her feet, pushing her soaking hair out of her eyes. She looked at her hand, it was covered in blood. She gently felt her scalp; it all seemed to be there. She had no time for a more thorough examination. She staggered down the slope towards the lighthouse. Its green door was open, light from inside pooled on a crumpled figure in the doorway. She knelt and turned its face towards her while feeling for a pulse:

it was Kat, there was none.

She glanced over her shoulder towards the higher compound. There was no sound now, just the rain. The explosion must have done for the MacLeans. She stepped over Kat's body and entered the lighthouse. The tight wound stair curved away above her; she ducked her head out to look up.

"Fraser? Are you up there?"

Nothing.

She started climbing the stair, pressing herself to the wall away from the wooden handrail. She suddenly realised that she had no weapons, excepting the sword on her back. She must have dropped her pistol during the chaos of the explosion. Her ears still rang with the echo of its kinetic force, seemingly amplified by the chilly silence of the lighthouse. Her sword would be useless in here anyway, the stair was too tight wound. Instead, she drew her sgian dubh and fumbled inside her armpit for her sgian aslaich. Their few inches of steel didn't feel like much protection. She slid her way up the stair, pressed to the wall, the red anti-slip paint on the treads spiralled downwards in a bloody sluice, the pristine white wall curved away above. But when she finally got to the top there was nothing there but the coruscating beam, blithely continuing its job of centuries.

Where was Fraser? She had to find him. Sheathing her daggers, she took the stairs down two at a time. When she got to the bottom she drew her sword and stepped out into the darkness and the rain. She could hear fighting at the foot of the cliff. If she leant over the wall she could just make out two figures ranged against each other on the narrow jetty below. A near vertical flight of steps led down the cliff face. The rain made the steps slippery, and the steel handrail was ice cold. She raced down the steps, arriving just in time to see Fraser take a blow to his upper sword arm. He recoiled, his arm hanging limp.

Without thinking she lunged into the space between the duellists, her blade catching and turning his opponent's fatal thrust. Capitalising on her momentum she vaulted into her Mako Leap, bringing her sword around her opponent's guard and chopping the blade down through his shoulder from above. The momentum of the blow carried it deep into his torso, nearly cutting his body in two. He collapsed without a word, a jet of hot blood spattered her face, mingling with the rain. She wiped it away with the back of her hand.

"Fraser! Are you OK? What the fuck happened to Kat?"

He waved her words away with his good hand.

"No time for that. Look." And he pointed into the night at the lights of a rapidly approaching boat.

28 – The Resistance

Charlie was the first ashore. The boat barely kissed the jetty before he was over the gunwale and racing towards the two figures standing at the far end. He covered them with his semi-automatic rifle as he approached. They both had their hands raised. He told the woman to put her sword down – he'd already seen how deadly she was with it; the remains of the dead MacLean still twitched at his feet.

"Who are you? Why are you here?" He barked.

"I'm Three Fingers and this is Fraser, we're with the resistance."

Before he could respond, Charlie felt someone brush past him as MacCailean Mòr stepped forward and grappled them both in a welcoming bear hug.

"It's so good to see you! Three Fingers, it has been far too long. When did we last meet? Was it at the National Championships last year in Lochmaddy? My God but you were fierce. Almost as fierce as the cut you delivered to that poor bastard…." He kicked contemptuously at the MacLean's corpse.

"Well, let's just say he had it coming. Can I introduce you to Fraser, a long-standing member of the resistance, ordinarily he farms over by Octomore. He's taken a bit of a blow."

MacCailean Mòr stuck out his hand but realised immediately that Fraser's arm was badly injured; he was pale and was going into shock. Charlie grabbed him before he fell down.

"Nin get over here you lump. We need to get him out of this goddam rain so we can dress this wound.

C'mon you take that side and let's get him up to the lighthouse."

Behind them the boat turned off all its lights before slipping its mooring and disappearing back into the night. As the noise of its engine faded, all that remained was the hammering rain and the slap of waves against the jetty.

The climb up the steep steps was difficult, it was dark, and they were narrow and wet. Fraser was slipping in and out of consciousness which didn't make it any easier. But they got to the top eventually and soon had him sitting in the shelter of the lighthouse where they could properly inspect his wound. Charlie cut the remains of his shirt and jacket away to get a clearer view. A large slice of muscle flapped open, seeping copious quantities of blood, the bone underneath seemingly broken too.

"Nin, get me something to support his arm, a splint or piece of wood, anything you can find." He looked at Fraser. "OK, I need to you to stay very still while we try and set this. Alright? Fraser nodded, gritting his teeth at the pain that was now beginning to override the adrenalin in his system. Charlie patted down his webbing pockets until he found a small bundle tightly bound in Velcro which he tore open. Inside were two stubby syringes, a small cannister and a few sealed wipes. He took the first syringe and without any ceremony jabbed it into Fraser's arm fully depressing the plunger.

"Morphine," he said, almost to himself. Within seconds Fraser's body relaxed as the drug's painkilling power took effect.

"Now, this will be a bit more difficult. Three Fingers,

MacCailean Mòr can you give me some light please – do you have a torch or maybe your phone? Right, OK, now just hold it there while I do this, I only have one syringe so I can't waste it." Charlie opened one of the wipes, carefully dabbing around the edges of the wound to clear away the dirt and grime. Then he tore open the other wipe and very delicately tried to staunch the blood flow in the flap of muscle and skin that opened deep into Fraser's arm. Charlie then took the second syringe and carefully injected the contents into the wound before binding it shut and using the can of spray-on field dressing to seal the outside. Nin returned with a splinter of wood which he quickly whittled into shape with his sgian dubh. Charlie bound it to the arm, before putting it in a sling.

"OK that'll have to do for now. He is going to need antibiotics and a proper set on that, but that will have to wait."

MacCailean Mòr turned to Three Fingers, "Where are the others? Do we wait for them here?"

"No, I think we need to get away from here as soon as possible. The MacLeans are going to have heard and seen the explosion; they're sure to have drones fly over and boats along here at first light. We need to be far away by then. The others are waiting at the foot of Beinn na Caillich, but we can't wait for them, we'll need to meet them en route."

"OK, let's go. Nin, you take his other side."

They shouldered Fraser's deadweight between them and walked him up the slope to the upper compound where the full devastation of Angus's explosion could be seen. The missile emplacement was completely destroyed. Mangled metal littered the ground along with various body parts, some identifiable, many not. The blockhouse had been demolished when the ammunition dump went up and apart from the occasional boot sticking out from under the rubble there was no sign of any MacLeans. Charlie poked around to see if there was anything worth taking, but rapidly decided that all the weapons were too damaged by the blast and there wasn't time, or appetite, for a more detailed search.

Three Fingers was standing by the wreckage as if looking for something.

"What have you lost?" Charlie asked.

"I was just trying to see if there was anything left of Angus that I could take back for his partner. You know his phone or watch, something, anything, for her to remember him by. But it's as if he was completely vapourised."

Charlie put his hand on her shoulder, "I'm sorry about your friends. They were clearly very brave."

Three Fingers looked like she might cry but swallowed hard. "What are you three doing here anyway? I was expecting a more substantial force if I'm honest. Don't get me wrong, I understand it must be important if he is here," she jerked her thumb at MacCailean Mòr who was picking through the detritus. "But I don't think three reinforcements is a good trade for two dead and one badly injured. And who the fuck are you anyway?" She grabbed his arm and twisted it so she could see the tartan panel on his forearm in the light. "That's not Campbell, that much I do know."

Charlie sighed, this was going to take a little explaining and he wasn't sure that this was the time or the place to be doing it. "No, it's not. I'm Charlie

Farquharson and that's my partner Nin MacNachtan, we are friends of MacCailean Mòr and more importantly of a mutual friend who's been kidnapped and brought here as a hostage. We are here as an advance party to try and rescue her before the main Clan force lands in the coming days. This missile station needed to be destroyed if there was any chance of that being successful. I'm sorry your friends died, but we need to get out of here now if we are to be far enough away before morning light. We can talk more later."

She stood for a moment gathering herself before nodding and turning towards the gate. Charlie and Nin followed, supporting Fraser between them, and MacCailean Mòr brought up the rear. The deep black of a highland night waited outside the compound. Through the rain Charlie could just see the steep slope ahead with its scraggy grass and clumps of heather. In the distance the deeper black of rounded hills rose ominously.

"Right then, best put on your night vision, I wouldn't want you to fall on your arse." Three Fingers then led them up the slope and into the night.

29 – Brighid's Choice

Brighid waited until deep into the night. She strained her ears to hear any movement in the corridors outside, but she heard nothing but the pelt of the rain on the windowpanes. Now was the moment, she could put it off no longer. She looked around the room for anything that might help her; there was nothing. She didn't even have a jacket against the cold and rain. She had at least eaten every scrap of food since the moment she broke the bracelet's hold. She knew she would need all the energy she could get.

She slowly twisted the door handle and opened the door a crack. Outside, there was a long corridor, with a dove grey carpet that flowed in both directions, occasional pendant lights cast their pools of light and shadow. She slipped out of the door. Which direction should she choose? Both looked near identical with a spiralled stair at either end of the connecting corridor. She chose to turn right.

She passed closed doors, uncertain of whether they held captives or captors; she had to stay focused, she could barely help herself, let alone others. She paused at the landing. Above a glass cupola, below the elegant spiral of the stairs winding downwards, the mahogany handrail, like a suspended thread, corkscrewed away leading her onward. She plucked up her courage, walking boldly down the treads as if she owned the place. No shouts or remonstrations came.

The stair disgorged her into a wide entrance hall. One corner was filled with a concert grand piano and pictures lined the walls. In front of the piano, in a wing backed chair, sat a sleeping figure. From the tartan panel on his forearm, she could immediately see he was a MacLean, and from his face that he was about seventeen. Too young for late night shifts on watch, too young for fighting too. The ambition of others had dragged him from his teenage years too soon. She wondered what she should do with him. She didn't doubt that Shonique or Kirstie would have probably cut his throat, after all, he was the enemy, wasn't he? For a second she paused and looked at the sleeping youth, his face carefree and untroubled by the years. He should be at school, chasing love, drinking and carousing, unthinking of tomorrow. Instead he was here, part of an occupying force, killing and burning strangers from their homes. For why? A victim of the ambition of others. Could she like Judith bring the sword of justice to sleeping Holofernes's throat? She tiptoed past him; it was his lucky night; she was no murderer.

Conveniently, he'd left his sword on the piano, along with a rifle. She soundlessly picked them up, the rustle of the webbing deafening to her ears. She then opened the inner door to the porch, a cold blast of air roiled around her, she was certain that her sleeping Holofernes would wake; but he stirred not.

In the porch were neatly ranked wellington boots and still dripping waterproof coats. She pulled on the smallest pair she could find; they were still too big but not comically so. She stuffed a pair of boot socks in her pocket to put on later, they would help. The first jacket was far too big, but eventually she found one that didn't swamp her and having buckled the sword onto her back, she pulled the hood up over her long blonde hair.

As quietly as she could, she turned the big brass door

handle and slipped out into the night. She was certain there would be other guards dotted around the grounds and that there would be motion sensors and infra-red cameras. There was no point in being too subtle. Instead, she walked boldly around the corner of the house and up a slope to a service courtyard. Here the detritus of an invading force was scattered casually around a large lot. Troop carriers, Kats and nondescript containers crowded with piles of boxes littered the area.

An arc light came on and a sentry called out from his shelter under the gable end of the building nearest to her. She almost walked right past him. She flicked a salute in greeting and flashed her forearm so he could see the MacLean tartan. She didn't wait for a response but walked on, not allowing the chance of further enquiry. The sentry clearly thought no more of it and settled back into his seat, more interested in keeping out of the wind and rain.

She walked steadily down the curved back drive, hedged in by tall trees that caught the wind in their branches, twisting and shaking under its assault. The rain pattered on the battered road; its potholes filled to overflowing with chilling water. Brighid was thankful for the boots. At the end of the drive she turned right, She could just make out a turning ahead and a signpost. She needed to figure out where the hell she was.

At the junction, a finger post pointed along the shore below her erstwhile prison to Port Charlotte, behind her was the road to Port Askaig and ahead to Bowmore. So she was on Islay! How the hell was she going to get away? She knew nothing of Islay, beyond whisky and wild weather. She had to find somewhere to lie low and figure out what to do.

She followed the road, passing a post office, with a forlorn petrol pump, and the burned out remains of a hotel, the gaping black of its smashed and charred windows shocking even in the dark of an Islay night. She hurried on. While she didn't want to be caught on the open road, she also needed to put some distance between her and her prison and the road was quicker than going across country. After half a mile, she found what she wanted, a side road that led off into the island's hinterland. Walking quickly, she put on a burst of speed before deciding it was now time to commit to the open hill. She climbed over the barbed wire fence that hemmed the road and set off over the scrubby grass to try and find a decent observation point. She needed to figure out where the hell to go. The rain began to ease, and the squally gusts died down as she trudged up the hill. As the slope crested she was confronted by a jabbing finger of stone, an obelisk, that stood defiant of the elements on a stone plinth guarded round by a broken-down iron railing. Despite her better judgement, she approached. There was writing on the monument, which she couldn't read in the dark, but on one side there was a bronze portrait in heavy relief of a bearded figure wrapped in a plaid. He stared out to sea, frozen in time, waiting and watching.

The site had been chosen for a reason and its commanding views of the surrounding landscape immediately helped her get her bearings. She could now see her former prison, below her to the right, above the shore of the large sea loch that she had spent so much time observing. Opposite was what she now knew to be the town of Bowmore, its lights twinkling cheerily through the night, a vestige of normality. To her left, she could just make out the pale line of a road cutting arrow straight deep into the heart of the island. Behind her was darkness, a darkness so total that not even a single light shone. She bit her lip in frustration. She knew she had to avoid the towns and the roads, but which direction should she follow? Where would the darkness take her?

As she watched, a distant burst of orange streaked the sky, the crump of a far-off explosion following ponderously after. The calm of the pitch black was torn apart for a few brief seconds before the Cimmerian shadow of the night descended once more. An explosion of that size did not happen by accident, especially not at this time of night. Realistically, it could only signal the presence of the resistance. While they were the only people that could help her, at the same time the explosion would obviously draw the MacLeans too and she didn't want to walk straight back into the custody she'd escaped from. No, her mind was now filled by a voice, that little voice, and it demanded dìoghaltas, vengeance on the man who had brought her here, vengeance for the wrong he had done her, vengeance for his cruelty and all the pain. The obelisk now became a pointer guiding her and putting it at her back, she set off into the darkest corner of the night.

30 – A Song On The Wind

Gillespie's days were spent in the data facility, supervising the mind-numbing processing of endless spreadsheets and data sets. He thought back to other penitential tasks he had read about, of digging and filling-in holes, or breaking and painting rocks, and while he could find some merit in the utter pointlessness of each of them, somehow the combing and ordering of data was even more depressing. Stuck inside in a large airless room, the serried ranks of tables and computers filled with hunch-backed prisoners pouring dead-eyed over their screens trying to meet their daily target, made for a soul crushing experience. The Sisyphean task was never done, every time he got to the end of one sheet, another would pop up to take its place. There could be no sense of satisfaction or even the exhaustion of physical labour, no endorphins were released in the soft press of the computer keys. Every day as he entered the room fresh from a night's sleep, he tasted the foetid air filled with stale sweat and loathing, the scent of desperation. More even than the wild and remote location, this is what trampled the spirit on St Kilda.

Early on, Robby MacRae told him that if you met your targets consistently, then you would be rewarded with datasets that might include words or names and not just numbers. Somehow the thrill of being able to connect the task with other humans made it more bearable, even if the mechanics were much the same. Gillespie worked hard in those early weeks to try and elevate himself up the pecking order. By contrast, he felt Davy MacSween's lifeforce being sucked from him a little more each day as he drowned in the data, unable to meet his quota and ever stuck in the bottommost circle of that pernicious hell.

When they met for their breaks, Davy would sit slack jawed, drained. Even the livid scar on his cheek had become a mere dribble of pallid flesh, a distant echo of a more muscular and vital past. In the early days he had joked and mocked the monotony, but not anymore, his head was in its coils and it was tightening its grip. When Gillespie looked at some of the older prisoners he now understood why they had that hooded, haunted look, broken down and shuffling when not even in middle age. St Kilda was cruel and no mistake.

At the end of a long shift he sought out Davy to check in on him. He found him sat alone at a table in the canteen, not even in the company of his MacSween kin. His face was grey and drawn, even his flame red hair looked subdued. As Gillespie approached, the corners of his mouth twitched as if to convey a cheeky aside, but words there came not.

"Do you want to come outside for a walk on the shore? I don't know about you, but I sure could do with some fresh air. I don't think the air in here has been changed since the 1970's."

Davy nodded and slowly got up; the sprung steel of his former poise now long dissipated. They walked along the corridor to the entrance and pushed bodily against the pressure of the wind to open the door and escape outside. They traversed the shore beneath the modest church and out towards the feather store, a small brick building at the end of the settlement. In centuries past it was where the St Kildans stored the feathers and fulmar oil that they harvested from the island's avian residents. Now it was an empty curiosity of days past.

With each lungful of fresh air, Davy seemed to come more to life and by the time they'd reached the feather store he was finally able to speak. They chatted for a while, throwing stones into the waves that pounded on the rocks. The human interaction felt good to Gillespie, even if he only heard about one word in every five, the rest snatched away by the ever-present wind which pinched their ankles and bit their ears. It was cold and every exposed patch of flesh felt the wind's rasp. A dank impenetrable murk clung resolutely to the peaks around the bay hiding them from view. Not a single shoot of green could be seen yet in the dun-coloured grass, spring was certainly taking her sweet time to arrive in the archipelago.

It was late in the afternoon, and soon they would have to get back to the prison complex for evening roll call, dinner and lock-up. As Gillespie was about to suggest they made their way back, he heard the snatched words of a song coming through the roar of the wind.

> *Sore sea longing in my heart,*
> *Blue deep Barra waves are calling,*
> *Sore sea-longing in my heart.*
> *Glides the sun, but ah! how slowly,*
> *Far away to luring seas!*
> *Sore sea longing in my heart,*
> *Blue deep Barra waves are calling,*
> *Sore sea longing in my heart.*
> *Hear'st, o' Sun, the roll of waters,*
> *Breaking, calling by yon Isle?*
> *Sore sea longing in my heart.*

Blue deep Barra waves are calling,
Sore sea longing in my heart.
Sun on high ere falls the gloamin',
Heart to heart thou'lt greet yon waves.
Mary Mother, how I yearn.
Blue deep Barra waves are calling,
Mary Mother, how I yearn.

Both he and Davy were caught by the sadness of the tune and the haunting half whispered singing that reached them from behind the feather store. Gillespie followed the sound, almost bumping straight into the black wrapped figure of Lady Lamont leaning against the wall and looking out to sea. She was clearly as surprised to see him as he was her, and she started as if to move away. Gillespie called to her.

"Lady Lamont, please wait. We mean no harm. We were just admiring your singing. What was the tune? If you don't mind me asking?"

The civility of his question seemed to catch on her conscience, and she stopped, turning towards him. "It's called Sea Longing, An Ionndrainn-Mhara. My mother used to sing it to me. Her family came from Barra."

"It's a fine tune and you carry it well. Please stay with us a while. I'm Gillespie MacNachtan and this is my friend Davy, Davy MacSween."

Davy looked embarrassed, his ears turning as red as his hair. "Hi, your ladyship, how you doin?" He mumbled.

Now that he was closer to her, Gillespie could see Lady Lamont's face properly. He was taken aback; the years of her incarceration were there for all to see. Her brown eyes were sunk deep in their sockets and gathered round with wrinkled pleats from squinting against the sea glare. With her high cheekbones, she might once have been called handsome, if not classically beautiful, but her features had been eroded and blunted by the elements, her skin scoured rough, her hair torn and shaggy. As if sensing his flinch, she once again turned to go.

"No, please stay. I know of your husband, well your ex-husband I guess."

"Do you now, and what makes you think I want to hear his name, to even think it, after all these years. After everything that he has done to me?"

"I'm sorry. I know a little of how much you must have suffered at his hands. He is a cruel man. He tortured and killed my friends and has sent me here."

She looked at him anew, studying his face closely to see if he was sincere.

"Aye, well you are not alone, many and more have endured his evil. And as for me? Seven long years have I been held here. For why? For nothing. Nothing except the foolish naivety to have married that monster." She studied him with her unblinking eyes, their intensity conveying hints of her rumoured mania.

It was Davy, surprisingly, that spoke next. "Where were you from? You know, originally, before you met Lamont? Do you not have any Clan or kin to help you?"

She looked at him strangely, muttering almost under her breath: "Torcastle on the bend of the Lochy, beneath Beinn Nibheis. A far cry from this godforsaken place."

"So you must be a Cameron then?" Davy continued. "Surely they could get you out of here somehow. What about your Chief, Lochiel, she must be able to raise it in the Comhairle, demand an enquiry, force him to release you?"

She laughed bitterly. "You think I haven't spent every night asking myself that? You think I haven't watched each time the ship comes to take prisoners away? Where is my Clan? Where is my Chief? Where is my father? Silence is all I hear, silence and the roar of this wind. In seven years I have heard nothing."

Her despondency hung in the air. It started to rain, the thick insistent rain of the open ocean, the heavy droplets quickly soaking them to the skin. Gillespie shouted to Davy that they should get back to the prison complex and by the time he turned back to Lady Lamont, she was gone.

31 – The Connection

The weeks passed and Gillespie saw no more of Lady Lamont. He couldn't get her out of his head though and he tried to gather as much information from the other prisoners as he could about her. It soon became clear that she rarely spoke to anyone and that her appearances were infrequent and unpredictable. She seemed to spend most of her time roaming the cliffs and the interior of the island. She wasn't bound by the same restrictions as the prisoners and could walk freely outside the walled perimeter. The cleit she lived in was apparently up on the ridge between the two glens, and while it was somewhat sheltered from the worst of the wind it was still a harsh and uncompromising place to live. When he had duties up at the radar station he would scour the mounds of stones that littered the landscape trying to figure out which one was hers. He once caught sight of her in the distance, a thin black figure bent against the wind striding along the southern cliffs determinedly walking to nowhere.

As he lay in his cell each night he thought about her and how she'd been incarcerated for no just reason and how the prison and the islanders were complicit. No one would pass a message to the outside world, to her friends and Clan, a conspiracy of silence that left her utterly isolated. He assumed that the Riaghladair had been bought off by Lamont and now that he was President that was not going to change. He wondered why Lamont hadn't just had her murdered like he had so many others. Perhaps there was a vestige of affection for her. Or perhaps he preferred the long drawn-out torture of her soul crushing isolation. Ultimately, he just didn't have enough mental rope to plumb the depths of Lamont's cruelties.

After a long day in the data centre, he and Robbie MacRae finally managed to get their turn on the Ping Pong table. Ping Pong was one of the few indoor activities that the Riaghladair approved of, largely because of the non-lethal equipment required to play it, and there were a number of tables dotted around the prison blocks that were hotly contested by the prisoners at break time. Robbie had a fiendish serve, but if Gillespie could at least get it back over the net then he knew he was in with a chance - the many hours he'd spent playing in the Bushmills community centre stood him in good stead.

It was while he was serving for the second game of their match that he saw a line of prisoners enter and shuffle through the room. They were ragged and broken down, with slumped shoulders, lowered heads and a crow footed stagger; they were a sorry sight.

"That's those feisty MacLeods and MacDonalds, back from their cleit time." Robbie said. "Doesn't look like they will be causing anyone any bother for a while does it. And frankly that Hector MacLeod of Brochel is a right cunt so he deserves everything he has coming to him." He shouted after the shambling line, "Not such a big man are you now, Brochel, you wanker!"

"Is it a good idea to bait him like that?" Gillespie asked nervously.

"C'mon Gillespie man, do grow a pair. You can't let those cunts push you around in here or else where will it end. Anyways, judging by the state of him he's not going to be doing anything that risks a return to a cleit anytime soon."

They continued their game which Robbie, seemingly fired up by schadenfreude, won easily.

"Want another match?" Robbie tossed the ball in the air, only to have it caught by a warder who appeared at the table unseen while their attention had been diverted. "Hey, give us the ball back...." Robbie remonstrated, adding a rather plaintive "Please?"

The warder threw the ball straight at Robbie's face and turned to Gillespie.

"You're Gillespie MacNachtan, right?"

Gillespie nodded meekly.

"OK, come with me."

Robbie started remonstrating. "Hey, we were playing a game here! He's done nothing wrong. He was just minding his own business. What's he done?"

But the warder didn't answer and didn't look back either. He just pushed Gillespie ahead of him, along through the games hall, out of the entrance doors and into the rain and windswept night. It was cold and as Gillespie didn't have a jacket he was soon soaked to the skin. He wanted to turn and ask why he was being singled out and where was he being taken, but his courage failed him. The warder didn't seem minded to hang around and pushed him onwards through the settlement towards the darkest end of the compound where the streetlights petered out beyond the feather store. They approached a line of large storage cleits. Gillespie was gripped with fear that he was going to be incarcerated in one. They stopped beneath a solitary bulb that illuminated the doorway, its pool of light shook with the wind's vigour. It was larger than many of the cleits, and over the entrance in red stencilled lettering it said Dry Goods Only. The Warder swiped the back of his hand against the chip reader to open the door and gestured to Gillespie to enter. He followed in behind.

The cleit was more spacious than most he had seen, but the ceiling was low and the lighting shadowy. The warder shut the door and pushed him up against some sacks of potatoes, putting his left hand on Gillespie's chest pining him in place. Like most of the St Kildans, the man was shorter than Gillespie, but powerfully built and stolid. Wild curly hair escaped his prison officer's cap in a cascade of greasy ringlets. His face was hidden but the whites of his eyes gleamed fiercely through the shadow. He pulled a stubby, dirty blade out of his oxter, holding it up to Gillespie's face, rather too close to his left eye for Gillespie's liking. Gillespie raised his hands in submission, trying to remain calm, waiting for the man to speak. He'd brought him here for a reason, if it was to be murdered then surely it would have been done already. The man was somewhat anguished and was struggling to marshal his thoughts. The blade fluttered around Gillespie's eye, the man's hand shaking with the effort of his concentration. Finally, like an uncorked bottle, the words poured out.

"I didn't mean to….. It wasn't my fault…..it wasn't fair…. Those bastards stitched me up tighter than a puffin's arse."

"I don't know what you are talking about," Gillespie stammered.

"It was just a game, a bit of fun…..just a game…..Is that so wrong? I can't pay…I won't pay…. they can't make me pay! Let them try. It is too much…. I don't have it, I'll never have that much. My mother…. if she knew, it would kill her. You must understand…. you must make them understand!"

Gillespie didn't know what to do, should he play along with the man's mania? It was a dangerous tightrope to walk blindfolded. He had to try and calm him down, before he took his eye out on the point of that knife.

"I will, I will make them understand. I know it must be very difficult for you and I am sorry. I'll help get them to agree." He poured as much empathy and emollience as he could into the words, even if he had no idea what the man was talking about.

The roving whites of the man's eyes stopped and through the shadow Gillespie could feel his face being read, all his defensive layers peeled away to get to the raw truth beneath. The man's face came closer, the umami funk of rotten gums and stale vape seethed up his nostrils.

"Now, listen MacNachtan. Your friends have sent you a message. They haven't forgotten you. They're looking at how to help and will send word through me. But you mustn't breathe a word to anyone. Not to your cellmate and especially not to that MacSween cunt you're so friendly with. Do you understand?"

The St Kildan's Gaelic was as hard and unyielding as the rocks the archipelago was carved from.

"Aren't you the lucky one to have such slippery friends. Just know this, we St Kildans have lived here for four thousand years, and this shitty prison has only been here for two hundred. Nothing will take me away from here but a long box. I'll pass you messages but don't think I'm going to lift one finger to help you. And if you get caught doing something, anything, I'll be the first to come down on you."

"And just so you know, no one has escaped from St Kilda in a hundred years, but plenty have died trying. Your friends think they're pretty smart. So let them try, and you too if you have the balls for it. But the cliffs are tall, and the sea is deep and if you don't want the black backs pecking out your eyes then you're going to have to be a lot smarter or a whole lot luckier than all those other cunts whose bones lie out there among the rocks. You tuig?"

"Your friends may have fucked me as good as any Stornoway whore, but if I ever hear that you've breathed a word of this to anyone I'll have your tongue out faster than I can gut a guga." He turned the blade to catch the dim light. "And this is a little reminder to carry with you." Gillespie tried to shrink from the blade, but the potato sacks resisted any further retreat. He held still, not wanting to risk his eye, the knife's flickering white point so close he couldn't even focus on it. He felt a sharp prick and a slow hot wet line drawn down his left cheek from his eye socket to his jaw. Gillespie tried not to flinch, returning the man's piercing stare. Its work done, the knife was withdrawn and wiped on his sleeve before being sheathed. The man removed his hand from Gillespie's chest and stood back. They turned to leave. Something dripped from Gillespie's jaw onto his shirt. He gently dabbed his cheek with the back of his hand: blood red. As they left the cleit, he was grateful for the fresh Atlantic air that chased out the foetid fug of the man's breath from his nostrils. The guard followed him across the compound, disappearing towards the strip of simple houses where the St Kildans lived. As Gillespie pushed back through the doors into the main prison block, he realised that he didn't even know his tormentor's name.

32 – The Rowan Tree

Shonique had to admit that she'd been a little terrified by how much information their Korean gangster connection had found out about Martin MacMartin. He seemed a pretty pathetic character, working in the prison by day and gambling away his nights in a succession of two-bit poker leagues. She almost felt sorry for him, his small-time winnings evaporated by chicanery into an eye watering loss. Initially, he'd resisted their approach, refusing to return their emails and then denying all responsibility. However, a scanned letter on heavily laid and embossed paper, stamped and sealed with the cartouche of the Senior Court of Justice of Macau soon changed that. Yes, his hostile tone had suddenly become much more pliant when they threatened an enforcement action against the house he lived in with his mother. It seemed she had transferred it to him to avoid tax, not knowing of her son's predilection for gaming, and the threat of them both being evicted was the key that unlocked his total capitulation.

They now had a channel to Gillespie, but still no idea of how to try and get him out. Shonique spent many hours poring over all the available information she could find about St Kilda and nothing she read made her feel any more confident that they could actually pull it off. The islands were stuck far out in the Atlantic and were only accessible in good weather. There was only one place to moor a boat and that was in Village Bay, right in front of the prison itself. The more she looked into it the more hopeless it seemed.

She sat in her kitchen and nursed a cup of Clansman tea, its bitter brown astringency only somewhat dented by the addition of milk and three sugars. She was missing Jamaica. She looked out of her window at the scrubby grass in her garden. It was limp and tired, waiting for summer sun to restore its vigour, much how she felt. The gloomy green was brightened by the neon pinks and oranges of a few fishing buoys she'd gathered from walks along the shore.

She went upstairs to what had been her father's room. The neatly made bed, with three extra folded blankets piled at the foot, filled the room. The eaves crowded in on her, gathering her into the middle, a cocoon of memories. She could still smell him faintly, his clothes hung in the cupboard. She went to the mahogany chest of drawers, running her finger through the dust collected on its richly figured surface. She pulled out the bottom drawer – she knew that's where it would be. Sure enough, a heavy brown paper wrapped parcel lay in the bottom. Their address was written on the front in heavy copperplate, on the back it simply said Ella, Hùisinis, Na Hearadh. She wondered who Ella was. She tried to picture her sitting at her loom on the wild west of Harris, braced against the Atlantic while she wove. The ocean's spraint still clung to the warp and weft of the tartan within, smashed sea salt and iodine from wave pounded wrack and rock. It was quite different from the smell of the Caribbean, which even in the wildest storm season didn't have the same tentacular fury. She took the kitchen scissors from her pocket and cut a long strip off the end of the bolt of scarlet tartan, using the sett lines to guide her straight. She pared off a two-finger wide ribbon onto the bed.

She then picked up the bolt to put it back in its wrapper, holding the tightly woven wool to her face, breathing in its ozonic magic a final time, before closing the drawer and the door to her dead father's room and going back downstairs.

The solitary rowan tree stood sentinel by the gate; its boughs still bowed with bright red berries. Strips of silvery gauze and brightly coloured MacNachtan tartan were tied to its gnarly branches. They caught the wind in silent prayer and shook like scarlet flames importuning the very zephyrs of the air to the service of their tier. Her father had started the tree when he'd bought the house all those years ago and it had been added to ever since, each strip tied carried a request on every passing breeze, until delivered or forgotten. She took the strip of tartan from her pocket, running it through her fingers, the kingfisher flash of blue, its emerald green, but mostly red, the cochineal of a thousand dead beetles, nature's blood sacrifice for a bright burning, living, colour. She looked at the tree, picking a branch and then, changing her mind, picked another. The rain fell soft and insistent; she didn't mind, the choice was important. Her decision finally made; she said a few words under her breath as her strong brown fingers tied the knot before releasing the scarlet streamer to the wind's grasp. It fluttered faster than its fellows, weighed down as they were by the falling rain, the wind picking it out, carrying her prayer. She stood for a moment more, regarding the whole, satisfied.

The Albany MacNachtans never wholly lost their connection with their mother country, despite their ancestor Gilchrist MacNachtan's capture in the War of Liberation and banishment to indentured servitude in

Jamaica. Following his escape, Gilchrist built a connection between the Windward Maroons and what was then the Kingdom of the Gaels under King Charlie the Liberator. As the then Chief's brother, he'd helped to forge strong trading links, smuggling sugar from the British Colony in return for the arms that the Maroons used to harass the Governor and maintain their independence. He also brought the distillation expertise of the Gaels to the island, where rum making was rudimentary, and most had hitherto drunk weak beer or imported brandy. Leveraging centuries of hard-won knowledge of distilling uisge beatha, the whisky so beloved of the Gaels, Gilchrist started producing rum and its fame soon spread throughout the island's mountain communities. To this day, Gilchrist's Lament was produced at Albany, the pot stills ironically fed by the very cane fields that he'd escaped from all those centuries before.

Shonique missed the rum and the wild full moon parties that they used to hold. The community coming together over a meal, each family contributing something for the pot – crabs or fish, plantain or callaloo, each brought what they could. Gathering at a different house each month to drink and eat and dance to the community sound system. Reggae and reels, bagpipes and bass driven dub, those Caribbean Ceilidhs were an important cement that held the community together.

Whether it was nostalgia for the Blue Mountains, keening for the loss of her father, or just out of a sense of duty, Shonique decided that despite the late hour she would go to the Infirmary and see her brother. LeroyMar had been making great progress recovering from the terrible wound he'd received from Alan Stewart and would soon be leaving their care to continue his recovery at home. With Gillespie away she was looking forward to having someone else around the house. She ordered a Tagsaidh and within half an hour was pulling into the car park of the Inveraray Infirmary.

LeroyMar was looking much better. He'd lost the deathly pallor that had haunted his face for so many weeks. His chat too had been reinvigorated and he was soon grilling her for all the information he could get on the outside world and the doings of the Clan and its members. She told him about what she had been doing with Kirstie and Fiona and their plan to try and spring Gillespie.

"Doesn't sound like much of a plan to me," LeroyMar said. "I mean, OK you have a link to him but that is quite different from actually freeing him isn't it."

"I know that well enough," Shonique replied, a little irritated at the perceived lack of respect for their achievements so far. "But it is a start, and possibly the hardest part. Without that we can't do anything."

"So, what's next then?"

"We are trying to figure that out. Nin and Charlie have disappeared, as has Brighid and to be honest, everyone else is pretty busy. We'll think of something, of that I am sure. Anyway, have you heard the latest from Oban and that mad bastard Lamont?"

"No, what's that bomba claat doing now?"

"He's ordered all Chiefs and Chieftains to the Riaghaltas to renew their oath to the institutions of the Republic. Really it is just a way for him to assert his authority as President and threaten those who might challenge him, but it's all dressed up in a pretty bow."

"Wow, that's incredible! Are they going to do it?"

"Well, if they don't, then they run the risk of being disestablished and replaced at best, killed or incarcerated on St Kilda at worst. It's the classic – you are either with us or against us – splitting his opponents into small easily picked off groups. The Black Watch wouldn't be able to take on MacDonald, MacLeod and MacLean all at the same time, but individually, that is much easier."

"And what about Kirstie? Does she have to go? She is our interim Chief after all?"

"I don't know. You should have seen her face when she got the news. For her to face Lamont again would be very hard after what he did to her. But if she doesn't go, we risk losing everything. Who's to say he won't just have her arrested on some trumped-up charge, he doesn't like loose ends."

An image of Kirstie's mangled fingers flashed into Shonique's mind. She couldn't imagine Kirstie submitting to Lamont, to face the man that had tortured her. Shonique had been in Honduras at the time, so she'd only heard the stories, but they were enough to chill her blood.

"How much longer are they going to keep you in here?"

"I don't know exactly, four or five days, maybe a week. I think they are keen to get the bed back, there is always a lot of pressure on space in here. Now that the wound is pretty much healed they think that I can do the rest of my recuperation at home – thank God."

"Where is home?"

"What do you mean?"

"I don't know, I was just thinking this morning about

Dad and what he would have done. I mean, I know he was keen to come back and stand for the Chiefship, but that was his dream not ours. I've been thinking a lot about Albany, about Jamaica. I am not sure the Republic is really where I want to be."

"What about Gillespie?"

"Yeah, I know, what about Gillespie? I like him very much, but we've only been together for a few weeks. It's not like we are married. He is stuck in prison for the next 25 years; am I supposed to sit around and wait for him? Wouldn't it be easier to just book in for another tour with the Black Tower Company? Travel the world, earn some Cùinn. No responsibilities, no pressure, none of this political bullshit that is tearing our Clan and this country apart."

LeroyMar stared at her, as if trying to read beneath the surface of her face.

"Sis, we have responsibilities too. We have a duty to help our Clan, our friends and family, to stick together. We can't just walk out now."

She looked away.

"LeroyMar, come on, this is the 21st century. We can only look out for ourselves, that's hard enough for fuck's sake. All this Clan bullshit. It's the past. I can' deal with it. Look, our Dad believed in it, came back to play his part, and look how that ended. We need to move on, leave this in the past where it belongs."

"You know I tied a ribbon on Dad's tree today. A ribbon for Gillespie. Asking for help, guidance, anything. I just don't know what to do. Should I stay and hope for something to happen, or should I go back to Albany."

"And?"

"And nothing. No blinding flashes of inspiration, I just feel empty."

"What are we without people though? What are we without friends and family? Yes each of us is trying to make their way in this goddam world and there are eight billion other humans trying to do the same. Without those relationships we are just drifting on the sea of life, waiting to be cast ashore wherever the tide takes us."

"Never had you down as a philosopher."

"C'mon Sis, I mean it, we can't run out on everything that is going on here. We have a responsibility to play our part, to help rebuild, to help Gillespie – he saved my life, we owe him. Albany can wait."

Shonique looked at him, his deep brown eyes, a little frown of concentration: imploring her.

"I suppose you are right. But why do I get the feeling that I'm never again going to be drinking shots of Gilchrist's Lament with Devon and Lloyd on their porch, or dance to some fire riddims with Tayshia. If I stay, will I ever see Albany again?"

"Who can say, Sis, who can say."

The walk through the hills in the dark had been long if uneventful. Neither he or Nin had night vision, so they were constantly stepping into boggy pools and tripping over tussocks of grass. The heather seemed to have a mind of its own, with gnarly roots reaching out to wrap around their ankles in a vindictive manner. Soon Charlie was wet and cold from the top of his head to the soles of his shoes. MacCailean Mòr, on the other hand, had been handed a set of Caddell's finest night vision goggles and was practically skipping across the terrain, all the while chatting earnestly with Iain Og.

They'd met up with the main body of the resistance about an hour after they'd landed. Charlie felt a little uncomfortable about the size of the group, it would be all too visible to watchers, if there were any. It was still night though and under the cover of heavy rain and thick cloud he felt that they had a chance of escaping scrutiny. The resistance was clearly buoyed by the success of destroying the MacLean missile emplacement and the unexpected presence of their Chief; there was a definite feeling of hope that now permeated the group.

They got back to the cave just before dawn. As a place of refuge it wasn't much, but Charlie couldn't remember being more grateful to get under shelter. He and Nin stood in front of the camp's solitary fire to try and thaw out their hands and feet, while MacCailean Mòr had to fulfil his chiefly duties by glad handing the group. He and Nin felt a little out of place among all the Campbells. They loitered on the edge of the group, drinking hot tea and trying to warm up. He was tired now. They'd been on the go for over 24 hours and his legs felt every mile of the yomp across the hills of Islay. After the pleasantries had been concluded, Iain Og called a planning meeting and disappeared deeper into the cave to consult with MacCailean Mòr and the resistance's leaders. When Charlie and Nin tried to join the meeting they had been politely but firmly ushered away.

"Ever get the feeling we are not really wanted here?" Charlie muttered to Nin.

"Ach, don't take it personally. They are the ones fighting for their homes and loved ones. I can understand why they might be sensitive to a few strangers blowing in. We just need to find Brighid and then get the hell out of here. I don't want to get involved in any more fighting than I need to."

"How are we going to find her though? It's not like we can just go round the island asking people if they have seen a tall good looking blonde."

"I am sure that MacCailean Mòr will be asking them. Just be patient."

Charlie sighed and turned his attention to wriggling his toes to restore some sense of feeling to them. He could really do with a rest, if he didn't catch a little sleep he would be good to no one. He found a dry looking spot and sat down against the wall; the rocks dug into his back and he struggled to find a comfortable nook, but eventually fatigue overtook him and sleep shuttered his eyes.

He woke after what seemed like an instant to a persistent tugging at his elbow. His head span with sleep and he grumpily pulled his elbow away seeking to return to the comforting blackness.

"Charlie," Nin's whisper came through the darkness. "Charlie, for fuck's sake man, wake up."

"What the fuck do you want? Leave me to sleep. I'm so tired."

"Don't move. Don't say anything. Look."

Charlie snapped back into himself, sleep evaporating as adrenalin coursed through his system. The cave was shadowy, but he could see enough to freeze his blood. There, hovering in the middle of the cave, was a swarm of tiny drones, each no bigger than a matchbox. The swarm was moving slowly but silently down the cave towards the chamber at the far end of the tunnel, its entrance shrouded by a heavy curtain. Two of the units separated from the swarm and moved towards Nin and Charlie. Each drone had four tiny rotors to sustain it in the air and propel it forward. The grey casing of their bodies gave no indication of their purpose, but you didn't need to be a rocket scientist to figure out they were an aggressive threat. They were mesmeric, hovering totally silent, moving slowly but inexorably towards them.

At that moment, the curtain parted and a man – Anndra? – came out. One of the drones swooped forward and hovered over his face for a few seconds as he gawped at it in surprise and horror. It then flew straight at the centre of his forehead and exploded with a muffled phut. The front of Anndra's head disintegrated in a wet shower of gore, his carcass dropping to the floor twitching in shock. He didn't say a word.

Charlie sat in shock as the approaching drone hovered above him. He was frozen as stiffly as any statue. The menacing insectoid threat paused momentarily as if scanning his face. He closed his eyes and waited for the impact.

He felt Nin's sword in the air it was that close to his face. Through his still closed eyes he saw the orange and white flash of the explosion as it lit up the back of his eyelids. But other than the passage of steel within millimetres of his nose he felt nothing, no hot, wet shower of death. He opened his eyes. Nin, sword drawn, was hacking at the remains of the drone, the still smouldering relic of the other was crumpled on the far side of the tunnel where it had been batted by Nin's blade. All hell then broke loose. The curtain to the operations centre was thrown open, revealing the group gathered round the table beyond. The swarm of drones seized their opportunity and flew straight at them. Several targeted Iain Og. He had no chance. He tried to swipe them away with his hands, like an enraged bear, but they were too agile, easily dodging his flailing arms. One swooped in, brushing the top of his head before exploding. Iain Og went down, bellowing a mad tortured scream. Another drone followed him beneath the tabletop; a further crump, the screaming stopped.

The room was chaos as drones sought out their targets. Even in the confusion it was clear that there was a method to the madness, it was as if the drones were seeking out specific individuals. Charlie saw a drone pass over Three Fingers to target a middle-aged woman - the teacher? − who manically waved her arms at it, as if to shoo it away. It was no use, the drone slalomed past her arms before flying into her face and exploding. She fell without a sound. Several of the last remaining drones had taken a close interest in MacCailean Mòr and were hovering just out of his reach, as if waiting for orders. Charlie could almost feel the datastream as they communicated with their operators over this unexpected target.

That moment of pause was all Nin needed, he shouted at Charlie: "Grab the fucking curtain, come on!"

Between them they ripped the heavy entrance curtain down and swept it over the hovering drones, the weight of the fabric taking them down to the floor where they detonated in a succession of muffled explosions. The last remaining drone now circled the room, as if confused over which target to choose. Before it could make up its mind, a flickering thrust of Three Fingers's sword shattered its casing and sent it spinning across the room to explode harmlessly in the corner.

For a second they stood staring at each other, trying to fully understand the horror of what had just happened. Charlie went to check on the teacher, but he didn't need to turn her body over to know that she was dead, the drone's explosive charge although small was very targeted and the flesh and bone of her skull stood no chance against it. He knelt down to check on Iain Og's corpse, but it didn't even need a second glance, the pool of gore was emphatic. He stood up. The cave stank of blood and death, they had to get out.

Three Fingers and MacCailean Mòr were ahead of them, running out of the cave mouth and into the glen. The ground was littered with the corpses of other resistance members, each suffering the same terrible head wounds from the cursed drone strikes.

Three Fingers shouted at a dazed couple who were standing open mouthed at the charnel house scene. "Mohammed, Needles, to me now. We need to move!

Grab anything in arm's reach and then let's go, right now!"

Charlie picked up an automatic rifle that was lying next to one of the dead bodies and swiped some bread off one of the plates on the table stuffing it into his pocket as they ran into the trees that lined the bottom of the glen. He was frantically scanning for more of the pocket-sized drones, terrified that he might suffer the same fate.

"Over!" Mohammed shouted, his finger jabbing at a large combat drone high up in the sky above them. Charlie threw himself down into the burn, the thick trees and undercut of the bank offering some protection. The drone hovered, unleashing a storm of automatic gunfire that shredded the trees around them. Then, just down the burn, a tree ignited in a sheet of flame. A cloud of white smoke then billowed around them in a thick blanket and the air was filled with the bizarre smell of acrid garlic and burned matches.

Charlie could remember enough from his active service to know that smell. He froze in horror. Surely, they could not be using such a banned substance here. In the Republic? The thought of Nin being fried by white phosphorus made his blood run as cold as ice. He'd seen its horrific effects, the deep, never healing burns, the suppurating sores, the agonies it inflicted on any touched by it. Those that were lucky enough to live, that is.

He clenched his fists tight to focus his mind, the steel of the assault rifle bit into his flesh. What the hell was happening? Where the fuck was Nin? The smell of barbequed pork floated through the clouds of smoke. He retched. Hot tears now blurred his vision as he tried to track the drone. Its inexorable, almost lazy, traverse of the burn was bringing it closer and closer, its relentless hail of bullets showering him with chips and splinters. Another puff of phosphorus engulphed a larch just beyond him, it went up like a Roman Candle, the ferocity of the instant blaze forcing him back beneath the bank of the burn. He couldn't move, he couldn't shoot back, he couldn't do anything but cower under the cover of the earth and think of Nin.

34 – Stalemate

Shonique hadn't seen Kirstie in such a state before. She was pacing the floor of the gaming operation like a caged lion, deep in thought and unresponsive to all enquiries. Shonique tried to ask her what the matter was but had been met with a stony silence. With Brighid, Ninian and Charlie all away and Gillespie languishing in prison it seemed that Kirstie was missing having someone to talk to. Shonique tried her best but was getting nowhere. She turned to Fiona to see what she knew.

"It was ever since she got that message from the Riaghaltas, something about a Presidential summons. She has been really upset about it. Mind you if the Lamontation has anything to do with it I can understand, given what she went through."

"Yeah, I heard about that. And seen the evidence of her fingers. Horrible. How did such a man become President anyway?"

"They say that for evil to flourish all it requires is for good people to do nothing, and I guess no one did anything to stop him. Mind you, sometimes I think this country needs a strong leader to keep these Chiefs in check – look at MacLean and MacDonald, not to mention MacLeod. Us ordinary folk have to go about our business, trying to earn a living and keep a roof over our heads while this pointless feuding and fighting wracks the country. Who gives a fuck about all this tribalism. I just want to earn my Cùinn and focus on helping Mara to get through her homework every day – that is the limit of my ambition."

"Worthy ambitions. I just want my brother to check out of the Infirmary. He has been in there too long. Anyway, what did this summons have to say? How does it affect us?"

"From what I have gathered from Kirstie, all Clan Chiefs have been summoned to Oban to re-swear allegiance to uphold the Republic or some shite. Obviously, part of that is an oath to support Lamont as President, something that no sane person would undertake lightly. He is really using it as a test - who will dare to stand against him? Its classic divide and rule. Also, each Chief has to travel to Oban to take the oath in the Comhairle Chamber and that will surely concentrate their minds for them, to be stood there in front of Lamont himself or one of his flunkeys. They know that he can pluck them there and then if he so chooses. The question is will he? He probably doesn't want more chaos in the country than there is already, who knows what the Kingdom might do if that happens. But he will also probably want to make an example of someone – pour encourager les autres, as they say."

"The goddam politics in this country are just too much."

"You would think everyone could just rub along, wouldn't you? But resources and opportunity have always been in short supply here and you have to make your own luck if you are to thrive – or take it from someone else. That's the way it's always been."

"Yes, that's as maybe. But surely that's what has to change. Otherwise you'll be stuck in a doom loop of mutual impoverishment forever. Maybe Lamont has a point after all?"

"Hmm, well Shonique, that is an idea that I think is

best kept to yourself, especially when Kirstie is around."

Shonique excused herself and went outside to have a vape and a slug of tarry expresso from the solar powered coffee stand that Dolina had set up in the Outer Ward. To the average clansman working at the castle, the travails of Oban seemed far away. It was a hive of activity, with carpenters and masons working on rebuilding the roof, as well as the ebb and flow of programmers from the gaming centre. She wrinkled her nose at the bitter coffee, it was hardly up there with the finest Sidamo, but it delivered the jolt of caffeine that she needed. She drew on her vape, billowing a cherry scented white cloud out of her nostrils, watching it be chased and scattered by the light breeze.

Kirstie and Fiona appeared at her shoulder.

"Hi Shonique, how are you doing?" Kirstie said. "Sorry I have been a bit distracted of late. It's the news from Oban."

"It must be hard dealing with all those politicians, not something I have the stomach for."

Kirstie nodded hazily, subconsciously wringing her hands as if checking her fingers were all still there.

"Shonique, we need to progress the plan with Gillespie. Now that we have established a way to communicate with him we shouldn't wait to use it. Who knows what might happen. Have you had any bright ideas on how we can extract him?"

"Not really. I've been studying the maps of the island and reading up on all the information I can find. We obviously need a boat, but you can't just sail into Village Bay and ask for him to step aboard. There aren't any other anchorages. It also needs to be done with stealth, something that is pretty hard to achieve when approaching isolated islands in the middle of the Atlantic. They are gonna see you coming. And as for a helicopter, even if you could find somewhere to land, you would be a sitting duck. Not to forget that with the winds they have there are probably only a handful of days a year when it would be safe to try."

"So, where does that leave us?"

"If I am honest, I'm fresh out of ideas. That goddam rock has got to be about the hardest place to bust out of anywhere in the world."

"Fiona – what do you think?"

Fiona drew on her vape and held it deep in her lungs while she thought. She closed her eyes briefly and said, almost to herself, as she breathed out: "Who do we know who is good at breaking out of things? Or into things? Who would have the balls to try and crack the toughest prison in the whole country if not the world? And who could get away with it?"

Her eyes flew open and locked onto Kirstie's as they simultaneously both replied: "Alasdair MacGregor!"

Shonique had heard a lot about Alasdair MacGregor, the leader of the feared Griogaraich, the outlawed MacGregor Clan. From their base in the wastes of Rannoch Moor, they plied a vicious trade as caterans and mercenaries wherever scruples were shallow and pockets deep around the world.

"And what makes you think Alasdair MacGregor would help Gillespie?"

"Alasdair owes him. Gillespie sheltered him in his house in Antrim before it got burned down by that bastard Alan Stewart. He also helped save his ass when he got shot escaping from Castle Ascog. If anyone can do it, Alasdair MacGregor can."

35 – Any Port In A Storm

Despite her thick jacket, Brighid was now shivering with cold. She'd been walking for hours through well-tended fields, clambering over fences and walls, and avoiding any houses. Dawn was starting to light the sky ahead of her, a grey lead streak that hung heavy on the horizon. Hardly a dawn to lift the spirits. At least the light allowed her to make more rapid progress. She would have to hole up somewhere discrete for the day; strangers walking across open fields being likely to attract unwelcome attention.

She was marching towards the dawn, so she knew that was the East. She knew enough of the geography of Islay that if she kept going East she would eventually arrive at the straits overlooking Jura. Ahead lay a ridge, where not a light was showing, she resolved to get behind it and then think about what to do next. She had been so focused on getting away from her erstwhile prison, she hadn't really thought about what came after. As she trudged her way up the ridge, the lush green grass gave way to yellowy tussocks, hard scrabbling heather and springy moss in a rainbow of colours. When at home in Stronshira, she always used to make tiny garden panoramas from moss collected on her walks: olive green, russet red, dirty yellow, lime green, an improbable kaleidoscope.

Her mind wandered back to her homeland. A tear rolled down her cheek, she brushed it away with the back of her hand, angry at her body's autonomous response. The tears kept rolling though, blinding her to foot-swallowing holes and snaring heather roots; she staggered and stumbled her way up that slope, all the while wanting to lie on the ground and sob. But she had to get to the top and over the crest and find some shelter out of sight.

Finally on the other side of the slope, she looked down on a wide shallow glen, with a further, taller line of hills beyond. In the far distance sat the rounded crests of the Paps of Jura. The valley was totally exposed and criss-crossed with rivers and drainage ditches; a track as straight as an arrow ran up the middle. There was no shelter that way, but to the north there was a stand of trees that closed in the end of the glen. She redoubled her efforts to reach it while carefully staying below the ridgeline and keeping an eye on the road for any suspicious traffic. She needn't have bothered, not a single vehicle passed. Even on Islay this was a remote spot.

At last she made it to the trees, as dull a stand of plantation as you could find anywhere, but at least they hid her from view and their gloomy ranks provided some shelter from the elements. She found a dry patch at the centre and in the crook of a tree root, wrapped herself tightly in her coat and closed her eyes. Sleep did not come immediately; her mind was whirring with too many thoughts and computations. But eventually fatigue won out and the frenetic machinery of her mind slowed and stopped as sleep engulfed her.

Many hours later, she woke to the sound of falling rain pitter pattering down through the boughs and branches of the conifers. She stretched and tried to stand. Her legs were stiff after the night's exertions and she stamped on the soft forest floor to get the blood flowing to her toes. She was hungry, and thirsty, not to mention cold. She would have to try and find shelter. She walked to the far edge of the plantation. Down below, tucked under the hill were a series of small fields and a solitary house. Smoke was coming from its chimney and the smell of woodsmoke cast a spell on her drawing her to the door as surely as any magic.

When she got down to the house it was very quiet. The yard in front was dotted with a few fish boxes and lobster pots but was otherwise empty. She knocked. The door was opened by an elderly woman, her grey hair tied back, deep graven creases on her cheeks and warm brown eyes. For a nanosecond the woman's eyes fluttered downwards – Brighid knew immediately she was looking at the tartan panel stitched to the forearm of the jacket. To her horror, she realised that it was MacLean tartan, as she had stolen it from her jailors. But the woman didn't react, and Brighid was too tired to try and explain.

"Oh my young girl, what are you doing out at such an hour. You look frozen. Would you be liking a cup of tea? Come in, come in." The old woman ushered her in, taking off her coat and hanging it on the back of the door. The house was warm as toast and Brighid gratefully followed her host through the hallway and into the front room. The room was neat and well used, with the chairs and sofa gently sagging under years of use, but their antimacassars were as white as snow. A fire smouldered in the wood burner and the woman threw a couple more logs on which immediately started to spit and hiss as they caught fire.

"Now you come on in through here and sit yourself down next to the fire, while I get us a nice wee srùbag. How do you take your tea? Would you like sugar? Milk?

Also, help yourself to some tablet, there is some in the tin on the table."

Brighid's eyes lit upon an old, battered shortbread tin swathed in tartan and portraits of King Charles the Liberator. She prized it open and took a few pieces of the crumbly, caramel brown cubes inside. It melted in her mouth almost instantly, the sugar swirling round her mouth in a treacly, vanilla tide. It was so good. She took a couple more lumps and sat back, putting her feet closest to the fire. The old woman came in carrying a tray laden down with mugs, jug, teapot and a plate of biscuits.

"Now you help yourself to what you want. I have some flapjacks there, and some shortbread too – mine is the best mind, all homemade. And if you would rather shop bought, there is some Milltear nam Fiaclan, I can't touch it myself as it plays havoc with my dentures." She smiled warmly, perhaps inadvertently showing off the neat row of white plastic teeth that jutted beneath her top lip.

The sugar-based snacks were very reviving and combined with the hot tea the feeling started to return to Brighid's feet and fingers. She looked around the room. The walls were filled with framed collages of family photos, seemingly all organised by year and mostly of smiling groups either squinting in the sunshine or wrapped to the ears in waterproofs. Some of the images were going yellow and blurry with age; they'd clearly been there a while. She wondered which of the figures was the old woman, they were all so young in the photos it was hard to tell. There were also rosettes from the Islay Show tucked behind picture frames of stern-faced sheep: Best Ewe in Milk and Best Shearling Tup and second place for Best Blackface Gimmer, not to mention a Highly Commended for Any Variety Cross Breed that was pinned to a picture of a tongue lolling dog of indeterminate parentage. This was clearly the house of a farming family. Brighid wondered where the dog was. Maybe it was outside, working dogs were often not allowed into the house. She sipped her tea gratefully.

"Now my dear, why don't you tell me what you are doing out so early? And being so cold. Have you been out the night?"

Brighid paused, she wasn't sure how much she should say, although kindly the woman was still a stranger.

"I was just up early, decided to go for a walk but got caught out by the cold. I'm ever so grateful for the tea."

"No bother. You just make yourself comfortable and warm up."

Trying to make small talk, Brighid asked: "Have you lived here long?"

"A while." Came the response, slightly more enigmatic than Brighid expected.

"Are these your sheep?" Brighid pointed at the ovine rogues' gallery on the wall. If ever stuck for conversation with a farmer, she knew that talking about their animals was generally a sure-fire winner.

"No, they're not."

Silence again settled on the room. However, the old woman was smiling and, as if to make up for the lack of reply, offered the plate of biscuits a second time.

In the far distance, Brighid could now hear a vehicle approaching. The woman cocked her head:

"Ah, that must be my son. He just went into

Bowmore for some shopping. Would you like another biscuit."

Brighid suddenly began to feel uneasy. She declined the biscuit. She looked at the photos again more closely, she was now certain the old woman wasn't in any of the pictures. Her mind raced. If this was a Campbell house then surely they would not have been so welcoming of a MacLean. But if it was a MacLean house then they would be in league with MacVey. She couldn't risk it. She got up to leave. The old woman leapt forward, her hands pinning Brighid's wrists to the chair's arms tighter than any manacle.

"No my darling, don't leave, not yet." Her wrinkled face pressed close to Brighid's, a glimmer of triumph in her eye. "Won't you wait a little longer, they are coming for you."

"Get off me, you bitch." Brighid tried to wrestle her arms free, but the old woman's grip was like iron.

"No, no, no. You must stay. They are almost here."

In desperation Brighid pushed herself as far back in the chair as she could and then slammed her forehead into the old woman's face. The woman fell back, immediately releasing Brighid's wrists as she clutched her broken nose that was bleeding profusely. Brighid booted her with both of her feet, cannoning the old woman across the table and into a heap on the far side of the room. Brighid knew she had to get out as quickly as possible. She couldn't be captured now, not after what she had just been through. She rushed through the house, grabbing her coat off the back of the front door. She wrenched it open to make good her escape and ran straight into the arms of Bruce MacVey.

As they drove back through the Islay countryside,

Brighid thought of all those hours of walking in the dark and cold, undone in just a few minutes. She was too angry with herself to put up any resistance to MacVey. He'd just cuffed her hands with a cable tie and she'd meekly climbed into the back seat of his car. They were soon bumping down the potholed back drive of Islay House, her erstwhile prison. The yard was a hive of activity, with troop carriers being loaded with personnel and their gear. Brighid's heart sank as she saw the blond lanky figure of Ardbreknish helping to direct operations.

Seeing them arrive, he approached their vehicle. She sat impassive, looking straight ahead trying to ignore him.

"Hi Brighid, welcome back. It's good to see you." She turned to look at him, his blue eyes carried a sad, wounded look, as if he could not believe that she'd actually wanted to leave, that he'd been disappointed by her behaviour, but that he would forgive her. She said nothing, returning her gaze to the back of the headrest in front of her.

"Are we ready to go?" MacVey asked.

"Yes, we were just waiting for you. Apparently, the nearest road access is at the far end of the Kildalton Road, a place called Ard Talla. It should take us about an hour to get there."

"Have we managed to recon the site at all?"

"Yes, it's all quiet there now, seems like we got most of them. There are probably a few survivors skulking around, but we can sweep them up easily enough. I don't think they are going to give you any more bother."

"Good, let's roll out. You can ride with me."

"What about her?" Ardbreknish jutted his chin at Brighid.

"We haven't got time to sort her out, we'll just have to take her with us."

"Anyway, she might be useful in identifying some of the bodies, particularly if we got you-know-who." Ardbreknish got in the front passenger seat and turned to look at Brighid behind. Brighid didn't show a flicker of emotion. The vehicles started to pull out of the yard, following the troop carrier in single file. "Do you know who that might be, I wonder? Maybe that was why you were trying to escape, so you could meet up with him? Do you know who I am talking about?"

Brighid shook her head.

"Your precious lover, MacCailean Mòr."

Brighid looked at him, he stared back, trying to read her emotions.

"What do you mean?" She said haltingly. "I don't understand."

"Really? Oh, I think you do. Your lover came to rescue you, along with those losers that you are always hanging around with - Ninian MacNachtan and Charlie Farquharson. The glorious cavalry dashing to your aid. Well, we don't live in some folk tale do we, one where Rob Ruadh pops up to save the day, steal the gold and rescue the fair maid." He laughed. "No, we gave them a dose of reality. I imagine it was quite an eye opener! You see, Catriona MacLean has been investing in tactical drone warfare for years and today we reaped the reward. We killed your lover and your friends, as well as the rest of the resistance, in one fell swoop. They didn't even know what had hit them. We're just going over now to clean up the last few stragglers."

Brighid felt like she had been hit with a sledgehammer. If she hadn't been sitting down already she would have fallen down. She tried to hold back her tears, burying her head in her hands to stop the flood of emotion that began pouring out of her. That her friends had died trying to rescue her, that MacCailean Mòr had been killed; she couldn't breathe, the air filled her lungs in lumpen gulps and gasps as her body shook. Ardbreknish said nothing, opening his window and putting his arm out. MacVey put on the radio, a Country and Western ballad floated through the air. Brighid pounded her fists on the back of the seat raging in her helplessness and fury.

36 – Lady Lamont

It was when he was crossing the prison compound that he saw her, her black robes fluttering around her like a funerial cloud. Gillespie had been keeping an eye out for her, but it had been days since she'd made an appearance. He called out and ran over. She looked at him, at once fragile but resilient.

"Lady Lamont, how are you? Are you OK? You look a little tired."

She didn't reply immediately but reached up and rubbed the heels of her palms into her eye sockets, before gazing at him anew.

"Ah, it's the MacNachtan. How are you and your MacSween friend?"

"Davy? Oh, I don't know. I haven't seen him in a few days. Just like I hadn't seen you. I was worried about you."

"And why should you be worried about me? No one else in this god forsaken place is."

"No particular reason, you know, just after our chat the other day. I wanted to check on you. You left rather suddenly."

"Instead of asking after me, you should be looking after yourself – how did you get that?" She reached out and turned his jaw so she could see the full extent of the cut that Martin MacMartin had wrought on his face. He winced at her touch.

"In here things just happen sometimes don't they."

"Yes, I suppose they do. Shame though, you had such a handsome face." She let go of his jaw.

"You don't think it gives me a dangerous allure

then?" Gillespie joked half-heartedly.

"No."

"Well, I am touched by your concern in any case." To change the subject Gillespie asked: "Do you mind me asking how you met Lamont? What was he like back then?"

She looked away and started to walk towards the seashore. Gillespie followed on her heels. She stopped just above the wrack line and looked down the bay, shielding her eyes as if she could see all the way back to the mainland beyond the horizon. She paused for a long time, until Gillespie was certain she wouldn't answer. But she did.

"What any foolish young girls wants, I suppose. Someone to listen to them, love them, support them. Someone they can love too, whatever that is. Someone that takes them out of themselves, believes in them." She turned back to look at Gillespie. "He was fun at the beginning. He had it all. Good looking, well off. Heir designate of a minor but ancient Clan, big enough to matter but not too big to count. But there was always something else too, a dark kernel buried deep within. It took me years to see, but once I'd spotted it, it grew and grew until, like cancer, it consumed us and our marriage."

Gillespie put his hand on her arm in solidarity. She initially recoiled, bristling at his touch, but then her shoulders slumped, and she sighed: "It was all so long ago."

"Why did he put you here?"

"I have asked myself that question a thousand times, ten thousand times maybe. Every night when I go to sleep and every day when I awake. Why me? Why here?

Why didn't he just kill me quickly, like he has done to so many others. I don't know the answer. Leaving me on this rock to go out of my mind. Yes, that would appeal to him, no doubt. He certainly wants me to suffer."

She stared hard at him. "He seduced me when I was too young and foolish to know any better. I remember it well. In the ballroom at Blair Atholl. With all those dead stags' heads staring at us, I should have realised that I was just another trophy." She spat on the ground. "And where are my precious children I ask you? Have they ever lifted a finger to help me?"

"Maybe they don't know you are here?"

She laughed, a crazed light dancing in her eyes. "You believe that if they wanted to find me that they wouldn't be able to get it out of him? Have they scoured the Republic looking for me? No, they are his creatures now. Ever since I caught him with that bitch, he wanted to get rid of me. He didn't have the guts to kill the mother of his children, so he stuck me here instead to rot. A small salve to the smallest of consciences."

The almost plaintive look that she'd had when they'd met had now gone, to be replaced with a fire that raged at the injustice.

"I think he hopes that I will do the job for him, hurl myself off a cliff or slit my wrists. That I will give up and leave his conscience clear. But I won't. I'll never give him that satisfaction."

"Do you have any other family?"

"I don't know who is left alive. All communications from here are controlled, nothing gets out without the Riaghladair's approval. Email, phone, text all of it goes through his server. Over the years I've tried, god knows

I've tried, but no one will risk helping me. In the past, several have tried to get messages out and have ended up marooned on Boreray or the Sea Stacs. I can't bring that fate down on any other. But enough about me, I live this life day to day, I'm heartily sick of it. Tell me your story."

So Gillespie told her about his life, about farming the North Antrim countryside and how at the time it'd seemed boring and mundane but now it was almost painfully desirable. About how he'd been kidnapped by his distant cousin and taken to Dunderave on the shores of Loch Fyne; about the Chiefly election and the attack engineered by Lamont; about destruction, murder and flight; and the rescue from Castle Ascog's deepest dungeons. About Allan Stewart and the child kidnappings and finally the duel with LeroyMar and Gillespie's role in Stewart's death, the subsequent trial and his incarceration. It all poured out.

The very act of telling the story to a stranger brought catharsis for the first time, draining some of the bitterness that had built inside. By the end, the fire in her eyes had been replaced with something closer to pity and she squeezed his shoulder in sympathy. When he finished they stood in silence and looked out at the sea. The wind was whipping white crests onto the waves rolling into the bay. Above, the gannets were circling looking for food and puffins could also now be seen. They'd just begun to return from their winter migration and were starting to crowd the cliffs of Dùn across the bay. Kittiwakes and Fulmars, Shearwaters and Skuas, the sky was filled with the caw and call of the island's avian residents, warmer days and better weather an invisible impetus to their partnering and procreation.

In the distance, the siren went off for the afternoon roll call and Gillespie turned to head back towards the prison block.

"I need to go, but before I do, I wanted to thank you."

"For what?"

"For listening. It's so hard in there," at which he jutted his chin towards the grey hulk of the prison block, "because you can never talk about how you feel. You keep it all bottled up. It's no wonder people go crazy or get violent. What other outlet do they have?"

"You should get along. You don't want to be late."

He didn't wait for a second invitation and he scurried over the rocky beach and up towards the prison entrance. He turned to look behind just once before he went inside. She still stood where he'd left her, rooted to the shore and staring into the mouth of the sea.

As he walked through the doors, who should he see in the lobby but Martin MacMartin. He was standing with another St Kildan warder and they watched him cross the room as he hurried to get to roll call.

"You're late." MacMartin said. "Is that how you choose to show respect to the Riaghladair?"

"I'm sorry, I was just taking a walk on my break. It won't happen again." Gillespie tried deploy as much ingratiating subserviance in his response as possible.

"I saw you, talking to that mad woman. You know she is out of her mind, right?" MacMartin muttered, his colleague adding for good measure: "You don't want the Riaghladair to catch you talking to her. He doesn't like prisoners snooping round her like a bitch on heat. You'd do better with your own right hand or one of the gumps, a nice-looking lad like you shouldn't have any bother." He and MacMartin sniggered at that. A second buzzer sounded.

"Oh will you listen to that?" MacMartin sneered. "You've only gone and missed roll call now with all your spraffing."

Gillespie briefly thought about remonstrating with them, after all it was their questioning that had delayed him and caused him to be too late.

"What do you think Stu, do we need to issue a punishment so that the prisoner remembers the importance of timely attendance at roll call?"

"Well Martin, that would be the normal procedure. Prisoner MacNachtan seems to think he is above the rules. I'm sure a little reminder wouldn't hurt."

"Wait, I think I have the perfect little job. MacNachtan, get yourself over to the South Block, ask for Danny. The toilets are blocked, and I think a little slurry duty will help focus your mind. I'll ring and tell him you are coming." Both of the warders started laughing.

Gillespie stood for a moment, unsure if they were serious, only for a red-faced and screaming MacMartin to yell him from the room, pursuing him with curses and threats all the way to the South Block.

It wasn't until many hours later that he finally crawled back to his cell. Robbie MacRae made him shower three times before he finally allowed him to step a foot over the threshold. For days afterwards Gillespie felt he could still smell under his fingernails the hours spent shovelling shit and hosing down the South Block. Whatever soap he used never quite seemed to expunge it, however hard he scrubbed.

Martin MacMartin clearly enjoyed seeing his

discomfort, pantomiming sniffing bouquets of roses whenever he passed. Gillespie knew better than to react. Martin MacMartin was the only link he had to the outside world and if he was ever to escape he would need his help, but there were days when he would willingly have wrung the bastard's neck just for the pleasure of it.

37 – Lamont's Vice

David Brown's anxiety had been growing for some time. As the weeks turned into months his exposure to Lamont and his nefarious plans had started to chafe away at his very soul. Lamont could be charming and persuasive in person, the objectives he espoused seemingly so reasonable, but it was in the dark of night that David Brown would wake in a cold sweat at the horrors being committed in the name of progress. As Lamont's right-hand man he had accumulated power like iron filings to a magnet. He hadn't had to do anything differently, but the deference that he now experienced from his colleagues in the Seanadh and the indulgence he enjoyed from the Chiefs in the Comhairle made his Republican bones uneasy.

Lamont's pitch to him had always been about modernising the Republic, about resolving the centuries old idiosyncrasies of Clan and Canun, about rebalancing the Republic's position in a European continent that had largely forgotten about the nation at its most western fringe; about containing the ambition of the Kingdom, the Republic's most ancient rival. Brown admired Lamont's skill at pitting the Chiefs one against the other, creating the power vacuum at the centre of the Republic which allowed him to take control. But what made Brown much more uneasy was Lamont's trips to Edinburgh and the discussions that were ongoing with First Minister Balfour and the Scottish and British Governments. Lamont played those cards close to his chest, but Brown had heard and seen enough to wonder what Lamont's real endgame was. Despite all the high talk of freeing the people from their anachronistic shackles and allowing the Republic to be reborn, what it was more and more resembling was a dictatorship. Even the epithet that was now being used of Lamont, that he was the Treòraiche, the Guide of the Nation, was more Maoist than Brown could stomach. He'd always known that when dining with the devil you needed a long spoon, but he suddenly found himself far too close to the Republic's Mephistophelean Machiavelli for comfort.

In the early days of his relationship with Lamont, some of his erstwhile allies in the Seanadh tried to warn him and turn him away from the dangerous path he was treading. But at the time he'd ignored them. He had to admit to enjoying the feeling of power, of previously closed doors being opened and the impossible becoming attainable. For so many years he had been treading water in the mundane humdrum of political life in the Republic, from planning issues and municipal waste management to stultifying arcane constitutional law, that his newfound authority was seductive.

It was when he got home that the doubts always used to set in. When he was at the Riaghaltas, surrounded by glad handers and brown nosers, it was easy to be swept along and to ignore his conscience. But when he finally got to eat his microwaved meal-for-one while looking out over the sleeping city of Oban, then his conscience became all-consuming and he found himself wracked with doubt and guilt, both for what he'd done and for what he was yet to do.

While Lamont kept control of Black Watch close, never allowing Brown to even visit their headquarters at Ruthven, other aspects of the Republic's security and intelligence service were available to him. Department 45 was the Republic's eavesdropping service, and while many of the Chiefs had powerful encryption services for their electronic communications, that did not extend to their face-to-face discussions at popular venues such as the Soused Herring which were heavily bugged. Department 45 used advanced lip-reading technology to allow simultaneous transcription of whispered conversations whether in a crowded room or even when walking down the street. Brown had been amazed by the Department's extensive use of low earth orbit satellites and their ability to capture high-definition footage of protagonists in the most unlikely or remote situations.

He knew that he'd been taking a bit of a risk when he'd asked Department 45 if they had a satellite over Edinburgh on the night that Lamont went for dinner with Balfour and the awful Guy Walker, the UK Government's Minister for Scotland, but it had been worth it. He'd made the request as matter of fact as possible – simple minute taking of an official meeting – but when he read the transcript he realised how explosive the contents were. If Lamont knew what he'd done then he wouldn't rate his life expectancy very highly, but fortunately Lamont's claws had not yet penetrated Department 45.

That was when the scales fell from his eyes about what Lamont was really up to. His endgame wasn't modernisation, but rather turning the Republic into some kind of personal fiefdom, subservient to, or possibly even incorporated into, the Kingdom. Dressed up in the fine language of modernisation, this was an ancient concept that was more to do with absolute power – for Lamont alone.

The summoning of the Chiefs to the Comhairle to re-swear their loyalty to the Republic, its institutions and constitution, had been a bold and clever move by Lamont. Essentially, they were swearing loyalty to him as President, the Head of State, and any that baulked at the oath would be dealt with. The more powerful Chiefs might have been able to resist if they banded together, but with the Republic in chaos and the magnates pitted against each other that was unlikely to happen.

Some of Lamont's most loyal Chiefs had already sworn their oaths, coming to the Riaghaltas in dribs and drabs to stand in the Comhairle under the eye of the Black Watch. As Prìomh-Chlàrc a' Bhun-reachd, he'd sat in to administer the oath when Lamont wasn't present. He had already sat to listen to Tam Matheson and Euan MacNeil as they sanctimoniously took their oaths. Others such as Dervoguila Farquharson and John Gunn had taken the oath through gritted teeth, noticeably focusing their emphasis on their commitment to uphold the constitution and muttering the part about obedience to the President very much under their breath. Others, especially those who had a beef against Lamont, were leaving it until the last minute, waiting to see which way the wind was going to blow, to see what would happen. Time was running down, and with only a week to go he was expecting a flurry of activity in the coming days with Chiefs scurrying to Oban to take the oath before it was too late. That day he had sessions booked in with MacAlistair of Loup, Sinclair, two different Fraser Chieftains, Cameron of Lochiel and Cameron of Erracht, obviously feeling security in numbers, and his biggest fish of the day, Murray of Atholl, the Warden of the March. He felt certain that Lamont would want to make an example of someone – that was part of the point of the whole exercise, to give him a reason. Who would be foolish enough though to risk his wrath?

He felt certain that his growing unease would be shared by others. Indeed, in the Seanadh, the more humdrum chamber of the Riaghaltas, where all the actual work to run the country was done, he knew of widespread alarm. Of course, the Seanadairean were just politicians, they didn't have heavily armed private armies behind them like the Chiefs did. They were there to administer and keep the wheels of Government turning, they had little real power. No, any opposition to Lamont would need members of the Comhairle on its side and preferably some of the bigger magnates who had real heft. He certainly wasn't about to stick his head above the parapet just to get it shot off.

He thought about leaking the transcript from Lamont's meeting with the Kingdom's officials – that would certainly cause a shit storm. Unfortunately, a major fly in the ointment was that Fionnlagh Fergusson, the Editor of the Oban Raven, was so far up Lamont's arse he couldn't see daylight. If he approached him, Lamont would know immediately and have it suppressed. As with so much in life, timing was everything and he would just have to wait for the right moment to make his move and hope that he could shake loose more support. Going up against Lamont singlehanded was not an undertaking any sane person would countenance – not if you valued your limbs and your life.

38 – The Burn

Charlie was struggling to see anything due to the smoke of the burning trees and the clouds of thick white phosphorus. The drone hovered high overhead, sweeping the burn and surrounding trees with a never-ending torrent of bullets, showering him with chips of wood and a blizzard of pine needles. The fire was so relentless and concentrated it was impossible to move. How much ammunition could the bloody thing carry? It started to circle round his position. Soon the protection of the burn's bank would be rendered useless. In a few short seconds it would be all over.

He desperately looked around, trying to find somewhere to run, anywhere there was some cover. Just up the burn he could see MacCailean Mòr, tucked beneath the shelter of its bank. Despite the hailstorm of bullets, he was hunched over his phone maniacally working the screen. With a look of desperation, he rolled out from the undercut of the bank, thrusting his phone upwards for all the world like a celestial TV controller while he mashed at the screen with his fingers. The combat drone immediately stopped firing and its rotors ceased turning. It hung motionless in the air for a moment, suddenly looking less like a deadly flying killing machine and more like a gravity bound imposter, before it plummeted from the sky, smashing into pieces on the ground.

Silence descended on the glen once again, but for the gentle patter of the burn, the rustle of the wind, and the lick of flames. The horror of the last few moments filled the air though: the acrid smell of white phosphorus, cordite and burning trees. Charlie hauled himself over the lip of the bank and staggered to his feet. He had to find Nin. He retraced their steps along the burn. The clouds of white phosphorous made it difficult to see more than a few feet. He called out; but got no answer. There were bodies lying scattered like nine pins, smashed and torn by heavy calibre bullets. He searched among them, dreading what he might find.

"Hey, shit for brains, I'm over here."

The unmistakable sound of Nin's voice came through the smoke. Charlie followed it to find Nin's face peering around a tree stump. He was haggard and pale, but Charlie had never been more pleased to see those blue eyes twinkle back at him. They hugged, they kissed. He didn't want to leave the cocoon of Nin's arms.

"I always said you were a lucky wanker."

"Like I always said you were a stupid bastard."

They laughed. Charlie looked him over for any injuries, but he seemed to have escaped unscathed.

"C'mon, let's get the fuck out of here! Where are the others?"

Nin scrambled up the bank and together with MacCailean Mòr they hunted through the trees to try and find Three Fingers or any other survivors. Charlie took out his phone and shot some photos and footage of the carcasses and what was left of the drones, he could scarcely believe what had just happened and they needed some kind of record. That this could happen in the Republic, to its own citizens, would ordinarily be unimaginable, but these were not ordinary times.

In the end there were fewer than ten of the resistance left, and that included Three Fingers, Mohammed and Needles. None of the leadership had survived the assault. MacCailean Mòr quickly took control.

"We need to get to the rendezvous. We need to abort."

"But what about Brighid?" Nin muttered, almost to himself.

"Yeah, what about Brighid." Charlie joined in. "We can't just leave her to Ardbreknish. You said so yourself."

"I know, I know. Believe me the last thing I want to do is to leave without her. But we have no chance of getting to her now. Our best hope is to try and negotiate her release or wait for us to recapture the island. With the missile battery destroyed, we can now launch our invasion force."

"Come on, you know as well as I do that he will probably stick a knife in her guts before giving her over to you. We can't just leave. In fact, I refuse to leave her to that blond haired Campbell cunt! And besides, do you really think your motley flotilla of boats is going to be able to land? Look at what she has just done to our party. She snuffed it out, like that." Nin snapped his fingers under MacCailean Mòr's nose. "You are more of a fool that I thought if you believe that you are going to take back this island by force of arms."

The group bristled at Nin's harsh words. Three Fingers and Needles both noticeably reaching for their weapons. MacCailean Mòr defused the situation, putting both of his hands on Nin's shoulders and looking him straight in the eye.

"I know how much you love and care for her, believe me I do. I feel the same way. She is the love of my life. But getting us all killed will achieve nothing and won't save Brighid either. She's tough. I am sure she will find a way to handle Ardbreknish. But look at our situation. Look how many have just been killed. We have no back up. We can't go up against an army."

Three Fingers now spoke up. "Not wanting to piss on your parade, but whatever we are doing we need to get a move on. Who knows if they have another of those combat drones to send over here. We need to get somewhere safe and to be honest I am out of ideas of where that might be on Islay right now."

"I agree," said MacCailean Mòr. "We need to get to an evacuation point where we can be picked up. Three Fingers, Mohammed, Needles where do we go and how long will it take us to walk there? I can call my launch to have us picked up, they are waiting just off Jura."

As the Campbell contingent gathered in a group to discuss the merits of different locations, Nin and Charlie stood apart. Nin's eyes were red with anger and frustration, not to mention a few tears. Charlie knew there was no sense in pleading with Nin, it was better to be direct and forthright:

"C'mon Nin, we always knew this was a long shot. We must be crazy motherfuckers to think that we were going to be able to waltz into this warzone and scoop up Brighid. We gave it our best shot, but now we need to leave. Brighid will understand, you know she will. In fact, she would be the first to tear you a new arsehole for even thinking about coming to the rescue. We can come back when we have some proper back up. Now's not the time to be foolhardy."

Nin looked away, as if studying the last whisps of white phosphorus as they were dissipated by the fresh Atlantic breeze. He said nothing, but as the group started to move off down the burn he followed, keeping a sullen distance. Charlie walked with him, but they said nothing further. The idea of leaving Brighid behind after everything they'd been through seemed like a betrayal, but it was the only option in the circumstances.

Three Fingers was in the lead, taking them down the glen, following the Leòra to the South. It was a swift and brutal departure, no one even thought about burying the bodies and everyone had one eye on the sky in case of further drones. As they walked under the cover of the trees, Charlie caught up with MacCailean Mòr:

"How did you do that? You know, with the drone."

"To be honest I had no idea it would work. I've never used it before. Our Independent Companies use a drone tracking app developed by some very smart Israelis. It helps them know when they are being observed in the field. Anyway, they gave me a special upgrade that disrupts drone systems. Basically, it fries their gyroscopes leaving them unable to fly, but it is directional and not very long range. With drones becoming so common place it has become more and more important to be able to take them down. I was very glad to see that it works!"

Charlie thought back to the horror of the cave. Now that the adrenalin was waning, he felt sick. The image of the dead bodies scattered where they'd fallen, the mutilated heads each lying in a scarlet puddle of blood, was seared into his mind's eye. The foolishness of their mission came home to him. Now they were nearly alone, isolated in enemy territory with little chance of finding Brighid and even less of getting out alive. It had been stupid to come. He thought of his mother and father, and Dorcha, his sister - would he ever see them again?

They trudged in single file behind Three Fingers as she led them downhill and towards the sea.

It started to rain.

He had never felt so alone.

39 – The Beach

The walk down the glen was uneventful. No one felt like talking much and Charlie was happy to keep his thoughts to himself as they stuck to single file along the burn trying to shelter under the few remaining trees. As they moved out of the low-lying hills cover was harder and harder to find. Charlie could now see the sea; deep sapphire and crested with white horses that sparkled in the afternoon sunshine. The weather had become increasingly fine as they walked, with even the wind dying away to leave space for spring birdsong to fill the air. The swish of their legs through the bracken was like a drumbeat and the damp musty smell of ferns and flag iris filled the narrow bed of the burn. The beauty of nature seemed in harsh contrast to the cruelties of man that they'd just experienced.

They stopped under the last of the tree cover while MacCailean Mòr called his launch; they didn't want to be caught in the open for a minute longer than necessary. The beach lay just below them, a white arc of sand gracefully drawn as if by a giant's hand to fill the bay. The tide was rising, but it was already plenty deep enough for the launch to come in close. Between them and the strand was a track and a narrow strip of rough grazing dotted with a few sheep and a weather-beaten horse.

MacCailean Mòr turned to Three Fingers and Mohammed: "What's the name of the bay?"

"Claggain. Tell him it is just down from Ard Talla, he should be able to see the point clearly enough on his charts."

"Ok, well he thinks he can be here in about twenty minutes. We'd better stay out of sight until then. Three Fingers, can you see anything on the drone tracker?"

"Nope, nothing."

"Good. OK, everyone, when we cross onto the beach we are going to be exposed, so now would be a good time to check your weapons."

Charlie patted down his pockets but unsurprisingly they held nothing more than they had earlier that morning; just a few magazines for the semi-automatic rifle, it wasn't much. He hoped they wouldn't be necessary. The sun shone down and the heat from its rays wrapped them in its somnambulant embrace; it felt good to just sit and wait for their pick up. There was currently no sign of any MacLeans, and he pictured himself strolling down to the lapping shore and stepping aboard the launch without a shot being fired. Nonetheless, he chambered a round in the rifle and patted down his sgian dubh and sgian aslaich. He squinted and watched the track. To their right, the grazing opened up into a decent sized field, hemmed in by the low hills tracking the southern end of the bay. The track bisected this as it followed the coast and meant they could see vehicles coming from at least half a mile away.

He heard them before he saw them. The grind of military metal on metal and the slap of heavily cleated tyre treads reached his ears shortly before the first of the vehicles made the turn and became visible across the bay. He called out to MacCailean Mòr, but he was already pressed flat to the heather and looking through a pair of binoculars.

"Fuckfuckfuckfuckingcuntbastards." Nin muttered.

"I guess it was too much to be allowed to just fucking leave. How many of them are there?"

"Two troop carriers, a scout and a passenger vehicle by the looks of it."

"Too many, too many. Fuck, what the fuck are we going to do now?"

The rest of the resistance survivors were looking pale and forlorn, Needles was slumped with her head in her hands and even Three Fingers looked exhausted. Charlie knew from his years of service in the Farquharson Company that someone needed to inject some steel or else they wouldn't have a chance.

"Right, Mohammed, I want you to take two people and circle around to the North, spread out and when we start firing, focus on the lead troop carrier. Controlled, enfilade fire, shoot anyone who moves but don't waste ammo, we want them pinned down. Needles, Three Fingers, you take another two and focus on the other troop carrier. Nin, MacCailean Mòr you take the scout car and I'll deal with the other vehicle. OK? Everyone got that? Watch for the boat, don't move until you see it round the bay, then lay down rolling covering fire as you move to the shore. Right? We've got this, they are not expecting us. We have the element of surprise so don't waste it."

They nodded dumbly and headed off to their appointed positions. The line of vehicles slowly crossed the bay, they didn't seem to be in any particular hurry. The column was led by one of the troop carriers with the scout car and passenger vehicle following and the other troop carrier in the rear. Charlie wondered how many troops were in each carrier. If they were full there could be as many as twenty in each, giving the

MacLeans a full complement of roughly five times their numbers. Not good odds. Yes, they had the advantage of surprise, but the enemy lay between them and the water; they were going to have to get past them to get to the boat. He caught Nin's eye, giving him the most cheerful thumbs up he could muster. Nin nodded in reply, returning his eye to the scope of his rifle.

The vehicles now passed in front of them, barely fifty yards from their hiding place. Charlie realised to his horror that in the back seat of the passenger vehicle was sat a woman with long blonde hair. He scrabbled for his binoculars, clutching them to his face. There could be no mistake, it was Brighid.

In the split second of that realisation all hell broke loose. Needles and her team opened fire on the rear troop carrier. The driver was an early casualty and lost control of the vehicle, slewing it across the track and into the drainage ditch that ran alongside. The troops struggled to get out of the back but were sitting ducks for Needles and her team. Meanwhile, the lead troop carrier accelerated away towards Ard Talla sustaining heavy fire from Mohammed and his team. The scout car pulled a hard turn taking it onto the beach and scurrying back the way it had come. Charlie shot out the car's tyres as it careened after the lead troop carrier. After briefly trying to continue on its wheel rims, it soon got bogged down in the mud and ground to a halt. The driver got out and fired a few shots in their general direction before running back to the stricken troop carrier.

Charlie's group were taking sustained incoming fire, mostly from the force that was in the lead carrier, the survivors of which had now managed to deploy further up the beach. The whine of bullets and the steady crack of automatic weapons filled the air. Only one thought filled Charlie's mind; he had to get to Brighid. He broke cover, weaving as he ran across the field towards the car. The thump of his heart filled his head as he crossed the open ground. As he got closer to the vehicle his brain struggled to understand why the two figures in it were not getting out – had they been hit? He ground his teeth in frustration at the thought that Brighid was so close. As he got to the vehicle he realised the horrible truth. Ardbreknish was in the front passenger seat and his limbs were thrashing and writhing. Behind him was Brighid, her cable tied hands on either side of his neck, her knees in the back of the seat, her back arched as she pulled with all her might, the cable tie biting into Ardbreknish's throat, crushing his windpipe. However much he tried, he could not escape her. His face started turning blue, his tongue protruding as the thrashing of his limbs subsided until they finally stilled forever.

Charlie wrenched open the door. Their eyes met. The single-minded fury in Brighid's tear filled eyes changed instantly into relief. He pulled her out and cut the cable ties that bound her hands. They sheltered behind the vehicle while he tried to gauge the state of the battlefield. Behind them, the MacLeans in the stricken troop carrier were finally getting their act together. The man that had run over from the car was busy helping the remaining troops out of the vehicle and they were beginning to return fire in a dangerously methodical manner. Up the track the remaining MacLeans were starting to spread out, causing greater problems for the Campbell resistance whose fire rate was much diminished; ammunition must be running low.

Charlie scoured the bay; MacCailean Mòr's launch should surely nearly be there? The problem they had was obvious. Once the boat arrived they would need to pass through the MacLean crossfire to reach the water and safety. It was too exposed; they wouldn't stand a chance. Charlie opened the front passenger door and pulled out Ardbreknish's rifle. He passed it to Brighid, and she immediately started squeezing off shots at the rear troop carrier, forcing the MacLeans there to duck under cover.

Where was the fucking boat? How much longer could they hold out? When would MacLean reinforcements arrive?

Bullets started peppering the car body as it drew MacLean fire. The protection it offered was meagre and they could easily be outflanked. The MacLeans were getting the upper hand. If they didn't move soon it would be too late.

Just at the moment that Charlie was contemplating a forlorn dash back to the burn, the hammering of a heavy calibre machine gun joined the fray. With delight Charlie looked out across the water and saw MacCailean Mòr's launch in the bay pouring fire into the MacLean positions from its foredeck mounted machine gun. Taken from two sides and unable to sustain the volume of fire, the MacLeans broke, scattering for cover.

Charlie grabbed Brighid and ran for the beach. Behind, he heard the others following and occasional burst of small arms fire. He was totally focused on the launch, they had to get there. He reached the sand, it sucked at his feet, cruelly robbing him of speed just when he needed it most. As they reached the water, he tripped and fell face first into the surf. The weight of his gear pulled him down and he scrabbled to try and get back to his feet. A strong arm helped him up, Brighid! They splashed through the water to the launch, each in turn laying down covering fire for the rest of the group. Bullets puckered the water around them throwing up mesmeric plumes, while overhead the rolling mill of the launch's heavy machine gun hammered out its response.

The launch was close in and brawny arms hauled them over the transom. Charlie gasped in the bottom of the boat flat on his back like an overturned turtle, trying to catch his breath. Bullets whistled through the air, occasionally biting chunks out of the gunwale and the doghouse. Pulling himself off the deck, Charlie started to return fire just in time to see Needles downed as she reached the water. Mohammed and Three Fingers were right by her; they took one glance at her body and then kept on running; there was clearly nothing to be done. Nin and MacCailean Mòr scrambled aboard, followed by Mohammed and Three Fingers. Two more Campbells were running across the beach, but neither even made it as far as the water.

"They were the last. Go, go, go!" MacCailean Mòr shouted to the helm who gunned the engine churning the water white as the propellers bit and thrust them forwards. The remaining MacLeans ran onto the beach firing wildly after them, but they were soon out of range astern as the launch carved through the bay and headed back to the mainland.

Charlie put down his rifle and slumped against the gunwale. His hands shook. He looked for Brighid, but she was already locked in MacCailean Mòr's arms, both were weeping. He turned instead to Nin, holding him tight and burying his head on his neck. He lost himself in Nin's cornflower blue eyes; they glittered back with adrenalin and relief. It had been close, too close, but that only made their escape taste all the sweeter.

40 – The Captain's Caper

The Clan was in a joyous mood. You could feel it, it was palpable in the vigour of the dancing and the cheers that were raising the roof, in the spraff and chatter that swept around the crowded room and in the volume of the music. Shonique felt it too, but her joy was muted by Gillespie's absence. She knew that the celebrations at the safe return of Brighid, Nin and Charlie from Islay were heartfelt, but she wished she could have Gillespie there too: to turn her, to kiss her, to hold her in his arms. She tried instead to enjoy the moment, consoling herself with a glass of Gilchrist's Lament, its pot-stilled, funk fuelled magic whisking her back to the Blue Mountains at the first sip.

LeroyMar joined her, chinking his glass to hers.

"Quite a party."

"Yes, after everything the Clan has been through I expect they are looking forward to quite a lot of dull humdrum."

She looked across at Nin and Charlie dancing wildly in a set of the Captain's Caper, the whole line shouting "Strip Charlie! Strip!", as he forgot to turn the relevant partner for the umpteenth time. She smiled. It was good to feel such unbridled joy after so much bitterness.

"How are you feeling?" She asked.

"The wound is healed; but I just feel so tired. After all that time in the hospital, I'm chewed up. I've been thinking about going back to Jamaica, to rest up in the sunshine, you know recharge."

"I can understand that. The Republic doesn't seem like a good place to convalesce at the moment. Who knows what will happen next."

"Will you come with me?"

"I can't. I've got to stay and try and help Gillespie somehow. He saved your life; I can't just leave him to rot in St Kilda. We've been making good progress. We now have a line of communication open through one of the warders. We're just trying to figure out how we can reach him. Now that Nin is back I am hoping we can leverage his relationship with the Griogaraich, apparently he has a bloodbond with their leader."

"I feel bad Sis. I should be doing more."

She put her hand on his arm, giving it a comforting squeeze. She knew he would if he could, but he still had the washed-out pallor of the bed bound and his usually muscular frame was depleted, even his dreadlocks were now frosted white.

"The most important thing is for you to continue to recover, there is plenty of time for everything else."

They continued to scan the room, occasionally catching someone's eye and nodding an acknowledgement. Shonique was waiting for the reel to finish so that she could speak with Nin. Ever since they'd got back he'd been hard to reach; he was always surrounded by so many well-wishers wanting to pump his hand and congratulate him on the rescue. She hoped that as the evening went on she would have her chance. In the far corner was a small group gathered around Brighid, and Shonique went over to welcome her back. Brighid was deep in conversation with Fiona and Kirstie, and Shonique hovered on the fringe of the group for a few minutes waiting for a pause to open and for her to be able to join the discussion. It was at moments like this that she felt like an outsider. She knew that they weren't deliberately excluding her, not consciously, but on a subliminal level the lifetime that they'd spent together had unsurprisingly created a bond that she could never share.

Fiona was the first to acknowledge her: "Hey Shonique, how are you doing? How's LeroyMar getting on? I saw him over by and thought about asking him for a Boston Two Step."

"Well I'm sure he would love to be asked, although I am not sure he is up to much physically. But a Boston Two Step is definitely more realistic than a Duke of Perth at the moment!"

Turning to Brighid, Shonique continued: "It's great to see you back, what an awful thing to go through. I'm so sorry."

Brighid nodded. "Thanks Shonique, I'm still struggling to take it all in to be honest. It was horrible. I still can't believe it. I've known Ardbreknish all my life, that he could have done such a thing…. well, it makes one question one's judgement about everything, let's put it that way."

"Is MacCailean Mòr here?"

"No, he decided to stay at home and let us MacNachtans celebrate in our own inimitable style. He needs to get ready to go to Oban to take the oath, there is not much time left. Obviously, he needs to go with a big tail of duine uasal; he can't risk Lamont snatching him and packing him off to St Kilda or worse."

"Have you been to take it yet?" Shonique asked Kirstie, who immediately started to look a little uncomfortable.

"No, not yet. As you can imagine, seeing Lamont is not something I'm looking forward to. Not after he gave me these." She held up her broken hands, a constant reminder of her time spent in Lamont's grip at Castle Ascog and the tortures he inflicted on her there.

"But you'll have to go eventually, no? You are our Chief, why put it off?"

Fiona and Brighid both looked slightly taken aback by the directness of Shonique's questioning.

Kirstie sighed. "I know, I know. I have to go, but I am trying to find a time when I can be sure Lamont won't be there to take it in person, so I can give my oath to David Brown or some other official. I can't guarantee that I won't do something stupid if I come face to face with Lamont. Anyway, there are still a few days left before the deadline."

"Do you really think that Lamont would grab you? Surely, he has other things on his mind? No disrespect meant." Shonique asked.

"None taken." Kirstie said crisply, before abruptly changed the subject: "Look, we were just talking about Gillespie. Now that Nin is back we need to get hold of Alasdair MacGregor to pick his brains. We can't leave Gillespie there a moment longer than necessary, there's no saying what might happen to him in that godforsaken place. I'll send him a message tonight asking him to get hold of MacGregor and set up a call or a meeting. Now that Brighid is back home, we need to focus on Gillespie."

Fiona took out her vape, drawing off a cherry flavoured lungful. "I'm just wishing for some quiet times to be honest. I want to take Mara to the Hydro and have a relaxing weekend splashing in the pool and having my back rubbed by they masseuses. You know, the ones in the skimpy white shorts and bulging biceps. It's the nearest I'll get to a bit of action round here anyways."

They cracked up laughing, hugging each other in an increasingly hysterical huddle; the tensions of the wider world dissipated momentarily by the bond of friendship. As if on cue, the Red Banner Band launched into a fast-paced medley of tunes led by Miss MacNachtan's Favourite, its urgent jig rhythm leaving the listener in no doubt as to what her favourite really was. In any case, the morning was early enough to worry about tomorrow, tonight was for drinking and dancing, music and laughter. Outside, the wind freshened, blowing from the North East over the Arrochar Alps, the temperature started to drop, and the taste of snow hung in the air.

41 – Oban

He checked his phone again, still no new emails. Dammit! Time was running out. MacCailean Mòr knew that if he missed the deadline that Lamont would unquestionably use it against him, after all that was the whole point of the oath taking, to isolate those who refused to submit to his authority. While he was obviously nervous about going to Oban at a time when Lamont had Black Watch crawling all over the capital, it was the perfect moment for the other task that he wanted to carry out. He'd discussed the legislative agenda of the Comhairle with David Brown and with the oath taking deadline rapidly approaching there was only really one remaining session when the house would be full. He needed a large audience to bear witness. In any case, he couldn't wait any longer. He would just have to hope the email would arrive in time.

He called Duncan, his steward, to summon his duine uasal. He needed a show of strength to show that he still had teeth enough. Over the next few hours they came in dribs and drabs, Lawers, Dunstaffnage, Skipness, Strachur, Otter, Barcaldine: his most loyal Campbell chieftains. They all came formally dressed in their finest plaids of dark green and blue tartan, pinned by brooches of fantastical knotwork, heirlooms of generations past. It was as demonstrative a show of unity as was possible to imagine. All bore their traditional edged weapons, but also carried an exotic selection of firearms attuned to their personal taste. Each brought their own tail of men and women, the best fighters that their companies could provide. They carried the languid threat of the supremely accomplished, relaxed in their ability to face down any situation that might arise. It was strength enough to put off all but the most determined assailant. As the long column of vehicles pulled away from the Castle and began the drive to the Oban Wade, he felt comfortable that no one would try and mess with him, no one except Lamont perhaps. But that was a gamble that he was going to have to take.

Snow continued to fall. It wasn't particularly heavy yet, but it was settling. It was a lambing snow, the cruellest kind. Just when you thought you had seen the back of winter, when new life was come to the hills, then the Cailleach would once again wrap them in her killing cloak of white. All the way over the hill to Loch Awe he was checking his phone, waiting for the ping of an incoming message, nothing. He wondered if it was the patchy signal as they rounded the haunch of Ben Cruachan, hugging the lochside as they threaded the Pass of Brander, where his ancestor of many generations had fought the MacDougalls and won hegemony over Argyll at the side of Robert the Bruce. Even as they rolled down the coast road and looked out to Lismore and across to Mull, when the bars on his phone showed full signal strength, no message came. He slipped his phone back in his pocket, it was no good staring at it; he shouldn't have left it so late. Anyway, there was nothing for it now.

As they rolled into Oban, the febrile atmosphere of the city was tangible, it hung in the air like a bad smell. The residents of the capital rushed about their business with pinched brows and pursed lips. Many of them were descended from incomers, come to service the needs of the Republic and its citizens. They might not even belong to one of the traditional Clans, either due to a reluctance to choose one and pay their Clan dues, or perhaps they did not feel the need for protection as they lived in the shadow of the Riaghaltas. It was at times like these that they felt the lack of a "roof" over their heads, when the city was filled with Chiefs and their proud and often pugnacious followers.

The Campbell cavalcade parked in the ferry terminal car park at the bottom of the hill and sauntered up the slope towards the domineering edifice of the Riaghaltas above. Its Bonawe granite arcades dwarfed the town below; it was an imposing sight, as it was intended to be. Several hundred duine uasal, well drilled, finely dressed in identical tartan, gleaming buttons and well-oiled weapons, was a display of Clan muscle that was rarely seen these days in the Capital. And the good burghers of Oban scurried past, giving them a wide berth with eyes very much averted. As they reached the Riaghaltas, the discrete presence of the Black Watch coalesced into a heavily armed and visible force. MacCailean Mòr had no intention of causing trouble though, his tail was just a show of strength. They would wait outside while he went into the Comhairle chamber with his key Lieutenants, each of whom were Chieftains in their own right.

Immediately on entering the chamber he looked to see if Catriona MacLean of Duart was present. He needn't have worried, she was there, in her usual place, surrounded by her own lackeys and supporters: Ardgour, Dochgarroch, Torloisk among others. She visibly bristled as the Campbell entourage entered, immediately turning to MacLean of Torloisk and whispering behind her hand. Torloisk nodded his head in response, his unblinking eyes fixed on MacCailean Mòr.

Ignoring her scheming, MacCailean Mòr scanned the other benches to see who else was present; Sorley MacDonald of the Isles was there, with the scar-faced Keppoch leering at his side; in the row behind, sat Clanranald, like the meat in a sandwich, squashed between Barrisdale and Glengarry. She was totally focused on working her phone, much to the annoyance of MacAlistair of Loup who was trying to attract her attention from behind. Further back, sat a swarm of MacLeods in their bright yellow tartan that shouted a warning as clear as any hornet's jacket. The room was buzzing as it filled with an endless stream of minor Chieftains, everyone pointing out new arrivals to their neighbours, each deciphering the tartan if they didn't know the face. Many of these were relative strangers to the regular attendees. Lamont's veiled threat obliged them to travel from the four corners of the Republic to take the oath. While some had already sworn the words in the previous weeks, and there were still a few days remaining, there was no denying that many had chosen that session to swear their allegiance, the perceived safety in numbers perhaps shaping their thinking.

MacCailean Mòr caught Speaker Urquhart's eye and submitted his request to address the chamber at the end of the session. He then sat on his bench directly across from Catriona MacLean. He gave her his best icy stare. She glowered back, her emerald eyes pools of poison that carried a tint of triumph, after all, she still held Islay.

He felt the buzz of the phone in his sporran, he took

it out to check – there it was, finally, the message he'd been waiting for. He checked it had downloaded correctly and then sat back, his mind turning over what he had to say.

The top of the hour approached, and with it the start of the session. The room quietened as it awaited the arrival of the President. As the Comhairle clock struck the hour, the large double doors were flung open and the room rose as President Lamont entered, preceded by the Gall-òglach carrying the great two-handed Sword of State. Behind came the diminutive figure of Camilla Brehon, the High Adjudicator, her pitter-patter trot echoing on the stone flags as she struggled to keep up. They marched to the dais and the President took his appointed place on King Charlie's Chair and the Gall-òglach placed the sword in its ceremonial cradle below the Speaker's throne. The Comhairle was now in session.

MacCailean Mòr hadn't known if he would be able to keep his cool when he actually saw Lamont. The last time they'd met face to face was when he'd been a prisoner in the Lamontation's dungeons beneath Castle Ascog. The horror of those days and nights had dimmed a little with the passing of time, but now it returned in a searing flash; his mind's eye momentarily cast back to the tiny cell and the weight of that soul-crushing darkness. He dug his nails into the palms of his hands, the sharp pressure dragging him back into the room, into the present. He had to stay focused, today was not about Lamont; his time would come.

Speaker Urquhart called the room to order and so began the long session of oath taking, with each Chief or Chieftain processing to the dais and, having rested their hand on the Sword of State, swore their allegiance to the Republic, to its laws and to its President. Lamont sat there drinking it all in, luxuriating in the sonorous declarations of his supporters, and scowling at the grudging, mumbled, mutterings of his opponents. At his side, Camilla Brehon scanned the face and retina of each Chief in turn, adding them to the formal record as incontrovertible proof of their submission, so that there could be no doubt or backtracking later.

Lamont seemed particularly focused on Catriona MacLean when she took the oath, nodding at her words as she spat them out like unpalatable gristle. But with the smaller Clans, like the MacGillivrays, or MacNabs, he could barely contain his boredom, often openly looking at his phone to pass the time; they were not a threat and he, and they, knew it. Hours passed as the shuffling line wended its way up to the dais and back; with the room full of so much ancient tartan the smell of mothballs hung heavy on the air.

Finally, as the session was drawing to a close, it was MacCailean Mòr's turn. He stood up and arranged his plaid before crisply approaching the dais. Placing his hand on the narwhal-tusked hilt of the Sword of State he swore the oath of loyalty and obedience to the Republic, her laws and her President. He then turned to Speaker Urquhart who called the Chamber to order to hear his statement.

"Mr President, Speaker, High Adjudicator, Lords, Ladies and fellow Chiefs. Thank you for your patience at the end of what has been a long session. A long but important session where we have all reiterated our loyalty to the institutions that make this country great. We have no Kings, but we have Canun, the laws that bind us and protect us. Part of what makes this Republic unique and enduring. Our institutions are robust, and they need to be, given everything we have suffered in recent months. At this moment, in front of my peers of the Comhairle and before the President, our Head of State, and the High Adjudicator, the upholder, interpreter and enforcer of the Canun, I want to bear witness to a terrible crime."

The atmosphere in the room changed instantly with the fug of boredom and dull process evaporating as the words left his lips. The whole room leant forward to better hear what he was about to say, none more so than Lamont, who suddenly looked a little nervous.

"I have just returned from the Isle of Islay. As you know, one of the members of this Chamber illegally seized my patrimony, killing and evicting its residents, house burning and widow making. All of these are in their own way flagrant and repeated breeches of the rules of war, the laws of Canun, and the laws of civilisation. There have been many terrible stories, but I wanted to see, I needed to see, the truth with my own eyes. And so I went to Islay and joined with a small band of loyal residents who had come together to resist the invaders. A small group of citizens, ordinary people, thrown together by extraordinary circumstances."

A ripple went around the room; this was not what they were expecting. Of course the Comhairle members all knew about Catriona MacLean's invasion and what that meant, but out-of-sight-out-of-mind was as true in the Republic as anywhere else. Everyone had their own problems to contend with and were happy to convince themselves that someone else, the President, the Black Watch, the Seanad, was responsible for managing the situation. But they could ignore the situation no longer, MacCailean Mòr had brought it to the Chamber and was laying it out in front of them. Catriona MacLean sat with her arms crossed and a face like thunder.

MacCailean Mòr continued. "And if I can just connect my phone to the Chamber's audio-visual system, I should now be able to show you exactly what MacLean hegemony entails." The large screen at the end of the Chamber flickered into life and started to show the film Charlie had taken of the dead bodies of the resistance, each with terrible headwounds and lying in pools of blood; of a tree burning like a candle under a jet of white phosphorus; clouds of heavy white smoke; the remains of tactical drones lying scattered among the bodies. All the while, MacCailean Mòr kept up a steady, dispassionate monologue describing the drone attack and the indiscriminate murder of so many of his Clan, the occasional crack in his voice the only giveaway to the emotion that was raging inside him. He outlined the numerous breeches of the Geneva Convention, of the United Nations Convention of Human Rights and the Canun. He read out the names of those killed by the drones, of the ethical atrocity of autonomous machines killing human beings; of the use of white phosphorus in the Republic against its own citizens, against every tenet of the Canun and the moral standards laid down in the Republic since the days of King Charles the Liberator.

The Chamber echoed with boos, murmurs and shouts for justice. Feeling the growing anger, Catriona MacLean stood to leave, surrounded by her supporters. She was shaking with fury at being ambushed in front of her peers. But before she could even make it to the entrance doors, Lamont's voice rolled down from the dais.

"No. I don't think we can allow you to just leave. I think I speak for us all when I say that I am shocked to see such war crimes committed by a member of this Chamber, in the Republic, against our own citizens. Whatever the situation, we will not sit by and watch our citizens slaughtered in this cruel manner."

Lamont was in his stride now, pounding the arm of King Charlie's chair as he pinned MacLean with his bulging-eyed stare. "Serjeant at Arms, please take Catriona MacLean into custody immediately. Yes, and all her accomplices too." He waved at the knot of MacLean Chieftains that surrounded her.

The Chamber erupted in jeers and shouted boos, as a squad of Black Watch entered to escort the MacLeans from the room. For a brief moment, it looked like they might try and resist, Torloisk's hand darting to his sgian aslaich. But common sense prevailed, and in the face of the heavily armed company of Black Watch, the MacLeans sheepishly followed her from the room. She was white with anger. MacCailean Mòr couldn't imagine that she was going to go quietly. Indeed, as she was frogmarched towards the exit, she turned to face the dais, her face contorted. But before she could say a word, Lamont waved her away: "Enough! There will be plenty of time to hear your justifications in court, we don't want to hear it now." And with that, she was bundled from the room.

42 – Sweet Sunday

Gillespie liked Robbie, he was one of the more laid-back prisoners and pretty much kept himself to himself. Occasionally, the relentless thud of four-on-the-floor dance music would get too much, not to mention the puffs of cannabis tinctured vapour that continuously erupted from the bunk below him, shrouding his bed in a befuddling murk like a zeppelin among the clouds. But on the whole, he was about the best cell mate Gillespie could have asked for. As it was Sunday, he didn't have to work in the data centre, and his eyeballs were grateful for the respite from spreadsheets and formulas. Lying flat on his bed, he lifted his head just enough to slurp the nut-brown tea from the mug perched on his chest. Fuck, it was as if the manufacturer had swept the floor of the cheapest tea merchant in China to pick and pack a blend fit for the scum of St Kilda. He would have added sugar to make it palatable if the Riaghladair hadn't banned all sugar, for health reasons apparently. Not only did it mean that inmates' teeth didn't rot, and that diabetes and obesity were somewhat curbed, but also the terrible injuries inflicted by thrown cups of burning hot, sugar-saturated tea were avoided. Gillespie began to feel a bit sick as yet another lungful of white skunk-scented smoke billowed around him. The thump of electronic music with its squelching acid bassline was also beginning to trip him out. Just when he was about to relinquish himself into its hypnotic embrace, a rough and ready call came from the open doorway.

"Fuckin' hell, what is you all doin in here, right

enough? I can't even see my hand in front of my fucking face."

It was Davy MacSween. Gillespie looked down on the milky white face of his friend, his impossibly red hair bound back in a ponytail.

"Come on you lazy cunt, time to get out and get some fresh air and stretch those fat little legs of yours."

For a moment Gillespie thought about trying to resist, the inertia of dope-fuelled lethargy pinned his shoulders to the mattress. But Davy was having none of it and a few short minutes later Gillespie found himself being bodily pushed out of the cell block and into the bracing outdoor air.

There was snow on top of the hills that surrounded Village Bay, just the lightest dusting. He didn't imagine it was going to last, but it accentuated the shadowy pits of the craggy rocks, bringing a crisp beauty to the scene. Davy dragged him across the compound to the northern gate which, as it was Sunday, was open to allow the inmates to exercise by climbing the shoulder of Ben Conachair and look across the short channel to Boreray and the Sea Stacs. The Riaghladair magnanimously allowed this in part to stop the inmates going completely stir crazy, but also to remind the prisoners of where they might end up if they behaved badly.

After they'd passed through the gate in the massive drystone wall, the slope rose steeply ahead of them. It was covered in rough grass that had been meticulously cropped by the islands' indigenous brown sheep. Tough little bastards they were. They had to be, living out on these hills all the time. Gillespie enjoyed the burn in his legs as they climbed the slope. So much of his time was spent cooped up inside, it was great to be out breathing the fresh Atlantic air. The wind, which was relentless for much of the year, had quietened to barely a whisper and the pounding of the blood in his ears and the ragged gasps of his breathing were the only sounds. He had to stop and catch his breath. They stood and looked down on the prison settlement below: the ugly concrete cellblocks and the neat and tidy ribbon of stone houses, the road that snaked its way out of the settlement and switch-backed up over the ridge of Mullach Mòr to the other side of island. It was a surprisingly peaceful scene.

Across the bay was the island of Dùn, and Gillespie could make out a couple of small groups picking their way along the cliffs. He wondered if they were locals catching or counting puffins? It was still early in the season, but the birds had started to return to the island after their winter peregrinations at sea. They were now busy feathering their nests and fucking hammer and tongs to hatch and fledge the next generation before autumn's arrival. Despite the best efforts of the Republic's Avian Appreciation and Protection Society, the capture and smoking of puffins and gannets for the pot had continued. Not that the St Kildans ate them much themselves anymore. No, like everyone else they'd evolved to prefer frozen lasagne and pizza shipped in from the mainland. Instead, they sold them as rare delicacies to a diaspora of ex-prisoners and overseas devotees who paid top dollar for the birds' pungent flesh.

Having caught their breath, Gillespie and Davy turned to climb the rest of the slope. As they crested the cliff top, the majestic sight of Boreray and the Stacs rose out of the sea below them. As if to reward them for the effort of their climb, the sun then came out from between the clouds, its golden shafts lighting up Boreray, like a crouching cat with its head between its paws, its peridot green flanks fell steeply into the sea. Just in front of its nose, the two teasing mice of the Sea Stacs: Stac an Àrmainn and Stac Lì. They rose straight out of the ocean, their jagged peaks painted white by the shit of a million birds.

"Anyone out there at the moment?" Gillespie asked Davy.

"Aye, I think there are a few MacIans out on Boreray, a Cameron on Stac an Àrmainn and old Dan Chisholm on Stac Lì, last I heard. Poor bastards. Well, actually I don't feel too sorry for the MacIans, those wankers deserve everything they have coming to them."

They laughed the hollow chuckle of schadenfreude, glad that they were not there in their place. Around them on the cliff top were dotted small groups of other prisoners. If Gillespie half-closed his eyes it was like looking at an Edwardian picnic. He settled down a little way away from the main groups with his back to a rock, facing the sun and well back from the cliff edge. Davy tore at bits of grass and absentmindedly tossed them into the void.

"What happened to your face?"

Gillespie gently traced the line of the scar down his left cheek. "It's complicated. Let's just say someone wanted me to give me a reminder."

"What bastard did it? Do you want them taken care of?"

"Nah. It's just one of those things." Gillespie thought about taking Davy into his confidence, telling him about the conversation with MacMartin, about his link to the outside world, about the prospect for escape. But he held back. God only knew how fast rumours would spread in this goddam pressure cooker of a place. He couldn't take the risk, not yet.

Changing the subject, Gillespie asked about the MacSween gang and how they were getting on with their innumerable schemes and scams.

"Oh, not so bad you know," Davy replied. "We've got old Murdoch MacDonald brewing up a new batch of vape juice at the moment. Something to keep the punters entertained what with spring on the way. Been trying to think of a name for it – maybe you can help?" Davy pulled a vape out of his pocket and took a drag, before offering it to Gillespie. Gillespie demurred, he'd never liked smoking at the best of times and the idea that he would entrust Stornaway High School's ex-Head of Chemistry with the inside of his lungs was not one he could entertain.

"How about St Kilda Kiss? Or Hirta Haze? You know, give it a local flavour. People love an alliteration too."

"Hirta Head-Masher?" Davy offered.

"Mmmm, that'll do it. Does what it says on the tin, I guess. Nothing like having a clear brand promise."

Davy laughed.

Amidst the soul crushing despondency of his day-to-day existence, this was the best Gillespie had felt since arriving on the prison archipelago. Amidst all the cruelties and uncertainties it gave him hope. Shonique suddenly filled his mind, her laugh, her lips, her firm lithe body, her smooth black skin and umber eyes. He wondered what she was doing? How was she sleeping?

Did she miss him between her crisp white sheets? How he missed her, her warmth, the thrill of her touch, her hips spooning against him, the cocoon of her arms. How he wanted to hold her, to feel her heart beating, her long fingers tracing whorls, tickling and kneading, skimming and skinning. Would he ever see her again? Would he ever feel her again?

He looked across at Davy. The moment hung taught in the air between them, pregnant with possibilities; it could go in a hundred different directions. The next thing he remembered was pulling away from Davy's astonished face. The chemical taint of Davy's vape fizzed on his lips and tongue. Shock and surprise, but also need overwhelmed him in waves. After so long, after so much stress and anguish, the touch of another human was overwhelming. Davy's eyes were wide. He said nothing. Tucking an errant strand of his cherry red hair back behind his ear, he broke into a wolfish grin and, leaning forward, he kissed Gillespie back, hard and long. They lost themselves in that moment filled with the distant screech of gannets and the soft whisper of the wind.

43 – Status Quo

John Lamont could not believe his luck. He hadn't known what to expect when MacCailean Mòr had stood up to address the Comhairle. He had fully expected it to be an expose of his time as Lamont's guest in the dungeons of Ascog. Of course, MacCailean Mòr had no proof to show of that, it would just have been his word against Lamont's and, as the President of the Republic, Lamont fancied his chances of winning that contest. No, it had been something altogether more unexpected and welcome.

Even though he'd had no hand in them, he had to admit that MacCailean Mòr's exposure of Catriona MacLean's war crimes had been perfectly timed for his needs. Barely a day went by without First Minister Balfour, or the ghastly Guy Walker, ringing him up and demanding an explanation as to what was going on. His plan had always been to encourage the natural jealousy and competition between the various west coast Clans to destabilise the Republic enough to allow him to take control. Now that he was President, and with the sweeping powers so recently created for his unfortunate predecessor, he had all the authority he needed. He now had to extinguish the conflagrations and show himself as the bringer of peace and prosperity.

Of course, he'd learned the hard way that even the best laid plans can run away from you. And so it had proven, with the unexpected intervention of MacLeod of MacLeod raising the stakes dramatically and increasing the disruption to Republic trade and commerce. Paul MacSporran, the Ministear an

Ionmhais, had told him in no uncertain terms that the tax take was down significantly and with reduced demand for Government Bonds the sources of finance to fund the Republic's public services were weaker than they'd ever been. If normality was not restored soon, then the Government could run out of cash. That would bring its own unpalatable choices, such as turning to the Kingdom for financial support; the kind of support that would inevitably come with conditions, conditions that he was all too happy to consider but only if they consolidated his hold on power. In his meeting with Walker and Balfour in Edinburgh, he had already explored the potential for the Kingdom to pay a significant sum of cash to the Republic if they were to consummate their partnership. Such a payment would be a formal recognition of the pooling of sovereignty, for the Republic surrendering its full autonomy to become a partner in something new. Some might see it as a bribe, an insult to the Republic's legacy of idiosyncratic independence, but he saw it as a douceur, a lubricant to salve the consciences of reluctant Clan chiefs and any Seanadairean that might try and stand in his way. It was only money, but that was something that they were always short of in the Republic, while pride and hubris were ever in abundant supply.

MacCailean Mòr's explosive testimony had allowed him to detain the MacLeans without a shot being fired. With Catriona and her key chieftains now languishing at Ruthven Barracks, the Black Watch's impregnable base, he could decide how best to unpick the chaos on the west coast. He summoned David Brown to the President's Suite to agree the best course of action and ensure he had the Seanadh onside to give it the fig-leaf of legitimacy.

He'd always liked these rooms; unlike so much of the Republic they were neither decorated in crude blocks of Baronial stone or cold Georgian classicism. No, they had been remodelled by President Angus "Bunny" Stewart in the 1930s and turned into an Art Deco masterpiece of sober luxury. The President's Suite was large and round with a shallow pierced dome in the centre that dappled the dove grey carpet below with light. The smooth wood panelled walls were richly inlaid with exotic woods; one wall had a tableaux depicting King Charlie the Liberator's victory at the Battle of Culloden, while on either side of the entrance door were two life-size marquetry Gaels, standing guard in all their finery, frozen forever in slivers of Cocobolo, Tiger Maple, Walnut and Padauk. Beneath the dome, with a fine view through a ribbon window over the city of Oban, sat the Liberator's desk. Bound in Macassar Ebony, framed with a golden Greek key frieze and inlaid with fantastical peacocks and exotic cranes, it was opulent, no question, but also grown up, almost sober in its restrained use of great luxury. He looked at his watch. Where was that goddam pen-pusher David Brown? He drummed his fingers impatiently, before idly picking up and discarding the papers that littered the desk. Finally, he heard footsteps and muffled words outside. The door opened and David Brown entered looking flustered.

"President Lamont, I apologise for being late. As you can imagine, the whole Republic is upside down after today's events."

Lamont resisted the urge to vent his annoyance at being kept waiting.

"Yes, indeed. And I don't want to waste the opportunity to consolidate our grip, especially now that I have MacLean and her cronies under lock and key. There are a number of important things I need to discuss with you. Not least of which is over what to do with Islay. Obviously, MacLean still has her troops there, but I am sure we can winkle her out. If she ever wants to see daylight again that is. But the bigger question is who do I give it to? Does it go to Sorley MacDonald? MacLeod? Should I get one of the East coast magnates to take it over? After all, Cawdor was there a few centuries back. Maybe an outsider would be good?"

David Brown sat lost in thought for a moment. "I don't think you can give it to MacLeod, he has no links there and already has plenty of power and land in the Outer Hebrides. No, we don't want to strengthen him further. MacDonald has been a useful cat's paw, but again we surely don't want to reward him for all the turmoil he has caused. If we want peace to return, then I am afraid we have to rebalance the west coast, return it to the equilibrium it has enjoyed for many centuries."

"What do you mean?" Lamont wasn't sure he liked where David Brown's thought process was going.

David Brown sighed, he clearly knew that what he was about to say would not be popular, but like the dutiful public servant he was, he ploughed on regardless. "I think you need to consider returning it to MacCailean Mòr. After all, the Campbells have held it for many, many hundreds of years. His control of the southern inner Hebrides counterbalances MacDonald and MacLean in the Northern Inner Hebrides and MacLeod in the Outer Isles. We have seen what happens when one of them gets too strong, we need to return to that balance if we are to have peace.

Lamont did not say anything immediately. Instead, he absentmindedly traced the nail of his index finger around the Greek key maze carved in the desk. Brown sat opposite, hands folded, that irritating, priggish half smile on his dull, grey face. Lamont briefly imagined having him as a guest on sub-level six at Castle Ascog, his mind instantly flooding with blood-red fantasies: a flensing blade, the ball-hammer, ligatures. He shook his head, banishing the distracting thoughts. Their time would come, but not now. Now he needed Brown and his influence in the Seanadh.

He turned Brown's idea around in his mind. MacCailean Mòr, yes there was a delicious irony in restoring Islay to his control after everything he had been through. In any case, he was weak at the moment, too weak to pose any meaningful kind of threat. Far less of a danger than Sorley MacDonald for example. Lamont briefly thought about leaving it outwith the control of any one Clan; but he knew that would never work. Influence abhors a vacuum, particularly in the Republic. With the abundant revenues available from global whisky sales there was no way it would be left alone. No, he needed to give Islay a "roof", someone who was strong enough to hold it and nurture it, ensuring that those tax revenues flowed into Oban's coffers.

Now that he held the Presidency and had hegemony over the Black Watch, all the key levers of power were in his hands; he had nothing to fear from MacCailean Mòr. In fact, he found the idea of MacCailean Mòr as supplicant almost erotic; the great man kissing his shoes in gratitude for receiving back what had always been his. This was also the fastest way back to stability. As soon as Sorley saw that there was no opportunity in the South he would come to peace with MacLeod; they both had too much to lose to fight over nothing. Lamont could then bask in the glow of peacemaker, something that could only enhance his standing in Edinburgh and London.

"OK, just supposing I agree. How do we know it won't go to his head? The last thing I need is MacCailean Mòr getting back on his high horse and trying to boss the Republic." Lamont continued to chase the Greek key with his nail. "But perhaps I have an idea. One that will also send a very powerful message to all the Clans to get back in line and behave. You know they only really understand and respond to strength, it's no good being gentle with them."

"Go on."

"Well, tomorrow is the last day for the oath taking and I must say our stratagem has worked very well, almost too well. All the usual troublemakers have come to Oban and taken the oath; Barrisdale, MacIan, Lochiel, not to mention Aodh MacSween, who hasn't set foot in the Riaghaltas in more than twenty years." Lamont paused as if suddenly having second thoughts, before continuing. "There are very few still to take the oath, but if one were to miss the deadline then we could use them as an example – pour encourager les autres, so to speak."

"Who do you have in mind? Who's left?"

"The one I have in mind are the MacNachtans. As you know, their last Chief was murdered, and their interim Chief is a certain Kirstie MacNachtan – do you know her?"

"I can't say that I do."

"They are an old but small Clan: too small for others to care enough about to intervene and yet well-known enough to send a powerful message, particularly to MacCailean Mòr, their next-door neighbour. If she doesn't take the oath in time, then we can make an example of them."

Brown whittered briefly about due process and the need for the transparent administration of justice, but he didn't disagree, and he didn't try and change Lamont's mind. As far as Lamont was concerned that was a green light. Ever since Kirstie had escaped from his dungeons he'd wanted his revenge on her. She had been able to shelter in the lee of Inveraray, under MacCailean Mòr's protection, but now he could make her pay. MacCailean Mòr wouldn't be able to help her against the full force of the State. All the other Chiefs would just be delighted it wasn't them. In the end, who would care too much if the MacNachtans were snuffed out. With the returning of Islay to MacCailean Mòr, this would allow him to cow the Chiefs while resetting the balance of the Republic.

Lamont tried to control his excitement at the perfection of his plan. He looked out of the window at the snow falling across the capital. Snow in April, the Cailleach could be cruel.

44 – The Lambing Snow

Charlie shivered, despite the near tropical heat coming off the cooking range. The snow falling outside the kitchen window was unwelcome. He'd already mentally shifted from winter into spring and had spent the last few evenings looking at flights to Mykonos or Ibiza. He and Nin needed a proper holiday to top up their vitamin D levels with some glorious Mediterranean UV rays, and the thick white flakes were a reminder that summer was still far away.

Nin slouched into the kitchen and poured himself a cup of coffee. He was dressed in his full finery; scarlet kilt, black horsehair sporran, crosscut jacket and matching waistcoat, his best silver buttons and a thick belt bound with a heavy silver buckle bearing the solitary tower of the MacNachtans and the slogan I Hope in God.

"You are certainly looking the part. I can barely restrain myself from ravishing you right here and now." Charlie cooed, plucking lint and brushing dandruff off the shoulders of Nin's jacket while straightening his tie.

"It's a total pain in the arse," Nin moaned. "Why Kirstie feels the need for us all to dress up just to go to Oban for her to take this stupid oath is beyond me. She's the one having to swear the words after all."

"Come on, she is just trying to project a bit of Clan pride. You know, we may be small, but we can raid the dressing up box with the best of them!"

Nin scowled and turned his attention to the white wrapped landscape through the window.

"Fuck. Look at all the fucking snow. How are we

supposed to get to Oban through that?"

Charlie stood next to him at the window. "Surely, it's not too bad? They'll have the snow ploughs out to clear the Wade. Its only really the Pass of Brander that might get a little sticky. After all, if it is settling here, there is no saying what it's dumping up on Cruachan."

"Aye, that's what I am worried about. Kirstie shouldn't have left it so late. There was no need. We could've gone and taken the oath days ago, weeks ago. Why the fuck she left it to the last day is beyond me."

"She couldn't have known it was going to snow, not like this." Charlie countered. "Besides, if I'd been tortured and nearly killed by that psychotic bastard, I wouldn't be rushing to pledge my loyalty either."

"That's as maybe, but you know the Lamontation as well as I do, he won't accept excuses."

As they both stared out of the window at the lead grey sky and the flurries of falling flakes, a line of Kats appeared on the track in the glen coming towards Elrig.

"That must be her now, you'd better get your coat. And don't forget these." Charlie thrust Nin's sgian dubh in the top of his stocking, before handing him his best dress sword. Nin grunted his thanks, wrapping Charlie in a farewell bearhug before heading out to meet the approaching vehicles.

Kirstie had rousted out as many of the Clan's duine uasal as she could find. What they lacked in numbers they made up for in visual impact, with Shonique, Jamie Ruadh, Davy Hendry and Archie Beaton and the other office holders of the Clan all dressed in matching belted plaids and dark blue bonnets carrying a single eagle's feather. Their weapons were a mixture of the latest assault rifles and heirloom basket-hilted swords and dirks that had been passed down many generations. The crimson red of the MacNachtan tartan stood out like fresh spilled blood against the snow. It was a fine sight, but Charlie couldn't help feel that it was feeble too. For all the fine clothes and bullish bonhomie, there was no getting away from their small numbers. It hardly spoke of a position of strength, quite the opposite in fact. He only hoped that the eye of Lamont had moved on from the MacNachtans to focus on greater matters of State.

It was around lunchtime that he saw the column of vehicles turn back into the glen and return to Elrig. He could see from his window that the mood in the group had changed utterly. A sullen cloud hung over them. The vehicles only stopped long enough to spit Nin out, before they turned around and disappeared back the way they'd come. Charlie went to open the front door for Nin who was stamping the snow off his shoes.

"Come on in, you look frozen. How was the oath taking? It didn't take too long."

"No, it didn't take too long, because it never happened. We never made it to Oban."

"What do you mean you never made it to Oban?"

"Exactly what I said. The road beyond the Falls of Cruachan was blocked by snow, just as I feared it might be. To be honest, I didn't think it was too bad. If the snow ploughs had been out then I am sure they could have cleared the road, but there was no way we get through it on our own."

"Did you speak to the Road Safety team? Did they say that they would be clearing the road?"

"Aye, we tried to get some sense out of them, but all they would say is that there were no available ploughs to clear the road until tomorrow. We tried to dig our way through, but we only made a few hundred yards in the last three hours, there is no way we could make it all the way along the Pass."

"Fuck."

"Aye, fuck indeed."

"What happens now?"

"Kirstie has gone to MacCailean Mòr to see if he can use his position as High Sheriff of the county to administer the oath. Obviously, he has been Warden of the West and Colonel of the Black Watch, so we hope that gives him some authority to oversee it. It should just be procedural after all."

"Hmmm." Charlie mused, not wanting to share his true feelings that nothing cooked up by Lamont could ever be considered as just a procedure.

"I don't know what else we can do. Kirstie has tried to reach David Brown without success. It's like we are hitting a brick wall, no one seems to want to know. Anyway, she has gone off to Inveraray to see MacCailean Mòr and try to sort it out."

They lounged round the house for the rest of the day, neither really wanting to talk about the situation again but both desperate for the phone to ring or an email to arrive saying that it had all been sorted. Nothing came.

That evening as Nin was trying to distract himself by cooking dinner, Charlie answered the phone to Kirstie.

"Hi Charlie, good to speak to you. Could you just let Nin know that it is all settled. I took the oath with MacCailean Mòr and he sent a recording of it to the constitutional committee at the Righaltas."

"Did they say that that was OK? If it was that easy why didn't everyone just phone in their oath?"

Kirstie's tone changed, her irritation palpable. "I don't know Charlie, OK? I can only do the best I can. We weren't able to get there in person because the road was closed, so what else can I do? That fucker David Brown was uncontactable, so I had to ask some fucking intern for their opinion, and they assured me it would be fine. As soon as the Wade is open I'll go to fucking Oban and take the oath in person, but until then there is nothing else I can do. And I would seriously appreciate your support rather than a litany of stupid questions. Good night!"

Before Charlie could get a word in edgeways, she'd hung up the phone.

He recounted the conversation to Nin who was busy chopping onions and dancing around the kitchen to the seething rhythms of Southside hip hop. Nin clearly wasn't in the mood to be distracted by bad news and waved away Charlie's concerns as he bounced to the breaks. "Don't worry. I'm sure it will be fine. Anyway, I can't believe that Lamont doesn't have bigger issues on his mind. We are just a minnow, and he is in the business of catching whales. You'll see. Anyway, come and chop the garlic – I want to give this some head - a whole head, fuck yeah!"

And with that, Charlie pushed the worries of the day to the back of his mind. Glancing out of the window, he saw that the snow had stopped falling. He hoped that would be the last they would see until deep into the following winter. Instead, he turned his mind back to the prospect of summer holidays still to come, of sunshine and warm water, good food and packed nightclubs, of the dawn rising out of the sea as the piano break hits the crowd.

45 – Rannoch Telegraph

Alasdair MacGregor was bored. He sat on the sofa and watched TV as the snow came down outside. He was absentmindedly tossing and catching his favourite Fairburn-Sykes stiletto while he half-watched the box, its blackened blade dully caught the light as it spun. His phone rang, momentarily distracting him, and he cursed as he caught the dagger's edge rather than its rough-milled hilt. Sucking hard on the resulting cut, he threw the knife at the dartboard mounted behind the TV, the point entering just beneath the triple twenty. He hunted for his phone, swiping it open just as it stopped ringing.

There was a message from Nin on the Rannoch Telegraph, the Griogaraich's private messaging system. He turned off the banal rubbish on the TV, his thick black eyebrows knitted in concentration as he read through the message.

He'd wondered why he hadn't heard from Gillespie for so long. Ever since he'd come back from Antrim there had been silence. Alasdair hadn't given it much thought. After all, he'd been busy trying to sort out the Griogaraich after their run in with the Black Watch, as well as trying to take advantage of all the national chaos to sell additional muscle and "protection" services to the smaller clans who otherwise might fall victim to bigger neighbours. But when he stopped to think about it, it had been strange. The last he had heard from Nin was a post ribbing Gillespie over his image as An Smàladair, the Extinguisher, after his duel with that bastard Allan

Stewart. But that had been months ago. Reading through Nin's message he was shocked to see that Gillespie was now incarcerated in St Kilda of all places. A hellhole that Alasdair spent his entire professional life trying to avoid. Now Nin was asking for his help to try and spring him, a prospect that even a Griogaraich couldn't take lightly.

He thought back to his halcyon few weeks at Gillespie's Northern Ireland home, of running the cliffs above the Giant's Causeway, of the craic in Bushmills' bars, and long nights in the tender arms of the loving ladies of Antrim. It had been a special time, particularly after all those weeks in the Inveraray Infirmary. The freedom of Antrim, where he was able to walk the streets without having to look over his shoulder, meant that it would always have a special place in his heart. And Gillespie too. He remembered their first meeting at the Inn at Gaur, the morning after the Dundee raid, he'd seemed as weak as water then, but in the months that had passed he'd been tempered into something much more robust.

St Kilda, though, that was a tough call. Sitting far out in the Atlantic, the archipelago had its own natural defences in the shape of wild weather and rough seas, that were as dangerous as they were unpredictable; one day it could be glassy calm, the next a raging sea with a swell so steep that it could swallow a ship whole. The Griogaraich occasionally had members incarcerated there, but they'd never seriously considered trying to liberate them. The risk of failure was too high. Besides, they generally rubbed along OK inside the prison, they had enough muscle on the inside, and on the outside, to be left alone to do their time in peace. The Clan welfare team made sure that they were paid, and their family cared for in their absence, so it was generally seen as an occupational hazard to be avoided where possible and endured when not.

Gillespie on the other hand was much more exposed. Even with the annealing he had undergone in recent months, he was still as green grass in comparison to the killers and cutthroats in there. The MacNachtans were also unlikely to be able to offer any kind of protection inside. Alasdair wondered how he was coping. He closed his phone and sat, thinking. The Griogaraich had a variety of vessels they could call on, including The Rose in June, which was fitted out and registered as a humble fishing boat. He imagined that they could sail close without drawing too much attention, but what next? They obviously wouldn't be able to sail into Village Bay and just collect him from the beach, but how else would he be able to get aboard. There was no way that Gillespie would be able to swim out; even on the calmest summer night it would be too cold and the swell too great. Could he steal a boat, even if only a canoe or dinghy to get him out to sea? Maybe, but they would also all be moored in Village Bay and looking at the map it was clearly impossible to get around the headland without being seen.

He pulled up a satellite image of the islands and spent hours poring over their jagged profile and close clustered contours. It wasn't just the rocks and the challenge of the sea, the cliffs themselves were so steep that even a mountain goat wouldn't be able to get down them. The more he looked, the more improbable any kind of rescue seemed. There was a reason why it was the Republic's toughest prison.

He went to get himself a pot of tea to aide his concentration. He scanned the jars of dried leaves in the cupboard: Orange Pekoe, Dragon's Well, Iron Buddha, nothing really appealed. He thought about a bog-standard cup of Highlander, the lowest grade Assam blend, but with a slug of milk and a tablespoon of sugar it had unmatched restorative powers. As his hand reached out to pick the box off the shelf, it knocked a slim gold packet onto the floor. He picked it up; Monkey-Picked Oolong, Fujian, was written in neat copperplate on the label. He burst the seal and smelled the rich grass and earth aroma, before taking a pinch and putting it in a cup. Monkey-picked? Did they really use monkeys to do their dirty work, poor bastards. He imagined monkeys scaling the inaccessible cliffs of Fujian. Ha! Maybe that is what he needed, just a few trained monkeys to scale the cliffs and carry Gillespie down to the waiting boat – it was so easy! He laughed inwardly, given the impassable cliffs those monkeys would need to have wings, like those monkeys in the Wizard of Oz; the evil bastards that swooped on Dorothy and carried her away to the witch's castle. He'd always found them creepy as a child, the idea that they could swoop from the air and carry you off like that.

At that moment, the Cùinn dropped; he almost let go of his teacup.

He raced back to the screen, pouring over the map with renewed enthusiasm before digging out his phone. There was only one person who might have a solution that could work, but it was still a long shot. He scrolled through his contacts before stopping at Natasha Caddell. He paused for a moment, gathering his thoughts and figuring out how he was going to ask the question. Despite their nefarious trade, he couldn't ask Natasha, as the CEO of the Atelier of Thomas Caddell, the Republic's leading arms dealer, to openly flout the law, he had to be a little more discrete than that.

He rang the number. After a few rings it was answered.

"Alasdair nan Sgàilean, to what do I owe this pleasure? It's been a while." She purred down the phone. He smiled, she sounded like a lioness and not a lap cat, it was powerful and alluring. He held her in his mind's eye, her mischievous eyes sparkling while she twisted a strand of her long hair between her fingers.

"Ah Natasha, if only you knew how much I miss you. Won't you come to Rannoch? We could have so much fun together. I can show you the Black Wood, or Buchanan's Stone, or we can swim together under the Fairy Arch at the Falls of Tummel, after which I could rub you warm in a bathsheet of finest Egyptian cotton. C'mon, you know you want to!"

She laughed teasingly, deflecting his invitation. "How can I help you, Alasdair nan Sgàilean, as you surely did not just call to invite me away for a romantic weekend in the wastes of Rannoch? However delightful that might be."

"For shame, that you could doubt me so! I'm cut to the core. But as you ask, I wanted to enquire about monkeys, flying monkeys. I need one and I need it now."

46 – MacMartin's Path

Gillespie was waiting in line at the canteen when MacMartin found him. He'd already been queuing for 20 minutes and was almost at the tray dispenser, an important way marker approximately five minutes before reaching the actual food. So he was more than a little cross when MacMartin frogmarched him out. He could feel the eyes of the room following him, an unspoken question hanging in the air – what had he done?

MacMartin enjoyed the power of his position, limited though it was. Like most St Kildans he was born and bred to the prison, it was the only real work that was available. There had been a time when the islands were threatened with depopulation, but the prison had changed that. With the prison had come electricity and telephones, regular ship services and food supplies. As the threat of famine and isolation receded, the islanders had clung on to their rocky home. Now, nearly a hundred years after that nadir, life for a St Kildan was grand, as long as you didn't mind being surrounded by violent cut-throat scum, the very dregs of the Republic, washed ashore and into their care by the penal system. This did mean that the St Kildans took their job very seriously. They were generally incorruptible, knowing that their community's survival depended on the prison and on its formidable reputation. Most of the time, life at the prison was fairly peaceful, with the threat of isolation in a punishment cleit, or on the Sea Stacs or Boreray, enough to ensure that all but the most foolish prisoners were submissive to their authority. And, as

Gillespie had found out, if a St Kildan wanted to make your life miserable, there were plenty of ways they could do it. He'd already had to gut a barrelful of Guga, dig guano out of the bird nesting gullies on the southern sea cliffs, and help on two burial details, one of which was some lecherous old paedophile who'd had his brains bashed out in the special unit at Glen Bay. Whenever there was an especially distasteful job, MacMartin would appear and volunteer him for it. To a degree, Gillespie didn't mind, because it was during these unpleasant interludes that MacMartin would give him news of Dunderave and his friends. It was almost as if MacMartin was so conflicted over his betrayal of trust, that he had to punish Gillespie while he was giving him the information. As MacMartin marched him out of the prison building and into the Village Bay compound, Gillespie wondered what the unpalatable quid pro quo was going to be this time.

"Where are we going?" He asked, trying to break the ice; MacMartin was being taciturn to the point of impenetrability.

"Never you mind. Just keep your mouth shut and walk on."

They skirted the islanders' meagre fields, avoiding the ribbon of houses on Main Street, and made their way to the western gate in the massive drystone wall that encircled the compound. MacMartin swiped the back of his hand against the chip reader and opened the gate. They then climbed the steep switchback road that snaked up the slopes of Mullach Mòr. Even after months of climbing this steep hill, Gillespie still struggled to keep up with MacMartin and had to stop every few minutes to catch his breath. Eventually, they were at the top, on the saddle that divided the island's two glens – Glen Mòr and Village Bay. Apart from the two radar stations that sat on the hill tops hidden beneath their golf-ball shaped cowlings, there was nothing else to see except endless cleits dotting the landscape, their grassy-turf tops waving in the ever present wind. The visibility was good for once, and Gillespie enjoyed looking out to sea, its azure mantle laced with white foam where it smashed on the rocks far below. They followed the sea cliff to the west, skirting the southern edge of Glen Mòr. Above them, a Great Skua shrieked and jabbered its fury at their intrusion, divebombing them repeatedly to drive them away from its freshly made nest. Low-flying puffins flitted along the cliff returning to their burrows from fishing at sea, only to slam on their brakes at the sight of the unwelcome human interlopers.

Ahead was a well found cleit tucked beneath a rocky outcrop and largely sheltered from the wind, despite being so high on the ridge. As they approached, MacMartin called out and the black shrouded figure of Lady Lamont emerged from the sepulchral interior. She nodded an acknowledgement at Gillespie and spoke for a few minutes with MacMartin in hushed tones while Gillespie patiently waited. MacMartin waved him over.

"Gillespie, this is Coira Lamont, she has been here a long time and helps tend the sheep. Coira, this is Gillespie MacNachtan – he's serving a 25 year sentence for murder."

"We've met before, I believe." Lady Lamont interjected, carefully looking Gillespie over from his feet to his scalp as if for the first time. "Anyway, the sheep generally don't need much tending. Most of the time they are just left to get on with it, but now is lambing and that is the one time that we are minded to lend them a hand."

MacMartin grunted. "Stupid bastards, sometimes I think they would just die out if we weren't here to help them. Not sure why we bother if I'm honest. They give us fuck all wool and taste like rancid seaweed. Plus the little bastards are always getting in among the crop and eating the best bits. Personally, I think they are more trouble than they are worth."

"As you can see," sniffed Lady Lamont, "Mr MacMartin has a low opinion of our ovine charges. However, they are protected under the Republic's Rare Native Species Act and so we are obliged to help preserve and promote the gene pool. As MacMartin says, we are now into the lambing season so it would be good to have another pair of hands. Have you ever birthed a lamb?"

Gillespie was so relieved to finally be asked something he knew a lot about that the next twenty minutes were spent in a rambling monologue describing the frequently complex parturition of his flock of Galway sheep. By the end, even Lady Lamont's eyes acquired a somewhat glazed sheen and MacMartin had given up all pretence of listening and was instead flicking through social media posts on his phone. Finally, losing patience, he interrupted.

"Fuck all that, just make sure you are here to help. For the next two weeks, you are working with Coira making sure as many of the dumb bastards get born as possible. Be here at eight o'clock each night. And if you give Coira any trouble, she'll be sure and tell me, won't you? And by god you'll find yourself on Stac Lì faster than you can imagine if that happens. Understand?"

Lady Lamont nodded sombrely, but Gillespie caught a spark of pleasure in her eyes for the first time. She was clearly going to enjoy having a bit of company, despite the antisocial hours.

Leaving Lady Lamont's cleit behind, MacMartin now strode off along the southern cliffs, bent against the wind. Gillespie was taken by surprise; they were walking in the opposite direction to the main prison compound. Below them, in the green bowl of Glen Mòr, he could see the brooding hulk of the maximum-security wing down by the shore. A shiver went down his spine despite the sweat that was pouring off him. He hurried to keep up with MacMartin who was now approaching a steep slope which ended in a sheer drop to the ocean far below. Skirting the summit, MacMartin edged down into a tight gully where a much-eroded sheep track led down an impossibly precipitous, winding path. The sheep clearly had no issues with vertigo, and had four feet to keep them from falling, but Gillespie found the narrowness of the path and the sharp drop almost overwhelming. He stopped and closed his eyes to try and banish his fear. The wind buffeted him as he clung to the rock unable to move.

MacMartin was unsympathetic. "Open your fucking eyes you idiot and stand up straight. If you cling to the rocks like that you are bound to slip."

"What the hell are we doing here anyway? I can't imagine there are any sheep to lamb down here."

MacMartin laughed. "No, you dumb bastard, we are not looking for sheep. Come on, it's not much further."

Gillespie gritted his teeth and followed after the rapidly disappearing figure of MacMartin who practically skipped down the narrow path impervious to the vertiginous drop and the skirling gusts.

As MacMartin had promised, it was only a little further until they came to an unexpected flat open space. It was little more than a ledge sunk deep in the socket of the surrounding cliffs, but at least it allowed them to stand without fear of being blown to their deaths. Around them, clinging to any meagre scrap of earth, were pink topped tufts of Sea Thrift which bobbed cheerfully in the breeze and brave clumps of Purple Saxifrage, their bright magenta flowers improbably garish against the monochrome rock. Below them, the sheep track picked its way on down between the rocks at an almost impossible angle before disappearing over the cliff and out of view.

"This is the Geo na Laise-suileach, the Gully of the Flaming Eye, so called because the setting sun in summer bounces off all these rocks, lighting it up as bright as midday just before it disappears into the sea."

Gillespie nodded dumbly, wondering why he was getting this scenic tour. MacMartin suddenly grabbed him roughly by the shoulders and shook him.

"Your blackmailing friends are coming to try and rescue you. Understand? That's why I have arranged for you to be on lambing detail, so that you can have the excuse to be out here at night for the next few weeks. When you get the signal you are to come here and wait, understand? They have a crazy plan which I cannot believe has a cat's chance in hell of working. But if they are dumb enough to try, and you are prepared to risk your neck, then so be it. I've kept my part of the bargain. I want you, and them, out of my life, now and forever. Understand?"

Gillespie nodded.

"And if you ever breathe a word to anyone that I've helped you I swear I'll stake your MacSween friend to the sea cliffs and let the Skuas rip him apart piece by piece."

Gillespie was taken aback by MacMartin's sudden vehemence.

"Just understand the risks I'm taking. If anyone finds out what I have done, I'll be feeding the fishes at the bottom of Village Bay with a block tied to my feet."

"What'll happen when they find out I've gone?"

Without immediately answering, MacMartin took the rucksack off his back and unbuckled it. Inside was a set of prison clothes which he put on the ground between them. Next he took the sgian dubh from his stocking and held it threateningly at Gillespie.

"Strip."

"What, here?"

"Just shut the fuck up and do as you are told." He waggled the point at Gillespie who hurriedly started to take off his prison issue jacket and kilt. He was soon in his stockinged feet. He started to remove those too but MacMartin shook his head.

"Right, pick up your kilt and rub it all around you. Go on, between your legs, everywhere. Make sure you give your arse a good wipe on it and all." He studied Gillespie closely as followed the bizarre instructions. "Right, now I want you to piss on it. Squeeze out whatever you can, it doesn't have to be a lot." Gillespie stood in the cold wind and tried to comply but the few drops and dribbles that came were whipped away by the wind. In his frustration, MacMartin thrust it at him. "Just hold the bloody thing. All I need is your fucking

DNA on it."

He then took his sgian dubh and drew it across Gillespie's forearm. The edge was so sharp that Gillespie didn't even feel it, but the scarlet line that welled up marked its passage well enough.

"Right, just get some of that on the shirt. Don't over think it, just smear it anywhere."

Gillespie used the shirt to staunch the blood until the cut stopped flowing and the once white shirt was splashed with carmine red. Finally satisfied, MacMartin carefully picked up the clothes.

"Right, get dressed in the clothes I brought while I sort this lot out." He scampered off out of sight down the sheep track while Gillespie pulled on the clothes. He'd just finished when MacMartin reappeared, for once with a smile on his face.

"That should do it. If you're lucky enough to get away with this crazy plan, I'll go and fish those clothes out in a few weeks' time. Just long enough for your DNA to still be traceable. Your name will then be added to the long list of prisoners that have fallen from the cliffs – either by accident or design. St Kilda's reputation will be preserved, and no one will ask too many questions."

MacMartin grabbed Gillespie by the shoulder again, holding his sgian dubh up to the scar he'd given him. "Just make sure you don't get caught, because if you do, and you come back here, you'll not last more than a few hours. Right?"

Gillespie nodded and MacMartin sheathed his sgian dubh back in his stocking. They started the steep walk back up the gully to the cliff top. He found the return journey easier, as he only had to concentrate on the few square feet of the path ahead of him, but he dreaded to think how he was going to negotiate the path at night, and potentially in a howling gale. He gritted his teeth and pushed the thought from his mind, there was plenty of time to be scared later. Right now he was buoyed by hope, that he hadn't been forgotten after all and that the MacNachtans were coming for him.

47 – Proposition

Lamont took the call in the Presidential Suite, his eyes flicking between his computer screen and the view out over Oban. His idea to keep the snow ploughs shut away and let the weather do its worst had worked perfectly. The Pass of Brander had been shut by heavy snow and that bitch Kirstie MacNachtan hadn't been able to get to Oban to take the oath. She'd escaped him once but would not do so again. So, he'd been a little surprised when his secretary called to tell him MacCailean Mòr was on the phone and wanted to talk about the MacNachtans.

MacCailean Mòr was trying to keep his voice calm and steady, matter of fact even, as they exchanged the pleasantries required of a call to the Head of State. While he listened, Lamont turned over some of the memories he had of when MacCailean Mòr was in his grip. He regretted that he hadn't had time to really work him over, but it still gave him a frisson of satisfaction to hear his squirming on the phone.

"Look here, Lamont…."

"President Lamont, thank you."

"President Lamont, my apologies," Lamont could almost hear MacCailean Mòr's teeth being gritted. "I am calling on behalf of the Clan MacNachtan, you know, based just outside Inveraray. I believe you are familiar with them. They used to be led by that old rogue Duncan Tapaidh."

"Ah yes, Duncan Tapaidh, as quick with his cock as with his blade, if I remember correctly. Who is Chief now? And why can't I remember them coming to take the oath? You know the deadline has passed."

"Well, yes, that is what I am calling about. You see, apparently they tried to go to Oban yesterday to take the oath before the deadline. But the road was closed because of the snow and for some reason it wasn't cleared. They tried their best but couldn't get through. They came to see me as the Sheriff of the county and senior regional government representative. We tried to speak with David Brown but couldn't get hold of him. Hence why I am calling you, to register their oath. They swore the words in front of me. I can send you a film of it."

"Remind me, what Government post do you hold at the moment?"

Lamont pictured MacCailean Mòr's discomfort as he ummed and ahhed. He'd been the Warden of the West for so long it must have been difficult for him to remember that that position had been stripped from him and given to Catriona MacLean a few short months previously. Lamont relished MacCailean Mòr's embarrassment but eventually had to step in and move the conversation on.

"So, these MacNachtans came to you to take the oath thinking that in some way that was a substitute for coming to the Righaltas and standing in front of their peers and putting their hand on the Sword of State to swear the words. Words of loyalty to the Republic and the organs of State that uphold her? Including, I might add, that of my own position. They really believe that that is in some way, any way, comparable?" Lamont poured cold-dripped venom down the line. He was enjoying this.

MacCailean Mòr gibbered at the other end of the

phone. He clearly hadn't been expecting such a hostile reaction. He'd probably imagined that Lamont would have allowed them to register their oath with a little slap on the wrist. After all, it was hardly as if they were in any way a threat. But that was the whole point of this exercise, he needed a sacrificial lamb. Someone who was expendable. And it was just too perfect that it was going to be the MacNachtans. Allan Stewart flashed into his mind's eye, those impenetrable eyes, unblinking and remorseless urged him on from beyond the grave. He wasn't going to let this opportunity slip through his fingers. No, he wanted to squeeze every last drop out of it.

For a while he sat and allowed MacCailean Mòr to try and sweet talk him round. For some reason he really seemed to care about that bunch of reprobates. But eventually tiring of all the false flattery, Lamont decided it was time to get down to business.

"I'll discuss the MacNachtans with David Brown and the other relevant officers of State, we will see what they decide to do to them. However, I want to talk to you about something much more important – Islay. With Catriona MacLean now in custody I have to decide who is best placed to take Islay under their roof. Obviously, you and the Campbells have performed that role admirably for many centuries, but you are obviously not the only candidate…."

Lamont left the sentence hanging while he allowed MacCailean Mòr's fevered brain to digest its meaning.

"Yes, that's right. I'll give you back Islay, but with certain conditions. First and foremost is that you don't interfere with whatever decision is taken in respect of the MacNachtans. They'll need to suck up their punishment alone. Secondly, I am not so stupid as to expect you to give me your full support in the Comhairle, but I do expect your total acquiescence. I don't care if you never come to the Riaghaltas again, but I don't want to see you vote against me or my plans, ever. Am I clear?"

MacCailean Mòr gave a strangulated gurgle, which Lamont took as the nearest he was going to be able to get to assent.

"Good boy. Good boy, you are learning. You see, life can be so easy if you just play for the right team. And just you remember whose team you are now on." Lamont then switched his voice from smooth emollience to a jagged hiss; "And if you break your word, I swear I'll have you taken to Ascog where I'll smash every bone in your goddam body one by one."

48 – The Cleft Stick

Brighid had never seen MacCailean Mòr so angry. As soon as he'd ended the call with Lamont he'd thrown his phone across the room and swept the papers that littered his desk onto the floor, before pounding his fists on its leather top, his lips pulled back in a snarl. She wasn't sure what to do. He didn't look in the mood for soft words. Instead, she calmly put her hand out and caught his clenched fist, tenderly wrapping it in hers and holding it. Her touch broke Lamont's spell, and MacCailean Mòr's demonic anger vanished as fast as it had come.

With the passing of his rage came a weariness. He looked at her, his pale grey eyes pained, the crow's feet that radiated out on either side deeper than ever. He held her hand between his.

"I don't know how to say this." He started.

"What do you mean? Would he not accept the oath?"

"I don't know, he rejected it initially but then said he would discuss it with Brown. God only knows what that desk jockey will say. Despite that, I very much get the feeling that he is planning something and that the MacNachtans are at the centre of it. He could never forgive you for wresting back Dunderave and killing Allan Stewart, never. His revenge was only a matter of time and form. You have been fortunate to escape his attentions until now."

"What the hell are we going to do?" Brighid stared at the fire. She'd only started coming to terms with the trauma of her escape from Islay. Her kidnap and

Ardbreknish, the rape and abuse, were still locked up deep inside her, a permanent weight she carried with her. She couldn't face them yet. This added tension was the very last thing she needed.

MacCailean Mòr sighed, "I don't know. There is very little we can do. We have to hope that Brown will keep him on the straight and narrow."

"Surely, we should talk to Brown then. We can't just hope that he'll do the right thing. Who is he? Do you know him?"

"A little, he is the Prìomh-Chlàrc a' Bhun-reachd - the Chief Clerk of the Constitution – and a leader of the Seanadh. He has become very close to Lamont ever since he seized power. I wouldn't say they were natural bed fellows. In my experience, Brown is a moderniser, someone who is keen to do his best for the citizens of the Republic. He doesn't have much truck with Chiefs or the Comhairle."

"What the hell is he doing with Lamont if he is such a moderniser?"

"That I can't say. But what I do know, is that Lamont has a horrible way of finding out your weakness and exploiting it. Before you've woken up to what is going on, you are in too deep. It wouldn't surprise me if he has got something on Brown, some leverage that he's using."

"Nonetheless, it seems to me he's our only hope. We are never going to persuade Lamont to do anything other than crush us. How do we get to him?"

MacCailean Mòr didn't answer but sat in silence. Finally, he drummed his fingers on the table. "You should go. Take Nin or Charlie. Go to Oban and try and get a meeting."

"Can't you help?"

"No. If I get involved it will only make it more complicated and risky. You know as well as I do that I can't go to Oban without attracting a lot of attention. Lamont has made it pretty clear to me that I need to stay out of it."

"What do you mean? That you are just going to let us swing, after everything we have done to help you?" Brighid felt her indignance rising, her face flushed.

"Not at all. Look…." MacCailean Mòr was clearly struggling to find the right words; there was something more to his conversation with Lamont.

"Spit it out." Her ears were burning red, her fists clenched, knuckles white. What wasn't he telling her?

MacCailean Mòr sighed and like a dam breaking it all came out, about Islay and Lamont's threats.

"You see, I can't get involved, not until I have Islay back. My people and the island have suffered too much. Once we have kicked out MacVey and his MacLean murderers I can then be more use. But, until then, you'll need to take the lead. It is my duty as Chief. My hands are tied."

Brighid felt white hot fury pour out of her. "How dare you. After everything we have done for you. Is our time together really so dispensable? You are going to sell me and rest of the MacNachtans out for the promise of a murderer. A man who would skin you alive at the first opportunity. A man who has butchered and tortured his way to the top leaving a long trail of dead innocent people. You disgust me. No, don't touch me, you can fuck off. I should have known you fucking Campbells are all the same, self-interested, morality-free bastards. Well you can stick your support and sympathy up your arse, and I hope it chokes you. I am going to try and save my friends with or without your help."

And with that, Brighid stormed from the room, slamming the door behind her as she fled the castle. Outside, she kickstarted her bike and tore off up the drive, scattering gravel, her long blonde hair streaming out behind and tears pouring down her face.

49 – Nan Sgàilean

Shonique was at Fiona's house when she met Alasdair for the first time. She could remember it quite clearly. She and Fiona had just put the fish fingers in the oven for Mara's dinner and were thinking about pouring themselves a hard-earned glass of clàireat, when the doorbell rang. She'd stayed in the kitchen while Fiona went to see who was at the door. The next minute she returned bringing with her the most extraordinary man Shonique had ever seen. Of medium height and slender, he had neat dark hair and thick brows above eyes of the bluest Caribbean water. He was as pale as a ghost. But there was something else, something that scratched at the edge of her mind, if only she could put her finger on it. He seemed to emanate an indistinct shimmer; if she looked straight at him she could see him clear as day, but if she turned her gaze away, even the slightest amount, it was as if he was behind frosted glass. She looked at the tartan on the forearm of his sleeve, the nine green squares on red – a Griogaraich!

"Shonique, this is Alasdair MacGregor, an old friend of the Clan. Alasdair, this is Shonique, Gillespie's partner."

Alasdair took her hand and held it between his long, elegant fingers, his hands were as tough and hard as old leather.

"Gillespie is a lucky man."

"You are too kind. I have heard a lot about you, unsurprisingly. Great to meet you at last. Can I pour you a glass?"

As the level of wine left in the bottle sank, the mood of the room lifted. Alasdair was great company, and Shonique caught herself feeling quite attracted to this raffish outlaw as he span them tale after tale of what he had been up to since his return from Antrim. She was no stranger to dodgy people, but for the Republic's most wanted man he was an unlikely figure. She'd been expecting some musclebound, shaven headed thug, the kind of man that could crush your skull one handed. She hadn't expected for a moment that the leader of the Griogaraich would be so charming. It was strange though, when she went to have a pee, she idly tried to picture him in her mind's eye but couldn't. She could recall everything else about him, but his face remained in shadow; like Tantalus's apple it hovered just out of reach.

They were soon joined by Nin, Charlie and Kirstie and the volume in the room rose as they all jabbered their welcomes and caught up on news. Nin and Alasdair clearly had a special relationship – she'd heard they'd made a bloodbond - and they greeted each other like long lost brothers. Eventually, Fiona managed to quieten the room enough to get them all sat down around the pine kitchen table, while she poured everyone a cup of tea to go with the clàireat.

It was Nin that spoke first: "I want to thank Alasdair for once again coming to help us in our hour of need. As we all know, Gillespie has been imprisoned on St Kilda for the last few months. Thanks to the incredible work of the digital team," at which he nodded at Fiona and Shonique, "we've been able to establish a connection with him through one of the St Kildans. We all know how tough that prison can be; we can't leave

Gillespie there a moment longer than necessary. We have asked Alasdair for his help and he has come up with a bold plan. However, we should be under no illusions that escaping from St Kilda is extremely dangerous. The number of those who have died trying is well known. Fiona, what can you tell us about our contact?"

Fiona took a sip of tea, a puff on her vape and a slug of red wine to fortify herself before addressing the table. "Thanks Nin. I wouldn't say he was the most willing tool, but we have been able to send messages to Gillespie and have regular updates on how he is doing. The reason for gathering you all together now − and many thanks Alasdair for coming at such short notice − is that we have a great opportunity to try and spring Gillespie over the next two weeks, as we have arranged for him to be outside the main prison compound each night."

Fiona took out her tablet and swiped open a high-resolution map of the St Kilda archipelago, zooming in on Hirta, the main island. They all crowded round the screen as she talked.

"As I am sure you all know, there is only one mooring spot on St Kilda, in the heart of Village Bay," she pointed at the deep crescent that bit into the south eastern end of the island, "which is obviously out of the question. However, we've been able to get Gillespie posted along the sea cliffs here on the southern shore." She traced her finger along the tightly packed contours. "The problem is these cliffs are extremely steep and almost impossible to descend, even for a local. Having spoken at length with our St Kildan, we have come to the conclusion that there is no way that Gillespie would be able to get to sea level, even if we could get a boat close enough."

A depressed sigh went around the table.

"However," Alasdair now interjected. All eyes now snapped onto him. "I've been speaking with my friends at the Atelier of Thomas Caddell, and I believe I may have a solution. They've loaned me one of their high-performance cargo drones. It is robust enough to carry a man but small enough to escape detection by radar. I know that some of you," at which he nodded at Nin, "are familiar with The Rose in June. She is a Griogaraich vessel and is a designated fishing trawler. She therefore has permission to fish the sea around St Kilda without attracting attention. The plan is for us to sail close enough to the island to be able to launch the drone and fly it in to pick him up. Obviously, this will have to be done with care and out of the direct beam of those radar stations, but we have found what we believe is the perfect spot." He pointed at the map of Hirta's southern cliffs. "Geo na Laise-suileach is one of the few gullies that you can descend far enough to get out of sight of the radar stations. There is a potential pick-up point about halfway down the cliff. If we can sail in close enough to fly the drone and Gillespie can get down to the pick-up point, then it should just be a question of him strapping himself in and flying him back to the boat."

"How close are you allowed to get?" Shonique asked.

"That is one of the problems, as in theory there is a two nautical mile exclusion zone. However, I understand from talking to the crew of The Rose in June that vessels can fish closer. The authorities tend to leave them alone, partly because there is no way of getting down the cliffs. As long as we don't attract any suspicion, and the drone stays low to the sea, we should be alright."

"OK, so when do we go and try to pick him up?"

"The weather forecast is always very changeable out at St Kilda, but tomorrow night it looks as though it is going to be overcast and cloudy but calm. That should give us our best chance of getting in and out in one piece."

Shonique was stunned, tomorrow night, it was so soon. Her mind swirled with the outrageousness of the plan. Maybe it was better that way, with crazy plans like this it was better not to have too much time to think about it. There was so much that could go wrong. But unless Gillespie wanted to spend the next 25 years rotting in the mid-Atlantic, there was no alternative.

50 – The Rose in June

They picked up The Rose in June in the small harbour at Connel, Alasdair being understandably reluctant to go to Oban. Shonique had been surprised at the ordinary boat that waited for them at the end of the quay. It was a sway-bellied, deep ocean trawler, pock-marked and streaked with rust with only the occasional swag of crudely painted roses to lift its battered appearance. However, as soon as she stepped aboard and went into the wheelhouse she could see that the interior was very different and furnished with obviously hi-tch navigation and radar equipment. The boat had an unmistakable smell of fresh paint, with the faintest tinge of old fish lying underneath; The Rose in June clearly had a few secrets up her sleeve.

As she was about to sit down, a middle-aged Indian man with burning black, red-rimmed eyes and wild hair proffered a mug of tea.

"Hello, my name is Daaku. I'm the Captain of The Rose in June, so don't hesitate to let me know if you need anything. Yes? Here, please take the cup of tea, it is going to be a little choppy out in the Minch, best to have something to calm your stomach."

She gladly took the cup and sat at the table while Alasdair and Nin loaded the gear onto the boat. Soon, they were motoring past the looming Dunstaffnage Castle, one of the MacDougall's many strongholds, before passing out into the Firth of Lorn. As they rounded the needle-tip of Lismore, they all looked across the channel at Duart, Catriona MacLean's base on the coast of Mull. It was dark and quiet.

The Rose in June made surprisingly good progress up the Sound of Mull which was once again thronged with sea-traffic. By imprisoning MacLean and her supporters, and giving Islay back to MacCailean Mòr, Lamont had finally restored balance to the west coast. With Islay off the table, Sorley MacDonald and MacLeod, who'd become bogged down in fighting a front line that never moved, came to their senses and agreed to return to their previously held positions. Like two bald men fighting over a comb, they struggled to remember why they'd come to blows in the first place; with no new territory now available, they both agreed that peace was preferable to war. The situation was calmer than it had been for many months and trade and traffic flowed once again.

The Rose in June made stately progress up the Sound, her comfortable lines belied her speed though, and without pushing her too hard Daaku was able to maintain a steady 12 knots. It was a grey day; occasional bursts of sunshine were quickly doused by rain showers. As the wind rolled the weather from the ocean onto land, dark black caps sat down on the peaks, their jagged tops raking open the passing clouds spilling their watery lifeforce onto the hills. It was quite different to Jamaica. Shonique suddenly felt a pang of homesickness. She missed the heat and the rich, fecund funk of the forest, that smell of rotting vegetation, the recycling of life as nature's hardest worker, the microbe, tirelessly reused and transformed the worn-out remnants of yesterday into fresh green hope for tomorrow.

She wondered if she would ever go back to Albany, to her life with the Maroon community high up in the hills. She missed her friends, the food and the music – probably in that order. The Republic was wild and had been fun and traumatic in equal measure, but in the end there is nowhere like home.

Nin sat down next to her and pulled out a deck of cards. He started laying them out in front of him in a game of patience.

"Doesn't that make you seasick?" She asked.

"Nah, it's a good way to calm my mind ahead of what is to come."

"Do you think our plan will work?"

"I wouldn't be here if I didn't. That said, it's hard to be certain. Flying a drone into those cliffs with the wind and rain is not going to be easy. We then need to fly it back to the ship while keeping it as low as possible to avoid spooking their radar. No cakewalk."

"Has anyone tried to do it before?"

"Nope. Apparently, several years ago the St Kilda Prison Service commissioned Caddell's to develop a signal jammer to stop people being able to fly drugs or weapons in, or people out. Of course, they've set up our drone on a different frequency, so we won't be affected by that, but for others it is pretty much impossible. There is also the issue of the weight of the payload and the flying conditions. The drone has to use a lot of energy to fly against the wind and the batteries are only now starting to be powerful enough. Fortunately, the weather is supposed to be calm tonight, so we should have enough juice to fly there and bring him back."

Alasdair appeared at the table, with a plate of sandwiches and the remains of a bottle of rum.

"Can I offer you a dram to keep the chill off? I'm sorry it's not Jamaican." He poured out three small shots and gave one to Shonique and Nin. She gripped the stubby glass between finger and thumb and chinked glasses with the others.

"To Lady Luck and Flying Monkeys!" Alasdair said, and they all dispatched their shots and slammed the empty glasses onto the table. The fiery liquor coursed down her throat leaving a trail of rich sultana sweetness, dry tobacco and nail varnish, while she demolished a ham and cheese sandwich.

The day passed without incident and she spent her time watching the spiny ridge of the Outer Hebridean island chain come ever closer. As night began to fall, they passed out through the Sound of Barra and into the Atlantic proper. As predicted, the Minch was choppy, but now they'd passed beyond the shelter of the Hebrides the ocean's mighty swell could be felt in full. It wasn't rough, but the relentless sway of the boat as it climbed each wave began to make her feel quite peculiar. She decided to get some rest before she started puking her guts up.

She woke after a few hours to find Nin and Alasdair hard at work assembling the drone. The main body was straightforward, it just needed its four rotor blades attached at each corner. The trickier part was threading the harness together. After all, they couldn't afford for any of the straps to come undone mid-flight and drop their precious cargo into the sea. To Shonique it looked too flimsy to carry the bodyweight of a fully grown man, but Alasdair assured her it would.

They were now coming up on the archipelago. Even though it was night, they could see the towering outline of its cliffs and mountains outlined by the light of the moon whenever it briefly emerged from behind the scudding clouds. The size of the Atlantic rollers made her wonder what a rough night on the water would be like. She clung to the handrail.

They were now in position and Daaku put The Rose in June into a trawling profile a couple of miles offshore while they waited for the signal. All that night they waited, the interminable hours of the early morning passing slowly, with the relentless swoop of the swell carrying them up and down the peaks and valleys of the Atlantic rollers. Shonique drifted in and out of sleep, wedged into one of the bunks. It was fine while she was asleep, but as soon as she awoke, she had to get on deck or else risk being violently ill. Daaku and Alasdair took it in turns at the helm, trying to keep the islands within range without arousing suspicion. But no call came, and as dawn threaded the distant hills of the Outer Isles with her pale golden light, the decision was taken to abort. Daaku turned the boat back towards Harris. No word of Gillespie came from MacMartin and their earlier euphoria at the assured success of their plan evaporated utterly in the morning sun.

Brighid stood with Kirstie watching the transports roll in along the Arrochar Wade. A long string of matt green and camouflaged trucks filled with unsmiling, heavily armed members of the Black Watch. She'd never seen so many members of the Republic's internal defence force up close. They looked as fearsome as their reputation.

She'd got the call earlier that morning from Kirstie who urged her to come to Dunderave as soon as possible. Brighid knew after her conversation with MacCailean Mòr that something was likely to happen, but nobody knew what. She'd spent all of the previous evening in an increasingly heated discussion with the Clan Council trying to decide the best course of action. While it was clear that they were now officially considered to have missed the deadline, no one knew what the consequence would be. Kirstie, understandably, was feeling responsible and was compensating by being unduly officious. She was beginning to piss everyone off. It was during the evening that Kirstie had taken the call from David Brown officially informing her that the Black Watch were on manoeuvres and that the Clan would be required to accommodate them while they were in the area.

After the call, there was much debate around the table over exactly what this signified, with the majority view being that their punishment was going to be extracted in the form of food and lodging. This was a common enough technique of Presidents past, who when they wanted to bring an unruly Clan or Chieftain to heel would descend on them for a two-week seminar or conference. The resulting bill could take years for most Clans to pay off and so was a healthy deterrent. What was unusual was for the guests to be the Black Watch; they were happy enough to be bivouacked on the hill under a tarpaulin, why did they need to be given food and shelter? In any case, as David Brown made clear, there was little that could be done about it and right on the allotted hour the Black Watch's vehicles rolled into Dunderave.

A bull-headed man with close cropped hair got out of the lead vehicle and stalked towards Kirstie and Brighid. He exuded 'don't-fuck-with-me' passive aggression and looked them both up and down as if they were something the cat had dragged in. Kirstie stuck out her hand in welcome, he ignored it, instead turning his attention to his clipboard.

"My name is Major Robertson, and I am in command here. As I believe you have been told, I need accommodation and subsistence for my men for the next few weeks while we are on manoeuvres. I will need men posted here in the castle, as well as at the following locations Clachan, Stronshira, Glen Shira. I want a minimum of five men per household, with fifty in the castle. There are 250 of us, so that means I need you to allocate forty houses for us to occupy. You will be responsible for all supplies and accommodation for the period. Am I clear? Good. We will wait for you to make your allocation."

Then, turning on his heel, he walked back to the troop carrier without waiting for a response.

Brighid felt her ears burning with indignation; how dare they just arrive and make such demands! Most of the Clan lived in variations of the classic west coast white harled cottage. They were small, modest dwellings and having to accommodate five hungry, lumpen soldiers was going to be tough. Even trying to accommodate fifty soldiers in the castle was going to be hard. While the Red Banner Hall now had a new roof and could probably host half that number if they squeezed in like sardines, where the rest were going to go was anyone's guess. The building just wasn't designed to hold so many people.

She and Kirstie scurried through the Outer Ward and into the Castle to try and figure out how best to spread the soldiers around. With such large numbers of guests, a high proportion of the Clan's households would be occupied. Kirstie immediately called Deirdre MacNitt the Clan Treasurer to ensure that the Hardship Fund could at least step in to pay the food bill.

Once in the gaming centre, they rapidly scrawled out a plan on the white board, carefully spreading the burden as much as they could, taking into consideration the age of the household, the presence of children, in particular teenagers, and their general financial robustness. Some houses which were larger, like Elrig, they felt comfortable squeezing in more men to try and lighten the load elsewhere. Finally, satisfied with the dispensation, they went back outside to find the Major.

There was something about seeing the columns of Black Watch filing into the Castle that pained Brighid. It just didn't seem right. They'd done nothing wrong apart from be late to the oath taking; it hadn't been their fault and they had nonetheless sworn the words. They were far too small to be a threat to the Republic, that was the preserve of the great Clans, the Campbells,

MacDonalds, Gordons, MacKenzies and MacLeods. So why this big song and dance? She wracked her brain to think of another occasion that the Black Watch had been used like this, but none came to mind.

The Major was as blunt and unforthcoming as a rock as he divided up his troops and despatched them to their quarters. Brighid was sent with a Captain Cameron to parcel out the Stronshira and Glen Shira allocations, going from house to house explaining the situation and placing the respective troops in each designated house. As she approached her own front door, she felt a twinge of anger at this imposition. She'd spent little time there recently; most of her time since coming back from Islay had been spent at Inveraray Castle with MacCailean Mòr. But her little house was her home, the only one she'd ever had. Having to open it up to a bunch of rough strangers was not just galling it was also upsetting. It was a violation of her private space and a violation by Lamont too, which made it all the worse. Would they never be free of him?

She showed the men around the house, gave them sheets for the beds and tried to tidy away her clothes and personal items. She couldn't bear the thought of losing her dad's sgian dubh and her mother's jewellery, both of which were likely to be too tempting to her 'guests' and she stuffed them into her bag. She knew that they would almost certainly pick though all her stuff. The idea of that voyeurism was unpleasant, and she resolved to stay with MacCailean Mòr, even if it meant having to apologise for her previous outburst.

Next, they drove down to the mouth of Glen Shira, distributing the soldiers in groups of five or six at each of the houses they passed. Eventually, they came to Elrig and Charlie appeared on the front steps to supervise the unloading. As they got out of the cab, Charlie came down to greet Captain Cameron.

"If it isn't Archie Cameron, you old wanker. How are you?" Charlie clapped Captain Cameron around the shoulder, an impish glint in his eye. "Aye, aye what's all this then?" He asked as he inspected the rank on Cameron's jacket. "Captain Cameron, well that has quite a ring to it doesn't it. Who would have thought Old Archie Cameron, a Captain in the Watch. Fuck me."

"Do you mind?" Captain Cameron replied. "I'm in command here and don't need any of your cheek. You'll be glad to know that ten of my men will be staying with you, and if you lay a finger on any of them you'll have me to answer to."

"Jesus, get over yourself, what makes you think I'd be interested in any of your brawny, spunk-pumped, numbskulls anyway? I am much more discerning these days I'll have you know." Brighid noted that Captain Cameron went slightly red and disappeared off to unload his men without saying another word.

She and Charlie watched the line of men with their kitbags as they pushed through Elrig's bright blue door.

"Will you be OK? With Nin away, you're all alone with that lot."

"I guess I will just have to make the best of it." Charlie winked.

"Seriously, Charlie. Come on. We have no idea what these cretins might do. Just keep out of their way."

"Don't worry, I fully intend to do just that. But if young Captain Cameron decides to come and stay then all bets are off; I'm not made of stone. We used to be at school together many moons ago, he was only the Captain of the shinty team then, but he was ever so masterful in his tight white shorts...."

Brighid smiled, she was glad to see he was taking it in good heart. She got back in the cab to finish parcelling out the last of the men up the glen. There were only a few more houses left to go. She began to feel tired; the stress of the day was taking its toll. As they pulled out of Elrig's front garden, she saw that Captain Cameron had indeed stayed behind. She was suddenly hit by an overwhelming and ominous feeling; why was Lamont doing this and where would it end?

52 – Balls

David Brown hated it when President Lamont summoned him. He was always half expecting to be 'disappeared' like so many others. Over the last few months, he'd realised that, like many powerful people, Lamont enjoyed keeping you guessing; were you about to be bathed in the warm glow of his confidence or were you about to get a punishment beating. Lamont could vacillate between these moods quite rapidly and Brown had learned that it was dangerous to ever be over-confident in his position. At the same time, when things went badly, Lamont's face was rarely set against him for too long. That was in part because Brown was the nearest thing Lamont had to a partner, although he was unlikely to see it that way. Brown knew that he'd made a pact with the devil, but he still hoped that one day he might be able to slip his leash; the good citizens of the Republic deserved better.

He arrived at Lamont's office door flustered, wondering what it was that Lamont wanted. Lamont was sat behind the Liberator's desk idly cleaning his fingernails with his sgian dubh. He waved Brown over but didn't invite him to sit down, instead he looked Brown up and down, like a heifer in the showring. Brown was wearing his grey, stay-sharp poly-wool kilt and jacket, as he did every day; it had been a while since he'd washed them, he hoped they didn't smell. His inspection over, Lamont turned to look out of the window.

"Does he have the balls for it, I wonder?" Lamont asked, almost to himself.

"I am not quite sure what you mean?" Brown responded, somewhat indignant.

"I mean, do you have the guts to follow through on what we have started? You and I, we have brought the country to the brink of change. We are standing on the precipice and looking over the edge. Do you have the balls to take the next step, or will you shrink back from the challenge?"

"You know that I am as committed to the modernisation of this country as you. Have I not backed you all the way, supported you in your bid to become President, helped you overcome your enemies and managed your negotiations with the Kingdom? Without my help you would never have got this far."

"True, true. But that is all just the hors d'oeuvres to the dish that we now have to prepare. You do understand that? We must break the Chiefs and their power over the people once and for all. The bonds of history and clannishness are an impediment to the order and control needed in a modern society. Why do people need Clans when they have the State! They must answer to us, not some inbred, entitled buffoon! You and I must take this crude iron and smelt it into fine steel, and that can only be done with fire and force – otherwise they will never achieve their potential."

Lamont was on a roll now and Brown braced himself for the unpalatable request that almost always followed these 'inspirational' monologues.

"Yes, Mr President, and what was it you have in mind?"

"I am delighted that the MacNachtans didn't come in to take the oath in time and I now want to use them as a signal to the others that those days are past and that any who brook the bridle will feel the whip. I've ordered the Black Watch to Dunderave and quartered them among the Clan. I want you to give the order to Major Robertson yourself that suppresses them once and for all."

"What do you mean?" Brown stammered, sensing the trap being laid out in front of him.

"Here, these are the orders." Lamont tossed a sheet of paper over the desk.

Brown picked it up, reading with trembling hands.

"You can't be serious? You want to kill them all, even the women and children?"

"All under seventy, and make sure that old fox Kirstie MacNachtan doesn't get away either. Consider it a work of charity to root out this damn set, the worst in all the Republic. Root and branch, root and branch; we need to prune away the old for new growth to come through. It may seem harsh, but that is the only language these people understand. Once we have shown what happens to those that stand in our way, we'll have no more problems with the others. Which brings me back to my first question; do you have the balls for it? Because, if not, I might need to find myself someone who does."

53 – Lambing

It had been a long night and Gillespie was exhausted when he finally was able to leave and return to the main prison compound. The St Kildan sheep were small and stubborn, hard to catch and even harder to help. After he'd delivered the third set of twins on the craggy clifftops, he was black and blue from being butted, kicked and stood on. He was beginning to agree with MacMartin; better to let the runty bastards die or be born on their own terms.

Lady Lamont was good company and a skilled midwife, she had clearly birthed plenty of them over the years. They seemed to endure her touch more easily than his, perhaps it was familiarity? He had been so busy that he hadn't even had time to ask MacMartin about the rescue and besides he was being unforthcoming. In the end, there was nothing he could do about it as he was totally reliant on MacMartin to pass on the details of the MacNachtans' plans.

He spent the day trying to catch up on sleep in his cell. At least when he was able to in between Robbie MacRae's junglist rhythms and relentless clouds of St Kilda Mist. That evening, feeling somewhat restored, he went to supper early to fill up on carbs ahead of the long night ahead. Having collected his tray, he went and sat at his usual table in the middle of the room. All the tough guys tended to sit in the corners, like spiders they kept their backs to the wall. They were the ones to watch out for. The saps like him clustered as far away from the troublemakers as they could. He was just finishing that day's stew of indeterminate origin when a shadow passed over the table. He looked up. A middle-aged man with receding hair and squashed nose stood over him.

"Are you the hard man, eh?"

"What do you mean?" Gillespie tried to remain calm, he didn't want any trouble, especially not now.

"Are you a deaf cunt as well as stupid? I said, are you the hard man? Are you the man that did for Allan Stewart of Ballachulish? My cousin Allan. That murdered him."

Gillespie froze; he'd been worried that this might happen, but as the days had gone by, he'd stopped thinking about it. He didn't say anything, steadfastly returning his gaze to the tray in front of him and continuing to eat. This seemed to perplex his interlocuter, who slammed a sharpened screwdriver into the table right by his hand and left it there quivering.

"Yeah, you understand that don't you, you cunt. Well, I've got another one of them for you. I've been sharpening it specially. And you see over there," at which the man pointed to a table in the far corner occupied by a scabrous mass of wild-haired caterans. "They are all Stewarts too. Stewarts of Garmoran, from the Rough Bounds. Allan Stewart was their Clan and their kin, and you've pissed on their Cliù with your gutless murder. You and us, we have a bloodfeud. You understand? Let's see how hard you are when we cut out your liver and feed it to the gannets."

Just as Gillespie was beginning to wonder if he was about to be slaughtered in the dining hall in full view of the entire prison, he saw a black baton appear from nowhere and crack the Stewart across the side of his head. The man went down, and MacMartin was on him, pouring blows down on his thrashing body, the flurry of blows only stopping when the man's limbs stilled. MacMartin stood up, wiping spatters of blood from his face, and pointed the baton at the body and then to the table of Stewarts who watched sullenly from the sidelines. He didn't say anything. Then he pointed at Gillespie and then at the door. Gillespie stood up and pushed through the silent rows of tables to the entrance with MacMartin following behind. As they left, the room behind exploded in shouts and laughter as the competing factions expressed their anger or amusement at the punishment meted out to Gillespie's aggressor.

MacMartin walked him through the prison to get his jacket and boots and then back to the main entrance. As they walked through the prison grounds to the west gate, MacMartin didn't say a word, but as they climbed the switchback, he gave him the news that Gillespie had been hoping for and dreading in equal measure.

"Tonight, 3 a.m. Where I showed you. Right? They are going to fly a drone in to pick you up. You just strap yourself in and off you go. Don't fuck it up. This is your only chance, there won't be another."

Gillespie nodded and they continued the steep climb to the ridge. Lady Lamont was waiting for them at her cleit, and she'd already laid out their supplies: torches, lubricant, disinfectant, ropes. The wind whipped around them, its Greenland chill gnawing at any exposed flesh. Gillespie couldn't imagine how she survived up here in all weathers, no wonder she'd gone slightly mad. She proffered a cup of tea to warm him ahead of the night's privations, and he greedily sipped it, clasping the mug tight in his hands. Night fell and having successfully delivered Gillespie into Lady Lamont's care, MacMartin left them, striding off along the southern cliffs. Gillespie wondered if he would ever see him again.

They gathered their gear and moved off, keeping an eye out for any ewes that were in distress. The hours passed slowly and after a couple of successes they had a run of failures. Gillespie was wondering if this was going to be his night after all. The wind was starting to get up, whipping off the ocean in bitter gusts; he was beginning to doubt that it would even be possible to fly a drone against it, let alone pick up a passenger. He kept glancing at his watch as the minutes crawled by. Eventually, and perhaps inevitably, Lady Lamont noticed.

"Why do you keep looking at your watch? What are you expecting?"

Gillespie groaned inwardly; she was no fool. He paused, how much could he, should he, tell her. He thought about lying or just fobbing her off, but in his heart he felt she'd been lied to enough. Instead, he said nothing, focusing on the ewe that they'd wrestled to the ground and were busy trying to help. Of all the people on the island, no one had suffered more at the hand of Lamont than she had; she'd been incarcerated in this most isolated and cruel prison for no reason. Perhaps Lamont had forgotten that she was still here, mouldering away, driven mad by the wind and weather. In his new position as President, she would surely be the ultimate inconvenient truth. How much longer would he tolerate her continued existence? Or would he just get Fergusson to have her pitched off a cliff on a wild night. It was a miracle that it hadn't happened already.

But that day would come, as surely as the sun sets in the west.

The lamb finally emerged, and the mother turned to clean it, licking its face and bleating until it answered her call. He tried to wipe the amniotic fluid from his hands onto the grass. He looked for the bottle of iodine to swab the umbilical cord that Lady Lamont was busy cutting and trimming.

"Some friends are coming to try and free me. Tonight. They are going to fly a drone in to pick me up. That's why I'm here helping you."

She wiped the blade of the knife on her sleeve and looked at him.

"I want you to come with me. I want to help you get away from this godforsaken place."

Her hands trembled as she looked at him. A slightly mad glint came in her eye.

"I can't leave. He will kill me if I leave."

"He'll kill you if you stay too. You know he's now the President. How can a President lock his wife away? Send her to this fucking shit hole to be held against her will, for years. Impossible! Even in the Republic. If word gets out, he'll be done for. And that's what makes me think that surely, when he has time to stop and think, he will turn his attention to you, and I don't like your chances."

"My life is here now. I can't just leave. This place, this island, I can't explain, it has become part of me."

"But this could be your only chance to escape, for freedom, to get your revenge. Come with me. What is there for you here?"

She didn't answer, instead she tucked the lamb up tight to the ewe before standing up and staring out along the pitch-black cliffs to the silhouettes of the island's peaks, the silver light of the moon casting long, jagged shadows. She gathered up their tools, putting the bottle of iodine, the birthing rope and the knife in her bag. Gillespie reached out to touch her arm.

"Coira, this might be your last and only chance to escape this place. You must take it. Forget Lamont for a moment, think of your children, surely you want to see them again?"

She nodded, dumbly.

"Come with me. Please?"

She gripped his arm in answer and together they walked away from the new-born lamb and its mother: new life and new beginnings.

Gillespie checked his watch again. It was half past two; they needed to get to the rendezvous. Fortunately, with Lady Lamont's knowledge of the cliffs they made good time and were soon at the perilous track down to the Geo na Laise-suileach. At least in the dark Gillespie didn't need to worry about the vertiginous drops down to the foaming ocean, instead he focused on following the black shrouded figure of Lady Lamont as she picked her way down the path as steady as any mountain goat. They finally reached the flat ledge in the rocky cleft and Lady Lamont tossed their bag of equipment to the ground. She stared out between the fold in the cliffs to the ocean beyond as if expecting to see the drone arrive out of the darkness at that instant.

Gillespie sat on the grass and tried to gather his thoughts while they waited. The idea of taking Lady Lamont with him had been spontaneous; he hadn't really thought it through. Would it even be possible for the drone to take them both? What would they do with her when they got back to the mainland? In his heart he knew it was not only the right thing to do, but that potentially it gave them a lever over Lamont, and they were going to need all the tools at their disposal.

Three o'clock came and went and no drone appeared, but the wind dropped away and the night became strangely calm, as if the archipelago itself was holding its breath.

"What's that?" Lady Lamont pointed into the darkness.

"Where?"

"There, you see? It looks like an upside-down flying table, its legs in the air?"

Although he couldn't see it, there was no question as to what she was describing. Sure enough, the drone finally came out of the night and hovered in the air above them. It was large, the biggest drone Gillespie had seen, and had a rotor at each corner. It was constantly adjusting its position in the air as the occasional gust of wind funnelled through the cleft in the rock. Underneath was strapped a harness and he immediately started undoing the straps.

"You've got to go first." He said to Lady Lamont.

"No! You should, it is your friends that have done this, they'll want to see you, not me!"

Gillespie insisted and ushered Lady Lamont into the web of harnesses and started strapping her in. While they'd been waiting, he'd realised that whatever happened to him, the Republic needed to get rid of Lamont once and for all, and Lady Lamont was probably the only way they could do that. It wasn't about him anymore, or even about the MacNachtans. He cinched the last straps tight and stood back. As the drone rose in the air, Lady Lamont cried out and reached for him, but he couldn't hear what she was saying. The drone disappeared over the cliff edge and off into the night.

Gillespie felt a slight sinking feeling as the drone disappeared. Had he just given away his one ticket off the island? He paced the confined space of the shelf waiting for its return. As the minutes ticked by, they seemed to slow even further. He tried to calculate how far the drone could probably fly and at what speed. Surely, it would be back soon? The minutes ground past as he stood looking out at the ocean far below, the smashing surf on the rocks illuminated by the intermittent moonlight.

The first blow caught him totally off-guard, and he was flat on his back before he even realised what had happened. It was MacMartin! Gillespie tried to shield his head and face as blows rained down on him.

"You stupid cunt, you stupid cunt, you stupid fucking cunt. What have you done you stupid idiot!" MacMartin shouted as he pummelled Gillespie's prone body. "The drone was for you, not her! How could you be so stupid."

Gillespie lay dazed, unable to resist. MacMartin sensing he had nothing to fear from Gillespie stood up.

"You're a stupid man MacNachtan! What have you done! To me, to you, to this island. What do you think is going to happen when Lamont finds out his bird has flown? Do you think he will just shrug his shoulders? Or do you think he will come down here and torture every last motherfucking one of us until he finds out what happened. And what do you think he will do to me when he finds out...." MacMartin lashed out at

Gillespie's torso with his boot. "Fuck! How could I have been so stupid. What do I do, what do I do?"

MacMartin started talking to himself as he strode back and forth across the gully. Gillespie tried to rouse himself. He couldn't open one of his eyes. He wiped it with the back of his hand. It was wet with blood. His licked his broken lips; his mouth was dry, and it only made them hurt more. He rolled onto his front and tried to draw his knees up under him.

Suddenly, MacMartin grabbed Gillespie's feet by the ankles and started to drag him towards the cliff edge.

"It's your fault, you made me do this. You've left me with no choice. If only you had taken the drone like you were supposed to!"

In horror Gillespie realised what MacMartin was doing, and he scrabbled, desperately trying to grab onto anything to stop his inexorable progress towards the cliff edge and the void beyond, but MacMartin was too strong.

54 – Trawling St Kilda

Shonique scanned the sky. Despite the weak moonlight, she could see nothing beyond the everchanging roll of the swell as it swept past them. Daaku put them in a very slow trawling profile just outside the exclusion zone. When The Rose In June was lifted by the rollers she could just make out the peaks and cliffs of St Kilda in the distance. The jagged, impenetrable curtain of rock rose sheer out of the ocean. It seemed incredible that there could be anywhere in those cliffs for the drone to make the pick up.

She'd been rooted to the handrail ever since they'd launched the drone. It took much longer to fly the short distance to the cliffs than she'd thought possible. Alasdair stood at her shoulder concentrating hard as he steered it to its destination. If they hadn't had the precise geolocation, she doubted that he could've found the gully, the cliffs looked so uniform, a hermetic barrier against the Atlantic's relentless assault. His brow beaded with sweat as the drone slalomed between the folds in the cliffs and into the gully. It's infrared camera picked up the outline of two figures, a welcome confirmation that they'd found the right spot. The return journey seemed to take even longer, if that was possible, and she became impatient, the unbearable thought gripped her that if something went wrong now, if Gillespie fell in the water, that there could be no rescue. The black unforgiving water of the Atlantic swept by, untroubled by her anguish.

"It's nearly here." Nin said, standing by her shoulder and scanning the wave tops with infrared binoculars.

"There, look there!" He pointed. Shonique grabbed the binoculars, zooming into the orange and red bundle swinging beneath the drone. She couldn't believe it. They had done it! Their crazy plan had worked.

The drone slowed as it approached the ship, Alasdair concentrating hard as he inched it over the deck and gently lowered its precious cargo. Shonique reached out to undo the straps, and that's when it hit her. The slumped figure in the harness was not Gillespie. She screamed. Nin and Alasdair rushed to her side, undoing the rest of the straps and catching the woman as she fell out of the harness. Shonique stood over the slumped figure, her arms akimbo; "Who are you! What the fuck are you doing? Where's Gillespie? What've you done to him?"

Nin took her arm, "Calm down Shonique, stop shouting. Let the woman speak."

The woman had a wild look in her eye and clung to Alasdair's supporting arm.

"Back, back …. you must send it back." She mumbled.

"Send what back? The drone?"

The woman nodded, "Gillespie is waiting, you must send it back, before it is too late."

Alasdair and Nin supported her on either side as they took her into the wheelhouse. Shonique was sent to make a cup of tea. By the time she returned with a steaming mug, Alasdair and Nin were locked in a furious discussion and the woman sat dejected and alone. Shonique slid the mug along the table and took the woman's hand and gave it a squeeze. The woman took the mug, tentatively sipping the life restoring liquid.

Ignoring the raging argument going on above them, Shonique asked: "What's your name?"

"Coira, Coira Cameron." The woman stared into space. "At least that is who I used to be, many years ago. Now I'm known as Lady Lamont."

Shonique started. "You're not related to the Lamontation? John Lamont – the President?"

The woman's eyes flitted to Shonique's face, scanning her emotions, trying to read her.

"Yes, the very same. My husband of some twenty years. It was he who incarcerated me on that godforsaken rock."

Shonique couldn't believe what she was hearing: the Lamontation's wife, here? She stood up and grabbed at Nin's arm, trying to get his attention. But Nin brusquely wrenched it out of her grip. She put her hand on his shoulder, physically turning him away from Alasdair towards her.

"Don't ignore me Nin. Do you know who this woman is?"

Nin shrugged and was about to turn back to Alasdair, when Shonique tightened her grip on his shoulder digging in her fingers so he could not ignore her.

"Nin! Listen to me! She's Lamont's wife."

"Shonique, she could be the Pope for all I care right now. I am trying to figure out what the hell we do about Gillespie."

"What do you mean? Surely, you can just fly the drone back and pick him up? He's there waiting in the same spot."

"You would think so wouldn't you. If it wasn't for the fact that the charge on the drone's battery is now below

50%. It is highly likely that it will never make it back. Alasdair thinks we should just take the risk. I am of the view that it is better for Gillespie to be alive on St Kilda, however tough that might be, than dead in the Atlantic Ocean."

Shonique's head swam. To leave him now, after they'd come so far, seemed impossibly cruel. How could they have come so close. Her mind spun, and then came to a juddering halt like the wheels on a one-armed bandit. There was only one option and the certainty of the choice spread through her like a smothering blanket of calm. She looked at Alasdair and Nin, the resolution on her face leaving them in no doubt of the strength of her feelings:

"You've got to try. You can't leave him there. I have the casting vote. Whatever the risk, you've got to fly it back."

55 – Archie Cameron

It had already been a long night and the mass of glasses on the table stood in testimony to the craic. Charlie felt exhausted. Having to host so many unexpected guests without any help had meant running from pillar to post all night. He had emptied most of the contents of the freezer to cook up sufficient food to sate the ravenous men who were lounged around his house. He'd then brought out several cases of beer and a few bottles of Black Tower whisky, the cheaper blend, mind, not the single malt. He didn't know how long the Black Watch were going to be staying with him, but he didn't want them helping themselves to all the booze in the house; it made sense to give them what he could spare.

Archie Cameron had spent most of the evening avoiding him. To start with, Charlie had been quite flattered that Archie had chosen to stay at Elrig. As a schoolboy, Charlie had always had a bit of a crush on him and there'd been an awkward snog and grope at the end of the school prom. But Charlie could tell that Archie's heart wasn't really in it and to his disappointment Archie had soon staggered off back to his date for the night, the ineffably poised Laura Mackintosh. To be fair, Charlie hadn't given it any thought in the intervening years, but now that Archie was actually sat in his house, his testosterone-fuelled teenage libido, dormant for so long, had started to stir.

He poured two glasses of Black Tower, carefully adding a splash of water to each, and went to find Captain Cameron. Given the hour, most of the soldiers had already gone to sleep, but there were a few gathered around the fire in the sitting room, including Archie Cameron. As Charlie entered, he proffered the glass, which Archie took with a nod of gratitude. The two junior soldiers suddenly looked a little sheepish and made their excuses, leaving Charlie and Archie alone.

"Well, isn't this just like old times!" Charlie ventured, taking the opportunity to have a proper look at Archie for the first time that evening. He was older than the picture in Charlie's mind's eye but given the intervening years and all the miles that was no real surprise. Crinkle cut crow's feet now radiated around each tawny-brown eye and his forehead was creased with a few deep lines, but the cheek bones and hump-backed nose – broken by Seumais Mackinlay's caman in Year Five – were still there. As was the sweep of blond hair, although much shorter and more severe than the boyish fringe of his youth.

The whisky pooled in Charlie's belly, its warmth radiating outwards. They spraffed for the next few hours, catching up on the news of their respective lives; reminiscing on teachers and school friends; who had married who, how many children did they have, who'd died. It was good to catch up. As the level in the bottle fell, the conversation became more animated, and Archie Cameron's stiff militaristic demeanour melted into twinkly-eyed conviviality. Charlie felt impossibly attracted to him.

Charlie stood up to tend the fire, chucking on another couple of logs and prodding the embers with the poker to revive the flames. He wanted to keep this moment going forever. He sat back down, this time on the sofa next to Archie. He put his hand on Archie's knee. He gave it a squeeze and started to trace his finger up Archie's thigh. Archie smiled and leant forward….

….and stopped. A puzzled look came on his face and he reached inside his jacket to take out his phone. Distractedly, he swiped open the message. That moment, as beautiful as a soap bubble in the summer sun, popped and vanished. Charlie sat back. It was after three in the morning, who could possibly be calling? He studied Archie's face; he was still handsome, he still had it. Just as he was fantasizing about kissing those thick, full lips, the expression on Archie's face changed from one of slightly addled geniality to flint-faced horror. He stood up. He paced the room, the anguish on his face writ large.

"What's the matter? Come and sit back down. Have another sip of whisky." Charlie tried his emollient best but was getting nowhere - Archie had evaporated and only Captain Cameron was left.

"You need to leave. Leave now."

"What do you mean? This is my house. Where else would I go?" Charlie felt his pulse starting to accelerate, something was clearly wrong. Archie Cameron's demeanour had changed utterly. Charlie stood up and went over to him.

"What's the matter? What's got into you? One minute I'm about to fuck you by the fire and the next you are telling me to leave my own house. What the hell is going on?"

Archie Cameron didn't speak, but turned his phone to Charlie, showing him the screen. Charlie read the message. They were orders, from Major Robertson, the words chilled his blood.

You are hereby ordered to fall on the rebels, the MacNachtans of Dunderave, and execute all under seventy. None must escape.

You must do this at 5 a.m. precisely. I will come with reinforcements, but do not wait for me. This is by the President's special command, for the good and safety of the country. No favour or quarter must be given or else you will be charged as a rebel and mutineer. Do not fail in this task.

"You've got to go. Get out of here."

"I can't just leave, what about all the others – are you really going to murder everyone in their sleep? This is madness, what the hell has got into you!"

Archie Cameron grabbed him by the shoulders and shook him.

"Don't you understand you idiot. They are going to wipe you and your friends from the face of the earth. You have got to get out now. Hide in the hills until this is over. I can't protect you. You must leave."

"Oh my god, what is the time?" Charlie looked at his watch – it was nearly 4 a.m. He only had an hour. He had to warn Kirstie and the Clan before it was too late!

56 – Gully of the Flaming Eye

MacMartin's wiry strength was too much for Gillespie and, try as he might, he couldn't shake himself loose from his iron grip. He tried kicking and twisting his body, digging his fingers into the stony ground, grabbing onto the scrawny heather that clung to the cliff face, but none of it made any difference; he was at the edge and there was nothing more he could do. MacMartin kicked his legs over into the void. Gillespie clung to the rocky lip of the cliff face, the sharp rock digging into his fingers. The wind pulled at him, his kilt like a sail catching the stiffening breeze. MacMartin loomed over him shrouded in darkness, he stood on Gillespie's hands and very deliberately started to grind his boot, slowly, as if to savour the moment. Gillespie screamed, the pain in his fingers unbearable. He desperately clung on; his mind completely focused on the single objective of keeping his fingers clasped around that rocky stump.

A flash of movement passed overhead. A shout came from MacMartin whose boot was suddenly removed. Gillespie's fingers found new grip as the blood flowed back into them. He scrabbled at the cliff edge, hauling himself back over the lip. The moonlight illuminated MacMartin on the rocky shelf, blood pouring down his face, as he thrashed his arms at the drone which now hovered above him just out of reach. Gillespie looked around, there were no obvious weapons. The bag with the lambing knife was on the far side of the shelf, beyond MacMartin, he would never be able to reach it. As he pulled himself upright against the craggy rock face, a loose stone came away in his hand. It wasn't big, about the size of a tin can, but it was heavy. Gillespie turned. MacMartin was still distracted by the drone, which made small darting manoeuvres as if it was going to try and hit him again. Gillespie launched himself across the shelf, bringing the rock down on the side of MacMartin's head with all his remaining might. MacMartin staggered. Gillespie hit him again, and again. MacMartin fell to the ground and Gillespie was on him, pounding the rock into his head and face until there was no more resistance from the crumpled body.

Gillespie rocked back on his haunches, surveying the bloody mess. He tossed the rock to one side and grabbed MacMartin by the ankles, dragging him to the cliff edge. Then, with no more ceremony than a casual boot in the midriff, he pushed MacMartin over the lip and down the precipitous drop to the ocean far below. No sound came, except for the whistle of the wind through the gully. Then he searched for the bloodstained rock, St Kilda's one and only gift to him. He weighed it in his hand before throwing it as hard as he could out into the void. Using the torch, he scoured the shelf for signs of the struggle. In the dark it was hard to see, but he scuffed over any obvious blood stains that he could find; it would have to do. Grabbing the lambing bag, he rummaged in it for the knife which he stuffed in his stocking – you never know when you might need a blade - the rest he would dump in the ocean.

He signalled to the drone which hovered lower to allow him to undo the harness. Stabbing pains shot up his arms as his bloodied and broken fingers tried to undo the clips. For a moment he thought that he wasn't going to be able to press hard enough. He screamed in pain and frustration; the clip came apart. He buckled himself in and without pausing for an instant the drone sped away, lifting him up and over the cliff edge before swooping down towards the black graven waters far below.

His adrenalin spiked as the water rushed towards him. Was the drone out of control? Just as he braced himself for the impending impact, the drone steadied itself into a stable flight profile with his feet suspended only twenty feet above the mighty Atlantic. If he hadn't been so terrified, he might have enjoyed his ten-minute flight over the waves, as it was, he spent most of it screaming into the wind, terrified that a passing wave was going to catch him by the feet and drag him down into the watery dark. When he wasn't looking at the waves beneath his feet, he was scanning the horizon ahead trying to see the ship. With the rise and fall of the rollers, it was hard to see anything that looked like a boat despite the feeble moonlight. The flight seemed to go on for hours, his desperation growing the further away from St Kilda they flew.

Suddenly, out of the blackness, came a bright light, low to the water. It went out almost as soon as it had appeared. It was the ship! At the instant that he saw it, the drone started to lose altitude, its flight path becoming lumpier as if it was consumed by hiccups. The waves rose up towards his feet. He lifted his legs, trying to keep them out of the water, his thigh muscles burning with the effort. But the drone continued to lose height and soon he was being dragged through the swell, bouncing from one wave top to the next. They were almost at the ship. Gillespie tried to pull himself up on the harness, but the drone's battery was now spent and with a graceless dive he and the drone plummeted into the ocean.

The shock of the water temperature constricted his chest, he gasped. The drone, which only a moment earlier been lighter than air, was now as heavy as lead, and as it sank beneath the waves it dragged him down with it. The water closed over his head. It was black and icy cold. He scrabbled at the harness trying to free himself, but his fingers didn't have the strength to open the clip. The silvery surface above receded in slow motion; he was falling into darkness. The knife! The lambing knife, was it still in his stocking? He brought his leg up, fumbling for the hilt. His fingers closed around it. The pressure in his lungs was becoming unbearable. In desperation he held the harness with one hand while he sawed with the other, working the blade away at the tough nylon webbing. The blackness of the ocean was all around him now. A voice in the back of his mind urged him to let go, to release himself to the deep, how bad could it be? But, just at that moment, the webbing finally parted, and he left that thought behind to sink into the ocean with the remains of the drone as he kicked with the last of his strength back towards the silvery light far above.

He broke the surface, his lungs tearing chunks out of the precious air. He was disoriented, where was the boat? Would they come for him? Could they find him? He gasped and trod water, the cold leeching away his remaining energy; blackness was crowding in on him. Then, the sound of an engine, voices, torchlight, hands and arms reaching, pulling, dragging, hard orange rubber, ropes, blurry faces, shouting, slapping, kissing, chest thumping, whining, clear!, kissing, more kissing, warm lips, hot breath, a face, close up, sharp, Shonique.

57 – Rousing the Clan

Charlie raced outside, only pausing to grab his coat, his broadsword and his phone. He took the front steps two at a time but stopped dead at the bottom. Where was the Kat? Where was the fucking Kat? *Fuckfuckfuckfuckwhereisthefuckingmotherfuckingcuntingbastardkat!* The yard was empty except for the Black Watch's vehicles. He staggered as if struck in the face; of course, Nin had taken the bloody Kat to Connel to pick up The Rose in June. His fevered mind flipped through the neighbours; did any of them have Kats, where was the nearest fucking Kat? What the hell was he going to do? He started running up the glen; Deidre MacNutt had a Kat, she was probably the closest, but was still a good mile away. As he ran, he started making calls. Most calls went straight to voicemail, it was four in the morning after all. How was he going to alert the Clan and save them from being murdered in their beds if they didn't answer the goddam phone!

Finally, he had a bit of luck, Fiona answered the phone with an almost inaudible mumble. "Who the fuck is this and don't you know what the fucking time is?"

"Fiona! Thank god. The Black Watch have been sent to murder us. At 5 a.m.! The whole Clan. You've got to get out of your house. I am trying to call the Clan to wake them, but their phones are all on bloody silent! You've got to get Clachan awake."

"That's absurd, why the hell would they do that?"

"It's Lamont, for fuck's sake, he doesn't need a reason, he's a psychopath. You can't fight the Watch;

you need to get out. Take Mara and whoever else you can and hide on Beinn Bhuidhe, anywhere. Go now!"

Swiping the call shut, he next called Don MacNachtan who like any self-respecting musician was clearly still awake and playing a few tunes too judging by the noise in the background. Charlie explained the situation.

"What the fuck do we do? We can't possibly get round all the houses, and if people have their phones off they'll never hear us. There are too many houses." Charlie was desperate.

There was a long pause, Charlie began to think that he might have lost the connection, but Don's steady voice came back. "Leave it to me, I have an idea." And with that he was gone.

Charlie was almost at Deirdre's house now. It was black as night with not a chink of light showing. He didn't know if there were any Black Watch inside, but he was going to have to take the risk. He hammered on the door, no response. He tried calling, again no answer. He ran round the house and tried the back door; it was locked and there was no key that he could find.

Fuck!whydidpeoplehavetolocktheirfuckinghousesallthetimewhyc ouldn'ttheyleavethekeyunderarocklikeanysensibleperson!

There was nothing else for it, he scouted the yard and found the biggest stone he could and hefted it through Deirdre's bedroom window. The light came on, and with it a barrage of shouts and abuse that would have turned any sailor's blood cold.

"Deirdre. Its Charlie, from up the road, you've got to let me in right now!"

Minutes later, having negotiated the Kat key from

Deidre and convinced her to take to the hill in whatever she could grab, he was tearing down Glen Shira in her antiquated Kat. He looked at his watch – where the hell had the time gone! It was coming up to 4.50 a.m.; they were running out of time. He called Brighid as he turned the corner at the bottom of the glen.

"Brighid, where are you? Please don't tell me you are at Stronshira? Are you with MacCailean Mòr?"

"Yes, I am, as it happens. Why the hell you are calling me at this time?"

Charlie gabbled at her, explaining the situation, urging her to alert MacCailean Mòr and to try and reach as many Clan as she could. She was gone in an instant; he knew he could reply on her.

He reached the bottom of the glen and pulled into Stronshira. Ahead of him in a blaze of headlights was Don standing on the back of his Kat behind the Clan's fearsome sound system. At that very moment, Don and his son started playing Women of the Glen, a well-known lament, on the bagpipes at full volume. The sound pierced the quiet of the night with a keening call of warning which Charlie thought would surely waken the Clan dead from the Dubh Loch cemetery, let alone the residents of Stronshira. As the residents started to stumble from their doorways wondering what the hell was happening, the pair tore into MacNachtans awa', a creach tune from cattle raiding times that all MacNachtan children were brought up on. The message these tunes delivered was unequivocal and at the volume that Don was playing unmissable too. Driven by the music, the residents of Stronshira started to gain momentum, scattering in every direction and dispersing into the pitch black of the highland night.

An Tùraidh Dubh, the Clan's intranet network, was now alive with messages and warnings that beeped and buzzed his phone every few seconds. His job at Stronshira done, Don gunned the engine of his Kat and sped off along the lochside with Charlie in pursuit. They peeled off at Dunderave which stood shrouded in blackness. Charlie swiped open the gates and they drove into the Outer Ward; the Black Watch's vehicles had vanished. Charlie raced for the Castle door, he had to get to Kirstie.

The Castle door was wide open. Charlie ran inside and up the steep entrance stairs. He burst into the Red Banner Hall; it was empty. Where was everyone?! He went up the stairs to the Chief's private apartments, where Kirstie slept. That was where he found the first body; Caty, one of the Castle's longstanding staff, dead on the floor, blood pooled around her corpse. Crying with anguish he pressed on, bursting into Kirstie's bedroom. She was lying on the bed, a single black bullet hole in her forehead, the pillow behind awash with blood. He was too late.

Hewastoofuckinglatethefuckingbastardshadkilledher.

He wept. After all she'd been through, after all she'd done for the Clan, it was bitter beyond words that she should be murdered in her sleep. She'd had the heart of a lion. He took Kirstie's broken hands in his before folding them across her dead body. But now was not the time to pause, he had to warn the others.

In a daze he toured the other rooms in the Castle, finding several more bodies, all loyal staff and Clan members who had been on duty at the Castle that night. They'd clearly not received any warning in time. Distraught, he left the Castle and returned to the Outer

Ward. Don could see from Charlie's face that they had been too late.

Charlie got back into his Kat to drive to Clachan while he sent Don away to finish rousing the more remote steadings. His heart was in his boots the whole way. Would Fiona have been able to wake the village? How many of the Clan would still be left alive?

Charlie caught up with the Black Watch just outside Clachan; their long line of vehicles queued up on the Wade. Clachan was in chaos. Groups of heavily armed men were standing around their vehicles surrounded by shouting groups of women and children. The MacNachtan men were nowhere to be seen, but Charlie felt certain they were there in the shadows, just out of sight beyond the reach of the headlights, watching and waiting. He pushed his way through the tumult looking for Major Robertson. He found him in a group of soldiers outside Tam MacNachtan's house; the old soak was lying dead on his doorstep. Charlie's anger was ice cold. Tam MacNachtan, everyone's friend, the heart and soul of the Two Stags, a man that was never sober long enough to harm a fly but never drunk enough to want to. What purpose could his death possibly serve? What harm could he do to anyone? Charlie took out his phone and started to film. He strode up to Major Robertson, barely able to control his rage.

"What the hell are you doing, you murderer!"

Major Robertson turned to look at him, his eyes lizard cold.

"Here's another one lads, who wants to deal with this traitor. Corporal Finlayson, you may have the honour."

Charlie froze. He couldn't believe what he was hearing.

"You are going to murder me here? In cold blood! Have you gone quite mad? What the hell has got into you? The Black Watch is the upholder of the law, not Lamont's assassin. Think of your Cliù, the Watch's Cliù; can't you see what you are doing?"

"We are just following orders, orders from the very top. You MacNachtan scum are the problem, and we are here to solve that once and for all. Corporal, carry on."

Major Robertson stared calmly at Charlie while the soldier unholstered his sidearm and slipped off the safety catch.

Charlie's mind went blank. He held out the phone in front of him like a shield, filming Corporal Finlayson as he raised the pistol and pointed it straight at his face.

"Wait!"

A voice came from the crowd. A little girl's voice. It was Mara, Fiona's daughter. She pushed her way through the press of bodies and put herself between Corporal Finlayson and Charlie. Barefoot and in her pyjamas, she put her hands around the gun, pressing her thumbs over the muzzle as if they alone could stop the bullet. She turned to Major Robertson.

"You don't understand, Charlie is not even a MacNachtan, if you kill him it will be murder! See?"

She took Charlie's free arm and rotated it so that the panel of tartan on his forearm was uppermost.

"He's a Farquharson. His mother is the Chief and everything. She sits in the Comhairle and if you murder her son she will be very angry!"

Major Robertson twitched, but said nothing. He leant forward and looked closely at Charlie's arm. The dark green and blue tartan was overlaid with red and yellow stripes, it was a world away from the scarlet, azure and green of the MacNachtan tartan; there could be no confusion. He nodded at Corporal Finlayson, who lowered his pistol.

Suddenly the momentum of the moment changed. The Black Watch seemed unsure of themselves and the crowd of MacNachtan women and children swarmed around them, driving them back to their vehicles under a barrage of insults and curses. As the soldiers retreated, clods of mud and stones started to be thrown, dustbins and bags of rubbish, anything that came to hand. The soldiers ran for the safety of their vehicles all thought of their mission abandoned. Major Robertson tried to rally them, but their heart wasn't in it.

Charlie continued to film, following Major Robertson and demanding to know why he'd murdered innocent citizens in their sleep. Major Robertson clearly didn't relish this and tried to hide his face with his hand as he got into his vehicle, hissing at Charlie to stop and that he was an officer of the Watch and was just following orders. The mass of vehicles now ground into life, and, as if spurred by the realisation of their terrible crimes, sped out of Clachan taking the Arrochar Wade away into the night.

The rise of the sun brought no cheer. As if in mockery of the Clan's mood, the sun rose out of the jagged peaks of the Arrochar Alps a cheerful cadmium yellow; big, fat and full of spring's potential. From where he stood, Charlie could hear willow warblers and song thrush, tree pipits and dunnock, while overhead the crossbills cracked pinecones in the treetops. It seemed a world away from the bloody reality that the Clan had woken up to. Kirstie, Caty, Peigi and Simidh were all found murdered at the Castle, Niall and the whole Scardan MacNaught family had been killed in their sleep in Glen Shira, and Muireall and Mànas MacNachtan had been caught at their remote steading over by Brannie. Last but by no means least, was the sorry figure of Tam, gunned down while opening his door in the night, no doubt selflessly thinking that it was someone in need of help or a dram; his house a refuge whatever the hour.

In truth, it could have been much worse. If Charlie hadn't raised the alarm then hundreds more could easily have been murdered. After all, that had been Lamont's plan, their total annihilation. The Clan wandered from house to house, as if in a daze, trying to take it all in. Their numbers growing as Clan members emerged from their hiding places, swelling the throng that shuffled from one murder scene to the next. With the growing strength of the sun came a profound anger that ripped from person to person, as white hot as any contagion. Charlie thought about trying to calm the crowd before it did something foolish but decided against it. Their anger was just, it needed to be expressed, to be vented, before it exploded.

It was LeroyMar that gave a focus to the angry mob, standing to address the crowd by the lochside.

"My dear Clan, what a bitter morning this is. That we should live to see the day that the Government of our own country should turn on us for no reason other than the psychotic vanity of one man. This horror must not stand. We cannot allow him to destroy this country, our nation, with his evil and twisted vision. We must show the world the true meaning of the Lamontation's word. We must show the citizens of Oban and the Republic what has happened here tonight. Because what happened here, could happen anywhere, to anyone and at any time. Is this the country that our forefathers fought for? Is this the future that we believe in and are prepared to accept? Are we to just sit here and allow them to slaughter us when we have taken them into our homes, fed and sheltered them? This horror must not stand! We will not allow them to murder us in our glens far from the heat and light of the city. We will not be out of sight and out of mind. We will take our dead to the city, to the people in power and show them the consequences of their actions; the old, the young, the innocent and sleeping that they murdered! Let them look on the corpses of our Clan, no longer friends and family, no longer the best craic or the wisest word, now so much dead meat to the grinder that Lamont has made out of this sweet nation. This horror must not stand! Come with me, bring our dead friends on one last journey, let us go to Oban. Let them try and stop us. Are we not MacNachtans! Does the Black Tower still stand?"

The fevered crowd shouted their affirmation back at the top of their voices and all turned to fetch their vehicles for the drive to Oban and justice.

Charlie took off one of Elrig's doors which he lashed to the back of the Kat to give a flat and elevated platform on which to lay Kirstie's body. Together with Brighid, he gently and respectfully laid her body out, putting the blood-stained sheets and pillows around her as they had been on her death bed. It was a vivid recreation of the murder scene. The other victims were similarly prepared and, once all were ready, the convoy set off at a snail's pace towards Oban.

As they passed through the countryside, onlookers began to crowd the sides of the Wade, peering at the dead and the ever-growing line of vehicles behind. The MacNachtans were a small Clan but even so when laid out nose to tail they made an impressive cavalcade as they wound their way up the Oban Wade. Their convoy was growing exponentially as neighbouring Clans now showed their support and joined them; Campbells, MacArthurs, MacLachlans, MacFarlanes and MacMillans, MacTavishes and MacNabs. By the time they rounded Loch Awe the line of vehicles stretched as far as the eye could see.

Charlie could not understand why their route was unopposed. Surely, by now Lamont would know what had happened to his plan. Charlie expected a roadblock at the least, a further and perhaps deadly confrontation with the Black Watch. But nothing slowed or stopped their inexorable progress towards the capital. As they entered the suburbs, quiet crowds started to gather on the pavements to watch. Occasional shouts of "I Hope in God" came from the onlookers, as well as snatched bars of Strong Stands the Black Tower. The citizens of the Republic were showing their solidarity and with that realisation came a surge of confidence in their cause.

They arrived at the ferry terminal car park. Above them, the Righaltas brooded on the hill, imperious, aloof, its granite arcades immutable and unmoving. The town was quiet, no Black Watch were visible. Charlie wondered for a brief moment if this was all part of Lamont's plan, to sucker them into a nice killing field – the car park was the perfect spot. But it was too late to worry about that now.

As he parked the Kat by the quay, he saw the battered, deep bellied silhouette of The Rose In June tied up alongside. His stomach fell away. With the drama of the previous night, he'd totally forgotten about the rescue mission. He grabbed his phone to call Nin, only to see there were 15 missed calls and a blizzard of increasingly angry texts. He got out and ran along the quay. There on the aft deck was the unmistakable figure of Shonique, then he saw Nin and Alasdair – where was Gillespie? Had they got Gillespie? After Kirstie's death he couldn't bear the thought that they might have lost Gillespie too. He bounded across the gangway and into Nin's arms. They kissed, and hugged, and kissed again. It felt as though a lifetime had passed between them.

"Where's Gillespie. Please God tell me that you managed to get Gillespie."

"He's sleeping, below. He's had quite a journey, but he's OK." Nin replied. "When we heard what had happened and that you were all heading to Oban, we decided to come straight here."

Alasdair came over to shake his hand. "That's quite a crowd you have assembled." Alasdair pointed at the car park which was now full to bursting with more and more people crowding down the hill and along the waterfront. "What happens now?"

"I don't know to be honest. It seemed like the right thing to do, to come here, to show the nation and the world what just happened. I think we should catch up with the others who seem to be setting things up."

Charlie went back ashore and pushed through the throng to Brighid and Don who seemed to have the logistics in hand. They'd lined up all the Kats holding the MacNachtan dead along the waterfront with the victims prominently visible to the ever-growing crowd. Don had also set up the Clan sound system. Thousands and thousands of people were now crammed into the ferry port, along every available space on the promenade and up the hill. The media had also arrived and were setting up their cameras to record the scene. Don thrust the microphone in Charlie's hand. "Say something for god's sake, I'm no good with words, I just do the music. You've got to say something to the crowd."

Dumbly, Charlie took the microphone and stood on the roof of the Kat. He looked out at the crowd. He'd never seen so many people in one place and the crowd was still growing.

"My dear friends and fellow Gaels. I can't tell you what it means to see so many of you here today. I know that you share my outrage at the terrible crime committed last night by our leaders. The leaders that sit up there," at which he pointed at the hulk of the Righaltas. "Are we sheep to be slaughtered? Are our lives so cheap and our rights, hard won over many centuries, cast aside so easily? There is a sickness in this country. But it is not the sickness of clanship. It is not the sickness of our heritage or bonds of family and friendship. It is not even the sickness of Cliù, although god knows that is not without its issues. The sickness lies there, in that building." He pointed up at the Righaltas. "I name that sickness John Lamont. John Lamont of the Sorrows, The Lamontation, our President. Never was a man better named. You may well ask yourself, how has he risen to rule our Republic? We may never know, but we do not need to tolerate his yoke of arbitrary cruelty. How low are we that we suffer his boot on our necks? It is time for us to rise up, rise up I tell you and cast him out."

The crowd that had been listening calmly now erupted with shouts and cheers of approval. Charlie gestured to Don to approach the microphone. "We will now hear a lament for the dead of last night and while we listen I urge you to think about how we can build a new and better Republic on the bones of the old. Our future is in our hands, let us grasp it now!"

Don started to play Grey John MacNachtan of Dunderave's Lament, the tune that was traditionally played at the passing of every MacNachtan Chief. A tune that had been played far too regularly in recent times. The tune held the crowd with its slow and brooding power, building in momentum as the variations of the pìobaireachd swelled in complexity. But instead of stopping at the end, Don segued straight into A Flame of Wrath for Squinting Patrick, its arrhythmic, halting opening metamorphosing into a fully-fledged roar of pain that flayed the crowd's emotions in a torrent of notes.

As he came to a close, the crowd bayed with anger,

the mood was turning ugly. The families of the dead now took it in turn to address the crowd, to describe their loved one in life and their fate in death. One after another they came and shared their story while the scene was live streamed to the nation and the world. When all the victims had been spoken for, Charlie turned to the crowd and shouted: "Who here still wants to bear witness to the cruelty of John Lamont? Who here will share their suffering?"

Above the hubbub a small but carrying voice shouted from the quayside: "I will."

The crowd turned to look for the speaker. Charlie hadn't been expecting this. He'd meant it as more of a rhetorical flourish at the end of the obituaries. But if others wanted to share their pain at Lamont's hands, that was fine by him. A haggard late middle-aged woman all dressed in black pushed through the crowd before clambering up onto the roof of the Kat next to him. He handed her the microphone. She turned to the crowd.

"My name is Coira and for the last two decades I have borne a name, a cruel name, the cruel name of a cruel man. And that man is John Lamont."

The crowd gasped.

"Yes, that's right. I was married to John Lamont for more than twenty years and what did he do to repay my love and the children I bore him? It's a sorry tale. When he tired of me, he had me taken to St Kilda, like a common criminal, and has had me held there for the last seven years against my will. A prisoner of conscience some might say, except he has no conscience. I'm shocked but not surprised to hear his latest crimes. He has all the compassion of a serpent. He must be stopped.

He will never change. He cannot be chided or browbeaten. He is merciless and cruel. He has no place in our nation, let alone at its heart and head. We don't need to beg from his hand what is ours by right already. Let us go, go now, to the Righaltas, our Righaltas, bought in blood and left to us by the Liberator. Let us go and cut out this cancer, cut it out from our nation, now and forever!"

The crowd roared its approval and immediately surged up the hill towards the Righaltas high above.

59 – The Moment of Truth

David Brown's face was grim as he strode through the corridors of the Righaltas towards the President's suite of offices. The news of the massacre had reached him at dawn, and he'd been working the phone ceaselessly since then making sure that everything was in place. Now he had to face Lamont. He stopped outside the doors to gather his thoughts. He noted that the Gallowglass that normally stood guard had vanished. Good, that was important; it showed that the Black Watch were no longer prepared to defend Lamont, he was running out of options. He didn't bother to knock but strode straight in.

Lamont was sat behind the Liberator's desk. He appeared shrunken, hollowed out, the scale of the desk making him look childlike, not magisterial. He turned to look at Brown, his needle-sharp eyes pinning him, a merciless rage burning inside.

"You should leave."

"What do you mean, leave? I'm the President of the Republic, I do not just leave because some lackey asks me to, or even because a riled-up mob is at the door. Where is the Watch? I want them to suppress that crowd, with live rounds if necessary, whatever it takes. They are rebels and revolutionaries that are trying to overthrow the State. They must be destroyed."

Brown felt his own anger rising; he tried to keep calm but the quaver in his voice gave away his true emotions.

"You are not the State. You are a murderous psychopath that has bludgeoned and bullied your way to that seat. But you are not the State. The Republic has been created by countless thousands who have given their service and their blood in the building of this nation. A nation for the Gael, free of outside oppression, a nation that safeguards our land and culture for future generations. You are not that State. Little did I know, that when I turned down your offer to massacre our own citizens in their beds, under trust, that you would press ahead and besmirch the good name of the Black Watch, the defender of our rights and liberties and in the process that you would drag our nation's name so low in the gutter of infamy. How could you have ordered so callous an act? You hear that shouting outside? Yes, that is the mob, and they are coming to tear you apart with their bare hands. They understand the meaning of your justice and that is what they will give you and nothing more!"

Fear now flashed over Lamont's face. He turned to the window, scanning the growing throng as they tried to force their way into the Righaltas. "Where are the Watch? Why is there no one here to defend me?"

"They've come to their senses. They'll not protect you. Now you must leave or pay the ultimate price."

Lamont stood at the window. Far below the doors of the Righaltas were being forced open by the mob. They would not hold much longer. Brown thought for a moment that he would come at him with his sgian dubh. If looks could kill, then Lamont's stare alone would have been enough to put him in the ground.

Lamont hissed. "You will pay! By god I will make you pay you jumped up little office clerk. I will skin you alive and feed you to yourself piece by piece. I'll make you beg for death. You'll see, I will have my revenge! I trusted you. I made you my partner! We could have achieved so much together. You will pay, you will pay!"

And with that, Lamont scurried sideways from the room, for all the world like a crab or spider dashing for the safety of its burrow. Brown didn't follow. Instead, he started gathering the papers off the desk. He wanted to collect as much evidence as he could before the mob arrived. He tucked Lamont's computer under one arm and a bag of papers under the other and set off for the entrance.

The hall was empty, the marble floor echoed to his footsteps as he walked past the great stone of Dunadd that stood between the two chambers of the parliament, the very source of authority for the Head of State. He hoped the next President to step into that ancient stone footprint would be more worthy of the rank. The entrance doors were bulging under the relentless assault from outside. It was only a matter of time before the mob broke them down. He went to the card reader and swiped them open. Surprised by the sudden release of tension, the leaders of the mob fell through them into a pile on the floor. The releasing of the pressure and the removal of the crowd's focus left a moment of calm for David Brown to fill. He raised his arms, shouting at the top of his voice.

"He has gone. The Lamontation has fled. We are free once more!"

The crowd was stunned; his words like oil on troubled waters calmed the tumult of emotion. For a few moments, the crowd stood dumbly wondering what to do. Then a cry came from outside; a helicopter could be heard taking off from the roof. Fists were raised once more and curses cast at the departing aircraft as it swooped low over the capital, buzzing the crowd once, before turning to the South East and disappearing. The scream of pipes filled the air as Ewen MacEunraig, the official Piper to the President, appeared at the entrance playing The Black Bear with such ferocity it was as if the tune itself was chasing Lamont over the hills.

With their animus vanished, the mood of the mob turned from focused rage to joy and the streets of Oban turned into a wild impromptu celebration. The good natured, bacchanalian scenes made it hard for David Brown to get to his home. But when he'd finally pushed his way through the cheering tumult, drinking umpteen mouthfuls of whisky and exchanging kisses and hugs of joy from all and sundry, he was relieved to be able to leave it all behind. He shut his front door, carefully putting Lamont's papers and computer in the safe. He would start building the case for impeachment tomorrow, but today was a day for justice and reckoning; it was a day to savour.

60 – Bloodline

In the end, the result of the vote for the new Chief was not a surprise. After all, he'd been the only candidate. Deep down, Gillespie wasn't sure how he felt about his sudden elevation to such a position of authority. Both Alexander and Kirstie had seemed worthy Chiefs, well suited to leading the Clan during difficult times. When Nin announced his candidature and credentials to the assembled Clan at Dunderave, he'd made much of Gillespie's sanguinary connection to Duncan Tapaidh and the line of Chiefs of old. But Gillespie didn't think that was why he was voted in with such unanimity. Rather, that after the massacre and the storming of the Righaltas there'd been a shift in mood, in the Clan as well as the nation. People were ready for a new way, a new vision of what the future should hold. That vision did not just reject the past but embraced it fondly while calmly looking ahead. For Gillespie there was an advantage in that he had no vested interests, he was dispassionate and level-headed; only interested in the wellbeing of the Clan. Similarly, for the nation, David Brown, the descendant of outsiders, brought a measured and authoritative dignity to the role of President. With no Clan to promote, he could make sure that the pork barrel of Republic politics was shared around equally.

A calm settled on the nation, the calm after the storm, when everyone that had been through the tumult placed even greater value on peace than before. Civility broke out like a national contagion, even among the hitherto ever-squabbling Chiefs in the Comhairle.

Ancient enmities and arguments were set aside, as all came together to reflect on how close they'd come to losing what really mattered. Their nation and way of life had hung in the balance, but it had been saved. Now it needed to be nurtured.

In sweet revenge, Lady Lamont returned to Castle Ascog, asserting her rights as the wife of the Chief. She emptied the Lamontation's dungeons and reshaped the Clan Lamont in an altogether more altruistic form. That she met so little resistance spoke volumes of how sick his own Clan were of Lamont's predations. By taking away his powerbase she also ensured that Lamont had no levers on which to pull from his exile in Edinburgh. Gillespie imagined Lamont's impotent fury; vengeance was certainly a dish best served cold.

The last months had been immeasurably hard on the Clan, but the MacNachtans had endured; the fire they'd passed through knitting them tighter than ever. His first act as Chief was to appoint Fiona as the Head of the Gaming business. There was no question she had the skills and expertise to take over from where Kirstie had left off. He made Don MacNachtan his Seanchaidh, knowing that he would never be without excellent music and wise counsel. LeroyMar became Curaidh Mòr, his bodyguard and Head of the Black Tower Company, while Brighid, Nin, Charlie, Archie Beaton and Shonique made up his inner council. He would need their guidance.

He thought of Antrim and the remains of his home there. He knew that he would never go back. He resolved to lease the farm to Eamon and Kate; let them make a go of it. But he wouldn't sell. In some ways it was only right to keep a MacNachtan foothold on both sides of the Irish Sea, it had been that way for many centuries, why change it now.

Shonique wandered the stairs and corridors of Dunderave, making plans and choosing colours. She tried to get him interested and involved, but he was quite happy for her to have her head; she knew what she wanted, and he wouldn't know where to start. The old castle was coming back to life. After having almost been burned down and stolen from the Clan the building now seemed to appreciate the rightful order being restored, its honeyed stone glowing with warmth and cheer. He wondered how it would feel when the screams of a tiny infant arrived to shatter the peace of the night. Surely, it would be relieved. After all, it had heard such disruption many times before in its long history. The cries of a baby signified continuity and the future, something the old building could only welcome. Shonique was beginning to show, and was basking in the glow of pregnancy, but that did not slow her down as she made all the arrangements for the post-election party. He enjoyed watching her dragooning Dolina and her team as they decked out the Hall of the Red Banner and the Outer Ward to make it a celebration for the Clan to remember.

After the votes had been cast and the feast despatched, came the music. The Red Banner Band tore into reel after reel, the four-to-the-floor thump of a thousand feet shaking the walls to their foundations. The infectious joy seeped into the stones and filled the air as the Clan gathered all-hands round, the heughs raising the roof as the lead couples dashed down the sets, the pulse of the band digging into the tunes, lifting the crowd on a rush of adrenalin: Reel of the Red

Banner, Dornoch Links, Edgefauld House, Dr Morrison's Seven Thistles, The Secret of Duncan Tapaidh's Sporran, tune after tune poured over the dancers. Gillespie caught Shonique's hand, their thumbs and palms interlocking, an unbreakable bond. He held her eyes in his as the room span around them, two joined as one. The tune changed and they broke apart, casting off in the set. He first turned Brigid and then Fiona, then thumbed his nose at Charlie and Nin, before catching Shonique's outstretched arm and turning her double-handed, elbows tight and head back. As they span he felt them leave the earth and rise in the air over the tumultuous floor below; how he wished this moment could go on for ever and ever.

Glossary

Alasdair nan Sgàilean - Alasdair of the Shadows
Àrd-Bhritheamhand - High Adjudicator
Beinn /Bheinn - Hill (there are no mountains in the Republic)
Cailleach – In Gaelic mythology the Cailleach is an aged crone, goddess of winter and weather
Canun - The honour code of the Republic
Canntaireachd – The sung notation of Gaelic music, especially Pìobaireachd
Cateran – Bandit
Ceann – Roof, also as in protection
Claidheamh dà Làimh - Two-handed sword
Cliù - Honour
Comhairle - Council of Chiefs
Creach – Cattle raid
Cùirt-Chanun – The Court of Canun
Curaidh Mòr - Personal bodyguard
Duine Uasal - Literally, gentleman - the elite fighting men of the Clan
Dìoghaltas – Vengeance
Gallowglass – Elite fighting unit – originally derived from Gall-òglach (see below)
Gall-òglach – Sword bearer
Gall-duine – Outsiders
Geo na Laise-suileach - The Gully of the Flaming Eye
Griogaraich - The MacGregors
Guga – Young Gannet, a gastronomic delicacy for some
Milltear nam Fiaclan - Tooth smasher (literally Destroyer of the Teeth)
Ministear an Ionmhais - Finance Minister

Pìobaireachd - Classical music of the bagpipe
Prìomh-Chlàrc a' Bhun-reachd - Chief Clerk of the Constitution
Redshanks – Gaelic mercenaries
Riaghaltas - The Parliament of the Republic
Riaghladair – Prison governor
Seanadh - Senate
Seanadairean - Senators
Sgian Dubh - Black knife
Sgian Aslaich - Armpit knife
Sìol-gin – Spunk / semen
An Smàladair – The Extinguisher (fire extinguisher)
Srùbag - Cup of tea
Tagsaidh - Taxi
Tapaidh – Brave / Vigorous / Clever
Treòraiche – Guide / Leader
Tuig – To understand

The song sung by Lady Lamont is Sea Longing, An Ionndrainn-Mhara, old fragment adapted and translated by Kenneth MacLeod, collected by M&P Kennedy Fraser from Ann Monk Benbecula and to be found in Song of the Hebrides, by Marjory Kennedy-Fraser and Kenneth MacLeod Volume 2.

Nick Bastin

Nick Bastin lives in London with his wife and three children and two cats. His mother's family come from Argyll in the West Highlands and the Island of Islay. He met his wife, who is from the Isle of Skye, studying Gaelic at an evening class in London – she was always much better at it than he was.

In 2007 he co-authored a Very Canny Scot – Daniel Campbell of Shawfield and Islay, a biography of one of Scotland's leading figures of the early 18th century.

The Book of the Black Tower Trilogy are his first novels.

Also by Nick Bastin

BloodBond

Scotland, the present day: the Gaelic Republic is the last place that you'd want to find yourself kidnapped, especially by your own family. A lethal web of ancient enmities, violence and vengeance leaves Gillespie MacNachtan running for his life in unforgiving terrain, dependent on his new-found allies to survive and turn the tables against the cruel and relentless John Lamont of the Sorrows.

"Well written, fast-paced.....the novel comprises well over 300 pages of intrigue and excitement, allied to a well-conceived plot.......I sincerely hope that the author's optimism of future tales is realised.....On this reading, those would be thoroughly deserved."
The Ileach
The Independent Newspaper for Islay and Jura

BloodFeud

BloodFeud is the sequel to BloodBond the fast-paced thriller set in an alternative contemporary Britain.

The Gaelic Republic is in turmoil; John Lamont's scheming has unleashed chaos all along the west coast as rival magnates vie with each other for power. Will he be able to seize control or will the Republic's institutions be able to contain his ambition?

The Clan MacNachtan's fortunes are at a low ebb; with the evil Allan Stewart in their stronghold of Dunderave their future looks bleak.

Gillespie wants to return home to Antrim, to continue the life he once knew, but he finds that leaving the Republic and its dangers behind is not so easy.

"The premise behind the Black Tower series is superb, as is the writing…..Compulsive doesn't begin to describe it…. There are few opportunities to catch your breath."

The Ileach
The Independent Newspaper for Islay and Jura